Cle
Clement, Peter, M.D.
Critical condition

$ 22.95

1st ed.

critical condition

critical
condition

peter clement

ballantine books
new york

A Ballantine Book
Published by The Ballantine Publishing Group

Copyright © 2002 by Peter Clement Duffy

www.ballantinebooks.com

Library of Congress Cataloging-in-Publication Data

Clement, Peter, M.D.
Critical condition / Peter Clement.—1st ed.
p.   cm.
ISBN 0-345-44339-X
1. Human experimentation in medicine—Fiction. 2. Brain—Hemorrhage—
Patients—Fiction. 3. Women television personalities—Fiction. 4. Manhattan
(New York, N.Y.)—Fiction. 5. Hospital patients—Fiction.
6. Critically ill—Fiction. 7. Physicians—Fiction. I. Title.
PS3553.L3938 C75 2002
813'.54—dc21   2002022151

Manufactured in the United States of America

First Edition: May 2002

10   9   8   7   6   5   4   3   2   1

To the constants of my life: Sean, James, and Vyta.

prologue

As a doctor, he knew how to wake up.

Especially when the phone was ringing.

Except it didn't sound like a phone. More like the whine of a mosquito, or a dentist's drill.

And he couldn't seem to come out of the sleep that held him.

In fact he knew he shouldn't.

There was pain waiting for him up there. Better he stay in the darkness down here.

But he was surfacing anyway.

First he felt his throat hurt. So what's a sore throat? Two aspirins and call me in the morning stuff. Nothing to worry about.

The pain burned across his neck and up his face. He swallowed, and felt he'd downed a mouthful of fire. What the hell, he said, but seemed to be speaking flames instead of words, their heat searing a hole out the front of his larynx with a loud hiss.

His head began to throb. And his arms. They were aching all the way from the shoulders, as if someone had grabbed his hands, yanked them over his head, and was pulling him out of the deep blackness where he wanted to stay.

He remembered. Waking up in the early gray of dawn and seeing someone by his bed who shouldn't have been there. He'd been about to shout, when a white explosion went off in his brain. He tried to call out again, alert someone now that there had been an intruder, but the hissing under his chin returned, and the pulling on his arms continued.

He attempted to run. His feet seemed stuck together.

And the noise continued. A high-pitched whir that he definitely knew was out of place.

Suddenly he was rocketing upward toward the light, unable to stop. His eyes flew open. He was in his shower stall, naked, suspended by his arms from the nozzle above, his ankles taped together. The whine of what sounded like a small electrical motor came from outside the frosted glass door of the cubicle, and he could see a shadowy form approaching.

He screamed for help, sending another gush of air wheezing out from below his chin. Someone had cut a hole in his trachea.

The door opened, and in stepped a figure clad in full surgical gear carrying a rotary bone saw. He had no idea who it was. The eyes above the mask were as glitteringly cold as any he'd ever seen. He began to writhe and buck against his restraints as the small spinning disc of steel was brought up to his sternum. His shrieks when its teeth tore through the skin and bit into the underlying ribs made no more sound than the morning breeze that stirred the bathroom window curtains.

1

She felt the sound more than heard it.

It came from deep within her brain, and in the first few seconds seemed to have no more significance than the tiny popping noise a congested sinus makes when it clears, or the slight creak that even a healthy neck can produce after the muscles and tendons have stiffened from being too long in one position.

So Kathleen Sullivan ignored it, automatically relegating the minute sensation to the background trivia of everyday life, deeming it part of approaching forty, unimportant, therefore not to be heeded, and resumed making love to Richard Steele, whom she sat astride watching his eyes glitter in the gray traces of morning light that had begun to creep into her still-darkened bedroom.

God, she loved him. Their sex seemed always such a celebration of how they matched each other in life.

Then the pain hit her at the base of her skull with the force of a two-by-four. "Oh, my God!" she screamed, clasping the back of her head and freezing.

She felt him initially increase his movements, then slow when she failed to respond, his flushed, smiling features growing puzzled.

A swirl of dizziness sent her reeling to the right as if she'd been slapped. She toppled off him. Nausea overwhelmed her, and vomit arched out of her mouth as if shot from a hose. She flopped down, half on and half off his chest. Blackness came quickly, but it took longer before she lost sensation enough to stop feeling the pain entirely.

And she could still hear.

"Kathleen! Kathleen, what's the matter?" he cried from somewhere far off.

Someone's prying open my skull from the inside, she tried to tell him just before the pressure squeezed all consciousness out of her.

The pain, like roots, ate deep into her sleep, and tendrils of harsh light ripped her out of the merciful dark. She tried to scream, but no sound came. She could see racks of bottles, bags of fluid, and coils of plastic tubing lining the walls of whatever little room they were in, yet everything looked wrong, as if outlined in double. She blinked to clear her vision; it made no difference. She couldn't shift her eyes from side to side, but she could look up and down. She tried to move her hands, but not even her fingers would budge. Had they tied her to the bed?

Someone loomed over her and placed a black mask on her face, then pumped air into her mouth and down her throat.

"Her breathing's labored," she heard Richard say from a place beyond her line of sight. "Step on it!"

"We're a minute from the door, Doc!"

She felt the room sway hard to the left, and realized they were in an ambulance. Probably on the way to Richard's ER. But why couldn't she look at him? Move anything? God, what had happened to her?

"It's okay, Kathleen," she heard him say. "We've got you. Just relax and let us help you breathe."

Volleys of air forced their way past the base of her tongue and down into her larynx. Each one felt big as a tennis ball and filled her with the urge to gag, but her pharynx stayed flaccid, refusing to respond. She wanted to shake off the mask and gasp for breath, yet couldn't.

"If you can hear me, Kathleen, we've called ahead to the hospital, and the chief of neurosurgery is waiting for us. You've suffered some kind of stroke, probably hemorrhagic from the way it's affected your eyes, but you'll make it okay, Kathleen. Count on it!" His voice trembled and broke, leaving her wondering if he'd sobbed. Squeeze after squeeze of air went down her throat. "Hyperventilating you like this blows off carbon dioxide and constricts arteries in the brain," Richard continued, his words coming in fragments as if they were catching on something sharp. "That'll slow the bleeding."

With a squeal of brakes the vehicle lurched to a stop. Instantly she heard the doors at her feet snap open and felt the cool morning air flow into the vehicle. Only then did she realize she was nude under a blanket.

The attendant went on ventilating her and a half dozen men and women in white clustered around to help lift out the stretcher. "Where's Tony Hamlin?" she heard Richard ask.

"In resus, ready and waiting with his neurosurgical team," someone answered as they raced into the ER and down a corridor, the sweep of the ceiling past her vertical stare adding to her dizziness. She could feel Richard's hands against her face as he took over holding the mask tightly in place around her mouth and nose. By straining her eyes upward she could see him. His expression grim, he snapped off orders to his staff as he ran. Even when he glanced down at her and tried to smile it was a miserable attempt to reassure her.

My God, she thought, *the poor man. He thinks I'm going to die, just like his wife.*

They wheeled her into a vacuous cool chamber filled with a dozen people in green gowns, masks, and surgical gloves. Everyone grabbed a part of her and worked on it as if she was a race car at a pit stop. While IVs went in her arms, a tube was shoved down her throat, and what looked liked tiny spigots were stuck into her wrists. Once more she felt she had to gag, but not even a cough or sound of any kind emerged. She lay as motionless as a corpse, yet aware.

"We've got her stable, Richard. Why don't you let us take it now?" said a man with long white hair standing by her head.

"Right, of course, Tony," she heard her lover reply, his voice more strained and uncertain than ever.

No, don't leave me alone, she wanted to cry out.

His face once more came into view, his handsome features as tense and pale as latex stretched over a skull. "Kathleen, our chief of neurosurgery, Tony Hamlin, is right here to take care of you."

"Hi, Kathleen," Hamlin said. "Sorry to meet you in such circumstances."

"These people are the best," Richard continued. "They'll get you through this." He leaned closer and whispered, "I love you."

Please stay!

He turned, and out of the corner of her fixed field of vision she watched him disappear.

Then a nurse whipped off her blanket and proceeded to insert a catheter up her urethra. "Did the event happen during intercourse?" she asked coldly, examining the secretions she'd picked up between her gloved fingers.

"Isn't that one of the classic presentations of an arterial rupture?" asked a curly-haired man in a short clinical jacket as he adjusted her IV. He didn't look much older than her daughter Lisa, who'd just turned nineteen. Christ, Richard had left her in the hands of a kid.

"When you've finished what you're doing, Doctor, why not step outside and get a proper history from Dr. Steele?" said the white-haired man behind her head as he proceeded to shine a penlight into her eyes. Despite the glare, she couldn't avert her gaze, only blink. His face looked to be in pieces, like a Picasso.

Richard stood in the corridor slumped against the wall. His taking charge in the ambulance had been both critically necessary and a retreat into action, his concentration on technique keeping his terror at bay. Now he had nothing to divert him from facing what had happened, not as a doctor, but as her lover. At the center of the domain where he'd spent his professional life resuscitating others from the dead, he began to tremble with helplessness.

A nurse with closely cropped gray hair and rectangular, gold-rimmed glasses came steaming out of the room he'd just left. "Dr. Steele, let's sit together in your office. I'll get you a coffee." Her name tag read Josephine

O'Brien, but she'd been around the department longer than he, and everyone with whom she was friendly called her Jo. "Dr. Sullivan's completely lined, we've wired her to every monitor we have, and her vitals are holding. A CT's next, so there'll be nothing new to report until then."

A much younger colleague followed on her heels. "She's in good hands with Dr. Hamlin," she added. "You're doing her and yourself no good hanging around the doorway."

They spoke with exactly the mix of firmness and compassion that he expected everyone in his department to use when dealing with frightened family and friends of patients. He mumbled his thanks for their support, and had he not been a physician, might even have felt reassured. The trouble was, like most good ER doctors, he knew the odds. No niceties on the part of his staff could stop the percentages from pummeling his brain.

Mortality for this type of intracranial bleed—eighty percent.

Morbidity or permanent brain damage in those that survived—almost certain.

Chances of a fatal rebleed—high.

A cold empty feeling settled into the pit of his stomach. As the two women led him down the hallway, he had to watch his step the way a drunk man does. The numbers literally staggered him. At his door he fumbled his keys until Jo took them and unlocked it for him.

Don't die on me, Kathleen, he kept saying to himself. *Please, don't die on me.*

As soon as he stepped into his own small sanctuary—a carpeted shoe box with an oversized metal desk, two chairs, and a potted tree—he quickly raised a hand to his eyes, not wanting the nurses to see the tears brimming over his lower lids. But the streams were halfway down his cheeks before he could wipe them aside. "Please, just leave me be," he said quickly, straining to keep his voice steady while looking up to avoid their gaze. The tiny perforations in the ceiling tiles shimmered like black stars in a white universe.

"Not on your life, Richard," said Jo, one of the few who would dare use his first name. Keeping her hold on his arm, she added, "Now sit down and let us take care of you for a change, starting with the mug of hot caffeine we promised you." A jerk of the head toward the door sent her junior running down the hallway to fetch it. "And don't worry about letting down in front of me," she continued when they were alone. "As for Kathleen, let me be telling you, us Irish women have a stubborn strength that adds up to an edge for seein' us through any ordeal. It probably comes from dealing with all the ornery men in our lives. From what I've heard she's as good a fighter as any, and that's sure to help her survive."

Richard looked up at her lined face and kind brown eyes. His wife had had fight in her, too. What good did it do her?

At that moment there was a knock, and a young resident stuck his head in the door. "Dr. Hamlin sent me to ask you a few questions, Dr. Steele," he said.

"Not now!" Jo snapped.

He disappeared back out again.

"These kids they make into doctors nowadays," she muttered after he'd fled. "Know all the facts, and nothing about people."

Because the people part's too painful, Richard thought.

"It's a pontine bleed," Hamlin told Richard an hour later in that same office, referring to a specific part of the upper brain stem. "Her pupils are pinpoint and, for now, unreactive. She's quadriplegic, has lost her gag reflex along with her ability to swallow. Control of her pharyngeal and facial muscles is gone as well, to the point she can't speak or show any expression. But she's conscious, and moves her eyes up or down on command. She can also blink up a storm. That's what tipped me off when I examined her."

"A locked-in syndrome?" Richard asked, the fearful sensation at the core of his innards turning to ice.

Hamlin nodded. "Her respirations haven't deteriorated any further, though she still needs an assist from a ventilator. We had to leave her intubated anyway, to protect her airway from an aspiration of vomit—she can't even keep her saliva out of her lungs. We've also sedated her—it's obviously a hell of a panicky situation for her—but she can still signal with her eyes. We're using morphine to manage the pain at the same time, and she's indicated the headache's lessened. You know, I was telling the residents that Alexandre Dumas was the first to describe this condition—"

"What's her prognosis?" Richard cut in, unable to take anymore clinical detail, nor Hamlin's pompous tendency to lecture even when he was talking alone with a colleague. "And don't bother me with the general outcome for brain stem bleeds. I know that. Is the pons any less dismal?"

"Only time will tell," said Hamlin, assuming an even more professorial tone. "On her CAT scan the hemorrhage seems confined to that area. If it stays there, without penetrating into the fourth ventricle that's nearby, and she survives the next few hours, she might have a considerable recovery. We'll get a better view when she's stable enough for an MRI, and of course I've scheduled an angiogram. But if she rebleeds and the hemorrhage extends into the ventricular space where there's no stopping it . . ." He let his voice trail off.

Richard didn't need to be told that these were the ones with the highest death rates. "What's a 'considerable recovery'? " he asked, his mouth so dry he could barely speak.

"Sometimes it means that patients regain sufficient respiratory function to get off a ventilator. Sometimes they do much better and are left with a deficit only in the legs, remaining paraplegic, or with luck, recover partial movement there as well. A small number actually walk again. In other words, I've seen instances where they win back almost full function, especially in the upper body, including the ability to swallow and talk. Of course, it's impossible to predict the outcome of any given case."

Hamlin's voice faded into the background as Richard's mind conjured an image for each scenario: Kathleen withering away on the end of a breathing tube, dragging her lifeless legs along on crutches; Kathleen feeding herself, garbed in a food-stained bib—nothing he hadn't seen before . . . in strangers.

"Her angiogram will give us a better idea of the reason for the bleed, which I suspect is a congenital arterial malformation, probably a capsular angioma, since she's no history of hypertension. Of course I don't have to tell you it's got to come out. Unless this underlying deformity is removed in its entirety, the risk of another hemorrhage will always be there. But first we have to stabilize her enough for the OR and verify with imaging that we can get at it surgically without doing too much collateral damage."

Richard shuddered. The term *collateral damage* was code for an even more chilling outcome. If the many neural pathways and centers that passed within millimeters of each other in the section of the brain Hamlin cited, those controlling breathing, walking, voluntary bladder or bowel control, finger-hand-arm movements, speech, and eating, had survived the bleeds, they might not survive the surgery. His cutting out the tangle of abnormal vessels, the capsular angioma that he suspected, while leaving the rest of the anatomy intact, was so tricky the operation itself could further destroy neurons, making her worse off and possibly killing her.

Again it wasn't anything he didn't know or hadn't already feared. But even doctors escape into false hopes when faced with a catastrophic illness that's personal. Hamlin's words slammed the door on anymore such retreats.

"Thank you for letting me know, Tony," Richard said, barely able to find his voice.

When he was alone, the well-practiced grip he usually kept on his nerve broke completely. Sobs came from so deep within they racked him with the cruelty of convulsions, wrenching the air out of his lungs and filling the room with a grotesque, high-pitched, hacking wail. He had cried like this only once before, years ago on the day Luana died. Then it heralded an eighteen-month spiral of grief, drinking, and denial that nearly lost him his son, his job, and his life.

"Not this time," he whispered through clenched teeth, still doubled over and struggling for breath. "Whatever happens, I won't cop out this time."

But the cold fear in his belly twisted as if to mock his brave words. Once a coward, always a coward, it seemed to say.

Others who loved Kathleen flew to mind—her daughter Lisa, and his own son Chet.

He had to let them know. He pulled himself together enough to reach for the phone and dial Lisa's apartment first. As he waited for her to pick up, he prayed the iron resolve he'd used when making similar calls to faceless next of kin would help him now.

"Hello?"

"Lisa, it's Richard."

"Hi! What's up?"

The youthful eagerness of her greeting hung between them. "Lisa, I've got bad news. . . ."

Where the hell was Richard? Goddamn it, Kathleen thought. Why didn't he come back? And why didn't anyone tell her anything. It seemed as though it had been forever since that Beethoven look-alike and his pack of apprentices finished their methodical tapping and prodding.

The tube down her throat continued to keep her perpetually on the verge of gagging, and still the choking never came. A new treat was the catheter in her bladder burning like a line of coals, leaving her feeling a constant urge to pee. The nausea never abated. And the unrelenting spin inside her head so tilted the room that she thought some masochist in white had strapped her to a table designed for training astronauts.

Worse was how they all talked over her, reducing her to a set of bodily functions and discussing her solely in terms of numbers. To them she wasn't even there.

"Respirations set at eighteen."

"O_2 sat's ninety-six."

"CO_2's twenty; pulse seventy; BP one-thirty over seventy."

Why couldn't she move? Why didn't someone tell her? She blinked furiously, wanting to catch the attention of a passing figure in white.

No one paid her the slightest heed.

What had happened to her?

"Some kind of hemorrhagic stroke" Richard had said. But he'd also promised she'd be okay. This sure as hell wasn't okay. Christ, they'd just parked her, plugged into a bunch of machines.

Then a woman with short gray hair and small gold glasses loomed into view. "Dr. Sullivan, my name's Josephine O'Brien, but around here they call me Jo. I know you're frightened, and it won't do you any good to

11

hear a bunch of lies about your being fine. But you are what we call stable, and that's the best we can hope for in this place. Richard's gone to get your daughter, Lisa. Blink twice if you're up to seeing her."

Hearing her name spoken with such simple kindness brought Kathleen hurtling back from the anonymity the others had cast her into. "Yes! Yes!" she blinked through tears. It took her a few seconds more to realize that at least she could still cry.

Dr. Tony Hamlin's gaze swept the crowded cafeteria until he spotted the man he wanted. He quickly weaved a path through the crowded tables where nurses, orderlies, and residents wolfed down the remains of breakfast. Those already finished raced by him, Styrofoam cups in hand, heading to the wards for the start of another day-shift at New York City Hospital. Everyone was more or less color coded—nurses of both sexes sporting pale green, orderlies powder blue, personnel from the OR and critical care areas garbed in scrubs of darker tones to better mask the stains from all the bodily fluids splashed about during invasive procedures. Doctors wore white coats of varying length—short jackets for students, mid-to-long ones signifying increasing seniority.

Hamlin's coat flowed out behind him like a cape. Matching his mane of white hair, it was a chieftain's regalia in any tribe.

His target, Dr. Jim Norris, had his own singular dress code—a dark brown bomber jacket, the leather cracked and weathered to the point it almost matched its owner's well-worn, bearded face. The man sat alone, his lean six-foot figure hunched over a porcelain cup of steaming water into which he repeatedly dunked a tea bag. When he saw the older man approaching, he narrowed his dark eyes, the way a bad-tempered dog might signal it doesn't want to be disturbed. "Now, why is the chief of neurosurgery descending on me at this hour?" he said as soon as Hamlin got within earshot. "Don't tell me you've another of your catastrophic cases, Tony, and I can't finish my tea."

"Go on, Norris. You love it when I pull you away from your rats and give you a chance to do some real medicine. Don't pretend otherwise."

The researcher flashed a smile that looked surprisingly brilliant amidst the wiry tangle of hairs in his salt-and-pepper mustache. "So what is it this time?"

"We've got to hurry," said Hamlin, leaning over the otherwise deserted table and lowering his voice. "I just examined the famous girlfriend of our esteemed chief of ER. She's had an intracranial bleed—I take it they were going at it rather vigorously in the sack at the time. The hemorrhage is localized to the pons, and she's got a locked-in syndrome. She's also young, not yet forty, and otherwise healthy with no risk factors, according to him. That makes her a candidate, just like the others—"

"You're not suggesting we do her!"

"Of course I am."

"Are you nuts? What if Steele finds out? We'll be finished."

"Not necessarily. In fact, saving her may give us a way out of our current mess."

"How?"

"If the infusion works in her case, we'll have a chance to get him on board. Think how beneficial it would be—his alerting us anytime a patient of ours comes into ER, before some other doctor or resident gets a closer look at the old records. It'll be one less way we can get caught."

"What if the infusion doesn't work?"

"Then she's probably dead anyway, or worse, a vegetable in a wheelchair. It'll be the outcome he expects."

"And if he still finds out what we did to her?"

"The only way he'll find out *is* if this stuff works. Because then I'll tell him myself. And make it clear that unless he goes along with us she won't get the second round of treatment she'll need."

"That's nuts. He could still refuse to go along and turn us in. How do you know he won't?"

"Because I'm betting he'll do anything not to lose this woman. Remember what happened to him when he lost his wife?"

Norris scowled, clasped his cup between both hands and took a sip of tea, then said, "I don't know."

"Damn it, it's my name on those patients' charts, and if anyone gets suspicious, it's me they're going to come after with all their questions. Shall I refer them on to you?"

The bearded man went still, his white smile once more coming into view, but slowly this time, tooth by tooth. "Threats don't become you, Hamlin, or did I misunderstand your point?"

"We're all under threat here. The only way you and the rest stay safe is to keep me safe. And that means we need Steele. Christ, if I'd known it was going to be like this I never would have gone along with your crazy scheme."

"My crazy scheme?" Norris's forced grin never wavered. "Hey, we're victims of our own success. Who knew our subjects would do so damn well at first that we'd have to let them go home?"

"You call what happened to them a success? Christ, it's got all of us living like fugitives. And you're damn lucky I've been able to talk the families out of autopsies so far."

Norris chuckled. Anyone paying him any attention would have thought him the happiest guy in the room. "So someday we'll be heroes, and you'll be a star in *Neurology Today* just the way you've always wanted." He downed his tea and shoved away from the table. "But let's just hope you're right about Steele being a good friend in ER. If you want me, I'll be in my lab, preparing what you'll need. I assume you're going to slip it to her during an after hours angiogram, as usual."

Hamlin bristled at the researcher's cavalier attitude, detesting the man's arrogance. Or was it sarcasm? With Norris he could never tell. Yet he remained professionally cold toward him, long resigned to being dependent on the brilliant prick. "That's right. And the rest during surgery, if she lives that long. I'll call you when we're ready."

"This is the last one I do for you, Tony," he said, his expression all at once deteriorating to a lipless grimace. The leathery features made Hamlin imagine fangs and venom concealed within.

She thought it was night, but wasn't sure.

"Hell of a time for an angiogram," said the nurse who wheeled Kathleen out of ICU and down a corridor.

"It's all that 'minimizing downtime' and 'maximizing efficiency' they keep harping on," Kathleen heard a man's voice reply. His job seemed to be steering the portable respirator they were pushing alongside her. Occasionally she saw his ebony-colored hand reach into view and steady the monitors they'd piled onto her bed for the trip.

The woman let out a hoot of laughter. "Tell me about it. Hell, I got a cousin over in Jersey who works in a hospital where they rent out their MRI machine to veterinarians from midnight till dawn."

"No! What about fleas?"

Their voices drifted in and out as the effects of the morphine they'd been giving her kicked in, and she watched the ceiling roll by. She felt them turn a succession of corners until they passed through a set of doors marked RADIOLOGY.

Wait! she wanted to shout. She needed Richard with her. Because only when Richard was around did they really take care and treat her with respect.

It had been good in ER. Richard's nurses had comforted her when they could, and Jo had taken the time to hold her hand, stroke her forehead, and explain whatever they were about to do to her. But once they transferred her to Intensive Care, soon as he left the room, the medical personnel became more inhuman. She'd overheard their snide remarks between Richard's visits.

"What gets me is how they expect special treatment for her."

"She's not even his wife."

"Just because she's some big shot geneticist on TV, and the chief of emergency's got the hots for her . . ."

Once even the word *mistress* came up.

How quaintly old-fashioned, she had thought during one of her more morphine-suffused interludes.

But in the harshly jagged interval after the medication had worn off when they left her shot long past its due, she took the delay personally.

Why not just carve a bloody *A* on her forehead, you self-righteous cows, she had wanted to scream, certain that they'd withheld the injection because of their resentment of her. Straining in mute fury against the unyielding sheath in which her failed nerves and muscles so brutally trapped her, she pulsed her eyes up and down and put her lids through a good imitation of a butterfly's wings. But the tiny movements caught no one's attention, and claustrophobia tightened its grip, suffocating her as surely as a pillow to the face. After what seemed an eternity, a perky young nurse with spiked blond hair and a diamond stud in her nose popped in. She emptied a syringe full of relief into Kathleen's arm through the IV line.

And Kathleen had drifted again.

Sometimes she'd thought of Lisa.

It had broken her heart to see the teenager trying so hard to be brave when Richard brought her to the bedside earlier in the afternoon. Lisa's eyes were as strikingly green and her hair was as vibrant an auburn gold as her own, but today, with her daughter's face drained white, ghostlike, her eye and hair color looked garish.

"Does it hurt?" Lisa had asked.

No, she had blinked, telling a lie.

"You're going to be all right, Mummy."

Yes, she had agreed, willing to join in any fabrication that would comfort her daughter, who hadn't called her "mummy" in the last thirteen of her nineteen years. Kathleen could see Richard standing behind Lisa, his hands on her shoulders. She liked that.

Yet she had felt relief when the visit ended and Richard led Lisa away. At least I kept from crying, she thought.

"Chet will want to see you as well," Richard had said when he returned, referring to his own fourteen-year-old son.

Will he? she'd thought, knowing the boy had endured watching his mother die of cancer a little more than three years ago.

Her eyes had flooded with tears despite her determination not to get weepy. One of her great pleasures during this past year with Richard had been growing to love Chet and discovering that he returned her love. Seeing her so near to death probably would rip open Chet's old wounds, and he'd be terrified about being abandoned again by death . . . her death. He might be even more devastated than Lisa.

"Are you strong enough to see him?" Richard had asked.

No, she'd blinked, thinking only of what an ordeal it might be for the boy. And the real question was whether Richard would be strong enough this time.

Feeling the stretcher come to a halt, she opened her eyes. They'd parked her under a bright OR lamp alongside a large beige-colored machine and what looked like a television screen. Hamlin leaned into view from her right wearing a surgical mask. He swabbed the side of her neck with something cold that smelled sickeningly medicinal. "Thank you," he called to the man and woman who had brought her. "We'll phone when she's ready for the trip back."

"I can't believe you're doing this," said a thin-faced man in a white coat who bent over her from the left. His name tag read DR. MATT LOCK-MAN and he, too, was masked, but the material outlined a pointed nose and thin receding chin making her think of a lab rat. A cornered one, she decided, given how wide with alarm his eyes seemed to be.

"Shut up!" said Hamlin, all trace of his elegant manners from earlier in the day gone. "Cases like this can hear, even when they're completely unresponsive, and sometimes they can remember."

Rodent-face studied her uneasily. "I thought you said she was full of morphine."

"She is. And IV midazolam. But you know how hard it is to tell just how deep those drugs have taken a stroked-out patient. Some only look gorked and remember the damnedest things."

"Christ," Lockman muttered, turning his attention to her thigh and giving her groin an equally frigid swab.

Straining to glance down, Kathleen saw in his gloved hands what looked like a three-foot length of tubing with a tiny wire loop on its end, the whole thing enclosed in a plastic sheath attached to a huge needle. She felt a piercing sting as he jabbed the point into her groin, and would have flinched if she could move. He proceeded to feed the long device out of its cover and through the needle, until only a few inches remained sticking out of her, the rest of it having disappeared up into her trunk. From her own work on lab animals she knew he was putting in some kind of central line, probably arterial, judging by the spurting backflow of blood she'd caught a glimpse of in the lumen.

"Tony, if you tell Steele even part of what we've done," Lockman said, "he could get us all sent to jail—and the fines. Jesus, we'd be ruined."

"Hey! I said shut up."

17

"But once more DOAs roll into his ER—"

"Can it!"

Lockman scowled. "I warn you, I won't let him or anyone else bring the cops down on us when it comes to homicide charges, understand? Even if it means silencing the man myself—"

"Jesus Christ, what does it take with you?" said Hamlin, shooting him an angry glance. "I told you to zip your fuckin' mouth!" Then he abruptly bent over her. As he brought his hand near her neck, she saw the glinting point of the large needle he was holding. It looked half a foot long.

Oh, my God! she thought, and strained her eyes further downward, yet couldn't see what he was doing. She felt a sting as the tip pierced her skin over the major arteries and veins in her neck, the pain making her eyes water. Terrified, and having no idea what they were up to, she blinked furiously in protest.

Ignoring her, Hamlin lifted up a small, threadlike catheter, connected it, plastic wrapping and all, to the needle he'd just inserted, and began to feed it from its sheath into her head. Lockman pulled the beige-colored machine closer until a cone-shaped cylinder protruding from it was aimed at a point below her ear. He pressed a button, and on the television screen she saw an X-ray image of a human brain in varying shades of black and gray.

He reached down and injected a syringeful of something through the larger catheter in her groin, then he and Hamlin turned their attention to the TV screen. A white lacework of pumping vessels branched into view. What appeared to be a large dark worm coming up from the bottom of the picture seemed to thread through the vessels. A much finer filament coiled horizontally from the front toward the "worm."

A sickening wave of fear roiled through her. It was her head they were looking at, and she was watching two catheters thrust into the depths of her brain.

What were they doing to her, she wanted to cry out, feeling the inside of her skull suddenly grow warm.

"Where'd you learn to fish about with a microline through the carotid like this?" asked Lockman, giving her another squirt from his syringe. He sounded annoyed.

She watched a new pattern of white spread into a morass of branches on the screen, and realized he'd been injecting her with dye.

"We once had a research project where we thought we could plug arterial leaks with a well-placed squirt of cyanoacrylate, the Krazy Glue they use on cuts in ER," said Hamlin, never taking his eyes off the screen. "It didn't work, but I sure got to know my way around the arteries in people's heads."

They weren't going to put Krazy Glue in her head! Kathleen screamed in silent disbelief. She was at the mercy of madmen.

"You think there'd be an easier way," Lockman muttered.

"There," said Hamlin, ignoring the remark. "That's the spot. Through the posterior communicating branch and into the posterior cerebral. Now bring your loop up, and let's see if you can snare me with your balloon. . . ."

She'd no idea what he meant, but the larger worm advanced vertically until the loop in its end was directly before the tip of the smaller horizontal line. Lockman said something about Hamlin threading the needle, and sure enough, the thin dark filament went forward, appearing to pass through the ring.

"Inflate the balloon," said Hamlin, his tone impatient.

Lockman fiddled with his end of the catheter in her thigh. Where the two catheters intersected, a tiny round sphere grew into the white dye like a small dark bubble. "That ought to trap it," he said.

"Gently pull down as I feed you some slack."

She watched in horrified fascination as the thicker line tugged the thinner filament lower, dragging it toward where the artery branched into what looked like a spatter of white dye. Was that where she'd bled?

"Jesus Christ! Will you get the tip at the opening of the pontine artery the way you're suppose to," said Hamlin.

"Goddamn it, you can be an asshole."

"Then hold it steady, until the flow carries it in."

The free end of the tinier line continued to weave around while the two men, cursing and swearing at each other, struggled to get it where they wanted. After what seemed like minutes, it swept sideways into the branch leading toward the white splotch.

"Take a little pressure off the balloon," said Hamlin, bringing up a glass syringe containing a clear liquid and roughly plunging it through a side portal on the catheter in her neck. Where the dye had made the interior of her head grow warm, this infusion had an icy quality to it, leaving her with what felt like an ice-cream headache.

Oh, God, what were they giving her now? Kathleen felt as if this nightmare would never end. Lockman had said they faced homicide charges. Were they deliberately murdering people? Doing away with others as they were about to do with her? But why?

Grisly stories about serial killers who worked in hospitals raced through her thoughts. No, that was impossible, she reassured herself, trying to dismiss the idea that these two could be such monsters and nobody know about it.

But the idea crawled back. Lockman in particular seemed dangerous. How could she not fear the worst about him? Hadn't he just threatened Richard?

Reflexively she thrashed and struck out at her tormentors. In reality she only blinked and shot her eyes up and down, all in a futile show of outrage.

Lockman kept taking wary glances at her over his shoulder. "You know, you're right in the way you describe her," he said.

Hamlin didn't reply, obviously still annoyed with the man.

"I mean that quote you told the residents. Where was it from?" persisted Lockman.

Hamlin emptied the syringe, let out a big sigh. "You mean Dumas's description of Nortier from *The Count of Monte Cristo*?" he said, disposing of the needle and snapping off his gloves with a flourish. His suave manner of speaking had returned.

"Yeah," said Lockman, seeming relieved to get things between them back to a more civil level. "She really is like 'a corpse with living eyes.'"

2

At fourteen Chet had already spurted to within eye level of Richard's own six-foot frame, and his voice had settled into the lower registers. But his curls, dark like his mother's, remained as unruly as when he'd been a child. His gaze, never failing to show exactly what he felt, held the same wide-eyed blackness that Richard had seen at the time of Luana's death, and something else. A determination that hadn't been there before. It suggested a newfound strength since the tragedy that had almost destroyed them both.

"Dad, I want the truth this time. Is Kathleen going to die?"

This time. As opposed to all the times he'd lied to him about his mother. "I don't know, Chet," he answered. "Kathleen's in real trouble, but there's a chance she'll make it."

Chet stared at him with eyes that were identical to Luana's. After her death when Chet looked at him, Richard had felt as though Luana stared from the grave, reproaching him as he fled the agony of his own grief by running from their son. Over the last year with Kathleen in their lives that same gaze had come to comfort him. Now was no exception, even mixed as it was with the needs of a man-child trying to be brave.

The boy swallowed. "You're pretty matter-of-fact about it," he said, his tone sounding an alarm.

Did Chet mean that if he could pull away from Kathleen, he might desert his son again? Richard wanted to reach forward and ruffle the boy's permanently tousled hair, then pull him into a hug the way he had before he'd made such a mess of things and the awkwardness of the teen years banished such open displays of affection. Instead, he said, "I love her as much as you do, Chet, and feel every bit as scared. It's just that in ER we're practiced at being matter-of-fact when frightening stuff happens. It doesn't ever mean I don't care." He left it at that, because as much as he wanted to assuage his son's fear, having wounded him once, he knew no amount of promises, pledges, or talk would ever convince either of them it couldn't happen again. Just as all the good intentions in the world couldn't make a coward brave. He nevertheless waited in silence, allowing Chet the choice of challenging him further or letting it be.

They were sitting alone in their living room, a place bright with paintings, lush with plants, and filled with family photographs, the legacy of Luana's instinct for creating a nest that was both beautiful and homey. She'd practiced her own art here, teaching music and playing at her prize possession, a magnificent grand piano that sat invitingly by the window. Occasionally one of her former students would drop by and perform a piece they'd worked on together, filling the house with her spirit. "I like the woman who did this," Kathleen had told him during one of her early visits. "She obviously had style and sophistication, yet it's all about family."

Chet let out a long breath, stood, and started to pace. "So do we tell Lisa outright how critical her mother is?" he said, lowering his voice and gesturing with his eyes toward the next room. She was holed up there, busily phoning everyone who had to be told what had happened—the staff at her mother's lab, close friends, the people who published her books and produced her television programs. It was a long list. "I know she already understands it's bad," he continued practically in a whisper, "but if she asks outright, the way I did, do we spell it out for her?"

Richard studied him. "I'd like to know what you think would be best," he said, going with an instinct that there might be another way to settle the wrong between them. "After all, I didn't handle this sort of thing so well with you when your mother was ill."

The boy started at the admission. At first he looked puzzled, as if trying to decipher if his father was being sincere. Then he swallowed a few more times, and seemed to stand a little more erect. "We're straight with her, from start to finish. Otherwise she won't trust us."

His voice had trembled, but there was a determination in his eyes that made Richard's heart leap. It was the same look his mother had summoned when she'd first been diagnosed with cancer of the pancreas and tackled the fight of her life. God, Richard thought, Chet had had her courage all along, and he'd never given him a chance to use it.

Thursday, June 14, 7:10 A.M.

He should have been in ER ten minutes ago. But he'd only just woken up, not having fallen asleep until five A.M.

"She's as stable as can be expected, Dr. Steele," the nurses had told him each time he called to inquire, their tone making it clear they thought him a nuisance.

He'd finally dropped off in front of the TV during a rerun of *Sea Hunt.* After two hours of fitful sleep and with his mind incapable of focusing on anything else but Kathleen, he headed directly for ICU figuring it better if he stayed clear of Emergency anyway.

Bypassing the usual morning congestion in front of the elevators, he used the staircase, taking the steps two at a time. He slowed for the strings of men and women in white who trailed like loose threads on the coat of the staff doctor leading them through rounds today. In the corridors he encountered similar processions, except they had been joined by nurses busily emptying bedpans and handing out food trays, the aromas of both hanging in the air. He noted a hush around one particular doorway through which the ward supervisor led a red-eyed, elderly woman to a motionless, sheeted figure lying on the bed. The nurses, on their final round before the day shift arrived, must have found a corpse, some poor soul who had died during the hours before dawn. He shuddered at his knowledge of how patients slipped away unnoticed even in a hospital.

In ICU there were no smells of eggs, bacon, or anything else to do with food, breakfast here served mostly through tubes. That left the scent of excretia pretty well unchecked.

From twenty feet away he could see Kathleen's eyes flicking, like joke eyeballs on a spring. "How long has she been doing this?" he demanded of the nurse as he strode to Kathleen's side.

"According to the report, all through the night, Dr. Steele," the nurse said. She looked odd to Richard with her spiked blond hair and a silver ring through her left nostril. He recognized her as being among the ones he'd made a point of speaking with yesterday to ensure Kathleen got the best care, but her laconic *I don't give a damn* tone suggested he'd wasted his time. Anger coiled his intestines into a knot.

"At first they thought it might be some kind of seizure," the nurse continued, not bothering to look at him, "yet she blinks appropriately when asked for a yes or no response to a question. Then Dr. Hamlin ordered an increase in the morphine, and that knocked her out for a few hours. According to the med-sheet, the evening shift hadn't exactly done all they could to keep her topped off enough. I made sure that's not the problem now."

Controlling his temper, he leaned over and asked, "Kathleen, are you in pain?"

She blinked once for *no*, the convention established between her and Jo O'Brien in ER.

"Is something else wrong?"

Her lids closed and opened twice, indicating *yes*.

"Are you feeling dizzy?"

No response.

"Yes or no?" he asked.

Nothing, except she raised her eyes upward and held them there. Even in her helpless state, they retained a sparkle, and their magnificent green color flashed under the overhead lights. If he didn't know better, he would have thought she was signaling her exasperation with him.

"Do you need more morphine?"

A definite *no*.

"Are you anxious?"

Her eyes shot toward the ceiling again.

She was getting impatient with him, he thought. Obviously he wasn't asking the right question. He leaned closer to her ear and whispered, "Is what you need a bedpan?"

This time he got a sharp blink and an elevated gaze. A cluster of monitors at the head of the bed flashed their warning lights to show a rise in her blood pressure, and her pulse ticked up to one-twenty.

"You're upsetting her with all your questions, Dr. Steele," said the nurse. "You have to let her rest. As you perfectly well know, any increase in her vitals could start a rebleed."

The pulse and pressure instantly rocketed higher.

No, Kathleen blinked over and over, a pause between each movement so there was no mistaking her.

No to what? His being sent away, or the prospect of a second stroke? He instinctively held her hand. It felt clammy and as flaccid as death, but he clasped it to his lips and gently kissed her fingers. He also placed a palm on her brow, then stroked her auburn-gold hair, all the while watching his touch coax her readings back to normal. "I'll be staying with her," he told the nurse, appalled by her cold insensitivity and finding it a stretch to speak calmly.

"No problem," she snapped, "except it's on your shoulders if anything bad happens."

Richard cringed at the woman's belligerence, but said nothing, continuing to sooth Kathleen with his hands. "Is that better?" he asked.

Yes, she blinked.

Her forehead was warm with fever, his clinical self noted. Probably from the usual effects of a pontine hemorrhage on the nearby thermoregulatory centers. Later he'd check and make sure they were giving her acetaminophen to control it. But it was as her lover that he must act now, he reminded himself, and went on caressing her.

When the nurse left, huffily drawing the white curtains behind her, Richard, asked, "Is *she* bothering you?"

No.

"It's something else?"

Yes.

"About your stroke?"

She blinked twice, waited a second, then once more.

"Yes, no?" He thought an instant. "You mean yes *and* no?"

Yes.

"But what?"

She kept directing her gaze downwards.

"You mean some other part of you hurts?"

No.

Jesus, this was getting them nowhere, he thought. He began to worry that despite her insisting nothing hurt, something else could be wrong with her. Any number of potentially serious symptoms—shortness of breath, numbness, even nausea and vertigo—might indicate a significant problem that didn't necessarily involve pain. The possibilities clicked through his head. Congestion in her lungs. Unrelieved pressure on a peripheral nerve from lying too long in one position. Maybe the nurses hadn't even turned her—bed sores were a real danger in paralyzed patients. Worse, it could be an extension of her bleed involving the pathways that control balance. Such an event could set off a new round of dizziness, foreshadowing a second major hemorrhage. She could be lying there, the stroke growing worse, but if he didn't ask the right question, she wouldn't be able to tell him.

Fighting his own panic, he rapidly queried her about each of the telltale sensations, yet she mostly answered *no*, except for dizziness and nausea, to which she gave both the single and double blink, a response he now took to mean yes *and* no. And when he demanded if that was what she had been trying to tell him, she gave him a clear-cut *no* and shot her eyes toward the ceiling again.

"Is there something wrong in a particular part of you?" he said, going back to square one, and trying another approach. "Besides the stroke."

Yes and no.

They were going in circles. "This 'something wrong with you,' is it what you want me to understand?"

Yes.

He had an idea, remembering a way he sometimes got patients in ER to tell him where they had a problem when they couldn't communicate. "I'll be right back," he said.

No, she repeatedly blinked.

"I'm just going to get some paper," he reassured her, and left the curtain open, so she could see him make his way to the nursing station where he picked up a prescription pad. Back in the confines of the cubicle, the curtain once more drawn, he quickly drew the outline of a human figure. "Now when I point to the body part where something is wrong, blink *yes*."

Again she looked at the ceiling, her eyes flaring.

"Please, Kathleen, humor me." He pointed to the drawing's head.

Yes.

"You mean the stroke?"

Yes and no.

Here they went again. "Is there anywhere else I need to know about that has something wrong?"

She hesitated a good five seconds, then blinked twice, slowly, as if unsure of her answer.

"Okay, then let's see. Chest?" he said, holding up the drawing and tapping the appropriate section with his pen.

No.

"Abdomen?"

No.

"Right arm?"

No.

"Left arm?"

No.

"Legs?"

No. No. No.

What had he missed? "Face?" he said.

She hesitated, then blinked *no*, but slowly.

"Am I close?" he said, feeling a flush of excitement.

Yes.

He looked at his crude picture. "A particular organ on the face? Nose, eyes, ears?"

No.

Then what the hell have I overlooked? he thought, once more studying his sketch.

Then he saw what he'd skipped. "The neck?"

Yes, snapped her lids.

He immediately leaned over her, his fingers instinctively palpating under her jaw and down the sides of the throat feeling for some abnormality. A small Band-Aid on the right, about midway down, caught his attention. Until now, looking so innocuous, it had escaped his notice. He lifted it off and saw a tiny clean puncture wound over her jugular and carotid vessels. She'd had a needle inserted in her neck. "Is this what you wanted me to see?"

Yes.

"They put a needle in here?"

Yes.

"Do you know why?"

No.

"Excuse me a minute. I'm going to check this out with the nurses."

As he turned to walk away, she started to bat *no* repeatedly.

"Kathleen, I'm not going anywhere," he said, then immediately regretted how curt he sounded. "I'll be right back," he added, making an effort to speak gently and giving her his best professional *everything's fine* smile. On his way to where the unit supervisor sat sticking bobby pins into her bun of gray hair as she stared at the central console, he chastised himself. He shouldn't have allowed his own fear and lack of sleep to make him testy, especially this early in the game. The real trials, he knew, lay ahead. If he couldn't keep a grip now, she would start to wonder if he would fold on her—just the way Chet doubted him. He swallowed hard, as if that could get rid of his own self-doubts.

"Nurse," he said, abruptly coming to a standstill at the console, "when did Dr. Sullivan have a neck puncture?"

The matronly woman perused Kathleen's chart. "It says here that she came back from her angiogram last night with the puncture site bandaged." She sounded pissed at having to take the trouble.

"But they usually go through the groin for an angiogram."

She'd already gone back to watching two dozen video screens reduce the latest progress of the souls in her charge to digital readouts and fluorescent squiggles.

Her sigh at being interrupted could have stripped paint. "According to Dr. Hamlin's note, her pressure fell during the procedure. Thinking she might be having an allergic reaction to the dye, he put in a central line, in case he needed to monitor her wedge pressure with a Swan-Gantz and give her fluids. But nothing happened, so he took it out." She spoke in the slow measured cadence nurses use when they want to make it clear they think the doctor's an idiot, and her face had *Now don't bother me anymore!* written all over it, just in case he didn't get the first message.

What she said did sound reasonable. If Kathleen had gone into shock, resuscitating her with fluid and pressor drugs would be tricky, since overshooting the mark could send up her pressure to the point it could cause another hemorrhage. He would want a central line to monitor her response, Richard thought.

"I hope you're not going to be second-guessing everything we do, Dr. Steele," the nurse added.

He turned on his heel and returned to Kathleen's cubicle, determined to be more laid back, then started to explain why Hamlin had stuck a needle in her neck.

No, no, no, she blinked, her eyes flaring. Alarms started to buzz on her monitors as her pulse and pressure climbed.

The curtains behind him whipped open. "Dr. Steele, what are you doing to her?" demanded Hamlin, gaping at her monitors.

To Richard's horror, her numbers shot higher.

"Nurse, get me IV midazolam!" snapped the neurosurgeon, shoving past Richard and moving to Kathleen's side. "Okay, Dr. Sullivan, we're going to sedate you, and all will be well in a New York minute."

The chippy young nurse who'd warned about upsetting her followed behind, giving an *I told you so* look as she swiftly reached into one of the medication shelves, retrieved a small, brown glass vial, and snapped it open. Within seconds she'd drawn the contents into a syringe, and Hamlin slowly injected the clear solution through a side portal in the IV.

Richard quickly tried to tell him what had happened. "I was just trying to explain why you had to put a line in her neck—"

"Yes, luckily we didn't need it." He continued to infuse the sedative. But why the hell are you bothering her with medical gobbledygook at a time like this, Richard? Act like family, for Christ's sake, not her doctor. Shit, you know it could be lethal, agitating her like that." Kathleen's eyes and lids slowed their movements, then drifted shut, and the numbers on the screens coasted back down into neutral territory. He stopped pushing in the plunger at that point, and withdrew the needle.

"Goddamn it, Tony, listen to me. I wouldn't jeopardize her for the life of me, but she seemed really upset about what happened during the angiogram, and I was simply trying to help her understand it so she'd relax—"

"From now on, Richard, I think it best she be more heavily sedated. These patients commonly have panic attacks as you can imagine, given the state they're in. And I don't have to tell you about the effects of morphine."

He meant how morphine, though it helps pain, can sometimes induce delirium and agitate a patient, even produce disturbing hallucinations.

"Look, our best hope is that she not rebleed, giving us time to wait until she's more stable before I operate. Now, I've tentatively scheduled the surgery for Tuesday, next week. That's seven days. Until then, no more upsets. You can give her head rubs, massage her hands, and whisper sweet nothings at her all you like, but nothing else, and certainly no interrogations. Agreed?"

"Interrogations?"

The nurse shot him a smug grin confirming that she'd ratted on him after all. Eyeing her pointy hairdo, he refrained from saying, "Thanks, Spike."

Everything Hamlin had said was absolutely right. Yet he still felt angry. Maybe, he thought, if Hamlin had explained things better the previous night, Kathleen wouldn't have been so upset about the needle in her neck. Richard wanted to rail at the pompous little man, but for Kathleen's sake he held his tongue. As far as technique went, especially for working in the brain stem, nobody had hands or experience like Hamlin's. Better to avoid a tiff with him than risk his taking offense and transferring Kathleen to someone with less expertise. "Agreed," Richard finally said, his face burning from being so thoroughly chastised.

Spike gave him another *I told you so* stare.

Holding her gaze, he added, "And I'm sure that from now on your staff will explain what they're doing before proceeding to touch Dr. Sullivan, also to avoid upsetting her?"

"Of course, Richard. We always do that," he replied. "Isn't that right, nurse?"

"All the time, Dr. Hamlin," she said, disposing of the syringe and broken vial in a plastic container before scooting out of the cubicle.

Yeah, right, thought Richard.

The entire incident fueled an icy burning in his stomach as he ran down the stairs to the ground floor. Why had Hamlin chosen to put the line in her neck anyway, he fumed, retreating to his office. He could have gotten the same information he needed to infuse her by going in under her collarbone, and wouldn't have frightened her nearly as much.

Not for the first time he found himself wondering how the man could have spent the better part of his life poking around people's brains and yet be so clueless about human nature.

With the medazzle whatchamacallit medicine that the white-haired creep had given her, Kathleen went floating off into darkness, but not quite out. At least not right away. She had feigned that part, deliberately closing her eyes just before he injected enough of the drug to close them for her. As a result she could still hear what he'd said. And Hamlin's statement that he intended to operate as soon as she was stabilized chilled her.

No way that son of a bitch was going to put a knife in her brain, she thought, feeling her heart start to palpate again despite the sedation. By shear willpower she brought her panic under control. Otherwise, she realized, she would set off those damn alarms again and bring back the ring-nosed she-beast with another shot. She struggled to remain calm as she wondered how she could make Richard, or somebody, understand Hamlin mustn't be let near her? How could she tell Richard he'd already put something into her he shouldn't have. And who would believe her? After all, she'd have to pretend that she was half-zonked most of the time, or they would medicate her into the twilight zone for real. She had to keep Hamlin and that rat-faced buddy of his fooled into thinking she was out of it, at least until she was safe from them. Plus it sounded as if there were others involved in whatever they're up to. How had rat-face put it? "Steele could get us *all* sent to jail—for homicide." Maybe if she was lucky, Hamlin and rat-face would let slip who "all" involved. Not that she'd be able to do a lot about it, she concluded, her head reeling. Considering my current repertoire of moves—look up, look down, and blink—how the hell could she say anything to anybody if they didn't ask the right questions?

She found it increasingly hard to think clearly as the medication gained the upper hand. Her head began to fill with darkness. She hadn't stopped him and his needle in time after all, only delayed its full effect, she realized as it sucked her down, whirling her faster and faster into a black sleep. And what a perfect lie he's told, she thought in the final seconds of her descent. Now even if she did figure out a way to say what the good Dr. Hamlin had done, everyone would dismiss her story as the ravings of a drugged-out lunatic.

3

Richard couldn't believe the change since morning.

As he watched, spasms snapped through her hands, arms and legs, coiling them so tightly he couldn't undo so much as her fingers. He knew it meant the brain's cortex was shutting down in the area of the bleed, whether from damage already done or a new hemorrhage, he couldn't tell. Either way, it left her folded into a ball, the way a child who is cold huddles in bed. Even her ability to understand him had become erratic. At times she no longer responded to his questions, or if she did, giving appropriate yes and no answers seemed beyond her.

"Kathleen," he said, again and again, as if his calling her name could penetrate her confusion when all the skills of his profession could not.

No response.

Images of their time together, fourteen months compressed into a flash, flew through his head. "We've beaten worse odds, you and me," he whispered into her ear, thinking of how they'd nearly died at the hands of a wacko terrorist who'd unleashed genetic weapons into the nation's food chain. "How many couples can say they fell in love escaping a would-be killer? And we've got such luck," he went on, hoping even if she couldn't understand, the sound of his voice would let her know he was there, "our kids taking to each other the way they have. Chet, he adores you, and Lisa, I love watching her big-sister him. He's exuberant again, I never thought I'd see that after his mother died. It's due to you, my love. You brought him and me back from the dead. . . ."

He continued his murmuring, keeping it steady as a heartbeat, driven by an insane fear that if he paused for so much as a breath, he'd lose her.

Yet it all seemed so horribly familiar. He'd stood at hundreds of bedsides observing people whose signs of life, like tenants about to vacate dwellings, hovered within for a last look around before departing. It always struck him how the work of muscles on automatic pilot—breathing, pulsing, contracting—had so little to do with who a person was, yet in the final hours were all that stood between sleep becoming death. But he kept talking, pulling her with words and pleading she not leave, sending any message of love he could think of into her ravaged brain to coax her back.

A half hour later the spasms cleared, and she continued to blink.

Over and over.

At first he thought brain damage had recruited her eyes into the same grotesque dance it had put the rest of her through. "Can you hear me, Kathleen?" he asked.

Her lids paused, then blinked yes.

"Are you trying to say something?"

Yes.

What he continued to fear most was that the hemorrhage had extended itself. "Do you feel new symptoms?"

Yes and no.

Not this again, he groaned inwardly, keeping a wary eye on the monitors showing her pulse and pressure. Above all, he had to keep from exciting her. "Is your dizziness worse?" he said, still whispering, knowing if the nurses overheard a repeat performance of his quizzing her they'd throw him out for good.

Her eyes shot up to the ceiling.

Wrong question, he thought, watching her pulse pick up a few beats. "Okay, so you don't want me re-asking all that stuff."

She resumed the steady, repetitive blinking, and her pulse settled down.

"Then what?"

The blinking continued.

After a few seconds he recognized that the movements had a pattern. He grabbed the pad of paper he'd used that morning to draw the human form, flipped over the page, and jotted down what seemed to be the sequence. Nine times she'd open and close her eyes in rapid succession, then look up. Three more times, pause, one time, pause, fourteen times, and then she'd look up again. Nineteen blinks in a row he counted next, followed by five, followed by twelve, two times. Then she'd repeat the whole cycle again. What the hell? he thought, once he'd been through the repetitions often enough to realize they weren't a fluke.

Did she know Morse code? he wondered. No, it couldn't be that. One blink wasn't longer than another to suggest dots and dashes. Then he got it, and kicked himself, it was so simple. He quickly jotted down the alphabet, and, starting with *a*, assigned each letter a number, from one to twenty-six. In less than sixty seconds, he'd translated all the different blinks into *icanspell.*

"Well, I'll be damned," he muttered, flush with excitement. "Looking up once is the end of a word, twice the end of a sentence?"

Yes.

"We can talk!"

Yes.

"What did you want to tell me?"

He carefully recorded a much more elaborate sequence of numbers. Occasionally she'd lose track of her count and signal "No" repeatedly, indicating she wanted to redo the word they were working on. After five minutes he'd written, *Hamlin gave me something bad.*

"Hamlin gave you something bad," he repeated out loud to make sure he had it right.

Yes.

Oh, Jesus, he thought. She must be getting confused by the medication.

"It's okay, Kathleen. Nothing *bad* is being given to you—"

Yes, yes, yes.

"Kathleen, everything's all right. What he's prescribed is to help you stay quiet—"

No, no, no.

Her pulse and pressure started to rocket again.

"Kathleen, calm down." He dropped the pad on the bed, grabbed her hand, and started to stroke her forehead. All four of her limbs curled even more tightly into spasm. Alarms began to sound from her monitors.

Two nurses ran into the cubicle. "What the hell's going on here?" said the one with gray hair.

"Christ, is she seizing?" her spike-haired companion asked, reaching for a syringe.

"She's becoming more decorticate," said Richard. "It may be a re-bleed. Get Hamlin, fast!" Bending down over her, he called, "Kathleen, can you hear me?"

No response.

Oh, Jesus, he thought.

The monitors continued to sound.

"It's a second hemorrhage," said Hamlin, shoving a film up on the view-ing box.

He and Richard were huddled in a tiny room outside the X-ray de-partment's magnetic resonance imaging suite, or MRI, peering at a string of small images showing Kathleen's brain in cross sections. They were like rows of snaps from a dollar-photo machine, except these, unlike any regular X rays, provided the detail of anatomy specimens.

Hamlin pointed to where the pons, a bulbous upper section atop the cone-shaped stem, peeped out from under the rounded cap of the cere-bral hemispheres. Or "an upright turnip stuck into the bottom of a cauli-flower" as Richard had always described the structure to first-year medical students. Tonight he had eyes only for the black sphere of blood that oc-cupied the center of that bulge, its edges extending to within a millimeter of rupturing through the cortex's surface.

"She won't survive a third," added Hamlin. "I'll have to operate as soon as I can get a team together, tonight if possible."

"Tonight?"

"Another bleed could occur at any second, even if we kept her com-pletely sedated. And by the way, one of the nurses gave me this." He handed Richard the pad where he'd been decoding Kathleen's blinking. "I can't believe you violated my orders and got her all worked up again with crap like that. He grabbed the paper back. "Well this time you might have killed her."

Richard felt as if he'd been bludgeoned.

"From now on you're not even going to be allowed near Dr. Sullivan," continued Hamlin, "provided she survives. And just so you know, the nurses are already urging me to lay a professional misconduct charge against you."

"Jesus, Tony—"

"I'm not going to, out of deference to your emotional stake in the case. But so help me, if you interfere with the well-being of my patient again, I'll do it."

"Please, stop, Tony," Richard said, his voice shredding.

Hamlin simply studied him, his expression impenetrable.

"Let me see her, I beg you, before you take her in to the OR. It won't do any harm. My God, man, I need to say good-bye!"

The neurosurgeon seemed to make a calculation in his head. "Of course. But keep it short. Now I've got to get scrubbed."

Richard walked through the doors of ICU and straight to Kathleen's bed without a glance at the nurses.

He gently kissed her on the side of her flaccid face, avoiding the airway hanging out of her mouth, "I love you," he said, over and over.

The gray-haired supervisor approached. "Dr. Sullivan's in no condition to give informed consent for her surgery. It says on her admission sheet the next of kin is her daughter, Lisa, but there's no answer at the number we have."

Richard found it obscene that life and death required so much paperwork. He could remember the thousands of dying he'd worked on who'd struggled for breath as a clerk pestered them for their mother's maiden name. He straightened, but kept his hand on Kathleen's. "Lisa is staying at our house now. Let me call her."

"Please make it fast. We just got word from OR. They want the patient up there in half an hour."

When he looked down at Kathleen, he was surprised to see her eyes open again. Ever so slowly, her lids lowered, then raised. Three times.

No, no, no.

Last-minute orders from Hamlin's residents ripped through the air.

"Up her O$_2$!"

"Set the respirator at eighteen!"

"Get me a blood gas!"

Lisa arrived within ten minutes.

Richard felt the thin young woman tremble as he guided her toward her mother's bedside. The nurses were too busy getting Kathleen ready for her ordeal to enforce Hamlin's order and keep him away.

Some hastily drew bloods.

Others adjusted her IVs and checked her monitors.

The older nurse with the gray bun rolled Kathleen on to her side and hastily sheared the back of her head with scissors and an electric hair-clipper. Hunks of auburn-gold hair tumbled over the pillow and onto the floor. Looking frightened, Lisa reached down and retrieved a lock of it, slipping it into her pocket. She then inserted herself between the crush of men and women around her mother, leaned down, cupped her face, and kissed her eyes. She whispered something.

"Everyone ready?" the supervisor asked.

Turning to Richard, Lisa said, "Chet's outside. He wants to see her, too."

His son approached the bed with the stiffness of a sentry, but he never faltered. "Can she hear me, Dad?" he said, eyes shimmering as he leaned over and kissed Kathleen on the temple.

"I think so."

He squeezed her lifeless hand. "I love you, Kathleen. I know you're going to be all right."

The nurses started to pile the various monitors onto the bed for the trip upstairs.

"Let's roll," said one of the senior residents.

"How long will the surgery take?" Richard asked him.

"At least six hours."

Richard managed to stroke her brow one more time before they wheeled her out of the room. As she vanished down the hall, the white circle where they'd shaved her head looked luminous under the dim overhead lights. Soon Hamlin's scalpel would slice through her scalp at that spot and his bone saw tear into her skull. It reminded him of a target.

He suggested they do their waiting back at the house, and told his answering service not to interrupt them. It was nearly midnight, and there shouldn't be any incoming private calls. Chet and Lisa might at least catch snatches of sleep without thinking the worst every time the phone rang. But there'd be no rest for him. Richard knew he'd be pacing until it was over, one way or the other.

At twelve-thirty he called the OR and got a report from the nursing station.

"They've just opened the cranium and are about to cut through the dura, a membranous covering over the brain," he said to Lisa and Chet after hanging up. "In other words, so far so good."

His two charges asked a few questions about what to expect next, then uneasily returned to the cribbage game they'd elected to play, the better to keep their minds occupied with the count and away from nightmare scenarios.

"I'll call back in an hour for another update," Richard added, hoping the prospect of not having to endure the full six hours without news would help relax them. Instead it only increased the frequency with which they kept sneaking anxious glances at the clock.

He moved his own nervous pacing outside onto the sidewalk of Thirty-sixth Street. Facades of the houses adjoined to his formed a three-story wall along the length of the block. The stones of each dwelling tinted a different color held and gave back the heat of the day. Warmth radiated across Richard's shoulders as he paused to lean against the deep brick-red front that distinguished his home from the rest.

The humid mid-June air enveloped him like extra clothing until his shirt grew sticky against his skin. He moved then, heading toward Lexington, hoping that something along the way would distract him from the curse of all doctors—knowing too well what could go wrong. But at the corner he could see the sprawling shape of New York City Hospital towering over the other buildings. By counting down from the top, he identified the OR floor. There being only a single set of lights burning at this hour, he found himself looking straight at the windows behind which Hamlin was at work on Kathleen.

He retreated back to his house, craving a cigarette as badly as he'd ever wanted one since quitting one and a half years ago. But he didn't yield. Giving them up had been part of a pledge he'd made, after having drunk, smoked, and grieved himself into a heart attack, almost leaving Chet an orphan.

He grabbed a fistful of carrot sticks from the fridge and crunched down on them.

At two o'clock he was back using the phone.

"They've raised the tonsils of the cerebellum, a rear part of the brain lying over the pons, and exposed the area they're after," he explained minutes later; the two teenagers listened attentively but with puzzled looks. "It means they can see the part of the brain stem they're after. It's swollen and has an underlying brown discoloration where the hemorrhage is. They're ready to cut into it as we speak."

What Richard didn't say was that this would be the moment of truth. If Hamlin opened the cavity of the angioma and set off a bleed he couldn't bring under control, Kathleen was lost.

Peering through his operating microscope, Hamlin carefully slit the cavernous sac containing the tangle of vessels that had bled and peeled back its edges using microretractors. Fresh blood surged out the opening, immediately flooding his surgical field and making it impossible to see anything.

"Suction!"

The resident opposite him, looking through the eyepiece on her side of the microscope, touched the tip of a tiny silver catheter to the welling red pool. With the sound a straw makes at the bottom of a milkshake, the fresh blood receded, enough to reveal lumps of old clots the color of liver, and a jet of crimson that pulsed up from deep within the cavity.

"Quickly, visualize the site of the bleed," said Hamlin, picking up his own microsuction. Together he and the resident removed more bits of gelatinous clot mixed with fresh blood, burrowing ever deeper into the small cavity. Their progress was slowed by the delicacy of the surrounding structures and the fact that the opening they were working in was no more than four millimeters, or a quarter-inch across.

"How are the patient's vitals?" he kept asking.

"Stable so far," the anesthetist assured each time.

As they got farther in, they came across the first of the abnormal vessels. It bled as soon as they lifted a piece of clot off it.

"I've got 'er," said Hamlin, zapping it with the point of his bipolar coagulator, a device resembling a minuscule soldering stick but which electrocutes blood in a vessel, instantly frying it to a solid. The bleeding stopped, but the culprit they were after kept pulsing bright red from below.

"Keep going," said Hamlin.

The two doctors worked furiously, setting off more bleeds and coagulating them as they went. Finally they lifted off a piece of clot and uncovered a ball of vessels the size of a raspberry. Hamlin spotted the crimson rivulet that they were looking for; it was coming from one of the lower vascular loops.

"Got you," he said, touching his coagulator to it.

They spent the next two hours coagulating and cutting away all the feeder arteries and shrinking down the central structure, until nothing but a shriveled husk of its former self remained, and this Hamlin removed in its entirety.

"Anybody see any bleeding?" he said, inspecting the now-empty capsule that he'd cleaned out as he irrigated it with a mix of normal saline and antibiotic solution. All the other residents around the table strained to see the video monitors where they'd been following the procedure.

"None."

"Looks clean."

"I think we're done."

"What a great job, Dr. Hamlin," said the sole female who had assisted him during the procedure. "You were fantastic."

Others joined in.

"Yes."

"Absolutely."

"Bravo."

"Okay, one last touch," said Hamlin, enjoying the accolades and eyeing his lady protégée. An attractive blonde in her late twenties, her name was Rachael Jorgenson, and beneath all her surgical garb she had a body he'd been impressed with from her first day on his service. Entertaining thoughts of inviting her back to his office to discuss her future, he picked up a small syringe he'd kept sequestered to one side of his tray. From it he slowly infused a few cc's of clear fluid into the still-open cavity.

"What's that?" she said, still standing across the operating table from him.

"Ringer's," he lied, referring to a colorless physiological solution intended for intravenous use that normally mimics the electrolyte and sugar composition of blood. "A little bath of the stuff at the site of surgery minimizes the swelling of brain tissue afterward. At least that's what a group out West are claiming. It's apparently got to do with osmotic pressure, the way a poultice of salt and water draws off the edema of inflammation. I do it on all my cases now."

As with most necessary deceptions, he'd kept the cover up simple and credible. Each new batch of residents, the nurses, and anyone else who happened to be in on his cases always bought it.

Flush with success over both the magnificent job he'd done on Sullivan and what he'd once more pulled off under everyone's noses with no one the wiser, he eyed Rachael. "Step over here to my side of the table and into the driver's seat, Rachael," said Hamlin, standing aside and offering her his place at the operating microscope, "Tonight, or this morning rather, the job of closing falls entirely to you." Groans of disappointment came from the rest of the group, "closing" being an honor coveted by all.

"Why, thank you, Dr. Hamlin." She moved into position, looked through the binocular eyepiece, and, using tiny silk sutures, proceeded to sew up the opening they'd made in the covering dura. As he leaned closer to inspect her work, she nestled into him.

Well, well, he thought. As pedagogical affairs went, this felt most promising.

4

Her mind cleared.
　　Voices came and went.
She recognized Lisa.
Chet, too.
Where was Richard?
All the voices reassured her that she would be all right.
They must be lying.
She wasn't all right.
She couldn't even see.
And one voice frightened her, yet she couldn't remember why.
"We have to keep you sedated, Dr. Sullivan," he had said. "Don't worry, the operation went fine. Just relax."
She wanted to scream at that particular piece of advice. But she was too drowsy to even open her eyes, let alone move any other muscle in her body. How had she gotten this way? She knew there was a good reason but couldn't recall what it was. Her mind clouded over.

She dreamed she was buried alive, submerged in quicksand, and pinned in a straitjacket. She awoke to the sensation she'd been imprisoned in cement that had hardened around her as she slept. Was she sleeping or awake now? She wanted to turn over—and panicked at her inability to move. Then the alarms on her monitors went off, loud as car horns it seemed, and frightened her even more. She heard the nurses running to her, the swish of the curtains as they swept them aside, and their chatter that sounded like shouting.

"When was her last dose of midazolam?"

"Two hours ago."

"Christ, she's going through this stuff like candy. Maybe Hamlin should change it to something more long acting, or she'll be addicted soon."

Why were they yelling? Had she done something wrong? She didn't want any more injections. And did they mean that Hamlin was trying to addict her to that medazzle stuff?

Oh, Richard, where are you? I need you.

"You're going to advise his maestro on what medications he should use?" intervened another voice, still awfully loud. "Good luck, sister!"

"I'm not about to advise Hamlin of anything," said the one who'd mentioned addiction. "That curvy resident he's always making rounds with these days is the one I'll speak with. Let her convince him. Looks to me like she's already got his ear, among other parts of his anatomy. Lord, the way that young woman is always brushing up against him."

Her companion gave a laugh that pierced the air like a shriek.

Get away from me! Kathleen imagined that she was surrounded by witches. They must have cast a spell on her, or injected ink into her mind, since everything in her head was black mush.

Was it day or night? She still couldn't open her eyes, despite knowing it was important she do so, that there awaited something for her to take care of out there where the shadows were. Again she'd no idea what.

Time passed. She realized she could perceive changes from light to darkness, even through her closed lids. And if someone loomed over her, she could tell that, too, as their shape caused her to see a darker gray.

A shadow crossed in front of her. "Can you hear me, Dr. Sullivan?" asked the voice she instinctively feared. Her ears amplified his words to the point they hurt her eardrums. She also found herself acutely aware of his smell—a mix of half-camouflaged body odors covered by a bracing flowery scent.

She struggled to look at him, and managed to raise her lids a slit. The lights in the room seared like a lash, and she shrank back behind her sole defense—darkness.

"I think you can understand," he said, this time in a whisper so close to her ear that she felt he had slipped into her skull.

He'd been there before, she vaguely recollected. And done something bad to her brain.

"The medication I've given you has mixed you up, given you troubling hallucinations. Forget them, for your own good. You'll get better faster if you put them out of your mind. You must not let those bad dreams get you excited and interfere with your getting well, understand? Otherwise I can't risk allowing you to see Richard or taking you off the drugs."

I want you out of my head! She was bursting to scream again.

Kathleen floated out of sleep, only to instantly recognize the smell of that awful man while feeling him poking and prodding her. *Leave me alone, you stinking pig!* she yelled, but once more no sound came.

After enduring his tapping her ankles and knees, then repeatedly stroking the bottoms of her feet with something sharp that sent her legs shooting into spasm, she heard him say, "So what do you think, Rachael?"

"That it's time to lower her sedation?" replied a woman's voice.

"Normally, yes. But in this case, since Dr. Sullivan already exhibited symptoms of acute paranoia after her first stroke, and the accompanying anxiety caused a rise in blood pressure that probably precipitated the second bleed, we can't afford to reduce her dose, can we?"

"I guess not."

"Guess? You'd be certain if you'd seen her, going on about me putting something in her brain. Of course Dr. Steele didn't help matters any, getting her all worked up and feeding her delusions by encouraging her to communicate them by blinking her eyes."

"You're kidding."

"A serious instance of a physician letting his personal feelings interfere with professional judgment. We don't dare let her regain consciousness again until we're sure we can wean her away from such upsetting ideas."

No, thought Kathleen. He was lying. She remembered now. He and the rat-faced man did inject something into her brain. And he was blaming Richard for making her worse. She tried so hard to protest that the alarms started to sound again.

"Look at her vitals take off," the woman said.

"If anything," Hamlin added, "we better up her sedation."

Moments later, Kathleen felt a warning swirl and plummeted, free fall, into a silent black void.

Saturday, June 16, 9:10 A.M.

"I still can't let you see her, Richard. I'm keeping my ban on all visitors. Even when I show up her pressure goes off the charts."

"But, Tony, I can calm Kathleen down, I know it." He'd intercepted the neurosurgeon outside the doors to ICU. The man's resident, a Dr. Rachael Jorgenson according to her name tag, moved a discrete distance down the hallway. "By all means keep the other visitors away. Well-meaning as they are, there have been far too many, and I certainly agree you should protect her from them." Because the comings and goings of doctors are recorded in ICU, the nurses had dutifully logged in Kathleen's chart the names of his colleagues who'd stopped by to inquire about how she was doing. On one level the list was personally gratifying. He particularly noted the physicians outside of his department who had taken the trouble to try and see her. Paul Edwards, chief of gynecology, Francesca Downs from cardiology, even Adele Blaine who ran her own rehabilitation institute on the upper East Side paid a visit. While he dealt with these people regularly in ER, he couldn't say they were friends. Their reaching beyond the professional to make a personal gesture moved him deeply. But no way was Kathleen ready for such onslaughts of thoughtfulness. "I swear, Tony, I'll put out the word myself that no one else is to bother her. And when I'm at her side, I'll keep my mouth shut, not make so much as a peep, and just hold her hand."

Hamlin shook his head, the white mane adding to his authority. "The vascular ends of all those arteries I sealed off are still fragile. They'll give way unless she remains completely quiet."

"She must be terrified."

"Not with what I'm giving her."

"Christ, Tony, I know I screwed up big-time—"

"Yes, you did. And by the way, so you're forewarned, I just learned one of the nurses reported you to Gordon Ingram."

"What!"

"Sorry. It wasn't my intention."

"But—"

"Look, do as you're told, and I'll have a word with him," said Hamlin, turning to walk away.

"Jesus, Tony, the last thing I need is to have Ingram on my back right now."

"I told you I'll speak with him. With any luck I should be able to make him back off. Of course it will have to wait until Monday morning, and you've got to behave."

Damn it to hell! thought Richard, shuddering at the prospect of being subjected to an inquisition by the most pugnacious ethicist and quality assurance expert that New York City Hospital ever had. But the man was sure to give him a fair hearing, he reassured himself. After all, Ingram championed excellence as ruthlessly as he ferreted out shoddy care. And, Richard remembered, the fact that he had saved Ingram's life wouldn't hurt his case any.

Saturday Evening, 6:30 P.M.

Ever since Doctor Francesca Downs read her first Wonder Woman comic she wanted a secret life, especially one that involved a trusted sidekick. But that was twenty-five years ago. As time passed, other dreams developed. The fascination she felt at dissecting frogs lured her into biology, then medicine, and finally to the rarefied world of cardiac surgery, where she had neither time for a life, secret or otherwise, nor a sidekick. Until two years ago. That's when she'd fallen in with the "sensational six," as they teasingly called themselves. But now, standing in the center of her walk-in closet and about to dress for tonight's dinner with her coconspirators, she realized that her once-happy childhood fantasy, sidekicks and all, had become a nightmare.

After pulling on the plain black dress she'd chosen, she padded into her bedroom and stared through the dusk at the lights of the greatest city in the world. In the distance she could even make out Times Square where thirty stories of dazzling neon necklaced the famous intersection with a crossed, thousand-watt strand of glitter. Her thoughts drifted to when all six of them had first got together at the place that had become their permanent meeting spot. A heavy rain had been pelting against the full-length windows at Lauzon's, a French restaurant with a private dining room overlooking Eighth Avenue. Droplets cascading down the glass rendered the gaudy points of color outside as insubstantial as a shower of chapagne bubbles. The cutoff setting proved a fitting bower for hatching a scheme so ripe with promise it blurred the prospect of consequences and made the risk seem remotely vague enough to be acceptable. The decisions they made that evening were the real intoxicants, so loaded were they with possible accomplishment. Together the six of them toasted each other, raising tall crystal flutes in celebration of their daring. As the pale golden fluid effervesced merrily in the light, Francesca believed she had finally arrived in the winner's circle.

She had even allowed herself a moment of feeling glamorous that night, having caught sight of her reflection in one of the full-length, smoky mirrors adorning the walls. Its flattering softness gave her white complexion and blond hair a golden glow that the harsh lights of the hospital never did, and she liked how her red cocktail dress showed off her breasts and hips the way no scrubs or lab coat ever could.

That dress was hanging in her closet now. She had so few opportunities to wear it that whiffs of stuffiness wafted off the material. Whenever she did put it on, that scent, she figured, served as warning to anyone who came near that she didn't get out much and therefore probably had something wrong with her.

But not back then.

She'd noticed early on the special smile Jim Norris kept slipping her during drinks as he explained to her and the others what he had in mind. He sat beside her, and she reciprocated his show of interest, gently laying a hand on his forearm whenever laughing at his jokes or asking him to pass her something. She knew he was at least fifteen years older than her, but his lean body and weatherworn features gave him a robust look that interested her, even if it might just be for a one-time romp between the sheets.

Why not? she'd thought. Men her own age weren't worth the bother, even for casual encounters. They seemed to be between divorces or finally wanting to settle down. Either way, once they got a taste of her lifestyle—twelve-hour workdays and being on call one in five—they dumped her for women with more time on their hands. She had left the restaurant with Norris that night, expecting nothing more than a little fun.

"You're a magnificent fuck," he'd told her after they had exhausted themselves in her bed.

"You sound surprised."

"Well, it's so at odds with your image at work."

"My ice-queen persona?"

"I didn't want to say it, but yes."

"It keeps the wolves from the door."

"Ah, you don't like hospital romances?"

"Despise them. All that gossip."

"Aha! So you listen to gossip, do you? I can't be bothered. But since you're a devotee, what have you heard about me?"

"That you're a notorious womanizer."

"And now that you know me?"

"I'm praying you won't be a scoundrel and let our secret out."

"Well, that all depends if you'll see me again."

And so it had started.

But over the next weeks it was his maverick intellect and rebellious spirit, not mutual lust that lured her much closer to him than she'd ever counted on.

"Damn him," she said, walking back into the closet to the line of shoes she kept on the rear wall, and angrily picking up a pair to go with her dress. She never should have become involved with the man, she told herself for the one-thousandth time. Everything seemed so right at first, and had gone so damn wrong.

Stepping in front of her mirror, she thought about what she'd say at tonight's meeting. Paul Edwards hadn't spelled anything out this afternoon when he phoned and summoned her to be at Lauzon's for eight o'clock, but his voice had the glassy hardness it got whenever he intended to ram what he wanted down everyone else's throat. "Well, good luck," she muttered, having already made up her own mind what to do. But could she count on anyone backing her?

Lockman would be the weasel he always was.

Norris wouldn't flinch from his original plan, holding as fast to it as he had from day one.

That left Adele Blaine. Maybe she'd be the sensible one.

Dark-haired, average in height, and ebony-skinned, she was so lithe that she was mistaken often for a dancer when she was off the premises of her institute. The Adele Blaine Residential Treatment Center occupied a lavishly renovated building on the upper East Side. In it she'd amassed enough Laura Ashley interiors, potted plants, and computerized rehabilitation equipment to rival any pricey workout emporium in town. But there was a difference: Her domain was the designer equivalent of a revival tent where the lame walked and cripples threw away their crutches.

"Do you know why I'm so great at what I do, honey?" she'd once asked Francesca when they were seated together during one of the group's more boozy dinners. "It's not the glitzy veneer of my place. I just play the high-society battle-ax because it's good for business. Puts the HMOs and everyone else on notice that they can't nickel-and-dime my black ass to death. No, my secret—and don't tell anybody, or you'll spoil my reputation as a hardnose—is I got a real passion for seeing past the wrecked bodies I inherit from the hospital and seizing on what they can still do. Then I trick the inhabitants of those ruined mortal trappings into believing it's possible. Once that happens, my charges work their butts off, and more often than not, whatever is the 'it' of their objective comes true. So there."

Francesca never had any qualms about sending her patients to the institute because, whatever the woman's "tricks" were, they must be sound, because she got post-op cardiacs back into form better than anyone. Hopefully she'd be just as practical about the business at hand tonight and see things Francesca's way.

Turning from the mirror, she rejected the thin belt that came with her outfit and chose instead the widest gold-emblazoned one she had. "You better go along with me, Blaine," she murmured, cinching it tight around her waist. "Because no one is going to take Wonder Woman down!"

"Goddamn it, Tony, you and Norris had no business taking Sullivan on without speaking to us first," Paul Edwards, chief of gynecology, was screaming when Francesca opened the door.

He abruptly stopped, and four faces flushed with extreme emotion swung and gaped at her.

She made her way to one of the two remaining places at the table.

Edwards made a show of looking at his watch. "You could have been on time."

"I'm sorry, but it was hell to get a taxi tonight—"

"And where's lover boy?" Edwards added.

She felt her cheeks grow hot. "If it's Dr. Norris you're referring to, I have no idea."

His lips parted as if he were about to say something more, yet he remained silent as she took her seat. His mouth always struck Francesca as ironically small compared to the size of the loose jowls and pudgy features surrounding it. Despite his being well past fifty, he reminded her of the baby picture on a popular brand of infant formula. Which seemed fitting she supposed, since he made his living by bringing the little cherubs into the world.

"Shall we order," she suggested, "to gather our strength?"

They rang for the waiter and expeditiously handled the process. White and red wines were brought in and poured, then they were alone again.

"I acted in the best interest of us all!" Hamlin said, picking up where they'd left off when Downs had arrived. He was on her left, and she could feel the anger coming off him. "If Sullivan lives—"

"Lives!" Edwards's voice immediately hit the decibels she'd heard coming in. "We've all seen her, Tony. She's a gorked, spastic, heart-lung preparation—"

"You didn't examine her—"

"And you didn't think! Trying to coerce Steele into helping us, I never heard anything so crazy in my life."

"But how else can we cover up the DOAs—"

"He's put me in more jeopardy than he has you, Paul," interrupted Adele Blaine, ignoring Hamlin even though she sat directly opposite him. "Hell, I'm the one who'll have to take her into rehab. Once she's in my institute, I'm implicated. My name's right there on her chart along with our genius neurosurgeon." She slapped her hand on the table with such a smack, Lockman, seated beside her, flinched. "So if he get's caught, I'm in for it, too, goddamn it!" She downed the remains in her wineglass, and finally turned her gaze on Hamlin. "And as for your idea of telling Steele anything, Tony, that's even stupider than what you've already pulled. I'm with Paul, and say no way!"

Even with the width of the table separating them, her ferocity made the white-haired surgeon cringe away from her. But it didn't diminish the anger in his eyes. "What I did, my dear Adele, was a miraculous piece of surgery on a woman who would otherwise have died—"

"Better she had of, Tony honey, than the can of worms you opened up—"

"Desperate measures for a desperate problem, Adele. We've all made that call as doctors. This is no different. Sure I took a chance, but everything is absolutely under control. I can keep her drugged until even she will think it was all a hallucination, and for the moment Steele will do what I say, which is keep away from her."

"How can you be sure of that—"

"Because he got himself reported to Ingram for his trying to question the woman—"

"Ingram!" interrupted Edwards. "He's involved now? Oh, my God, this is out of control."

Blaine looked as if she were about to fly across the table at Hamlin.
Downs felt her own heart start to race.

"No, no," the neurosurgeon said, flapping his hands at everyone
to settle down. "It's Steele who's on the carpet. He's even begging me to
smooth the whole thing over with Ingram, and in return has promised to
stay away from Sullivan. It couldn't be better."

Blaine rolled her eyes to the ceiling. "Mother of God!" she muttered,
just as a discrete knock sounded at the door, which immediately opened
so that two waiters could serve them. That done, Blaine said. "Hamlin,
you're out of your mind."

Lockman leaned his pointed face toward hers. "I told him he
shouldn't say a word to Steele."

"Oh, shut up, Lockman. You and Norris both ought to be shot for
having gone along with helping him do Sullivan in the first place."
Swinging her fury back to Hamlin, she added, "Let me tell you something else, fool! You've been taking far too many risks from the beginning,
what with that asshole technique of yours."

"Couldn't agree with you more, Adele," said Edwards. He turned
toward Downs. "And why Norris also went along with him yesterday, I
just don't understand. I mean, if anyone should have known better—"

"Shouldn't you be saying this to Dr. Norris yourself?" she interrupted, refusing to let him or any of them use her as a conduit to Jimmy.
It wouldn't be the first time. They seemed to think it went with the turf
of her having slept with him, and she resented it.

Piss off and deal with the man face to face, Francesca wanted to scream
at them. She wasn't his keeper or anything of his now, but she'd be
damned if she would reveal such a personal thing about herself.

"We'd like to know where you stand first, honey," said Blaine, reaching for one of the open bottles of red wine. She poured herself a refill,
then swallowed a third of it in a single gulp.

This business was getting to her, Downs thought.

Edwards delved into the fillet of sole that sat in front of him. "Yes,
Francesca. What do you think?"

No one else showed the slightest interest in their food.

Hamlin glared hard enough at the middle ground of the table to set it on fire.

Lockman, always one to gang up on whoever he sensed was about to be picked on by the rest, joined the other two in locking their sights on Downs.

"What do I think? I think I was on cloud nine until Hamlin's patients started to die," she told them, speaking as if the neurosurgeon weren't even in the room.

Hamlin leapt to his feet. "Jesus Christ, I've had it with the lot of you! Like it or not we set out to save lives, and that's what I'm trying to do with Kathleen Sullivan. Now if any of you have a way to protect our work other than forcing Richard Steele to cover for us, then tell me now."

No one answered.

As if for good measure he went around the circle, fixing each with a good dose of venom from those black eyes of his. Lockman looked away. Edwards and Blaine gave back as good as they got. Francesca went on watching the others, still trying to pay the neurosurgeon no attention, but it was like attempting to ignore a volcano.

"Then as far as I'm concerned the matter's settled." Hamlin said, exuding the authority of a man used to imposing his will at meetings. He threw down his napkin as if it were a gauntlet, and strode from the room. His white hair streaming after him reminded Francesca of an era when another of the men present would have met him at dawn by the East River to mark off twenty paces and use their pistols.

"He's up shit creek, whatever he does," she said the instant he slammed the door behind him. "By trying to cover up he'll only make matters worse, for him, his patients, and us. As for Steele, you know as well as I do that he's sharp as a whip. But I've probably dealt with him more than any of you over cardiac cases in Emergency, so I've seen for myself how the man won't back off once he gets a whiff of something not quite right. Throw into the mix that Sullivan's his lover, and I think we've got a real problem hurtling right at us. In fact, I've been figuring maybe it's time we all cut our losses and came clean."

Blaine paused, her wineglass halfway to her lips. Edwards's full fork dangled from his hand. Lockman's little eyes bored onto hers. Their faces seemed to hang off them in disbelief.

"Look," Francesca continued, "I'm getting downright fed up with Hamlin trying to tie his fuckup to us. I didn't kill his patients. And you know my situation's precisely the opposite of his. The technique I used on the cardiacs was exactly the same procedure I'd have elected to follow even if we had approval, not some untested improvisation. My success rates stand for themselves."

"Hey!" Edwards said. "Don't get any ideas about paring yourself off and somehow avoiding the hammer here, Francesca. If Hamlin goes down, I go down. So does Adele, Lockman, and your boyfriend, Norris. Speaking of whom, does he know you're thinking this way, or is it a surprise you're planning to spring on him?"

"You asked me what I thought. I told you."

"Well, here's what I think," the portly man continued. "We're in the same mess together, period. I hear talk like yours, and I start getting afraid that maybe someone's considering making a deal with the cops, going after immunity in return for tossing the rest of us to the wolves. I warn you, I'll no more let that happen than I'll let Hamlin reveal our little secret to Steele." His teeth chiseled sharp edges onto the words, and his eyes grew hard as flints.

Francesca felt her cheeks grow hot for the second time that evening.

Blaine carefully set her drink back on the table, folded her hands in front of her as if she were about to say grace, and gave a tight smile. "That's right, sweetie. Don't get any ideas about playing Miss Goody Two-shoes on us. Besides, there's a little matter of your having helped Hamlin modify those customized catheters from the heart lab that he uses."

"I never touched a patient with them—"

"You aided and abetted, honey, with full knowledge of what he intended. I'm no lawyer, but you're definitely no Snow White. And may I remind you, whatever scheme you might work out with the police, you'll be finished as a doctor, for life. I'll personally offer testimony to make sure of that."

The heat in Francesca's cheeks spread to the rest of her face, and sweat formed on the skin between her shoulder blades. She struggled not to lunge at the woman.

Blaine smirked, apparently content with the obvious discomfort she'd caused, and took a triple swallow from her wineglass.

"You've both given me an idea how we can deal with that pompous jerk Hamlin," said Edwards after a few seconds of arctic silence, "and Steele, if necessary . . ."

A half hour later Blaine was downing her fourth glass of wine. Edwards scowled at his half-eaten fish, shoved it aside, and joined her in ordering a drink. Lockman looked nervously from one to the other, as if unsure who to side with.

Francesca excused herself, found a toilet, and threw up. Rinsing her mouth out at the sink, she studied her drawn face in the mirror. The thought of rotting in a cell, her life as a doctor over, left her trembling.

Returning to her table, she saw a man at the bar watching as she passed, his eyes moving sideways like marbles in a slot. Any other time she wouldn't have given his stare a second thought. These days the sight of anyone singling her out was enough to set off her fears that somebody had discovered her secret. That Edwards and Blaine had already made their own deal with the cops to save their skins. That the police had her under surveillance. That they were about to lead her away in handcuffs. Whoa, girl, she told herself, marshaling the same iron discipline she'd used for over a decade to keep her nerves steady in the OR. I can't afford to be paranoid right now.

The man went back to his drink.

5

Dr. Gordon Ingram leaned back in his chair after closing Kathleen Sullivan's chart. His dark suit was immaculate and, like all his other dark suits, had been selected to emphasize the leanness of his physique. Likewise his intellect hadn't an ounce of fat on it. And his prowess at sorting out ethical dilemmas was equaled by the formidable clinical skills he had honed during the decade he'd served as chief of ICU—until a heart attack felled him at the age of forty-two, only three years ago. Degrees and commemorative plaques honoring the superb quality of his work during that portion of his career filled the wall behind his desk. They were testimony to his suitability for the other half of his current job—sniffing out other people's screwups. Hanging above the gallery of his own accomplishments was a framed poster with red printing that read INCOMPETENCE KILLS.

Otherwise his small office was spare, containing no personal mementos and not even a plant. What items the hospital had issued him—a utilitarian metal desk with a modest computer, a laminated bookshelf in imitation oak, and a pair of distinctly uncomfortable visitor's chairs covered with black Naugahyde—were at the low end of the status continuum. There were even snide jokes told behind hands about Ingram decorating the place in "early police station," all the better for "questioning suspects." But nobody felt much like laughing when they found themselves seated across from him, accounting for complaints that had been leveled against their work, or worse, trying to explain away mistakes that he'd discovered during one of his infamous random chart audits. As usual, Ingram delivered his penetrating stare that could unsettle both liars or innocents and exuded the contented aura of a man who liked his work. Liked it too much, as far as Tony Hamlin, the person currently seated across the desk from him, was concerned.

"I agree with you," Ingram said. "What happened with Dr. Steele was obviously a lapse of judgment, but it certainly doesn't merit an official inquiry. Clearly the man is too emotionally involved, but that's understandable."

"Thanks, Gordon," Hamlin said, greatly relieved that he'd headed off Ingram before the big snoop could look too closely at Sullivan's case. "Which nurse reported the incident? I'd like to have a word with her, to point out that I merely threatened official action against Steele to drive home that he must follow orders this time. She'd no right to follow through on her own."

"Sorry, Tony. You know my rules. Anybody who comes forward to report potentially unethical behavior is guaranteed anonymity."

The better to encourage snitches, thought Hamlin, getting up to leave and reaching for Sullivan's chart.

Ingram slapped his hand on the document. "Not so fast. There's another issue here that we have to address."

"Pardon?"

"It's whether you should continue your ban on Richard's visiting her. I also see you only allowed her daughter and Richard's son a quick look at her immediately post-op, and nothing since. Hell, it's over seventy-two hours since surgery. Why shouldn't she see those closest to her?"

"Because her vitals go haywire whenever anyone gets near her, including me, and the cauterized vessels won't hold—"

"Hey! Remember who you're talking to here." His boyish crown of curly dark hair did not offset the severity of the expression on his face. "Patients in ICU need contact with loved ones, especially if they're agitated. Lay down the ground rules about what they can and cannot do, so as not to excite her further, but get them in there."

"Gordon, she's my patient. I think I know the state of mind—"

"Don't make me quote the data on ICU psychosis. Also, don't make me officially question the amount of sedation you've been using on this patient. A medical student could see it's the most likely cause of her being so inappropriately agitated. It's time to use family as a sedative, and wind down the drugs."

"But—"

"I can go through channels, and make that an official recommendation, Tony."

The thought of all that scrutiny stopped Hamlin. The OR greens he was still wearing suddenly felt very heavy and hot.

"Now do I tell Steele, or do you?"

"I'll tell him," Hamlin replied, determined not to give the man an additional chance to become anymore involved than he already was.

"And you'll speak to the nurses about allowing as much family contact with Sullivan as possible?"

"Yes."

"Good. If you start tapering the doses of midazolam tonight, we should have a sea-change in Kathleen Sullivan's mentation by week's end. Have you arranged for someone to trach her?"

Hamlin felt the temperature crank up another few degrees, and a ripple of perspiration broke out under his scrubs. Ingram referred to cutting a hole into her trachea through the front of her neck and ventilating her lungs by that route rather than using the tube down her throat. Patients likely to require long term airway protection or breathing assistance found it more comfortable, and the arrangement also allowed them to talk, recovery of speech often being one of the first functions to return, if it came back at all. But that was a risk Hamlin couldn't take at the moment. "Of course I have," he said, and got up to leave. Retrieving Sullivan's chart, he smiled at Ingram while silently cursing the man.

12:10 P.M.

The Hospital Cafeteria

"You're going to tell Steele now, without even waiting to see if she recovers? That's absolute lunacy!" Lockman whispered. He leaned so far across the table toward Hamlin that he almost upset their untouched cups of coffee. "If she dies, which there's a damn good chance she may do, and he knows, he'll turn you over to the cops for sure."

Hamlin hunched forward as well, drawing close enough to catch the sour aroma of the day's NOON SPECIAL, cabbage rolls, off the radiologist's breath. "If you'd kept your mouth shut, she never would have suspected anything."

"What's done is done," interjected Adele Blaine, looking nervously around her and motioning the two men to quiet down. "But you're not thinking straight, Tony honey. Down in Tennessee where I was born and raised we sure believe in letting sleepin' dogs lie. So, if she's going to go, best you let her die with no one the wiser."

"And you're a fool to ignore our usual precautions not to be seen together," Edwards added. "Summoning us all here like this is plain nuts." The large man kept his voice low, but it rumbled the length of the table.

"It's an emergency, for Christ's sake," Hamlin said. "I can't drug her any longer, thanks to Gordon Ingram. The woman's bound to keep on spelling out to Steele what she remembers from the angiogram, and once she's not so sedated, maybe he'll believe her."

Downs said nothing. She kept hoping Norris would walk in the door and bring the others to their senses, the way he always had when they'd clashed before. But back then their problems had been scientific in nature and were solvable. What loomed now seemed as insurmountable as fate.

"So what do you suggest?" Hamlin continued. "Wait until he finds out for himself? Get real! Because if that happens there's no chance he'll listen to our side of the story before going to the police, whether she lives or not."

Edwards exchanged glances with Blaine, then swung his beefy face around to Hamlin. "Here's how we see the situation, Tony. If you persist in your insane idea to confess all to Steele, then Adele, Francesca, Matt, and I figure it's not just you who'll be arrested, but the bunch of us. That would force us, in the interest of keeping ourselves out of prison, to take drastic measures."

Hamlin tensed. "Meaning what?"

"Either you keep your mouth shut, or we'll approach the cops now,

61

before you give Steele the opportunity to do it for us. And we'll offer them you in exchange for their granting us immunity."

Hamlin looked poleaxed, the color drained from his face, leaving his complexion as white as his hair. "You wouldn't!"

Blaine, Lockman, and Edwards remained defiantly silent.

"Francesca?" he said hopefully. "You can't be serious."

She glanced up at him, as disgusted with herself as she was with the lot of them, but too frightened by the prospect of prison not to go along. Casting around for something to say, she decided anymore words would be futile and, resigned to the trap she was in, simply shrugged.

The gesture infuriated Hamlin. His slack features instantly coiled into a show of contempt. "You—you—wouldn't dare." A crimson flush spread over his cheeks, up to his forehead, and down his neck. "You'd all lose your licenses to practice."

"Try us!" said Blaine, her pupils growing wide as buttons and making her small head appear doll-like. "It's better that than jail."

"You bitch!" Hamlin sprang to his feet and towered over the little woman. His high-pitch whisper had been sibilant enough to shush conversations two tables away.

"Shut up, Tony, and sit down!" said Edwards, rising to grab him by the shoulders and plunk him back in his seat. "You're attracting attention. Now listen up. I've got another way to buy us all some time."

"Oh, really?" He tried to shake off the gynecologist's massive grip.

"Yes, really," the big man said, maintaining his hold.

Downs looked around nervously. A half dozen people were staring at them.

Edwards's large face broke into a forced smile, and he released his captive with a friendly slap on the back, as if they were the best of pals. "Why shouldn't I get an operating slot from you? I could do a week's worth of D-and-Cs in the time it takes for one of your brain jobs. Now you're not leaving this discussion until I tell you my plans for dividing up the summer OR schedule in favor of my department." This time his over-loud voice carried the length of the room.

The onlookers lost interest.

Edwards brought his head up close to Hamlin's and whispered, "Have

Sullivan add a few more features to her story that will make the whole thing so implausible no one will believe anything she says, not even Steele."

"And how do we do that?" said Hamlin, sarcasm curling off his lips.

"Not we," said Edwards. "You."

While passing the cafeteria, Richard spotted Hamlin's distinctive head of hair. He'd been trying to catch up with him all morning to find out how his conversation with Gordon Ingram went, but the man hadn't answered any of his pages. This was his chance, as soon as he had finished talking with the people at his table.

But as Richard watched, the conversation seemed to grow quite intense. "Probably hospital politics," he muttered, recognizing each person at the table as a prominent figure in their respective departments. Knowing from bitter experience that such dustups could go on at length, he bought a coffee and sat down at a table between Hamlin and the exit, intending to intercept him on his way out. He soon realized that even by New York City Hospital standards, this argument was especially heated. At one point it looked as if Hamlin would throttle Blaine, the rehabilitation specialist, but Edwards settled him down. What could have them so worked up? Come to think of it, they were an odd group. Lockman from radiology and Blaine with her rehab unit would obviously work with Hamlin on neurological cases. Lockman would work with Downs doing coronary angiograms. But why was Edwards, chief of obstetrics and gynecology, with them, and what was he so intent on telling Hamlin that could make the neurosurgeon blanch? Turf battles between those two specialties weren't common.

Ten minutes later Hamlin pushed away from the table and headed for the door, a dazed look on his face.

Richard jumped up and cut him off as he passed. "Tony, can I have a word with you?"

"Richard!" he said, appearing startled. His eyes darted ever so slightly in the direction of the group he'd just left. "Why? What do you want?"

Was he ever rattled, Richard thought. "How did your conversation with Ingram go?"

Hamlin didn't answer. For a second it seemed he was too distracted to make sense of the question. Then he swallowed and said, "Quite well, actually. I got him to agree that no official inquiry into what happened would be necessary."

"Whew. That's a relief. Listen, thank you—"

"I also agreed that you can begin to see Kathleen. Ingram insisted on it, despite it being against my better judgment. He also strongly recommended we taper down her medication, as part of reinstituting family visits, again against my advice. But don't visit her before tomorrow morning. Perhaps by that time, though I seriously doubt it, she'll be better prepared to see you." He then abruptly walked away.

Richard stood speechless watching him go. At the doorway the man paused and stole a backward glance in his direction. He looked frightened. Even stranger, when Richard turned to retrieve his empty coffee cup, he saw scowls on the faces of some of the people Hamlin had been arguing with. But Francesca Downs didn't scowl. She had the puckered look of someone who'd just caught the scent of an exceedingly rotten odor.

Must be the cabbage roll special, Richard thought.

From the opposite side of the cafeteria, Gordon Ingram also viewed the disapproving tableau that monitored Hamlin's exit. He, too, found the grouping odd. He made his judgment with a statistician's sense for recognizing things outside the norm, especially their vehement arguing. Trouble, he figured, but what kind could they have in common?

Anyone else might have left the observation at that. But he was a born muckraker. His remarkable clinical skills had not only given him a podium from which he could pronounce on lesser lights, his aptitude for doing things right made it easy for him to spot things done wrong, and he'd made a career of routing out mediocrity wherever he found it. Since his heart attack, he'd become all the more zealous. "If I can't practice medicine, I'll be damned if anyone who's screwing up the privilege will either," he told anyone who complained he was coming on too strong. The truth was he hadn't given up practice altogether, simply curtailed his hours by confining himself to consults. It gave him some satisfaction that those same complainers were almost always among the first to seek his opinion as soon as a case got the better of them. But none of it replaced the exhilaration he'd felt at the helm of ICU. Not a day went by that he didn't chafe at how he hadn't the physical stamina for it anymore.

Within minutes he was in his office unlocking the bottom drawer of his desk and taking out the computer he actually relied on, a black laptop barely an inch thick with a thousand times the power of the puny antique the hospital provided. "It's my book of secrets, just like J. Edgar Hoover's," he used to joke to his wife, before she got fed up with his long hours at the hospital and left him.

Over the next hour he ran a morbidity-mortality analysis for the last few years of each physician at the table, including Hamlin, looking for any patterns suggesting a higher rate of complication or death than was acceptable.

"Interesting," he muttered.

Lockman's record was littered with mistakes, as Ingram expected. All the other numbers were within normal limits, except Hamlin's and Down's. Their rates of adverse incidents were far below national standards, indicating the two physicians were much more successful in treating their patients than most other U.S. doctors in their respective fields, Downs even more so than Hamlin.

So why would these two superstars be so unhappy with their colleagues in the cafeteria? Judging from the expressions on their faces, they appeared the most upset by whatever the group was arguing about. Come to think of it, Hamlin also seemed rather unusually defensive during their meeting over his problems with Kathleen Sullivan. And his medicating her so heavily, especially in the context of a clear-cut ICU psychosis, was of questionable judgment, to say the least.

Ingram used his authorization to access the hospital's computerized records of prescribing patterns by physicians and punched up Hamlin's profile for ordering narcotics and tranquilizers.

It seemed in order. His overmedicating Sullivan was an isolated event.

So why the scene in the cafeteria?

He went after another indicator that often signaled trouble, pulling out the incidence of unexpected patient readmission back into hospital shortly after discharge for the two physicians. Again, they both had exemplary records. Two entries for Hamlin, however, caught his attention, because they were both similar and relatively recent. Both were men who had been readmitted to emergency with fatal hemorrhagic strokes, but more than a year had elapsed since their previous surgery. The neurosurgeon couldn't be faulted for that. Especially since the initial diagnosis in each case was a hereditary vascular malformation, one being a Berry aneurysm, or sacular weakening of an artery that was leaking blood, and the other a capsular angioma, same as Kathleen Sullivan had. Whatever led to their second bleeds couldn't have had anything to do with the first. Once congenital malformations were removed, they didn't reoccur.

But why had they rebled? Intracranial hemorrhages only comprised 20 percent of all strokes, whatever the cause, and vascular malformations were way down that list. Yet here were two men who'd both had two bleeds.

Perhaps they also suffered from hypertension, he thought, identifying the most common reason for strokes of all kinds. But he couldn't tell without pulling their charts, the computerized record listing only their principle admission diagnoses. Any contributing secondary problems, such as high blood pressure, should have been added as well, but staff pressed for time often failed to enter such data. Even for a suspicious mind like his, the absence of the secondary diagnosis on a couple of charts didn't seem much of an indicator for something being seriously wrong.

Still, attributing a pair of hemorrhagic strokes in the same patient to more than one disease process bothered him. To explain away two patients that way left him even more uneasy, because he knew the statistics. When doctors resort to more than one diagnosis to account for a recurrent sickness, they're usually wrong.

He shoved back from his desk and rubbed his eyes, the glare from the computer screen along with the harsh white light from the overhead fluorescent tubes giving him a headache. But he continued to puzzle over what he'd learned.

Years of uncovering bad practices had taught him another important lesson in the quality assurance business. The more successful things appeared to be, the less critical attention people pay to what's going on, and the greater the possibility that a serious problem could escape detection for a long time.

Maybe one of our two superstars warrants a closer look, he thought, shutting down his computer. The trouble would be finding the time. Today alone he had three disciplinary hearings to chair.

8:20 P.M.

Silver needles of rain danced off the asphalt as Richard ran for his car, his coat pulled over his head.

"Hey, Richard," called a voice from behind, barely audible above the noise of the downpour. "Wait up."

He turned and recognized the sleek form and familiar slow walk of the man approaching him carrying an umbrella. "Evening, Gordon," he said. "Have you got room for me under there?"

Ingram grinned. "Come on in."

Richard hurried up to him and stepped beneath the black brim. As they both were tall, he didn't have to duck. He did have to reduce his pace a little, so as not to pull ahead of Ingram, who had the measured step and slightly labored breathing of an old man.

"Everything straight between you and Hamlin now?" he asked, puffing a little.

"Yes. I was going to thank you tomorrow for smoothing things out for me—"

"My God, Richard. What's the point of sorting out ethics all day unless I enforce a few of my rulings now and then? You know, win one for the good guys and all that. You're certainly one of the 'good guys' around here, and among the few I can talk with equal to equal. Think nothing of it. Just take care of Kathleen. How's she holding up?"

"As to be expected, I guess. She's pretty dazed."

"Well, that ought to improve quickly. I remember how I felt as a patient in ICU. Like I'd had my teeth kicked in."

Richard thought back to the night three years ago when the man had arrived at ER in cardiac arrest with a massive heart attack. "Half the battle in saving your sorry ass was getting the residents and nurses settled down," he'd told him weeks later. "They were already freaking out at having to resuscitate one of our own, but after coming around, you started giving orders on yourself. Everyone was so intimidated and used to taking what you said as word of law, they very nearly carried them out." Richard now chuckled at the memory. "You were a real son of a bitch as a patient, I seem to remember."

Ingram's normally ascetic expression burst into a smile. "I was, wasn't I?" he said, beaming with pride.

"The worst."

"Well, I wouldn't wish the experience on anyone, but it taught me a ton about being a doctor. Having someone around to hold your hand can count for a hell of a lot."

The sudden edge in his voice made Richard wince. It had been the talk of the hospital how lots of colleagues and residents dropped by to wish him well or sent him flowers, but the man's wife barely managed to visit him a half dozen times. Even then, according to gossip from the nurses, the woman barely touched him. A year later she had filed for divorce.

"A lot of the fools around here, such as Hamlin, could stand to learn from a stint at the opposite end of the stethoscope," he continued. "You were one of the few who were not only competent but never stopped dealing with me man to man. I even heard your voice trying to reassure me I'd be fine when I was clinically dead. I'll never forget it."

"How are you doing now, by the way?" To Richard's expert eye and ear, he seemed to be puffing a bit more than usual as he spoke.

"Me? Can't complain. Just this muggy weather makes my breathing hard sometimes. Bit of asthma is all. But I sure miss the action."

Ingram, like most doctors, had always been secretive and dismissive about his own medical problems, so Richard had no idea of his current state of health, heart or otherwise. Respecting the man's privacy, he didn't press the point. "You still do a lot of good, Gordon. I see it in ER. You being around pulls everybody's socks up. Nobody rides herd on the place better than you." As prickly a personality as Ingram was, there wasn't another chief in the hospital who championed the practice of quality care the way he did. The man could literally raise the dead, and more than once he'd pulled off a save when everyone else, Richard included, had called the resuscitation off. "You know all the residents nickname you The Lazarus Man."

He grinned again. "Yeah. I kind of like that."

"It's well deserved," said Richard.

"Thanks. "

"Here's my car, but it's me who thanks you."

He gave a dismissive wave. "If you have anymore trouble with Hamlin, let me know."

As Richard crawled in behind the wheel and started the motor, he watched Ingram's slow progress between the vehicles until the slightly hunched figure reached his silver Mercedes parked at the opposite side of the lot, well out of the way from where the two men had run into each other. *Well, I'll be damned,* thought Richard, realizing the man must have engineered their meeting just so he could check if Hamlin had rescinded the no-visitor ban. Shifting into drive, he plowed through a large puddle of water, cutting it in two as he headed for the exit. *Take that, Hamlin,* he thought, feeling a tiny surge of triumph at the "good guys" having won something for a change.

She dreamed Richard was making love to her.

The feel of him stroking her breasts and thighs seemed so real, she thought for a moment that they were back in her bed at the apartment, and that everything else had been a nightmare.

But her head had felt so much clearer since they'd stopped giving her the injections every few hours. She shouldn't be mixing up fantasy and reality anymore.

A familiar whiff of tangy aftershave infiltrated the haze.

Her eyes flew open.

The cubicle was dim, the curtains closed.

Hamlin stood over her, running a gloved hand between her thighs, inserting his fingers into her. He also reached up, took one of her nipples between his fingertips and gave it a squeeze. The whole time he stared straight ahead, not even looking at her, his profile carved still as a mask in the dim light.

Disbelief, revulsion, and rage swept through Kathleen, warring with each other until, unable to do anything, she thought she'd explode. His casual manner of violating her made the deed seem even more monstrous. Feeling her heart pound its way into what had to be triple digits, she looked up at the monitors to see why the alarms weren't sounding.

He'd turned them off.

He continued to touch her, coldly, almost clinically, his gaze remaining fixed in front of him and away from where he prodded.

She started to cry, her mind racked with sobs, but only silent tears escaped her body-prison and rolled down her cheeks.

Beyond the curtains she could see the lights in the rest of the department.

Nurses and patients were talking together as casually as ever.

". . . do you need your pain medication now . . ."

". . . yes, please . . ."

". . . and how about glycerine for your lips . . ."

". . . that would be nice . . ."

Hamlin still continued to touch her.

People answered the phone.

Overhead the PA announced that visiting hours were over for the evening.

She thought she'd go insane.

Please, someone help me, she screamed into the impenetrable vault her skull had become.

The woman in the cubicle next to her asked for an extra pillow.

I'll survive this, Kathleen repeated over and over. *And I'll nail your sorry ass. Nail it.*

Finally Hamlin glanced at her.

Even with the low light she could see his face. His eyes looked dead, and his face was the color of paste beneath his crown of white.

The instant he saw her looking at him, he snapped off his gloves, dropped them in the wastebasket, and strode from the cubicle. "Give her a few minutes before you turn the monitors back on," she heard him say to the nurses. "Halfway through my neurological exam, she woke up, and she went crazy again at the sight of me."

6

When Richard saw her the next morning, she looked completely vulnerable, lying on her side and curled tightly into a ball again, her limbs once more severely flexed and her hands again twisted into claws. He knew he should expect such spastic contractions, but still he felt a sense of foreboding as he knelt by her head so she could see him.

"Hi, Kathleen," he said, fighting to give a smile and conceal his fear for her. He knew it was a pathetic effort.

Her cheeks and mouth sagged deathlike onto her pillow, lips pulled into a leer by the endotracheal airway, nostrils misshapened by a feeding tube. But in brilliant contrast to the chalky pallor of her loosely hanging skin, a spark of fiery green from the depths of gaunt eye sockets told him that she was in there and very much alive. Instantly she started to blink at him.

He glanced up at her monitors in alarm. "Stop, Kathleen! No more trying to spell out words." To his relief and surprise, both readings, pulse and pressure, stayed rock steady. But when he met her gaze again, she persisted to blink at him. He tried to take her hand, having difficulty inserting his fingers into the rigid grasp. "No, Kathleen. Just relax. There's no need to tell me anything right now."

She stopped, just for a second, then blinked. Yes. Yes. Yes.

Oh, boy, he thought, starting to stroke her brow. "Listen, Kathleen, if you set off those alarms again, I'll be kept from seeing you until God knows when, so cut it out!"

72

No.

"Damn it, Kathleen. I'm not kidding. You're four days post-op. All those severed vessels haven't healed yet and won't take your jacking up—"

She cut him off by starting to blink out a long sequence again. A quick glance at her monitors showed everything remained perfectly normal. "Oh, man," he muttered, "You're not going to quit until I decode this, are you?"

No.

He reluctantly dug out a paper and pen. "I'm only going to do this on one condition. That you promise to stop if I see your vitals changing. Is that a deal?"

Yes.

He began to count. She'd spelled out *Ham* when he guessed, "Hamlin?"

Yes.

When she added a *t* to *moles* he became uneasy. This might be more of her paranoia again. By the time she'd blinked *Hamlin molested me*, he was already figuring the gentlest way to convince her it couldn't be true. Seeing her readings on the monitor remain steady, he stroked her forehead, intending to explain about ICU psychosis, and reassure her that it was a common reaction that would pass. Poor Kathleen, this was already such a nightmare for her. The last thing she needed were hallucinations to make it worse.

But before he could start, she resumed her blinking. Maybe it's best I hear her out, he figured, and once more picked up his pen and paper.

You don't believe me, do you?

Oh, Jesus. "It's not that, Kathleen. I just don't think you understand how this place and the medication you've been on can affect your mind." As he proceeded to tell her about the side effects of intensive care, the pupils of her eyes smoldered hot as pitch, and he knew she was furious at him. She made no more attempts to tell him anything, even when he asked.

Sitting by the bedside, holding her stiffened hand and stroking her head, he felt increasingly helpless to do anything for her. He kept up a constant chatter, describing how Chet and Lisa were coping, that they'd be in shortly to see her, stressing how much they all loved her, how well the operation went—anything positive he could think of. When a physiotherapist arrived and began to work on her, extending her legs and uncoiling her fingers, to his shame he almost felt relieved for an excuse to return to ER and escape into work.

Whenever the smell of Hamlin came into the cubicle, she would open her eyes and stare straight ahead.

If he asked her to blink *yes* or *no* to his questions, she held her lids immobile.

Most of all, she kept her emotions cold as ice, determined to control her pulse and pressure, denying him an excuse to oversedate her again.

Sooner or later, Richard would believe her, she kept telling herself.

Sooner or later.

She took particular pleasure in the fearful glances Hamlin started to give her as another day passed and she continued to ignore him during his rounds.

Sooner or later, she would think, *I'll blow the whistle on you.*

But Richard didn't believe her.

I didn't imagine any of it, Richard, she told him each time he arrived.

Concern would flood through his haggard face, and he'd continue to reassure her that nothing was amiss.

If she weren't paralyzed, she'd brain him, she sometimes thought. But she kept her frustration in check and the alarms on the monitors silent, still resolved never to give anyone the slightest excuse to load her up with those hideous drugs.

Sooner or later, he would have to believe her.

The next day she saw doubt in his eyes and knew her persistence was getting to him.

The following morning Hamlin arrived to find him at her bedside. Until then, he'd avoided doing rounds while Richard was about. The alarmed look in the neurosurgeon's eyes spoke volumes. At one point he took Richard aside, obviously intending to keep her from overhearing. "Is she continuing to show signs of paranoia?" she heard him whisper, her hearing still hypersensitive.

Richard hesitated, swallowing a few times the way he always did when he wasn't sure about something. "A little, but it doesn't seem to up-set her anymore," he replied. "Certainly her vitals are stable. I guess she's starting to realize that her mind was playing tricks on her."

She watched relief creep ever so slightly into Hamlin's face. "Why, that's wonderful!" he said.

Yeah, right! she thought, more set on getting the bastard than ever.

By the time he finished his neurological exam, her fixed stare had him looking nervously at her again. More importantly Richard seemed to be studying Hamlin, his forehead gathering into the faintest hint of a frown. He's asking himself "could it be true?" she thought. He was starting to suspect.

That night she moved the fingers of her right hand.

The following morning when she did it in Hamlin's face, he looked as if he were about to run screaming from the room.

Later That Same Day,
Friday, June 22, 1:10 P.M.

"She's going to get me. And the more she recovers, the more convincing her accusations will seem. Why the hell did I let you and the others blackmail me into touching her?" Hamlin paced the length of the phone cord as he yelled into the receiver.

"Now, Tony," Edwards said, "you don't know how many complaints I get a week from women who claim they've been diddled by one of my staff. Half are crocks, and even the ones who aren't rarely prove anything, so they shut up."

"I tell you she won't back off!" he said to the gynecologist, this being the third time in as many days he'd violated their policy of not contacting each other in the hospital.

"So what! The important thing is Steele doesn't believe her, just as I predicted, and more to the point, neither is he liable to believe her if she again starts harping that you put something into her brain."

"But if she keeps it up—"

"If she dares keep it up while benefiting from a miraculous recovery the whole hospital attributes to your surgical skill, everyone will slot her as a crazy ungrateful bitch. All you have to do is maintain a steady demeanor and a closed mouth. Now settle down, and don't call me anymore."

"You don't know her. She's got to be tough as nails to keep her nerves under control around me the way she does. Once she's able to write, or speak, I'm dead."

"Shut up and get hold of yourself!"

"You bastard. That's easy for you to say. I was a fool—"

Edwards hung up on him.

Enraged, he tried to call him back.

A busy signal buzzed in his ear like an infuriating fly.

He slammed down the receiver, then raced into his adjacent examining room, and threw up in the sink.

A man wearing a white smock over a patient's examining gown sat outside Hamlin's office door. A portable stand suspended an intravenous bag and tubing that ran into his arm. No one paid him much attention as there were half a dozen doctors's offices along that stretch of corridor, and at least fifteen other people waiting to be seen, some in hospital gowns, too. He was clean shaven with a very short buzz cut, a stark contrast to the beard and full head of hair he'd worn when he used to work in pathology, or years later, as an orderly on the obstetrical ward, until the bastards had fired him. Even his name was different now, thanks to his phony ID and fraudulent Medicaid card, so he was sure that anyone who'd known him back then wouldn't recognize him.

His wristband indicated he'd registered in ER earlier that day as Robert Lowe. He had complained of symptoms to make them think he had renal colic. When they asked for a urine sample, he surreptitiously pricked his finger with the safety pin he'd brought for the purpose, and added a few drops of blood to the cup. As soon as the nurse saw the test strip, she sent him to the ultrasound department, where he knew he'd be left waiting, completely unattended, possibly for hours. From there, pushing his IV bottle, he could wander unhindered through most parts of the hospital.

It had been easy for him to find Hamlin's office and park himself in front of it. He wanted to get a good look at the man he'd received the anonymous tip about. It wasn't that he didn't know him—everybody who'd ever worked in New York City Hospital over the last decade had probably seen the guy with his flamboyant white hair—but he hadn't laid eyes on him for two years and needed a close-up look. Not that he thought the man would have changed much. His worry was that the information he'd been given about the neurosurgeon could be part of a trap—one intended to lure him and other members of his cause into the arms of the police. So he thought it wise to scout out this situation, starting with the target.

Hamlin had looked like hell when he finally appeared, rushing into his office and slamming the door behind him. A doc that frightened hardly seemed like someone he should fear. Curious, he moved from opposite the entrance to a place close enough to hear what was going on inside. Minutes later he was rewarded with the shouts of a one-way conversation. Obviously Hamlin had phoned someone. Then he heard the bang of a receiver being slammed down.

Hamlin was terrified all right, the phony Robert, Rob, Lowe thought. But was he meat for the crusade—or bait?

Three floors above, Paul Edwards picked up a toasted bagel, lathered it with cream cheese, and lopped on a slice of smoked salmon. But when he bit into it, he felt his stomach churn as the fishy taste spread through the grooves on his tongue to the back of his throat. "Shit," he said, throwing it back on the lunch tray his secretary had brought him. Even then the smell of it lingered, playing with his gag reflex. He pushed his black leather chair away from his mahogany desktop, carried his tray across an expanse of pastel green carpet, and shoved the offending food out the door.

"Not hungry again today?" his secretary called. The middle-aged woman, dressed in a canary-yellow suit, looked startled as she studied him from her desk.

In reply he shook his head, locked himself in, and returned to his desk.

Edwards had been hoping against hope there was a chance Hamlin might have just enough nerve to hang tough against the Sullivan woman and at least get them past their present catastrophe. Now he was sure Hamlin would crack.

He looked around his office, the bookcases full of articles he'd published, the plaques on the walls paying him tribute for his research in high-risk obstetrics, and the many, many photos of him receiving checks for endowments to the department. The business of birthing babies brought in more bucks to the hospital than all the diseases combined. While people were grateful for the treatment of an illness, they'd give the sky and moon to assure themselves progeny, the only certain way to outlast one's death and leave a living legacy. In fact this luxurious suite, provided at the institution's own expense, was a trophy, awarded to him for the skill with which he mined this most fundamental of human drives to procreate.

He would lose it all.

Worse, he had nothing else that mattered. There were no offspring of his own with their pictures on the walls, and the space he'd kept for a portrait of whoever happened to be his wife—he'd been through three divorces—had remained empty for the last five years. Without his prestigious position at this hospital he'd be lost.

Time to cash in his chips and bring the game to a close, he decided, reluctantly going to the drawer where he kept his private phone. It was a safe line, one with no extensions that he used mostly when dealing with lawyers. If delivering babies to barren couples was the most lucrative of professions, obstetrics in general was the most litigious. It was on this phone he wheeled and dealed, trying to achieve out-of-court settlements to avoid bad PR. Even to his hardened ear these conversations could be crass beyond belief, and he'd never want anyone to overhear them.

"... a dead baby's worth a few-hundred grand, tops. It's the brain-damaged ones that will cost you millions, so for God's sake, whatever you do from now on, don't resuscitate a vegetable . . ."

It was also the line he used to talk with his new business partner.

He dialed the long-distance number he'd come to know by heart.

"Fountainhead Pharmaceuticals," said a receptionist with a heavy Spanish accent.

"Extension two-six-five, please."

After a few rings a man answered "Yeah?"

"It's Edwards. That matter we discussed. I think it's time to bring the deal to a conclusion."

Sunday, June 24, 10:35 A.M.

"Dr. Sullivan's making wonderful progress, Dr. Hamlin," Rachael Jorgenson said during her Sunday morning phone report.

He'd gone on tearing himself apart with worry well into the weekend, and had avoided the hospital altogether by letting the residents do the daily rounds on his patients.

"She's more than ready for her trach."

His stomach tightened at the news. "Really," he said, toweling off his forehead. He'd been working out on his treadmill downstairs when his wife had yelled for him to come up and take the call.

"Yes. Dr. Ingram was in to see her as well today. He asked about when we were going to do it. It would be more comfortable for her, and she could try talking by covering the opening. Though she can't flex or extend her wrist or support her arm at all, she's actually able to hold a cup in her right hand, and her fingers are beginning to move in her left, so—"

"We'll do it Monday," he said, his innards churning at the prospect of Sullivan repeating her charges against him for all the nurses in ICU to hear. It marked the first time he admitted to himself that Blaine and Lockman might be right, that his only way out would be if the woman died. Not that he'd ever think of deliberately harming her. After all, he was a physician. But even in experienced hands, a tracheotomy could be a tricky procedure. In the hands of a resident, anything could happen. "In fact, I'll let you do it. Go ahead and make the arrangements," he said on impulse. No sooner were the words out of his mouth, than he recoiled at the idea. *What am I doing?*

"Why, yes, Dr. Hamlin . . ."

"Is there anything else?"

"Well, not about the patients. But I'd like to see you, privately."

Hamlin flushed, and turned his back on his wife who sat nearby reading the Sunday paper. "I can't talk about that right now," he whispered.

"It's not talk that I had in mind, Tony," she said, her voice all at once temptingly husky. "I thought maybe we could meet in your office again, to rate my performance under your tutelage."

Despite his misery, or perhaps on account of it, he found the offer irresistibly appealing. "I'll call you back." He felt himself grow hard even as Rachael hung up, so he had to keep his back to his wife.

"Trouble with the hospital, dear?" she asked.

"Oh, the usual. You know. Residents complaining we're always looking over their shoulders during the week, then they can't get through the weekend without calling one of us in."

"Ah, no, don't tell me you have to go on duty today? I planned for us to have tea at the Plaza this afternoon. You know how I love all those little sandwiches and cakes they serve with it."

Yes, he was afraid he did, he thought, as he eyed her varicosed plump thighs protruding from the hem of a yellow floral housecoat and a belly that seemed to billow through its folds. He absently patted his own flat abdomen, something he was proud of at sixty-one. It validated him as a man as much as his stature in neurosurgery did as a doctor, and he worked equally hard at keeping both. His wife annoyed him, the way she seemed comfortable with growing old. Not him. He knew how to feel young. And he needed a dose of Rachael Jorgenson right now. But when he got to his office about an hour later, an unexpected message was waiting for him on his hospital e-mail.

We have to discuss your patient in ICU, privately. Meet me at the film showing in Bryant Park Monday evening. I've booked a table in your name for eight-thirty on the upstairs terrace of the restaurant there. I'll slip in after the movie starts. It's essential no one sees us together.

P. E.

The date showed it had been sent Saturday afternoon, but not from Edwards's usual hospital service. He'd used an Internet café near the university in the East Village.

He could only hope Edwards would be more helpful this time. Hamlin deleted the passage as Rachael let herself in his door without knocking. She was wearing OR greens and, he soon found out, nothing beneath.

Monday, June 25, 9:15 A.M.

"I tell you, Jo, I know drug-induced hallucinations can be so vivid people can't distinguish them from reality at the time, but after a while, they at least acknowledge what they saw could have all been in their minds. She's been so coldly persistent, her story never wavering, that I'm beginning to think the unthinkable."

"That he actually molested her?"

"I feel nuts even saying the idea out loud, it's so preposterous. But it's as if she's sucking me into her paranoia. No matter, I just can't dismiss what she's saying."

Richard had asked Jo O'Brien to have a coffee with him in his office, sworn her to secrecy, then unburdened himself of what Kathleen had been saying about Hamlin for nearly a week now. They were sitting across from each other at his desk. "I'm sorry to dump this on you, but if I don't talk it out with somebody, I'm going to go nuts."

The woman leaned forward and patted his hand. "I'm glad you did Richard. It isn't the kind of thing you should keep to yourself."

"But she's got to have imagined it," Richard insisted. "At least that's what I kept telling myself. Now I'm not so sure anymore."

"I'd err on the side of Kathleen. Report him!"

"But you know how it is with a sexual-assault allegation against a doctor. Even the rumor of it can be a career-ender."

"Would you sit on this if another of your patients told you the same thing?"

He was startled by the question. "No, I wouldn't sit on it. Neither would I leap on the guy. I'd check it out, the way I am now."

"So what's keeping you from doing something about it?"

He didn't reply. The truth was, Kathleen's initial claim about Hamlin and Lockman putting something in her brain had seemed so crazy, it primed him to dismiss anything else she signaled as out of whack. But if Hamlin did touch her, he wondered, could her first story have something to it as well? No, that part was really too weird, he told himself, deciding he wouldn't say anything about it to Jo.

"You know as well as I do," she continued, "the guy's a notorious skirt chaser. I can't count how many nurses and female residents he's gone through."

"But that's between consenting adults. Have you ever heard a whiff of gossip that he's ever accosted a patient? That any of those women you mentioned who went to bed with him weren't willing and ready."

She pursed her lips and stared at the ceiling, presumably consulting her storehouse of hospital gossip. After a few seconds she said, "I have to admit, the answer's no."

"Well, neither have I. And that includes stretching my power as head of ER to sneak a look at his personnel file. It's squeaky clean. There's never been a single complaint of that nature."

"So what are you going to do?"

"Christ, I wish I knew. I mean, the guy saved her life with a masterful piece of heroic surgery, and here we repay him by—"

"Have you seen him lately? Is he behaving as if he has something to hide? Is he acting peculiar in any way around you?"

"Things were a little tense last week, but that might have been me. I mean, half the time I wanted to grab the guy and demand what he'd done. The other half of the time I felt ashamed at ever having thought him capable of something so creepy."

"When did you last talk with him?"

"Early this morning. It was a brief phone call, to tell me he'd arranged the tracheotomy on Kathleen for this afternoon."

"Have it out with him afterward. Clear the air, or bring the matter to a head. Better still, once the tube is out and Kathleen is finally able to talk, listen to her first. When you can actually hear what she has to say, you'll be better able to judge whether it rings true. Then confront Hamlin. If his side of the story smells fishy, nail him."

Monday evening arrived, and Kathleen still hadn't had the procedure. It had been booked for three P.M., but a series of emergency surgeries had bumped her time in the OR. Richard had ended up hanging around the whole afternoon and into the night, determined to be with her.

At nine-thirty the call finally came to ICU that they were ready for her. But now Hamlin, who'd been around during the day, was nowhere to be found and wasn't answering his page. Normally someone from ENT, or the ear, nose, and throat division, would have overseen the procedure, but the neurosurgeon routinely waved them off, having a reputation of never letting anyone else touch his patients.

"Goddamn it," Richard muttered. "Do I have to do it myself?"

Jorgenson had been in and out all afternoon, obviously as impatient to get the job done as he was. All at once she reappeared at the curtains and announced that she'd had authorization from Hamlin to start the job so as not to lose the slot, and he'd be along.

"Will the anesthetist be present in the meantime?" Richard asked. Residents did tracheotomies, but their skills varied greatly, and by law they were never to do them without supervision. He'd be damned if he'd let some novice bend the rules and possibly butcher Kathleen.

"He's waiting for us now," Jorgenson replied.

Richard took on the job of ventilating Kathleen with an Ambu bag as they made the trip through the hallways.

Once they rolled into the OR and centered her under the harsh glare of the operating lamp—anesthetic equipment on one side, equipment trays on the other—Richard explained to Kathleen what would follow, stressing that she'd receive an injection to put her asleep while they worked. He didn't mention it would be midazolam again, the same agent that had made her paranoid.

She blinked, yes, which he took to mean she understood, and when he held her hand she gave his a weak squeeze.

"Wow!" he said, beaming down at her, delighted at the lift he got each time he felt her fingers move. Even though her hand was still a misshapen claw, her grip was a little stronger each day, and he used every incremental improvement to try and convince himself recovery was possible.

Once the anesthetist had administered the sedation and taken over bagging Kathleen, Richard discretely withdrew to the doctor's lounge. He didn't want to hang around and make everyone nervous. To pass the time, he looked through a stack of magazines. They were so old they had articles about the Bush-Gore recount and market watchers predicting a quick turnaround of the Nasdaq toward ever new highs.

Jorgenson had been thinking about the tracheotomy all day. In real life the procedure wasn't at all like in the movies or on TV, where George Clooney would say, "Hand me that ballpoint pen and find me a straw."

"Trachs" were special. Infrequently performed, not every trainee got a chance to do them, and those who did bragged about the number over lunch in the cafeteria. As personal stats went, it was a claim to prestige against which there was no argument, like an earned run average or a tennis ranking. Those who hadn't "done one" yet would grow silent or laugh nervously as they listened, doubt flickering in their eyes and betraying the worry that they wouldn't make the grade when their turn came. She knew there wasn't a man or woman in the entire surgical program who hadn't coveted getting the nod, and when Hamlin announced he'd assigned her the case during rounds that morning, she could feel the heat of envious stares.

Rather than miss the opportunity now, she'd lied about Hamlin's imminent arrival. She actually had no idea where he was or why he wasn't answering his page. But what could it matter, she reasoned, if an anesthetist were to watch over her instead? After all, both were qualified teachers. Nor did she see a problem in having said Hamlin was on his way. The operation usually took less than ten minutes, and if he wasn't coming at all, she'd be finished before anyone would realize. Tony, of course, would back her story up afterward. Of that she could be certain.

Holding her hands up in the air, she gave them a final rinse under the taps, turned from the sink in the scrub room adjacent to the OR, and walked authoritatively into the operating theater. Already masked, she quickly slipped into a green surgeon's gown that one of the nurses held up for her and pulled on a pair of sterile gloves with a decisive snap. She moved precisely and quickly, wanting everyone to know that tonight, though just a resident, she was in charge. Nobody was going to interfere with her proving herself by undercutting her authority. Neither did she want them to suspect it was her first with a live subject.

She'd only ever practiced a tracheotomy on cadavers in the pathology lab. Both times she got the tube in the wrong place, missing the trachea and wedging it in the subcutaneous tissue between the skin and the structures of the neck, much to the derision of her fellow house staff. She hadn't told that to Hamlin. Why should she, and risk his giving the nod to somebody else?

"She's ready for you, Doctor," said the anesthetist, adjusting both the volume and rate of Kathleen's ventilations after hooking her up to a respirator. "Everything's set. I'll be in the next room doing another induction."

"You're leaving?" Jorgenson felt a twinge of alarm as she stepped up to the table and stood over Kathleen's exposed neck.

"Of course." He gave her a wink over the top of his mask. "We always work two rooms at night. The anesthesia technician here can handle switching the machine from the old tube to the trach. Besides, you said Hamlin's on his way, right?"

"Yes, but—"

"You're all set then." He turned and walked into the scrub room of the adjacent OR.

Her mouth went dry, and she rested her hands on one of the sterile drapes to keep anyone from seeing the slight tremble that had developed in her fingers. She shouldn't be doing this without supervision, a voice cautioned somewhere at the back of her mind, but the stares of the nurses waiting for her to begin and her previous humiliation at having failed with the cadavers only increased her determination to proceed. She picked up the scalpel.

The nurse standing opposite swabbed the front of Kathleen's neck, turning it brown with proviodine, washing it clean again with alcohol, then placing a sterile towel with a hole in the center over the area where the trach would be performed.

Jorgenson quickly felt out the landmarks of Kathleen's voice box—beginning with her thyroid cartilage, or Adam's apple, moving below it to the semicircular shape of the cricoid, another cartilage piece, and beneath that to the top ring of the trachea. Counting down to the one below it, she brought the scalpel point to the surface of the skin, pressed the blade in and made a horizontal cut an inch wide. As with most novices, though, she hadn't pressed deep enough, slicing too superficially and missing the windpipe. But now, unlike in the cadavers, the tissue bled profusely, obscuring her view for a second try.

"Sponges!" she said, far too excitedly.

The nurses gave each other uneasy glances.

Jorgenson pressed four-by-four pads into the incision, but the blood continued to flow.

"Here, someone hold the pads while I complete my opening."

Willing hands reached into the field, and after a minute of swabbing and pressing, she could see her first cut, and the still intact tissue of the trachea underneath. Using her left hand to steady the structure, she felt the endotracheal tube still inside. Should I remove it first, she wondered, only then realizing that her practice and instruction on a corpse hadn't involved there being a tube already in place. Having no idea how she should proceed, she resorted to an old resident ploy. "How do the anesthetists do this here? Cut into the trachea with the tube in place, or remove it first?" Phrasing a question to imply that her ignorance embraced only the local practices of New York City Hospital had saved her ass before.

"Leave the old tube in place, cut down to it, then pull it back until it clears your incision," said the anesthesia technician, "then you can put the new trach tube through the opening." He was a big man with ebony skin and kind eyes who spoke in a calm matter-of-fact way, but the completeness of his answer told her she hadn't fooled him about the extent of her inexperience.

"Thanks," she said, and sliced the gray band of connective tissue that stretched between the glistening-white rings. The cut parted, revealing the bright orange surface of the tube beneath. "Pull back," she ordered, her voice still way too loud.

He did much more, first shutting off the respirator so that it wouldn't be blowing air out through the opening she'd just cut, then deflating the cuff that wedged the tube solidly in place, a preliminary step preceding removal.

She should have ordered the nurses to do that, she realized as the orange airway slid up out of view. *Settle down,* she told herself, *or you'll really screw up.*

"Quickly now, Doctor," said the technician. "Remember she's no longer breathing."

Her face flushed. He was now telling her what even a medical student would know. More flustered than ever, she picked up the curved tube she was to slide into the trachea and tried to insert its tip through the opening.

It wouldn't fit.

Prickles of sweat emerged between her shoulder blades and across her forehead. "The opening's still too small!" she said, her voice skipping even higher.

"Then cut it wider!" snapped the technician, his gentle calm vanished.

The nurses started to call out readings.

"O$_2$ sat is dropping!"

"Pulse and pressure falling."

"I'll get the anesthetist!" added a third, racing from the room.

Jorgenson got the scalpel into position, and gingerly extended the cut. Again the tube wouldn't fit.

"Patient's turning blue!"

"Pressure's sixty over thirty; pulse forty."

"Shit!" said the technician, struggling to re-advance the original endotracheal airway.

All her poking around had got it hung up.

The door flew open from next door as the nurse who'd gone for help returned at a run and raced for the wall phone. "The other case is a bullet wound to the heart who's crashing, and nobody can leave him. See if Steele's still here. I'll page anybody else who's around." She grabbed the receiver and punched 0.

Someone hit the intercom. "Dr. Steele! We need you in OR C stat!"

Her hands shaking more than ever, Jorgensen took another slice at the trachea. This time she used too much pressure, and the blade slashed through another half inch of skin. Blood flooded out of the opening. Once more unable to see anything, she tried to insert the trach tube by feel alone. At first it didn't go, and she increased the pressure. It gave a sudden lurch, and went into the neck. "Got it!"

The technician attached a ventilating bag to the protruding end and pumped hard.

Bubbles gurgled up through all the blood with each compression.

A nurse placed her stethoscope to the base of Kathleen's lungs. "No air entry!" she called out.

It was interstitial, between the skin and the trachea, like she'd done on the cadavers.

"Any surgeon or intensivist, OR stat!" blared the overhead PA speakers. It kept repeating over and over.

Jorgenson felt as if she would faint.

Richard barged into the room, his eyes wide with fright. "What the fuck have you done?" he shouted, seeing the carnage at Kathleen's neck.

The nurses had him masked, gowned, and gloved in seconds. "Get ready to reintubate her," he told the technician.

"I'm set," the man said, already holding a laryngoscope and an endotracheal tube a size smaller than the one he'd just removed.

Shoving Jorgenson to one side, Richard stepped to Kathleen's head and grabbed a wad of gauze pads from the surgical tray full of equipment.

Handing them to Jorgenson, he said, "Put pressure on the trachea with your fingers using a gauze pad, to seal the opening."

She stood, frozen.

"Now!"

She did as he'd ordered, reaching into the blood and finding the opening with her fingertips, then slipping pads into position.

"Got it?"

She nodded.

"Pulse is thirty. No pressure," said the nurse beside her who'd been reading the monitors and checking vitals with a cuff and stethoscope.

Scissoring open Kathleen's mouth, the technician slid the blade of the scope along the side of her tongue with one hand and reinserted the tube with the other.

He connected it to the ventilating bag, and gave it a squeeze.

A few bubbles came up around Jorgenson's fingers, but nothing like before.

"Good air entry," said the nurse listening to Kathleen's lungs.

"Pulse and pressure coming up."

"O_2 sat rising."

Whistles and sighs of relief filled the room.

At that instance, Dr. Gordon Ingram rushed in, his face flushed and gasping for breath. "What's going on?" he said. "I was chairing a meeting and heard the call for an intensivist. When it kept going and no one seemed to be answering it, I thought you might need me."

Richard looked over at him. "Can you still perform a tracheotomy, Gordon?"

"Of course. It's like riding a bicycle. One never forgets stuff like that."

"Then please do me the favor of completing one on Kathleen."

"Of course," he said. "Give me a second to scrub up."

"And when you're finished with that, you can launch an investigation into what happened here, including why the hell Hamlin didn't show up." Richard then turned to Jorgenson, his blue eyes like ice. "As for you, I'll leave your fate to Dr. Ingram," he said. "But Kathleen Sullivan is off limits. Go near her again, and I'll personally make sure you won't get a license to do as much as cut patients' fingernails, let alone their brains."

She swallowed, said nothing, and left the room. She could fix this, she kept thinking as she made it to the surgical lounge on legs as insubstantial as Jell-O. She poured a cup of the stale coffee, slumped into a chair, and began to figure out how she could protect herself. After all, it was the anesthetist who left her on her own. If there were an inquiry, he would be the one who'd have to admit being at fault for failing to supervise her. As to her assertion that Hamlin's arrival had been imminent and that she was to start so as not to lose the slot, surely Tony would understand and corroborate the claim. She'd simply tell him it was her reasonable expectation of what he'd have wanted her to say, since they'd both been hanging around all day ready and waiting to do the case. Just trying to buy him some time so he could get to the OR, she would insist. He couldn't hold her responsible for his not showing up at all, could he? And as it was he who did her evaluation, she reasoned, none of this need follow her on her career path.

Bit by bit she cobbled together a strategy to keep the disaster off her record. Not once did she blatantly acknowledge her biggest advantage in any future battle, that her staffman was fucking her. Rather she avoided thinking through such base thoughts, never putting into words that neither Tony nor the hospital administration, both following their baser instincts to preserve their image and avoid bad publicity, could afford to do anything but bury the incident as quickly as possible. Her disconnect from overt scheming served her need never to see herself as being manipulative or coarse. Instead, she instinctively grasped the fact she had them by the balls, her more venal side able to read a hostile terrain like radar and intuitively plot her position on it with soothing clarity. It was all a reckoning by the subconscious, the defensive reaction of a cornered animal, nothing rational she need ever acknowledge or bother herself with. Nevertheless, the sense she won from all this—that she'd be okay— comforted her, the way a heartbeat does a child.

One thing she couldn't deny—any chances she might have had of a future position at New York City Hospital once she completed her residency were finished. Whisperings of how she blew a trach on Steele's lady, the famous Kathleen Sullivan, would be all over the floors by morning. That would invite counterwhisperings from those who suspected her affair with Tony. By week's end the story would be woven into the fabric of hospital lore like a scarlet thread.

Bryant Park, an acre of green space that fits like a postage stamp behind the New York City Public Library between Fortieth and Forty-second Streets, was packed for the Monday evening outdoor film series. Hamlin skirted the hundreds of people lounging on the grass in front of the large movie screen erected for the occasion and approached the restaurant Edwards had chosen. It was the most prestigious of the eateries huddled under the magnificent stone facades and high windows of the library building. Of course it would be, Hamlin thought. Edwards was always sure to pamper his stomach whatever the occasion.

The waiter showed him to his table, one at the corner of the upstairs terrace that commanded a perfect view of the throng below. He barely looked at the menu, ordering the first item he saw. He wasn't in the least hungry, but saw no other way to appease a jittery waiter who kept hovering over him and jabbering about the kitchen closing soon. Edwards would probably eat whatever Hamlin ordered anyway.

The evening air hung motionless, the trees trapping the stagnant heat of the day and the brown fumes from the continually circling traffic. Tasting the benzenes, he wondered how many other pollutants would seep into his system tonight.

What did Edwards want? He fretted, taking a gulp of ice water. Surely by now Edwards realized that his crazy idea to discredit Sullivan had backfired, that if she lived, it would be the ruin of him, Tony Hamlin. Did the big fool think he could persuade him to take the fall alone? If so, he had news for the idiot.

Hamlin looked at his watch. Eight thirty-five. Rachael should have taken Sullivan to the OR by now. Would she botch it?

He'd wrestled all day about tricking the ambitious resident into trying the procedure on her own. On the one hand it would have been easy enough to set in motion. Simply fabricate some reason to be held up on the floors at the last minute, and hope her eagerness, plus the usual impatience of an anesthetist to keep the cases moving, led her to start in alone. On the other, he hadn't the stomach for even so minimal a degree of premeditation, because despite everything else he'd done, he wouldn't commit murder. Then as they kept getting bumped, he realized he didn't have to arrange anything. If he just let events take their course, it would be after regular hours when they got to Sullivan, and he'd be out of the hospital meeting Edwards. If a resident was stupid enough to try something so risky as a trach without her staff supervisor present, and the anesthetist agreed to oversee her, albeit spottily while running between ORs, it wouldn't be his fault.

He could live with that, or at least rationalize it to the point where he wouldn't feel guilty, he'd initially tried to convince himself, so desperate was he to escape Sullivan's informing on him. Now he wasn't so sure. Killing was killing, and clever moral semantics couldn't protect him from his conscience. Nor could he say for certain his troubles would subside if Sullivan did die. He'd still have Steele to contend with. Besides, the chances that an anesthetist would be so irresponsible he'd let Rachael proceed, yet he wouldn't actually stay in the room with her, were pretty slim. He took another belt of ice water, and savored the cold as it cut a path through the burning in his gut.

At eight-forty the crowd below began to whistle and clap rhythmically, delivering their verdict that it was as dark as it would ever be in downtown Manhattan and time to get on with the show.

Once the movie started he barely paid it any attention, continually rechecking his watch and scanning the sidelines for Edwards. The silvery glow from the black-and-white images made it relatively easy to see, so he shouldn't have any difficulty spotting him walking toward the restaurant. But where the hell was he?

Brooding theme music filled the night, making him feel edgy. Up on the screen Fred MacMurray lurched into a deserted office building and began taping a message intended for a man named Keyes. Flashbacks rolled.

Again he thought of Sullivan. By some fluke could she have had the trach after all? And made it? He checked his cell phone to make sure it was on. Surely they'd have called him if she had died. He found himself waiting for either result with equal dread.

By nine-thirty Hamlin started to suspect that maybe Edwards wasn't coming. Had he met with the others instead? Decided to turn him over to the cops after all in exchange for a deal? No! Surely they wouldn't do that yet, not while they still believed there was a chance no one would take Sullivan seriously. The cost to themselves would be too great.

He tried watching the movie to distract himself, but the menacing score swelled louder, feeding his uneasiness, and the story, one of shadowy characters pursuing a fated scheme of murder and treachery, only increased his sense of doom.

Feeling as slated as the characters were for a bad end, he nervously peered past the fringes of the crowd in yet another vain attempt to spot

Edwards. Staring into the dark, he heard Fred MacMurray say, "Walking down the street, suddenly it came over me that everything would go wrong. It sounds crazy, Keyes, but it's true, so help me. I couldn't hear my own footsteps. It was the walk of a dead man . . ."

He lay in the dark, listening for the watchman. Even in the heart of the stone building, he could hear the distant strains of music and the murmur of dialogue.

After observing Hamlin on Friday afternoon, he'd figured it safe enough to at least lay the groundwork for taking further action. The accusations, e-mailed to him from an unknown source, were serious enough to warrant that. Whether they were also true never once entered his mind.

Anonymity was the fundamental tenant and key to security in his army, messages and directives arriving from untraceable informants the standard practice. As to authenticity, as long as the information gave fodder to their preformed beliefs and didn't seem to be a trick by the cops, his brothers in arms took it as true. The indictment regarding Hamlin fit his suspicions about doctors to a T, and the instructions detailing passage of sentence whetted his appetite for justice.

He had selected the spot later that same day, carefully reconnoitering the building, still not entirely certain if he'd go through with the scheme, intending to back off if anything interfered with his preparations. But they went flawlessly.

As a result, on Saturday he had set the plan in motion, using an Internet café to send the e-mail signed P.E. that he had been told would bring Hamlin running. Sunday he spent collecting and preparing the equipment he would need. Again everything went without a hitch.

Four hours ago, around five-thirty, he had slipped into the library's Forty-second Street entrance. In his hand was a briefcase, over his arm a raincoat, the pockets containing a bottle of water, a penlight, and a library floor plan he'd picked up at the information desk on his previous visit. Sewn in to the lining of his coat was the gun barrel of a disassembled M-4 carbine positioned to remain upright when he draped the garment over his arm. The rest of the weapon, stock, trigger works, and magazine, were in the case, along with two large suction cups, a glass cutter, and a box of hollow-point bullets. The only uniformed guard stationed at the door sat in a little wooden booth reading a magazine. She didn't even look up.

Instead of going upstairs to the massive Astor Hall foyer, he had turned left and entered an area of beige lockers where the staff kept their personal belongings. No signs told him to keep out. Several men and women resting on benches while drinking coffee and chatting not so much as glanced at him. He walked on through, unchallenged, into the bowels of the building.

Eventually he had reached a massive indoor loading dock big enough to fit a transport truck. It was empty at the moment, the entire space closed off from the street by a pair of giant iron doors that could have kept out King Kong. Stepping down into the parking bay he crossed to the other side, avoiding the large patches of oil so as not to slick the soles of his shoes and leave tracks. He then mounted a short flight of steps, ending up in front of an entrance marked SHIPPING AND RECEIVING. He peeked in. A group of workmen moving crates at the back of a voluminous storage area paid him no heed. He slipped inside and navigated around head-high stacks of boxes. Finding a staircase at its far end that led upward, he went over and quietly climbed to the first landing. The entry hallway was deserted. He was at the doors of the microfilm reading room on the main floor. He quickly retreated down to the storeroom, found a stack of boxes near a back wall, and sat down behind them to wait.

At six the lights had started going out. The chatter of workers slowly subsided in the distance, then ended altogether as they slammed doors behind themselves, entombing him in the utter silence and darkness of the place. At nine he crept halfway back up the stairs to the microfilm reading room, this time using his penlight to find the way. There he waited, listening for the approach of a night watchman above.

At nine-fifteen he heard some echoing footsteps approach in the hallway, and retreat just as they had when he'd hidden in the building overnight on Friday to time the rounds of the guards. He waited another ten minutes, and when he heard nothing more, crept the rest of the way out of hiding. The corridor itself was dimly lit, but on his previous scouting trip he'd noted the complete lack of video surveillance here, so he knew he wouldn't be seen.

The reading room door was secured by an electronic lock that he guessed would be on an alarm system, but its upper half was essentially a window. He stepped up, secured the large pane with a suction cup, and removed it with his glass cutter. Using his raincoat as a padding along the remaining glass in the lower edge of the frame he hoisted himself up and crawled through the opening. On his right a wall of mahogany behind a long wooden counter infused the harsh white probings of his light with a rich hue of red.

He shone his beam toward the far end of the room. Illuminating bench after bench loaded with rows of viewers the size of computer screens, he satisfied himself that nobody had made any surprise changes, such as moving a giant bookcase up against the rear window that he needed access to. He'd seen on Friday that it could be opened by hand and looked out on the terrace of the restaurant outside.

But before going over to it, he inspected the row of windows to his left overlooking Fortieth Street and located the fifth one from the end. When he'd cased the building from outside, he had spotted an aluminum awning about five feet below the sill. From there it was an easy jump to the top of a stone wall and a final seven-foot drop to the sidewalk. In the pandemonium that would be going on back at the movie, no one would notice him escaping out there, he figured. Once more using his suction cup and cutter, he made himself an opening, then tiptoed the length of the room to his chosen vantage point and looked outside.

The silver screen in the distance dominated the night. The light from it rippled back over a thousand heads, but he sought only one. Turning the crank to open a tall narrow pane that would give him a good angle of sight, he felt the warm air against his face as it filled his nose with the scent of exhaust fumes.

The constant honking of horns and sounds of cars formed a backdrop to Edward G. Robinson's giving Fred MacMurray a stark prognosis for all killers: ". . . They've committed murder. It's not like taking a trolley ride together where they can get off at different stops. They're stuck with each other and they've got to ride all the way to the end of the line and it's a one-way trip and the last stop's the cemetery . . ."

From the dialogue he could immediately tell how much time remained for him to get ready. He'd already watched the video version a half dozen times in order to pick the scene that would best cover the noise of his shot. Yet he didn't hurry. In fact he deliberately took his time assembling his gun, experiencing an odd sense that his success tonight was inevitable, since everything so far had gone perfectly. He almost felt like testing his good luck, seeing if his lack of haste could make him miss his cue. After all, for the last few days he'd half considered the whole exercise as little more than a dress rehearsal, a trial to see if he could actually pull it off. Yet here he was, everything successfully in place, and only the act itself to be done. Working leisurely, he had the weapon put together within five minutes.

Up on the screen, in glorious black and white, Barbara Stanwyck was issuing her ultimatum: ". . . Nobody's pulling out. We went into this together and we're coming out at the other end together. It's straight down the line for both of us. Remember?"

He got up on the bench that ran under the window to better see the terrace of the restaurant. Using his scope to survey the seated patrons from behind, he began to think the mission might end because he wouldn't spot Hamlin given the size of the crowd. It was also possible the man hadn't come at all, or if he had, he'd grown impatient and left. Such a shame, he thought, to fail at the last minute. But he also felt a twinge of relief. For as much as he was prepared to serve his cause, he preferred to be a hero in waiting, not one on the run.

Then he went still. There Hamlin sat, at a table near the front, not the one in the rear nearest his vantage point that he'd insisted on when making the reservation. But there was no mistaking the man's white hair as it bathed in the silver light cast from the flickering images overseeing everything. Crouching in a shooter's position, he slowly brought the rifle to his shoulder and focused its sight on the back of the man's head.

All at once the heat seemed to suffocate him, and his skin grew damp under his clothing. So the deed was to be done now after all, he thought.

He only had to pull the trigger at the precise moment, the chosen scene fast approaching.

From the beginning he'd accepted that the shot would change his life forever, launching him into a deadly cat and mouse game with the police as he went after the rest. For the e-mail indicting Hamlin contained the names and crimes of others to be taken care of. Even the seed of his targets would be punished, if necessary, for as usual when on a hunt, his network had tracked down their children and provided him with the schools they attended. And if he succeeded, once everyone pieced it all together, he would have opened a whole new front in the war that consumed him. He carefully placed a long twig on the windowsill, then waited without moving a muscle.

Barbara Stanwyck pulled a gun.

His own finger tensed on his trigger.

They fired together.

Tony Hamlin never saw the surprise on Fred MacMurray's face as Stanwyck put a bullet in him.

Instead he fell sideways, his head flopping onto the shoulder of a woman at a table beside his.

At first she must have thought he was drunk, until she saw that the back of his skull was missing.

7

The killing made front-page news in New York's three major papers.
PROMINENT NEUROSURGEON SHOT BY SNIPER IN BRYANT PARK.
UNKNOWN SHOOTER BLOWS OUT SPECIALIST'S BRAINS.
MURDER AT THE MOVIES!

No one knew any reason for the man to have been targeted by anyone. His wife didn't even know why he'd been there. "He hated the cinema," she said to the media. "The last picture show he ever took me to was *The Sting* back in the seventies." When asked to comment on reports that he'd told a waiter he was waiting for someone, the woman looked bewildered.

The nurses had their own ideas.

"He was probably meeting one of his residents—female of course," one nurse said, expressing the commonly held view.

Some unloaded their disapproval on Rachael Jorgenson, treating her to cocked eyebrows and icy sneers.

She in turn, armored with the righteousness of what she'd convinced herself was grief for her lover, refused to feel shame. Defiantly she went about her business, head erect, posture rigid, acid tongue at the ready to enforce a pyramid of power in which even she, a resident, outranked nurses. Under ordinary circumstances they would have let experience teach her the reality of the teaching hospital's food chain—that it's nurses who can save a resident's ass, or bust it, depending on how the doctor in training wheels wants to play the game. She however, got their backs up, and smirks graduated to snickers whenever she walked onto a ward.

But nobody had any reason to call the police.

Except one.

"If you don't . . . get me . . . the detective . . . I'll ask Lisa. . . . She . . . Chet . . . will help me . . . find McKnight."

In order for her to speak Richard had to cover the tracheal tube sticking out the front of her neck with a small rubber pad. "It redirects expelled air up through the vocal cords, allowing you to say short phrases," he'd explained to her. Between each fragment of speech he would remove the cover, she'd ponderously inhale the next lungful, and out would come the next few words. Watching her pulse and pressure creep up on the monitors, he grew tense. She was in no condition to meet with an NYPD homicide detective. "Kathleen, you're not up to it."

"Liar," she whispered.

"No! Your throat's been too traumatized for the kind of grilling that would turn into." He had listened to her painstakingly tell how Hamlin had touched her. She'd embellished nothing, whispering her account a detail at a time in cold, clinical terms that burned away all his doubts and branded images of what she'd endured into his mind's eye. When she finished he could hardly control his rage, and had to grip the side rail of her bed to keep his hands from trembling.

"I don't . . . believe you!"

She took in a breath.

"You still think . . ."

She drew in another.

". . . I hallucinated . . ."

Her next effort was even more laborious.

". . . he put something . . . in my brain."

He swallowed twice, then a third time. "I swear that's not true. And for what he did to you I'd have killed him myself if he had walked in here this morning. All I'm saying is let me handle the police."

"What you're saying . . . is you believe . . . he diddled me . . . and not the rest."

He eyed the monitors again. Her vitals revved up a few notches more. "Kathleen, I believe you saw and heard what you say. But what does it prove? That part of the story is so bizarre no one else, including the police, are liable to think it credible. Yet it won't stop them from bombarding you with questions there are no answers to. Which is why I should be the one to deal with them."

"I'll convince McKnight . . . that it's true."

He watched her vitals spurt higher still. Better he just stop talking. Every time he opened his mouth she got more agitated.

Her eyes watered over. ". . . Get out . . ."

"Kathleen . . ." His voice trailed off into another grotesque silence and he sank back in his chair, taking the rubber pad with him. He felt disgusted with himself, able to fix airways, insert IVs, even jump-start a heart, but incompetent at regaining her trust.

She curled her hands into fists where they lay. Unable to move her wrists or arms at all, she was totally dependent on him to cover her trachea for her. Her frustration raged at him through her eyes, until once more he leaned forward and closed the opening in her airway, bestowing on her the power to say, "Go to hell!"

He removed the small rubber pad he used as a seal only long enough for her to take yet another breath. But clearly the effort was starting to exhaust her, and he knew she wouldn't be able to go without the respirator much longer. Her own breathing muscles, though beginning to function, were still far too weak to sustain her. When she did talk, her pronunciation was thick and slurred, the result of a lingering paralysis in the right half of her tongue and the rest of her mouth. It broke his heart to hear her once-lilting voice hobbled. Earlier this morning he'd mustered an appropriate show of enthusiastic delight at her first words and what, clinically speaking, was deemed remarkable progress considering she'd started with zero function of anything except her eyes. Privately he found it such a puny advance he couldn't stop the physician in him from taking inventory of her chances for ever talking normally again. They were dismal.

Nevertheless he quickly replaced the pad on the opening, not wanting her to feel anymore impeded than she already did.

"I want McKnight!"

She took a quick short gasp, and started to sob. A succession of loud, blowing noises full of gurgling came out the tracheostomy site as secretions from her lung pooled in her airway. Without suction, he knew, she could drown in her own juices.

Jesus Christ! he thought, reaching for the small plastic catheter that hung on the wall. The nurses didn't clear her out nearly often enough as far as he was concerned. Yet they resented it when he did the job himself. Well, tough! Opening the intake valve to activate it, he threaded the tip of the flimsy device down through the much bigger orifice of her tube and into her lungs. The pain and anger he saw in her eyes as he emptied out the accumulated fluid nearly stopped him. "Hold on, just a few seconds more, Kathleen," he kept saying as he worked. "But it's got to be done." Feeling guilty about already having upset her so much, he added, "I'll get you McKnight. I promise."

When he finished, her face and lips were turning a dusky gray from a lack of oxygen. He quickly reconnected her to the respirator and reinflated the seal around her tube to block any leaks. Cutting off the flow of air out her larynx rendered her silent again.

Her skin quickly pinked up, but she wouldn't look at him, keeping her lids clamped shut. Nor would she respond to yes and no questions by squeezing his hand the appropriate number of times. When he inserted his fingers into hers, she feebly opened her grip, rejecting him.

"I told you I'd get McKnight," he said, feeling more helpless than ever. The man would unquestionably pay very close attention to anything she told him. Whether he believed her, would be another matter. "I'll phone him from my office. And while we're waiting for him, I'm going to radiology and do some serious damage to Lockman if he doesn't tell me what they did to you—"

The curtains behind him parted and Gordon Ingram swept into the cubicle.

"Morning, Richard. Some news about Hamlin, eh? I guess we know why the poor bugger didn't show up last night." He went right to Kathleen's side.

Her eyes flew open,

"Hello, Dr. Sullivan. I'm the fellow responsible for this little doohickey in your neck. Thought I better check my handiwork." He quickly undid the pads of dressing surrounding the tube and exposed a thin line of stitches where he'd repaired Jorgenson's hatchet job.

Though the area appeared bruised and a little inflamed, Richard thought it looked surprisingly good. "You did a hell of a repair, Gordon."

"Shouldn't be much of a scar. Nothing an expensive diamond necklace won't cover up."

Kathleen gave them both a *who is this man* stare.

Ingram smiled and disconnected the respirator. "Let's hear what you've got to say, Dr. Sullivan. Shall we send Richard shopping, bigtime?" Releasing the seal and adjusting her tube so she could once again speak, he added, "I know a terrific jewelry store on Fifth Avenue."

"You did . . . my neck?"

"Guilty as charged."

"What happened . . . to Dr. Jorgenson?"

"Richard didn't tell you? She needed a little help," he said.

"Will there . . . really be a scar?"

"In truth, nothing too noticeable," he whispered. "But let's tell him to start looking for a forty-carat stone, maybe call Elizabeth Taylor."

Kathleen's eyes twinkled. "We're having . . . a fight."

"Are you now? Well that sounds healthy. I'll leave you to it."

"Are you . . . my new doctor?"

"No, the neuro people will take care of you still. But I'll be your tracheotomy doctor if you like."

"I'd like."

"Good. Well, happy battles."

And he was gone.

So was the icy silence.

"I like him," said Kathleen when Richard had again covered her airway.

"Me, too."

"Will I really . . . need a . . . necklace?"

"Absolutely."

A half hour later he'd contacted Lockman's secretary.

"That man," she said, issuing a sigh that nearly fried the telephone line. "Not only has he not come in today, I can't reach him at home either."

"Well, when he shows up, tell him Richard Steele called, and to phone me right away." If he knows what's good for him, he nearly added.

"But Dr. Sullivan, it's not my case," said the giant ebony-skinned detective at her bedside.

She gave his hand a squeeze. How small her own fingers looked in his massive palm. She and Richard had met him over a year ago, during the bioterrorist attack on New York City and a dozen southern states they had tried to thwart. Although the country was still dealing with the consequences of the assault, the one thing she knew she had with this tough skeptical cop as a result of that previous escapade was credibility. His appearance within hours of being sent for proved just how quickly she could get his attention.

"But first let me say how sorry I was to read about your stroke," he continued. "They had a mighty fine article on you in the *Times* a few days after it happened."

Lisa had read it to her only last week. "Sounded too much . . . like an obituary . . . for my taste," she whispered. "And thank you . . . for coming." Richard stood opposite the detective, humble as a manservant, covering and uncovering the opening in her throat, enabling her to speak. "I'll have . . . to be brief."

"Then I'm ready to hear what you have to say. Dr. Steele told me you have information that you think might have a bearing on the murder of Dr. Tony Hamlin. I also understand he was the neurosurgeon who operated on you, is that correct?"

She stole a glance at Richard, wondering if he'd already editorialized on what she had to say, undermining it as drug-induced ramblings. But he looked her right in the eye, gave a wan smile, and she knew he hadn't interfered. "Yes . . . my first night here . . . he infused something . . . into my brain . . . intravenously . . . and he didn't want . . . anyone to know. . . . He's done it before . . . to other patients. . . . Some must have died. . . . His radiologist said . . . they'd face homicide charges . . . if Richard found out."

"Me?" said Richard. He hadn't heard that part of the story before. "What did I have to do with it?"

"They were arguing . . . feared you'd somehow . . . realize what they'd done . . . from DOAs in ER."

"DOAs? But I haven't noticed a rash of patients brought in dead on arrival."

"He said . . . 'more DOAs'. . . . Most . . . are yet to come . . . I think."

"You didn't know about any of this?" said McKnight, glancing over to Richard, incredulous furrows forming lateral swells across his brow.

"Well, not specifically—"

"Not specifically?" The folds deepened toward outright dismay. "For starters, I would have thought the mere mention they'd done something not aboveboard to Dr. Sullivan here would have had you on the warpath. Yet you did nothing?"

"Hey! Morphine, or even a stint in ICU can cause paranoia," Richard said defensively.

McKnight shook his head at him. "I suggest you start checking your records on DOAs, Doc, especially any with Hamlin's name on them." Retrieving a pen and notepad from the breast pocket of his suit, he then turned and leaned close to her. "Now, what's this radiologist's name?"

Before answering she savored the pained expression that had slid across Richard's face at the detective's rebuke. Good, she thought, and would have added an ever so sweet *I told you so* smile had she the muscles for it. "Matt Lockman. . . . And he implied . . . others are involved."

"Did he say who?"

"No."

She felt Richard's hand at her neck tense, and glanced at his face in time to see it light up as if he'd been caught in a camera flash. Whatever had crossed his mind he kept to himself.

"He also . . . threatened . . . he'd do anything . . . to keep Richard . . . from telling . . . the police."

"He threatened Dr. Steele?"

"Said he'd silence . . . him and anyone else . . . who might talk."

"My God," said McKnight, getting to his feet with remarkable quickness for such a large man. "I want to speak with this guy, tonight. What a lead! The people working the case were beginning to think it had to be some sicko picking off a random target."

"You think Lockman shot Hamlin?" Richard asked.

McKnight looked at him as if he were an idiot. "I think the man's got a lot of explaining to do, don't you? I also think you'd like to ask him a few questions yourself, no?"

"You've got that part right. In fact, I already tried to reach him today. He didn't come into work, and wasn't answering his phone. His secretary was suppose to have him call me soon as she reached him."

The detective turned back to her and took her hand, his dark eyes narrowing as if he'd already drawn a bead on the ratlike radiologist without even having seen him yet. "Whatever he tells us, Dr. Sullivan, I'll bring you some answers, I promise. And thanks for the information. You're an amazing woman." He returned her weak grip with an affectionate squeeze.

"There's more," she said.

"Oh?"

"Monday . . . eight nights ago . . . Hamlin fondled me. . . . I think . . . he did it . . . to make me . . . discredit myself . . . make anything else I said . . . seem crazy . . . from sedation . . . and morphine."

McKnight swung around to face Richard. "She told you this, and you didn't believe her?"

Richard's expression remained still, his mouth grim and his face growing crimson. "Not at first. But I do now." She thought she saw his hands, usually so rock steady, tremble slightly as he began reconnecting her to the respirator, signaling that the interview was over. He brought his lips up to her ear. "I'm so sorry," she heard him say, his voice shaking, and he brushed her temple with a kiss. She saw as sad a look as she ever wanted to see in those eyes that already had known far too much pain. "I'm so sorry," he said again, grabbing her hands and caressing them with his mouth.

McKnight discretely looked away. Then the two men strode from the cubicle.

My avenging angels, she thought.

Lockman still wasn't anywhere to be found in the radiology department. Those who were there working late said that they hadn't seen him all day. When Richard reached the hospital switchboard to ring his home number, he got a busy signal. A check with the phone company revealed the receiver was off the hook.

"Do you know where he lives?" McKnight asked.

"I can find out," said Richard, leading the way to his office in ER. Rifling through his hopelessly disorganized drawers and a shelf, he found a copy of the staff directory.

McKnight gave an appreciative whistle when he saw the address. "That part of Long Island is pretty posh," he said, copying it down. "I've got a big bust coming down tonight and have to get back on duty, but I'll radio this in to the detectives who are on the Hamlin case. They'll want to talk with the guy for sure, maybe even tonight. Care to tag along?"

"Wouldn't miss it for the world," he said, imagining having Matt Lockman in his clutches for a few hours before the police got to him.

"They'll need time to liaise with the Long Island precinct to arrange proper backup for the visit. I'll give them your cellular. They'll phone you when they're ready."

"Of course," he said, smiling agreeably. But he'd already settled on a better plan.

It took him an hour to get there. Though the time was only seven-thirty, it was well on the way to dusk where Lockman lived, thanks to the trees overhead. They were the kind that old forests and neighborhoods with old money had in common, spreading over everything like a thick canopy that shut out the light below. And just as on the floor of an old forest the new growth was usually stunted, the offspring in such places often failed to live up to the parents. Matt Lockman was no exception.

His father had once been chief of radiology at New York City Hospital, a giant in his field. He'd died shortly after Richard first came on staff over twenty years ago. Lockman Junior had tried to follow in his father's footsteps, not only becoming a radiologist, but aspiring in loud, obvious ways to succeed him as head of the department—except his peers had never deemed him to have the right stuff to be put in charge. Richard had good reason to share their opinion. More than once the man had landed the emergency department in court by misreading an X ray for one of the residents, thus failing to pick up a lung tumor, missing a fracture, not catching a subtle sign like free air under the diaphragm indicating a perforated bowel. These were just a few of his transgressions. In each case the proceedings pinpointed Lockman as the culprit, and as a result Richard had discouraged anyone in ER going to him for an opinion on anything.

Except money.

In a speciality renowned for earning top dollar, Lockman very definitely had the right stuff as far as billing to the maximum was concerned. Yet the joke around the hospital was that he needed the cash to pay off all his lawsuits, and though he lived in "Daddy's" former mansion, he did so without servants. He was also the only guy on the block who drove a Camry.

A few minutes later Richard found the street number. It was a gated property, as were most of the houses in the district, except these wrought iron barriers were open.

"Convenient," he muttered, pulling into a straight gravel driveway that ran a hundred feet before widening to serve a three-car garage. Lockman's ordinary looking vehicle was parked outside, its nose to one of the doors like something that didn't belong sniffing to get in, Richard observed. A tall unkept hedge blocked his view of the house.

He got out and walked over to where an opening in the shrubbery gave access to a gently curving sidewalk leading to the front door. Even in the twilight, Richard could see the old homestead wasn't what it used to be. Made of stone, swathed in ivory, and, like most of the elderly houses he'd caught glimpses of on the way, it was of a size that made it clear just how much old money had once been at stake here. But the splits and peels of white paint on the numerous window frames and shutters revealed the graying wood underneath, a thousand open scars on the corpse of whatever lifestyle once flourished within. The front garden held no flowers, just ornamental evergreens, each in as much need of a trim as the hedge he'd just passed through, and an abundance of weeds. The lawn at least had been mowed, but resembled a bad haircut where there were bare patches that had been sheared too close while other spots could have used a trimmer.

House rich, cash poor, Richard thought.

He arrived at the doorway, an ornate wooden entrance bound on either side by narrow full-length windows. A push of the bell produced a two-tone chime deep in the dark interior.

Birds sang from the trees as he waited. There wasn't so much as a puff of breeze, and though it had been hot during the day, under all that foliage the air felt cool, almost clammy.

He pushed the bell a second time.

Still no reply.

He looked in one of the windows, cupping his hands around his face to cut down the reflection. He saw no movement, only a display of antique chairs and small end tables in the foyer.

"Come on," he murmured, imagining the little man scurrying around there somewhere afraid to answer. One way or another, he'd get his hands on that scrawny neck and choke it out of him. Otherwise, once the cops and lawyers got to him, due process would protect him to the point the little weasel might never tell what he and Hamlin had done to Kathleen.

Seeing no one, he started pounding on the door. "Matt!"

Nothing.

He angrily grabbed the handle, and wrenched it clockwise, hoping the lock might be in the same state of disrepair as the rest of the structure.

To his amazement, the door simply opened.

He stepped inside. "Matt?"

No reply.

The house smelled stale, musty even. He obviously still didn't have a housekeeper. Whether the man lived alone, Richard didn't know. Certainly he'd never brought a Mrs. Lockman to the hospital social functions that included spouses, only a series of women he'd introduced as "his companion." Richard couldn't recall meeting the same one twice.

"Matt!"

He walked through the foyer he'd surveyed earlier and entered a large, richly furnished living room to the left.

Empty.

He saw it opened into a long dining area where the centerpiece was a gleaming mahogany table that could easily seat twelve, but there were no takers tonight.

Continuing toward the rear of the house, he found a kitchen that looked recently updated, full of new appliances.

Passing the entrance to the basement he spotted a pair of rat traps, loaded and ready to spring, guarding against visitors from those lower depths where it was pitch black. *Old-moneyed vermin?* he wondered, or upstart interlopers that were new to the neighborhood, along with the dot-com millionaires who'd moved out here, all the trophy digs in New York being taken. Having fought his own battles with the city breed of rodents at his home on Thirty-sixth Street, he decided against having a look in the darkness below.

He continued circling the ground floor, striding through a den decked out in leather, a magnificent library that looked so undisturbed it appeared as if nobody had ever taken a book off the shelf let alone read one of them, and an extensively equipped entertainment center dominated by a shiny, black TV screen the same size as one of the garage doors he'd seen on the way in.

But no Lockman.

Back in the foyer, he headed for the large central staircase. As he climbed, he wondered at how much better the house appeared inside than out with all its rich interior trappings. Lockman's way of hiding assets perhaps?

As he neared the landing, he paused, stopped by a familiar smell. Either someone had forgotten to flush, he thought, squinching up his nose at the scent of stale urine and excrement, or Lockman should sell off some of his goodies and hire a housekeeper to clean the toilet. Reaching the second floor he found himself at the center point of a long hallway.

Much of the passageway was already in deep shadow from the increasing dusk, and he wondered which direction to take. He took a few steps to the left, the hardwood floor creaking under his feet. The odor, both cloying and sour, grew stronger as he moved, forcing him to swallow a few times, then breathe through his mouth in order not to gag. He also thought he caught a whiff of something else he recognized, and wondered if one of the basement dwellers hadn't died somewhere nearby.

The rooms off the corridor were illuminated by the ghostly gray of twilight. Through the first two doorways he saw sparsely furnished bedrooms where drop cloths draped the chairs like shrouds and the mattresses were stripped of their sheets. The third looked like the master suite, given its size and the four-poster that occupied most of the inner wall. The rumpled covers and men's clothing draped over a pair of matching sofa chairs suggested that someone had at least slept here recently. But what struck him most was the stench. It had trebled.

"Jesus!" he muttered, the force of it staggering him. In the far corner he could see partially into a lit bathroom—the front curve of the toilet bowl, a bit of the sink, a portion of a bathtub—everything gleaming white. Through the frosted glass of a shower stall he saw the blurred, flesh-colored form of someone standing completely still.

He felt the hairs go up on the back of his neck, and his breathing slowed to a stop.

The only sounds were the evening birds chirping outside the bedroom windows, one of which, he absently noticed, was partly open.

Not taking his eyes off the human shape in front of him, he started to back away, wanting to get out of there. Let the cops handle this, he thought, having already identified the aroma of early rot.

He froze.

There was movement behind the glass. Something chest high and dark swirled in a circle across the skin tones. Then the black shape went lower, and settled at the person's feet. Another seemed to appear from behind the right shoulder.

What the hell? he thought, exhaling his held breath. Steadying himself, he slowly walked toward the cubicle.

As he entered the small room, as familiar as he was with the smells of death, the stink became so overwhelming his stomach did a flip into his throat and he nearly vomited. Refusing to yield, he reached for the handle on the glass door and pulled.

Matt Lockman, his arms lashed to the shower nozzle, hung naked against the tile wall, his feet trailing in a mush of human waste and blood that was up to his ankles. His left ribcage had been cut open top to bottom, the severed ends of the bones sticking outward to reveal the chest cavity within. As Richard recoiled from the sight, a pointed, beady-eyed head of a rat poked from the opening.

"Jesus Christ!" he shrieked, jumping three feet back.

The rat retreated around behind the body and disappeared through a hole in the tiles.

At the same instant, something brushed by his pant leg. He looked down in time to see a second creature, this one glistening red, its fur matted with streaks of congealed blood and strands of tissue. It was scurrying by him, pulling something nearly as big as itself along with its mouth, something that resembled a raw hunk of beef.

Richard bellowed at the animal and stomped his foot, startling it enough that it dropped its grisly load and scuttled into the bedroom. He then bent down to examine what it had been carrying. From the arteries and veins hanging out of it like tiny hoses, he instantly recognized a human heart.

8

Richard felt he couldn't breathe.

Revulsion played at the back of his throat.

No stranger to human remains, he struggled to quell the sensations and force himself to think clinically. After all, he'd been trained to remain unfazed around body parts in ER and on autopsy tables.

But this was the stuff of slaughter, not science. It breached any professional distancing he could muster. Feelings he would normally keep in check ran riot.

Outrage at the savagery of it.

Disgust at so obscene a violation of another human being, even a creep like Lockman.

Who could have done such a thing?

He moved to take a closer look at the open chest cavity, approaching it cautiously in case there were any more rats.

The ribs had been severed cleanly, the way they were by a bone saw at autopsy. Even the curve of the cut matched the usual incision line followed during a dissection.

His gaze worked upward. Lockman's head had dropped forward onto his chest, but Richard thought he caught a glimpse of something white under the line of the dead man's jaw. He leaned in to get a better look, and saw a plastic tube sticking out the front of the man's trachea.

But this was a very special type of tube.

What he was looking at was the instrument used in ER to do a cricothyroid punch, a type of emergency tracheotomy, except it's designed to provide a temporary measure, and is inserted through the membrane just above the trachea with a single stab, a much easier procedure for un-skilled hands than the regular technique. But why would anyone intent on butchering Lockman go to the trouble of giving him an airway?

The answer crept to mind, slowly, like the chill it brought crawling up his spine. Whoever did this wasn't concerned with Lockman's breath-ing. They wanted him mute, so no one would hear his screams while he or she worked on him.

Presuming the killer was alone.

He spotted a clotted laceration leading from Lockman's left temple to behind his ear.

A solitary attacker could have knocked him out first, stuck in the cricothyroid punch to render his voice box useless, then tied him up be-fore he came to.

Richard glanced down at the body's feet and saw, just above all the fe-ces, the upper edge of masking tape wrapped around the ankles.

The thought of the man being conscious while they cut him open sent his head reeling, and he finally succumbed, leaning over the toilet bowl ready to vomit.

That's when he heard the floorboards in the hallway start to creak.

He felt high with success.

Now it was on to the third name in the list. That it was a patient didn't phase him. They too must make payment for sacrificing a child of God. That she was a famous geneticist would better spread the terror, when the truth would be told. Unlike for the other executions, however, the in-structions he'd received were very specific about the means of her death. It had to appear natural.

This he found puzzling, disconcerting even. He couldn't see any rea-son why her murder shouldn't be public immediately, and though he'd sworn blind obedience to the Lord, he found it altogether something else to carry out orders he didn't understand that came from mere mortals. But having made a soldier's pledge to follow all such commands, he nevertheless got on with it no matter how difficult he found it not to question the logic.

Among the many items he had stolen during his years at the hospital were uniforms—those of orderlies, male nurses, porters—any number of sorts. Tonight he would play the roll of a cleaner, the most invisible job in the work hierarchy. He'd worn the drab, olive-green outfit under his jacket when he signed in earlier tonight, as a visitor. Finding a washroom stall, he attached a forged name tag, one modeled after his old one, to his shirt, and emerged as Harold Glass, janitor. He arranged the clip so that the picture portion partially slipped into his breast pocket. No one, he was certain, would pay it the slightest attention, as long as it was there. He then headed for where the housekeeping staff kept their carts, and in no time was dutifully mopping the floor outside the entrance to ICU.

The doors slid open from time to time, as nurses, doctors, residents, even visitors came and went. On each occasion he surreptitiously glanced up from his work to look inside, studying where the staff were, whether the supervisor was at the central station, and most of all, trying to spot which cubicle Kathleen Sullivan was in. This was difficult, because depending on the instability of the patients, ICU cases were always being switched around, the more critical ones being kept in easy view of the nurses in the charting areas. With the side curtains drawn for privacy, from his advantage point he could see only the foot of each bed. I'll have to get a look inside, he decided, to learn where she was. Then he could time his attack when no one was paying her any attention.

He put down his mop, pressed the round disk that activated the doors, and strode toward where patients' records were stored. He spotted the nearest wastebasket, picked it up, and headed back to the exit as if to empty the trash. But he took a slightly more circuitous route this time, slowing his walk and looking into each bed as he passed. That afternoon he'd bought one of Sullivan's books to get a picture of her, but found it difficult to recognize the woman once he saw her. Only the auburn gold of her hair tipped him off. Otherwise the pale flaccid face bore little resemblance to the radiant looking woman on the jacket he'd studied so carefully.

He returned to his cart, dumped the papers into a disposal bin, and started back, his left arm swinging the empty receptacle to and fro, making an obvious show of carrying it to where it belonged so no one would wonder what he was doing here. On the way he felt in his right pocket for the capped, fully loaded syringe of potassium chloride. "Okay to mop in here now?" he said to one of the nurses at the desk.

"Sure," she answered, not even bothering to look up.

"I ought to have let them lock you up, pulling a stunt and sneaking in here on your own like this," McKnight said, scowling down at Richard.

"I'm sorry," he replied. He left it at that as McKnight seemed angry as hell and any attempt to explain would likely make him madder.

The Long Island police and two NYPD homicide detectives who had been creeping up the hallway first scared the hell out of him, then read him his rights, having assumed he was the killer.

It had taken McKnight coming all the way out from Manhattan to convince his colleagues they should back off.

The two men were now alone in the kitchen, Richard seated, the detective pacing back and forth, both waiting for the crime lab people to finish going over the scene upstairs.

"I mean, who knows what could have happened if you'd stumbled in on the murderer." The big man's voice had become a growl. "We might have found you strung up like that."

"Lockman's obviously been dead since this morning. Whoever did it is long gone."

"You know what I mean. What were you in such an all-fired hurry for anyway?"

"You guys were coming after him with a murder charge. I needed him to tell me what they did to Kathleen. I figured once you got to the man his lawyers would make him clam up about everything."

"And what made you think you could make him talk by getting at him first?"

"Don't ask."

The detective stopped midstride, a look of surprise on his face. "Really, Doc, I didn't think you'd go in for rough stuff—"

"I'll do whatever it takes to help Kathleen. Now if you'll let me out of here, I'll go after Hamlin's charts, not just the DOAs, but all of them. Maybe I can figure out what's going on."

The detective brightened. "Wow, Doc, now you're talking. I'll tell the people upstairs where we're going—"

"Wait a minute. I said I can go through the charts. As a chief I'm authorized to do any audit I want—it's called quality assurance. Bringing you in, however, it becomes a violation of confidentiality, as you already very well know, Detective McKnight. No, sir, this is something I do alone."

The man shrugged, and turned away.

Most cops, Richard had found out in dealing with them in emergency, would take a shot at asking to see a medical record if they thought it would help their case. They also backed right off as soon as the legality of the issue got thrown at them. It was a game they played, never crossing the line of blatantly breaking the law themselves, but willing to try and lure an overtired, distracted ER doc into letting something slip.

"So can I get out of here?" Richard asked.

"Yeah, I guess. But first I want you to tell me what you think of that handiwork upstairs."

"Whoever did it knows how to wield a bone saw. I also figure the heart was cut out by someone who knew his or her way around a chest cavity. All the major vessels were severed like in an anatomy dissection—"

"You mean you think it was done by a surgeon?"

For the second time that evening Richard refrained from telling the detective about the odd trio he'd seen arguing with Hamlin and Lockman last week. If they were "the others," the same reasoning he'd had about getting to Lockman before the cops applied to them. Instead he answered, "Or a pathologist. Maybe even somebody taught by one—"

A man's scream came from upstairs.

Richard was on McKnight's heels as the two raced to see what had happened.

They burst into the bedroom to find a crowd of officers clustered around an ashen-faced policeman seated on one of the chairs. He was cradling his bleeding right hand in his left, and a pair of bloodstained examining gloves, one of them torn, lay at his feet.

"What happened?" Richard asked as he stepped forward to look at the wound.

"There was a fucking rat hiding in the chest cavity," he answered, his face growing even more drained of color.

Oh, shit, thought Richard. In all the excitement when the cops had descended on him, guns drawn, patting him down, cuffing him, he'd forgotten to warn them about the rats. "Here, lie down before you faint," he ordered the bitten man, figuring there was no point in confessing yet another wrong, everyone already being mad enough at him.

"Hey, I don't faint," the cop said just before his eyes rolled up and he pitched face forward onto the rug.

"Jesus," Richard muttered, checking the man's airway to make sure he hadn't swallowed his tongue. "Somebody get his legs up."

A man and a woman at his feet complied, each raising one of his lower limbs and holding it there. Almost immediately he started to come around.

"Does anybody have a first-aid kit?" Richard examined the injured hand. It was a small puncture, but probably dirty as hell, considering where the rat had been. "He'll also need an injection of antibiotics, and a tetanus shot, so after I dress the wound, take him to the nearest ER."

"Hey, Detective McKnight, look at this," said one of the plainclothes detectives who was peering into Lockman's open chest with a flashlight.

"Is that rat still in there?" McKnight asked.

"No, it escaped out the window."

"You're sure there's not another one hiding inside somewhere?"

"It's safe, I promise."

McKnight nevertheless approached the corpse very warily.

Someone handed Richard a small white box filled with basic bandages and plasters. As he wrapped the hand, he watched what was going on in the shower stall.

McKnight took a peek in the gaping cavity, and his eyebrows shot skyward, his forehead folding up like an accordion. "What the hell?" He reached over to where someone had left a box of fresh latex gloves and pulled on a pair. As his colleague held the light, he gingerly reached inside the opening and retrieved what from a distance looked like a blood-covered twig from a tree or hedge.

The detective grabbed a zip-lock bag from a nearby case and placed what he'd found inside it. He looked up and saw Richard watching. He hesitated, then brought the bag over to where Richard was finishing bandaging his now fully awake patient.

Up close Richard saw it was indeed some kind of branch.

"What do you think this might mean?" McKnight asked.

"Mean?"

"Yeah."

"Probably that our little furry friends planned to set up house inside Lockman and were building a nest. I mean, give me a break."

McKnight didn't smile.

"You don't seriously think the killer would put it there, like some kind of message, do you."

"Yeah, I do."

"Why?"

"How do I know? Maybe whoever did this is after doctors who are cruel to plants and shrubs."

"I meant why do you think its being there has anything to do with the killer at all?"

"Because at the New York City Public Library we found a branch just like it on a windowsill. Right where we figure the shooter knelt to take out Hamlin."

He was nearly at her cubicle, no one paying him any notice. He'd even made it a point to clean around the beds of the other patients so as to not attract attention when he would make a similar approach to her. He shouldn't have any trouble. As far as he could see, the nurses pretty well left her alone.

He pushed his cart to the foot of her bed and proceeded to run the mop under it. After a few strokes for show, he moved up to where the IV bottle hung suspended on a pole dangling from the ceiling, continuing to wipe slowly. All the while he kept an eye out for a moment when no one had a line of sight into the cubicle. But too many people were about. Better to wait.

As he worked, he stole a glance at the woman he would soon dispatch to God's justice. Given her complete stillness and absolutely expressionless face, he wasn't prepared for the alert, steady gaze that studied him in return. He gave a small start back, feeling uneasy for an instant, then recovered enough to offer her a big smile.

Her only response was to blink at him a few times, then open and close her right hand.

"And hello to you, too," he said, continuing to grin at her. "No one to visit you tonight?"

She blinked once.

"Does that mean no?"

She blinked twice.

"And two is yes?"

Two more blinks.

"Well, aren't you clever."

He hated women like her. Independent. Not married. Defiant of the Lord and His plan. Her work in genetics in particular was the work of Satan. It pleased him no end to see her laid so low, struck down by the mighty Jehovah for her sins. And no way must she, or anyone else, be allowed to survive His wrath by benefiting by measures that compounded those sins and defiled His works.

He put aside the mop and, keeping his back to the rest of her room, retrieved the syringe from his pocket. He waited a few more seconds, watching her eyes shoot wide open at the sight of it, enjoying her dawning realization that it was all wrong, that cleaners didn't give needles, that he shouldn't be taking the cap off a syringe. He also watched her for any movements other than of her hands and eyes, wanting to be sure that she was as helpless as his information had led him to believe. He'd have to inject her in a split second to avoid being seen, and couldn't afford having her struggle. His smile widened. Apart from her starting to furiously bat her eyelids and make clawing motions with her fingers, the rest of her never budged.

He turned his head and scanned behind him.

A pair of residents were bent over a chart at the central console where all the monitors were located. The unit supervisor stood beside them, and all three had their heads down in an earnest discussion. But if any one of them so much as glanced up, he'd be seen. Better hold off some more.

He recapped the syringe, pocketed it again, and resumed his mopping, keeping an eye on the trio, ready to act the second he was in the clear.

She was at his mercy.

Who the hell was he? What was in the syringe? And why the hell didn't anyone notice he was hanging around her so long? *Stop him, someone! Don't you see him? Doesn't anyone spot the needle? For God's sake. Stop him, please, before he injects me with it!*

But her mute pleas were, of course, fruitless.

No one seemed to realize that he was even there.

Oh, God, she wailed in her prison of silence, the panic growing.

Was he associated with Hamlin? Did Lockman set him on her? Did the person who killed Hamlin also want to silence her? Her mind was too scrambled by fear to sort it out. All she could think now was how she could stop him.

She knew enough as a scientist to guess at what might be in the syringe.

Insulin? It could send her into hypoglycemic shock, knock off her brain, and leave her convulsing to death.

Cyanide, to destroy the oxygen transport system in her blood?

Potassium maybe, to stop her heart?

Or would he infest her with something to give her a more lingering death?

Such as AIDS perhaps?

What difference did it make how he intended to kill her?

She had to stop him.

The nurses had pinned the cord of a call button near her hand, but the device itself had gotten away from her and slid under the covers.

Increasingly terrified, she tried to move her fingers, thinking she might drag her hand toward it.

At first she couldn't get any traction, the tips of her nails slipping on the surface of the bedsheet, and she was unable to budge the weight of her arm. She dug her nails in and tried again. Her right hand crept forward—but she needed to back it under the covers to reach the call button. This time she pressed their tips into the bed and shoved, extending her fingers.

Her hand slid backward slightly.

The man continued to eye the rest of the room.

Probably waiting until no one was in sight, she thought, quickly repeating the process. Her fingers suddenly lost their grip and splayed out flat, making a tiny brushing sound. It was barely audible above the hiss of the respirator.

The man's eyes darted toward her.

He heard her! She held her hand perfectly still.

After a few seconds he went back to watching outside the cubicle.

She tried again.

Her fingers once more flew out straight, their quiet sweeping noise again attracting his attention.

Damn! she thought, waiting for him to look away. But he continued to watch her, a puzzled expression on his face. It seemed forever, but he finally went back to scrutinizing the room.

She had to go for a smaller distance at a time, she told herself, and flexed her fingers only halfway closed. When she extended them, her hand moved a half inch backward.

She did it again.

A quarter inch.

On her third effort she lost traction and gained nothing.

The man fired her an angry look. "What are you doing?" he asked in a very low voice as he took a step closer.

Surely he wouldn't notice such a minuscule change in the position of her arm, she tried to reassure herself while fixing her gaze on the sheets, unable to bear the rage she saw in his eyes as he towered over her. Please, why didn't someone see him and come to help? But in her isolation she heard only the pounding of her heart. It was racing so she figured the monitor's alarms must be shut off, or they surely would have rung by now.

All at once she heard him move and went cold with fear. Was he taking out the syringe?

She snapped her eyes upward, only to see him working the mop at the end of the cubicle looking to the right and left as if he were about to cross a street. Or making a final check that no one could observe him.

She dug in her nails and extended her fingers, over and over, no longer caring how quiet she was. Ever so slowly her hand slipped increasingly under the covers.

He took one more quick look in both directions and propped the mop against the bed.

The son of a bitch was going to do it, she squeaked, flicking her fingers open so roughly that her hand jerked completely from view with a series of little leaps, like spiders jumping. She felt her forearm brush against the call button as she pushed by it, then her wrist. In just a few more moves she'd have her palm over it.

He reached into his pocket, and brought out the syringe, shielding it from view with his back.

Oh, my God, she whimpered, trying to aim her movements. The button fell off to one side, against the fleshy part of her thumb. She pushed with her pinkie, attempting to bring her palm more in line. She ended up sliding the device to the side. *No!* She tried furiously to get her fingers wrapped around it. The activity made the overlying sheet squirm.

He leaned over her, removed the cap, and brought the needle up to a side portal in the IV tubing.

Knowing she was out of time, with one big effort she managed to plop the center of her palm over the device, and with another push, grip it between her index finger and thumb. Desperately she felt for the button.

"What the hell?" he muttered, looking at the motion under the covers. He quickly lifted the corner of them and snatched the call button from her hand before she could press it. "Well, aren't you the crafty little bitch," he whispered, laying it back near her pillow, well out of her reach.

This was it, she thought. The only choice left now was how to die.

Stare down her executioner, or retreat behind closed eyes for want of a blindfold as he killed her.

No. That would make it too easy for him. Better defy the bastard. Stare him down. Let her face haunt him until the end of his days.

He reached again for the side portal.

Thoughts of Lisa, of Chet, of Richard raced through her head. *Take care of them for me, my love,* she said to Richard, knowing it was a silent prayer.

"Is everything all right in there?" called the familiar, imperious voice of her spike-haired nurse with the ring in her nose from somewhere over near the central console with all the monitors.

The sound of that irritating woman usually set Kathleen's teeth on edge, but at this moment it sounded as sweet as a bugle call heralding the arrival of the cavalry charging to the rescue.

The man, his back still turned to the room, immediately slipped the cap back on the needle and shielded it from view as he pocketed it. "Yes, ma'am. Just finishing up," he said over his shoulder. "The patient's call button had slipped away from her, and I was getting it is all."

The nurse glided up to Kathleen's side. "Awake, are you?" she said. "The monitors showed your pulse and pressure going sky high again."

Kathleen made frantic grasping movements with her fingers and blinked so rapidly she created a strobe for herself.

"Now calm down, Dr. Sullivan, or I'll have to sedate you."

No!

"I told you, get hold of yourself."

He was going to kill me.

"You've been doing so well lately, with almost no panic attacks since the night of your surgery. It would be a shame to go back on midazolam now."

Then don't give it to me, you dimwitted, pill-pushing, needle-happy cow, and pay attention to the man behind you.

"I'm sorry, you'll have to leave your cleaning for now," she said, as if on cue. "I want her to rest."

He simply leaned on his mop. "Perhaps I should come back later after you've sedated her?"

"Yes, that would be fine," she answered, without so much as a flick of her eyes in his direction. "But make it a couple of hours from now, will you? Just before change of shift, when most of the visitors are gone. That's when the whole place really needs a sweep up, given all the dust they track in. It's twice as bad since they extended the times for having families underfoot in here."

He stood stock-still, staring at the woman's back, then at Kathleen, his pupils dilating with fury at being sent away. His eyes looked so big she imagined peeking into his head, looking around inside, and getting a firsthand glimpse of a madman's brain.

"Whatever you want," he said after a few seconds, turning and walking over to his cart.

"And don't wake her or anyone else when you do return," she called after him. "It's hard enough getting them bedded down without you lot banging about."

"I'll be quiet as a ghost," he answered over his shoulder, still gazing directly at Kathleen. "The last thing you've got to worry about is anyone waking up when I'm around."

"Then how come you guys always bang down the wastebaskets?" she muttered, reaching for one of the medication trays and taking out the familiar brown vial. In seconds she broke it open, stuck in a syringe, and loaded a few milliliters of the clear fluid into the barrel.

Please, don't, Kathleen begged.

Without hesitation, the nurse plunged the needle into a side port on the IV, and slowly pushed in the plunger.

Kathleen felt the familiar icy headache creep across the inside of her skull, followed by a smothering cap of darkness pulling itself down over her eyes like a black hood.

Richard hunched forward, straining to see through cataracts of rain sheeting down his windshield, knuckles as luminescent and white as a dashboard ornament. The deluge had accompanied him for most of the drive back to Manhattan from Long Island.

Damn wipers! he thought. Might as well try and part the Red Sea with them.

He glanced at his watch. Even after having broken about every speed limit on the way back, it was still well past ten-thirty. Would Kathleen be asleep? As anxious as he was to get at the records of Hamlin's patients, he wanted even more to tell her about Lockman.

He was driving north on the elevated FDR Expressway that skirted Manhattan's east side. On his right the East River was little more than a black smudge. On his left the core of the city seemed to be nothing but soaring lattices of flickering lights in a watery gloom.

The carnage that he'd seen at Lockman's house kept seeping into his head. He tried to block it out, but found himself wondering, What was the motive? Why carve him up so brutally? A bullet to the back of the head to silence a threat, yes, but to dissect a man while he was still alive? That went way beyond just keeping him quiet. And what the hell was the business with the twigs?

Spotting his exit, he headed down, unable to slip the sensation he was at the controls of a submersible.

"Christ!" he muttered, gripping the wheel harder still as the vehicle plowed through a deep puddle at the foot of the ramp and lurched to one side. Its wheels planing over the water, it sent arches of spray cascading onto each side of the street. After a short zig and a zag, he turned on Thirty-third and pulled into the hospital parking lot.

He took the steps up to ICU a pair at a time, hit the metal disc, opening the doors with a hydraulic whoosh, and crossed the distance to Kathleen's bed in half a dozen strides.

She lay on her side, much as he'd left her over four hours ago. He felt a slow burn in the pit of his stomach, angry that the nurses obviously hadn't turned her since. Nonhealing skin ulcers the size of drink coasters would be the result if they didn't get with it and regularly change her position to relieve the pressure points on her shoulders and hips. He knelt beside her and ran his hand through her hair.

"Hi, love, it's me."

No response.

The respirator steadily hissed and caused her chest to rise and fall, but her eyes, usually quick to spring open whenever he spoke to her, remained closed.

"Kathleen?" He took her hand, inserting his fingers into her palm. Lately she'd give a little squeeze of recognition even when she was half-asleep.

Nothing.

He reflexively glanced at her monitors, his ER instincts leaping to the worst of possible conclusions.

They showed her vitals were completely normal.

In the wastebasket by her bed, he caught a glimpse of an empty brown vial.

Midazolam.

Shit! he thought. They'd sedated her again, and ignored the need to reposition her.

Seething, he whirled about and headed to the charting area where a half dozen nurses were busily writing in assorted black binders. It was the usual ritual at this time of night during the lead-up to shift change at eleven. But for Richard, the sight meant they had put paperwork above their tending to Kathleen.

"Is that how you do things now?" he said in a coarse, raw whisper, his vocal cords strung as taught as the tendons in his neck. "Knock your patients gaga, so you can leisurely sit around and document their numbers? What about real care, such as turning them before they get pressure sores?"

Six jaws dropped in unison.

The supervisor half rose from her chair, her bobby pins glinting under the fluorescent lights and making the bun in her hair look baled. "I beg your pardon," she said, summoning her wrinkles into a portrait of disapproval.

He waved her down and leaned over the table at them. "Who's taking care of Dr. Sullivan tonight?"

"I am," replied the young woman with whom he'd had his initial confrontations and had since entered into an uneasy truce. Her pretty face tilted toward him, her blond spikes providing a fetching setting for her most striking feature, a pair of lucent aquamarine eyes.

Shark waters, thought Richard, reminding himself to watch his step since it was probably she who'd complained to Ingram about him. "Why is Dr. Sullivan sedated?" he asked as politely as he could.

Her tightly drawn lips curled upward at the corners. "Because Dr. Sullivan had another panic attack, Dr. Steele." Her tone had an insolent sweetness to it. It reminded him of the way addicts talked when they were stringing a line in ER to score drugs—half smirk, half menace.

"Did you bother to ask her what was wrong?"

"Ask her? She was freaking out. Why should I ask her?"

"Because, she probably was afraid of something. Something that you should have taken the trouble of finding out by removing the respirator, covering her trach tube, and letting her talk."

"Really Dr. Steele, I've seen the signs of panic in patients here often enough before—"

"Dr. Sullivan hasn't been having panic attacks. She's been frantically trying to tell us that on her first night in this place Drs. Tony Hamlin and Matt Lockman did something to her during her angiogram, and all of us, myself included, were too ready to write her off as delusional from morphine to pay her any heed."

She reared back, gaped at him with mock incredulity, and took a slow glance around at her colleagues. Recruiting a similar show of disbelief from each of their faces, she soon had all of them regarding him as if he was nuts. Cocking a hip and perching her hand on it, she said, "Surely you don't believe—"

"Yes, and so does the NYPD. In fact, Hamlin was probably killed to keep whatever he was up to secret."

"Why, this is preposterous—"

"Is it? I just got back from Matt Lockman's home. Found him strung up in the shower with his chest cut open and his heart taken out. It appears whoever killed Hamlin killed him as well."

It took a few seconds for this tidbit to register.

Spikehead remained speechless.

One by one the other nurses dropped the smug little smiles they'd been exchanging with each other.

The supervisor went rigid where she sat, stiffly leaning away from him as if putting distance between them could let her ignore what he'd said. Better watch it, he thought, or the weight of all those bobby pins will topple you backward.

"You . . . you . . . you're not serious?" she managed to stammer.

"I'm afraid so. And the police will be questioning whoever's been associated with any patients those two have worked on together, so get ready."

The woman swallowed and took a big breath, then exhaled long and slow. Richard could smell the residue of cigarettes. "Oh, my God," she murmured.

Kathleen's nurse looked away.

The rest glanced nervously at each other, the way people do when they hope someone in their midst can explain away bad news.

"I want to know what was happening when Dr. Sullivan became frightened," Richard said. "What set her off?"

Everyone turned toward Spikehead. She diverted her gaze to study the middle distance of the room, as if the answers he wanted from her might appear there.

He grew impatient. "I'm waiting."

"It was nothing," she said. "Her call button had slipped away from where I had pinned it near her hand." Her voice bristled with resentment.

"And yet you didn't bother to find out what she was trying to call you for. Just knocked her out."

She made no reply.

Richard fought his urge to hoist her off her chair by the ring in her nostril. "Is that how you prefer patients? Gorked and on machines, so they don't bother you?"

The others gasped in unison.

She snapped her head up and locked eyes with him.

"Dr. Steele!" said her supervisor. "You're out of line."

"Oh, no, I'm not, and you know it. This woman's been hostile to Kathleen from day one." Turning back to the younger nurse, he added, "I don't know what your problem is, lady, but I advise you to keep it out of the workplace. And if you have difficulty with the fact that she's a well-known celebrity or that she's dearer than life itself to me, or that as chief of ER I'm in a position to be a pain in the ass making sure she gets what she needs, that's just too goddamned bad. Now get over there and reposition her before she ends up with a hole in her skin." He pivoted and made for the door. "The minute she wakes up, phone me," he called over his shoulder. "I'll be in medical records all night."

He was so angry he nearly bowled over a cleaner who was mopping the floor in the hallway outside. "Sorry," he said, stepping around him and hurrying off down the corridor.

9

"Where is it?" muttered Richard, rifling through his desk. He'd dropped by ER, needing the pass card that gave him access to the hospital computer network and the electronic records of all patients admitted through ER.

A solitary yowl from a siren outside announced the arrival of an ambulance. It was the heads-up signal alerting the nurses and staff to get ready for trouble—not a cardiac arrest, because then drivers arrived with everything going full blast. No, now they were bringing in somebody only half-dead who was going the rest of the way fast.

Instinctively he tensed, twenty years in the pit having conditioned him to go on full alert at the sound. But this was someone else's problem at the moment, since his shift was long over. He returned to his search, finding what he'd been looking for in a petty-cash box. He could keep his department in order, but his desk defeated him on a regular basis.

But instead of heading toward the elevators for the basement, he walked through the sliding doors that separated his administrative cubbyhole from the bustle of emergency proper. Better check out that ambulance, he thought, unable to shake entirely his tendency to be a mother hen.

At least he handled it better than he had years before when Luana had died after a six-month battle with pancreatic cancer. He shuddered under the sting of a thousand memories flying out of the past and striking deep, fixing themselves like barbs inside his head.

"So what if I still take small hits of the same fix," he'd rationalized to

Jo O'Brien recently over one of the many cups of tea they'd begun to have together most afternoons.

"In the few shifts I still work, dealing with the pain and tragedy of strangers gives me a sense of being in control for a few hours. Otherwise I sit around helpless, feeling suffocated, afraid that Kathleen will die. I tell you, Jo, even the air clings like a shroud then."

But he repeatedly promised himself, as all junkies do, that he'd never let his need to kill the pain get out of hand again, that he'd not fail Chet, Lisa—or Kathleen—this time. Images from the past of his son looking at him—eyes bleak with misery and panic as they searched for comfort; eyes demanding at least a clue as to what wrong he, Chet, must have committed for his father to have preferred work over him; eyes shimmering with fear that he, Chet, was somehow a disappointment—all bore witness, floating watchfully over him and keeping him in check each time he fled to the pit now. Even so, Chet sometimes still watched him as if the fault lines along which he'd once cracked were visible and might open again.

Tonight however, it wasn't a need to lose himself that made Richard detour. His sole focus remained on getting downstairs and digging out some answers. But as chief, he couldn't ignore his department for the night anymore than a parent could fail to look in on a sleeping child. He simply intended to do a walk through and let everyone know that he was "in the house" as the old-timers at NYCH put it. When the nurses and staff knew he was around, it had a leveling effect that made the work go more smoothly. Might as well take advantage of it, he figured, since he was going to be nearby anyway.

"Dr. Steele," said Jo O'Brien. "What are you doing here? Is Dr. Sullivan all right?" A frown creased her face.

"Apart from some needle-happy rookie oversedating her again, she's no worse." He deliberately said nothing about Lockman. He wanted to keep his visit short.

Her generous chin-line stiffened. "You're not serious."

"Afraid so."

"I bet I know the one. Well, looks like I'll have to pay her a visit and let the woman know that she's dealing with a friend of mine."

Despite everything, Richard smiled. "I'd appreciate it, Jo. All of them up there are mighty pissed off at me right now."

"Pissed off at you, Mr. Diplomacy? Come on," Jo said with a wink.

As she spoke, her eyes slid past him toward the triage area. He turned to see two ambulance attendants wheeling in a plump man about his own age sitting bolt upright on a stretcher. He wore a lime-green sports jacket and a straw cowboy hat. A pair of white-tipped shoes stuck out from the bottom of the sheet. An oxygen mask adorned his face.

Jo hurried down the hall to meet the new arrivals.

From fifty yards away Richard could see the patient's labored breathing and could tell by the way he clutched his fist in front of his chest as he spoke that he was probably complaining of chest pain. Out of habit he stepped into the nursing station and took a look at the on-duty sheet for cardiology. Spotting Francesca Downs's name, he knew if the man needed an angioplasty or emergency bypass procedure there'd be no delays the way there were with some of the surgeons. She was tops as far as that stuff went. But maybe he could catch her later and ask if she'd also been up to any extracurricular activities lately.

He walked back into the hallway in time to see Jo wheel the new arrival into one of the cardiac monitoring rooms. A dumpling-shaped woman dressed like Dale Evans trotted along behind, saying, "We were in our line dancing class when he suddenly felt dizzy. So I called 911 and made him lie down right on the floor. He's a pilot, you know, flies 747s . . ."

Not anymore he won't, Richard thought.

A couple of residents ran through the doorway after them, followed by the staff doctor on duty. They didn't even seem to notice he was there.

Glancing into the rest of the treatment areas he saw that everything else was pretty much under control.

Before leaving he used one of the phones at triage to call Chet and Lisa, saying simply that Kathleen remained stable, but he'd be staying in the hospital to catch up on some paperwork. He wasn't about to tell them over the phone all that had happened.

"No problem, Dad," Chet said. "Lisa's made popcorn, and we rented *The Mummy* again."

Richard smiled despite everything. "Remember, it's a school night," he warned. Obviously he wasn't missed there either. At least Chet sounded secure when Lisa was around.

The hospital, like most large midtown structures built in the 1950s, had a multilayered basement. Medical records were at the very bottom, like sediment. *The bomb shelter* one of the clerks had initially christened it, at a time when Eisenhower was president and movies advocating *Duck and Cover* were being shown at schools throughout the nation. The label stuck.

On the ride down, as he planned how to tackle Hamlin's charts, his dread of losing Kathleen spiraled after him with the persistence of a vulture. Stepping into a long lime-green corridor that had a low ceiling lined with pipes and square metal ducts, he felt the silence weigh as heavy as the fifty feet of stone into which the foundation had been sunk. The walls seemed to close in on him, the air stuffy and unbearably hot; the harsh fluorescent lighting overhead hurt his eyes. He turned right and walked briskly, his leather soles slapping against the concrete floors with a loud echo.

Reaching a solid metal door, he punched in a four-digit code he knew as well as his own phone number. As confidential as it was supposed to be, it hadn't changed for years, and there wasn't anybody, practically, in the whole hospital who didn't have it. Everyone—from ward clerks, through the nursing staff, all the way up to doctors—had cause to come here, either to fetch charts, return them, or sign off some forgotten piece of paperwork. This shuffle of records and people in and out matched the comings and goings of patients upstairs. The hospital attracted a quarter million visits a year, what with the ER, the clinics, and ten floors of eighty beds each. It was a wonder they didn't lose more files than they did.

The soft rushing noise of air-conditioning replaced the silence in the darkened room, and he welcomed the coolness. A slightly sharp odor made the inside of his nose tingle, proclaiming that the acid-free-paper movement hadn't made a dint in this realm.

Reaching along the wall he felt out a long array of switches and flipped them up three at a time. Lights flickered to life one section after another as far back as he could see, illuminating rows and rows of shelves, each stuffed with manila folders, all of it holding a half century's worth of medical histories, a chronicle of New York by its diseases. He'd never failed to feel overwhelmed by how many stories of so many lives were deposited here, all of them beginning with the uncertainty of a tentative diagnosis, each sustained through the hope of treatment, and, ultimately, everyone of them with a conclusion, for better or worse. Sometimes, late at night while working alone on an audit, he would think he'd hear whisperings, and wonder if the souls whose journeys had ended here were trying to tell their tales. A running quip around the hospital predicted that if the Internet gurus ever did manage to do away with paper charts and finally compact all this information into microchips, the resulting space would solve Manhattan's parking problems. But to Richard, the real joke would be if the subsequent underground lot was full of voices and forever haunted.

He walked over to a bank of computers in a big open section that served as a reception area, sat down at one, and inserted his card. The screen welcomed him by name.

He typed in *Hemorrhagic Stroke*, added *Dr. Tony Hamlin*, and got to work.

"Damn them!" he muttered, peering through the ICU doors when they next slid open and seeing the nurses still hovering over Sullivan.

"Harold Glass," as he'd called himself tonight, began to mop farther down the hall, afraid that his hanging about any longer would attract attention. He'd already pressed his luck, taking as much time as he could when he'd gone back in to clean the floor just before change-of-shift. But the nurses had remained clustered around Sullivan the whole time, turning and attending to her, making it impossible to approach her again. And so far the new crew seemed intent on checking her every few minutes. He had no idea why she'd suddenly become the center of attention, but it was ruining his plans. He had to rethink what he was going to do.

Not that the alternative was hard to figure out. The list had sentenced Steele to be the fourth to die. And yet here the man was. It was as if God had offered him up instead, even to the point of having him announce he'd be in medical records. A more secluded, isolated part of the hospital at this time of night he couldn't imagine, perfect for a kill, in case things got loud.

Growing excited, he parked his mop and bucket in a corner and walked briskly down the hallway, trying to keep a clear head. It was no small matter to disobey orders. But could it be God was presenting such a golden opportunity because the mortal who had drawn up the list had been in error? After all, why was it important to the Lord that Steele should die after Sullivan? It certainly made no tactical sense, because if he killed her first, even if no one else realized she'd been executed, surely Steele would know, and his rage, fed by the wrath of Satan, would make him all the harder to destroy. Wasn't it better for him to do God's work by taking Steele out now? In fact, this might be His steering a clear path through the man-made agendas that contaminated the mission.

His heart racing, he pivoted and headed back to where he'd left his cleaning equipment. But what about a weapon? Should he first bash him unconscious, the way he did Lockman? But that was different. The stupid bugger had left the window open, and all he had to do was climb up the vines and clobber him with a hammer in his sleep. Even then it had taken more than a single whack to knock him out, and he'd fought back a bit. If the first hit failed to take Steele completely unawares, "Harold Glass" could end up having to finish him off while dodging about trying to protect himself. Besides, he hadn't brought anything heavy with him this time, and he might not find something lying around down there big enough to finish the job in a single blow.

Then he thought of his training when he'd first joined the movement, the month he'd spent five years ago with combat instructors in the Blue Ridge Mountains. He could snap Steele's neck, the way they taught him. Doing the feat for real would be different from performing it on a mannequin, sure. Yet as long as he got the guy from behind, it shouldn't be too difficult. And he could come back to dispatch Sullivan afterward.

Because chances were, if he hid his body in some back corridor, they wouldn't find him until the morning staff came on duty at seven. That gave "Harold Glass" plenty of time to revisit ICU. Six-thirty would be best. He'd offer to clean up before the end of the night shift. The nurses would be too busy getting their charts in order for the changeover to notice him getting close to her again.

Breathing quickly, he reached the elevator that would take him downstairs and pushed the button. A distant motor whined into action, but the wait for the car seemed to take forever. He shifted nervously from one foot to the other. He had to slow down, he told himself. He couldn't rush this. But the prospect of action had him on edge.

When the door opened, he hesitated before getting in, his enthusiasm to go after Steele all at once wavering. Was his deviation from the original plan really the Lord's wish? How did he know Satan wasn't tempting him to stray by playing with his impatience to get the job done.

The elevator door closed in front of him, and he looked over to the mop and bucket against the wall. The corridor was very long. He estimated he could spend another hour or two pretending to mop it end to end and no one would find it out of the ordinary. That was it. He'd trust in God to show him the way, he decided as he walked over and pulled the pail of water, its wheels squeaking, to the middle of the floor. He grabbed the wooden handle and hoisted the wad of dripping gray strings, then slapped it onto the linoleum. If He hadn't provided the opportunity to kill Sullivan by the time he'd finished, he would know He meant for him to move on to Steele. After all, he had the whole night.

The metal wheels gave another little squeal as he nudged his way back toward ICU.

Hamlin had operated on four types of intracranial hemorrhages in the last two years. There weren't a lot.

Capsular angiomas like Kathleen's caused only 2 percent of all hemorrhagic strokes. As for the other kinds requiring surgical intervention, even the most common—subarachnoid leaks, or bleeding onto the surface of the brain from congenital aneurysms—showed up in ER only about a dozen times a year. Hemorrhages into the cerebellum, the large spheres hanging over the brain stem at the back, might arrive eight or nine times. Arterial-venous malformations—arteries pumping directly into weaker-walled veins until they burst—were slightly more common, especially in hypertensives, but only in a fraction of the cases could they be reached with a scalpel. And Hamlin wasn't the surgeon of choice in all of them. He had a department full of hungry competitors with whom he had to share any goodies amenable to the knife.

In every category his patients did twice as well as those of any other neurosurgeon in the country. If he and Lockman were killing people, it didn't show here. "So what the hell were they up to?" Richard muttered. The sound of his own voice was a welcome respite to the steady sushing noise pouring out of the air ducts.

Armed with a list of seven files for the year so far and thirteen for the period January 1 to December 31 of last year, he went into the maze of open-sided, ceiling-high shelves to track them down. Overhead the pipes let out a moan, then gurgled and thumped as if they were the intestines of some angry beast.

He found it tedious work. First he had to locate each chart according to its seven-digit listing. That entailed wandering about deep within the stacks while keeping ten-digit numbers straight in his head. Some of the dossiers were reasonably slim, but others were three-volume affairs, each the size of the New York phone book. Might as well round up everything at once before looking through them, he decided, taking the first half dozen to the table where he'd been working and going back for the rest.

Once he had them all, he began by arranging them in four piles according to diagnosis—nine patients with subarachnoid leaks, one of which had deteriorated into an outright bleed; six with cerebellar hemorrhages; three with an AV malformation; two with a capsular angioma in the brain stem. He started with the turf where he would be most at home, the patient's arrival in ER.

In each instance they'd been seen promptly by his staff, stabilized, and transferred to Hamlin's care. But one case from over a year ago, the subarachnoid leak that had deteriorated into an outright hemorrhage, leapt out at him. Richard himself had done the resuscitation. Immediately he remembered the patient, a young man of forty-two who had come in complaining of the worst headache in his life. His wife, a slight blond woman so pale with fright that her face seemed brittle as porcelain, ran out of her husband's cubicle to get help when he suddenly slumped down on the stretcher, unresponsive.

Richard had rushed to intubate him. As he worked, the man's bulging right eye seemed to seek him out and stare at him, its pupil dilated big as a blackened dime, a sign that the pressure of the hemorrhage was squeezing the brain out the bottom of his skull like so much toothpaste. The mouth twisted into a one-sided sneer and emitted grunting noises along with frothy spittle as he seized. For an instant Richard allowed himself to think his patient was trying to tell him something, trying to protest against having his memories, his mind, his ability to think, his very self reduced to a gray-and-white puree being emptied out like the pulp of a plant.

He'd obviously let that one get under his skin, he thought, surprised by how clearly it all came back to him. Let too many horrors in where they could work on you, and it was burnout time, the end of most ER careers. He'd counseled enough husks of formerly good physicians to know, and had been through his own near brush with the flame.

It wasn't just the victims who ate into your dreams and stared back at you if you let them. He could still see the young wife's eyes. Already dilated as black as her husband's in terror of losing him, they had seemed to recede into their sockets as she tried to prepare herself for the worst. Yet against all odds, he and Hamlin managed to save the man's life. In ER they had shrink-wrapped his brain down to three-quarters its size by running a half liter of concentrated mannitol through it. Hyperosmotic, it sucked the brain tissue dry, collapsing it around the ruptured vessels, slowing the bleed, and relieving the pressure that was emptying his skull of white matter. That bought enough time to get him on the OR table within a few heartbeats of being alive. Hamlin did the rest. Six hours later the woman returned with the good news, pitch embers of hope glittering where earlier there'd been hollow despair. Maybe it was the sight of her so transformed that helped him put all thought of her husband's grotesque ordeal out of mind and escape with one less haunting, for he hadn't given a thought to either of them from that time until now.

Richard turned to the section detailing the man's course in hospital. As with most medical records the world over, the initial notes belonged to the doctors and residents. Their terse, dated entries, the handwriting varying from day to day according to the rotation of house staff who took care of him told the tale of his physiological recovery, defining the extent he was alive with a string of numbers that documented his vitals, his O_2 levels, and his coma scale. Next came all the lab results, the cardiograms, and finally the X-ray reports—MRIs, CT scans, angiograms—all peering into the state of his brain. But to really see the progress of the person as opposed to the body he read the nursing notes. They were more subjective, and therefore more pertinent regarding a return to life.

  . . . *recovering movement in arms and legs* . . .

  . . . *asking for his wife* . . .

  . . . *swallowing water through a straw without choking* . . .

Richard marveled at what he read, never having imagined that the extent of brain damage he'd witnessed could have been reversed enough to enable the man to perform even such basic tasks. The progress notes for the second week he found more remarkable still.

  . . . *patient able to feed himself* . . .

  . . . *sits in chair* . . .

  . . . *speech much less garbled* . . .

The final note deemed him stable enough for transfer to rehab, in this case at the Adele Blaine Rehabilitation Institute. Nothing unusual about that—except there were no follow-up visits to the hospital. The patient simply dropped off the radar as far as NYCH was concerned.

Strange, thought Richard. Most people saw the treating surgeon at least once or twice after discharge. In this case, who knew how the man did afterward? Maybe this was how Hamlin ended up with such good statistics. Even if the guy died, it wouldn't show up on his NYCH record.

He made a note of the man's name, intending to contact Blaine's rehabilitation institute in the morning and request that they give him whatever they had on file about the guy's outcome. If he said it was part of an ER audit, they might fall for it and tell him, he figured.

He got up to walk around a few minutes, the coolness he'd found so pleasant on arrival having seeped into his bones. As he warmed up, he noticed that directly overhead where he'd been sitting was an air duct. "No wonder," he muttered, and pulled the desk over against a partition that separated the work area from the rest of the room. Not only did it seem warmer there, he felt more comfortable having his back to something solid. It always unnerved him a little to sit alone in such a vast open space. Tonight he felt especially jumpy, due to the aftershock of discovering Lockman's body.

Getting back to work, he found that the admission notes in the remaining files showed a pattern similar to what he'd seen in the first. A timely, successful surgical intervention, a remarkable post-op progress, a transfer to Adele Blaine's rehabilitation institute with no follow up.

Except on two occasions.

One involved a man whose surgery had been a year and a half ago for a subarachnoid hemorrhage: the other was a woman who, like Kathleen, had a bleeding capsular angioma removed in April of that same year. Both of them had returned to ER, the man two months ago, the woman a few weeks later, except they were DOA.

Intracranial hemorrhage read the death certificates signed by Hamlin. In neither case had there been an autopsy.

His own staff hadn't seen any cause to challenge this. According to the nursing notes, the families had expressed their extreme satisfaction with Hamlin for the remarkable recovery their loved one had made from the first stroke, and didn't feel any need to confirm his diagnosis of the terminal event.

Richard found it odd that none of his ER doctors had questioned why a person who'd had a congenital vascular malformation removed over a year earlier should have a second bleed. After all, these things didn't grow back. To suggest that both had a second vascular anomaly Hamlin had missed on the first workup invoked impossible odds.

Were they hypertensive? he wondered, willing to grant that they could have suffered a second hemorrhage from otherwise normal arterial sites if they were already weakened by chronically high blood pressure. But he couldn't see any record of elevated BP readings on their previous admission, nor did their ER record indicate a prior history of it.

He added these two patients and their particulars to his list, intending to see what their charts at Blaine's institute said about subsequent blood pressure readings as they became more active. He also found the names of their family doctors on the initial admission sheet. After all, it wasn't impossible the readings remained low here, what with all the morphine and bed rest, then returned to previous highs after discharge.

Something flushed through the pipes overhead, making them groan in protest.

Still feeling stiff, he arched his back, crossed his hands behind his head, and continued to think. Certainly these two hadn't died as an immediate result of their previous surgery by Hamlin. It had been over a year between the operations and their deaths. So how had they done in the meantime?

He flipped through the ER documents to the names and phone numbers of their next of kin. He'd also phone them tomorrow and ask.

Again he leaned back in his chair. Could Blaine be in on some kind of cover-up with Hamlin? If so, why? His previous numbers for morbidity-mortality were completely respectable.

Once more recalling the heated exchange he'd witnessed between her and the neurosurgeon along with the others in the cafeteria, he played with the idea of specifically confronting her before setting McKnight on the bunch of them. Or might his asking about the two killings make the woman shut up completely and hide behind a lawyer just as quickly as the police speaking to her would?

Rather than single her out just now and jump to any conclusions that she was part of something he couldn't yet identify, he'd better check the files of those patients at her institute and see what really happened to them. In fact, without evidence of any wrongdoing, she, Edwards, and Downs could all claim they'd been fighting about anything. Certainly the last thing he should do was antagonize her at this point since even if she wasn't involved, his getting at those rehab records might still be crucial to figuring out what Hamlin and Lockman were up to. He should approach her as a colleague, requesting her help to uncover Hamlin's secret without suggesting he suspected her of involvement with the surgeon. He completed a list of all the people whose records he'd ask her about, recording their names, birth dates, and phone numbers.

Something else he should look at, he thought, flipping back to the section for X-ray reports in each dossier.

Sure enough, in every case the patients had an angiogram, the radiologist on record being Lockman.

But Richard couldn't spot anything else out of the ordinary. So what had the neurosurgeon done to them that he and Lockman feared he would find out? The OR reports, the record of what Hamlin had actually performed during surgery in all twenty cases certainly didn't suggest anything, at least nothing causing obvious harm. The majority of these lengthy accounts were dictated solely—and in mind-numbing detail—by his residents, then checked and signed by them, which seemed to rule out the possibility of Hamlin having altered them.

Assuming his statistics were true, did it mean that whatever he'd done to improve them had occurred solely during the angiogram?

Not necessarily, if Hamlin had managed to pull a fast one right under the residents' noses.

What sort of fast one?

Something that, after making everyone do so extraordinarily well, also killed them. Killed them with another bleed, the way these last two died.

And if it killed them, would it kill Kathleen?

Rage tumbled through him like a flash flood. What if he never found out what they'd done to the other patients and Kathleen in time to help her?

Crazy ideas screamed through his head. He suddenly didn't feel so sure about pussyfooting around Blaine. An hour alone with her might be all he needed to make her tell what she knew.

And if she along with Edwards and Downs were the "others" that Lockman had referred to, were they also the ones who killed him and

Hamlin? Visions of the radiologist's body reinforced for Richard the idea that the killer's handiwork itself indicated he or she was someone with a medical background. Certainly Downs could have managed it. Edwards, too, for that matter because after all, a surgeon was a surgeon, even if he normally operated only on females between the navel and the knees.

But despite his desperation to pounce on a definite answer, his instincts as a physician pushed him to consider all logical solutions, the same way he would entertain all reasonable diagnoses in a sick patient. Again he vacillated between his suspicions about the three and the possibility they'd nothing to do with the whole affair, that someone about whom he'd no idea held the secret of what had been done to Kathleen. Without proof to the contrary, he was back to admitting Lockman's killer could have been anyone with training, just as he'd initially told McKnight.

I'll hunt them down, so help me, and make them tell me what Hamlin did to Kathleen, even if I have to grill everyone in this hospital. He gave a shudder, a flurry of faces and names flashing through his head, until he suddenly thought, *Oh my God, look what I'm doing.* He felt sick to his stomach.

Leave the trapping of the murderer to the cops, he tried telling himself. Yet his sense of being personally responsible for doing so—something from the realm of a "Hail Mary"—persisted. In the pit he'd pulled his share of desperate moves resorted to only when all else had failed and there was nothing to lose. He also knew when it wasn't going to work. He'd feel as if an icy hand reached up to rake through his own innards before it pulled whomever he was working on into his, or her, grave.

He'd have to be careful who he fingered to McKnight, he finally decided, still unclear about what he should do on his own. Yet he was determined to keep his options open, ready to try anything that would help Kathleen, even if it meant working without the cops.

Looking at his watch, he saw that it was four A.M. Since ICU hadn't called him, he figured Kathleen must be sleeping normally, the drug having worn off by now. Better she rest, he decided, seeing no advantage to waking her. She could tell him in the morning what upset her so. Besides, there was more he could do here, and he proceeded to follow up on a hunch. If he concentrated on the years just prior to the spectacular fall in Hamlin's morbidity-mortality rates, he might twig to what was done differently, however insignificant it might seem, around the time of the change. That might be the key to whatever *fast one* the neurosurgeon had pulled.

Punching the appropriate keys, he asked for the list of Hamlin's patients corresponding to 1998 and 1999. When he had the numbers of the files, he arranged them in ascending order to make his retrieval of them more systematic. As a result, the more actual dossiers he picked up, he found himself having to go further and further into the warren of charts and aisles. The steady noise of the air-conditioning and the industrial carpet underfoot dulled any sounds he made as he walked until he seemed to be moving about in virtual silence. "Like one of the ghosts I've heard down here," he muttered, once again trying to find comfort from the sound of his own voice. But the muffling rush from the overhead ducts increasingly bothered him, as did the realization that if anyone else ever did come in here, he wouldn't hear them. However useful a conversation with the killer might prove to be, Richard's having conceded the person could be anybody from the hospital had him feeling edgy and looking over his shoulder.

Shit, he was being ridiculous, he chastised himself. Better keep his wits about him, or he'd scream at the sight of some poor clerk from ER trying to find a chart. He started to whistle, as much for solace to his jumpy nerves as to warn any unsuspecting newcomers that they weren't alone.

When his cell phone rang, he leapt into the air and dropped the folders he was carrying.

"Jesus Christ!" he said, fumbling the instrument out of his pocket and putting it to his ear.

"Find anything?" McKnight asked, sounding sleepy.

"You scared me to death."

"By calling you? Man, you must be getting skittish."

Sheepish was what Richard felt at the moment. "Hey, you caught me off guard is all. My damn phone hardly ever works down here. I wasn't expecting it to ring."

"What have you got for me?"

"I told you, I won't breach confidentiality—"

"Fine! Fine! I don't have to know a single thing about any patient. Just what our two dead men were up to."

Richard thought a moment. "Yeah, that might be possible."

"So what have you discovered?"

"Nothing yet. I got sidetracked by something with Kathleen."

"Is she okay?" All at once McKnight sounded wide awake.

"Yeah. I mean, physically. But earlier tonight she got really agitated by something, and one of the nurses shot her full of tranquilizers again."

"What upset her?"

"I don't know. She's sleeping it off. Why all the questions?"

The detective said nothing for a few seconds. "A team of detectives will be over at the hospital first thing in the morning to start interviewing people about Hamlin and Lockman. I'd like to talk to Dr. Sullivan then, too, if I may. Will you be there?"

"Sure. I'll meet you in ICU. I take it you're officially part of the investigation now?"

"Around seven?" he said, not answering the question.

"See you then," said Richard, wondering if the detective was involved formally, or out of his attachment to Kathleen. "And thank you," he added, welcoming the big man's special interest in any case.

After punching the END button, he kneeled down to pick up the spilled charts.

He'd recovered half of them when the room suddenly went dark.

"What the hell," he said.

Must be a power failure, he thought at first. Probably from the storm outside.

Then he noticed that the vents continued to breathe ice on him from overhead. Air-conditioning didn't work when the power went off to the whole building. Plus, a general outage should have automatically brought on the emergency lights.

"Hey!" he yelled, wondering if somebody from ER actually had come to get a chart without his hearing them. On the way out, figuring no one was here, whoever it was might have flicked off the switches.

But no one answered.

A passing night watchman perhaps.

"Hello?" he called.

Only the noise of the vents filled the silence.

But wouldn't someone have heard him talking on the phone, even with the air-conditioning going? After all, it wouldn't have covered up his voice.

He began to grow uneasy.

And how could they have turned off over a dozen switches at once?

His mouth went dry.

Maybe it was only that a fuse blew, just for this area, he reasoned. The emergency generators wouldn't have come on for something so local. The explanation relaxed him a little. It seemed reasonable enough, and put to rest the creepy crawlers that had started racing through his brain.

Sort of.

The plumbing clunked and clanked the way it always did, as if someone were hammering on it with a monkey wrench. The sound reverberated off his skull.

He got down on his hands and knees, feeling for the remaining files scattered around him. If the electricity was fine in the rest of the hospital, he thought, he'd take what he'd collected upstairs and look at them in his office.

He had quite a load in his arm as he felt his way along the files. He wasn't entirely sure he was going toward the door, since he'd been pacing and turning while talking with McKnight. He figured it didn't matter, since the aisles ran perpendicular to the exit. He'd walk until he hit a wall, then go left until he either found the exit or hit another wall. At the worst, if he was going opposite to what he thought and heading for the back of the room, he'd simply have to keep following the walls until he eventually came to the way out.

He walked quickly, knowing that there was nothing he could trip over. When he came to a break between sections of the cabinets, he clutched his load to his chest with one hand and flapped the other in the intervening space until he made contact with the next line of shelves. He was moving so swiftly that when he finally did reach a wall he nearly banged his face into it before stopping. Undaunted, he turned in the direction he thought the door would be, and felt his way toward it.

The pipes along the length of the room gave a shudder.

He figured he'd know when he reached the open reception area. There'd be no shelves at all in that part. Then the door would be directly in front of him. He couldn't remember if it had a lit EXIT sign or not, but it should, one with its own circuit. Whether he'd also see a light coming under the frame from the outside hall he'd no idea. It was of no importance. He'd feel his way to the door handle if he had to.

A few minutes later he began to suspect he had gone the wrong way after all, since he hadn't come to the clearing that he'd expected. "Shit," he again muttered, the inky blackness weighing in on him.

He passed the end of a cabinet and hit another wall.

Feeling disoriented, his heartbeat quickened. "Okay, just focus on getting your bearings," he said aloud to help settle himself down. "This means I'm at the far corner in the back of the room. I turn left, go straight until I reach the front wall, and left again to the door."

He'd taken three steps when he thought he heard something rustle behind him.

It had been just loud and harsh enough to be distinguished above the steady whoosh from the ducts above him.

Already primed to jump out of his skin having seen what he had at Lockman's, and being in a basement, he sent a screamer into his brain with the first answer that came to mind.

Rats!

"Get away!" he screeched, and started running blindly ahead, "Get back, you filthy little creeps!"

In his imagination he pictured the darkness teeming with them, and when the sounds behind him increased, he became certain packs of them were on his heels.

In full panic and without thinking, he hurled his heavy bundle of charts behind him.

"Aggh!" he heard someone yell, followed by the sound of a heavy thud.

"What the . . ." He went another ten yards before it registered that his pursuer was human.

His first thought was to pull up and see who it was. But before he could even slow his stride, the image of Lockman's corpse popped back to mind. *Oh, Jesus, what am I doing?* he asked himself, his second thought being to get the hell out of there.

He accelerated into the dark, careening off the sides of shelves.

10

He ran blind. His hands fluttered along steel edges and guided his flight like a pair of startled birds, losing bits of skin on the sharp metal corners. He swept his fingers further in, until they stuttered over the cardboard spines of the records, and, reaching deeper, scooped an armload of them onto the floor as he passed. A series of grunts and sliding noises came from behind him, like someone trying to run on wet leaves.

He poured on the speed, and, as he flew by, hooked onto more clumps of folders and wrenched them out. Yet another round of curses and slips sounded on his heels. At the end of the next cabinet he cut left. If he reached the open reception area, the door would be to his right, he figured, taking advantage of the wider aisles that ran parallel with the front wall to go even faster. Once he was through it and into the hallway outside, he could get to the stairs.

The exertion made his ears plug. Unable to see or hear beyond the confines of his own body, he fled in a vacuum, his heart hammering pure adrenalin to his brain and the rasp of his own breath becoming the only sounds to fill his skull.

He imagined a bullet from behind.

A gutting.

Or something worse?

He hit the receptionist's counter at full tilt, the waist-high barrier delivering a perfect punch to his solar plexus and jackknifing him into a forward somersault. His breath exploded through his cords in a roar as he flipped through the air. From inside the sealed confines of his own head, it sounded as if it could curdle blood, but he doubted it would frighten off whoever was after him. He let out a second bellow when he slammed, back first, onto the floor and slid into a desk.

Fighting to get his deflated lungs working again, he staggered to his feet and stumbled in the direction of what as near as he could guess would be the exit. Any moment he expected to feel the hands of his hunter come out of the darkness and grab him. That he wasn't already in his clutches meant he must have lost the creep by ducking left when he did, instead of continuing straight to the front wall.

To his dismay there was no illuminated EXIT sign. He scanned the blackness, looking for any hint of light coming from under the doorframe.

None.

Find the handle by feel?

But the killer might already be waiting there, expecting him to try just that. His scream sure as hell told the man where he was.

Fighting to breathe normally, he crouched down, taking slow shallow gasps through his mouth to make himself as silent as possible.

He needed a strategy.

And he needed to hear.

Pinching his nose and blowing hard, he made his ears pop, the rush of the air-conditioning breaking over his head like a wave.

But there was no sound of the man.

Get back into the stacks, Richard told himself. Far enough away that he could call for help over his cell phone without being heard. Then he'd have to start moving again—and fast.

He got up, bent over, and crept away from where he thought the exit was. He went about ten yards before clunking headfirst into a wall that shouldn't have been there.

Shit!

Immediately he figured he'd taken the wrong way again. But by feeling around beside him he discovered a desk, then another, and realized he'd hit the partition behind the work area.

Remaining absolutely still, he strained to pick up any noises to suggest the man was approaching him.

Again he heard nothing. Maybe the whoosh from the ventilation ducts was covering up the sound. He knew the man was out there, probably listening equally as hard. Better move, he told himself, and gingerly made his way to the end of the partition. He turned right and skittered across the floor, reaching an aisle between two rows of shelves that he moved along. With every stride he anticipated steps coming from behind.

No one followed. For good measure he zigged left for a few rows, then right again, always moving farther from the door, and, he hoped, away from whomever was after him. Finally he stopped, figuring it was as good a spot as any to call for help, and reached into his pocket for his phone.

It was gone.

No! He patted himself down as if it might have traveled someplace else in his clothing.

Nothing.

Oh, my God. It must have fallen out when I took my somersault.

He went very still. Should he try to go back and find it?

He began to feel very cold, as if icy fingers were worming their way through him.

What if he hadn't lost it in the reception area? It could have worked its way out of his pocket and dropped to the floor anywhere while he was running. With his ears plugged, he wouldn't have heard it fall.

He swallowed, his mouth completely dry.

And where was the man? He must have figured by now what he, Richard, had done, so should he keep moving?

The thought of blundering into that killer kept him from budging. He simply stood and listened, knowing that whoever was after him was surely doing the same. A silent standoff, he thought, like two submarines, each waiting for the other to make a mistake and give himself away. And time was on his enemy's side. It would be impossible to stay completely quiet for the hours it might take before someone came to his rescue. Something would be bound to give him away, especially at close range. It could be as little as his bones creaking, an untimely gurgle from his stomach, or a sneeze from the tickle inside his nose.

His hunter, on the other hand, didn't so much have to keep silent as be patient.

As he remained motionless, bent over and uncomfortable, he thought he heard a shuffle off to his right.

He waited.

The unmistakable growl of an empty stomach came from about ten feet away, somewhere near the entrance to the aisle where he was hiding.

Richard brought his respirations down to practically nothing.

What to do?

If he comes closer, I'll try and coldcock him with a punch, then maybe I can run for it again.

He got ready, drawing back his fist, breathing silently through his mouth, slowly standing upright and adjusting his stance.

But the man withdrew, until he could hear him moving a few rows over.

Richard stayed where he was a few minutes, allowing the slight sounds that marked his adversary's progress to fade away completely. All at once he felt an advantage. There was no one between him and the door. He might just creep back and get out. But another thought came to mind. What if he got his stalker?

Kathleen woke to tugs on her IV tubing. She shot her eyes open expecting to see the janitor from hell injecting her. Instead she gazed directly into the eyes of a nurse who changed her intravenous bag.

"You awake, Dr. Sullivan?" the woman asked.

Kathleen didn't blink a reply. If she started on about one of the cleaning staff who tried to kill her with a syringe, they would knock her out again. She needed Richard!

Summoning the use of her fingers, she tried to point at her tracheostomy, hoping the nurse would understand and remove the tube, then help her to conduct a conversation.

Unexpectedly, she moved her wrist as well.

Staring at it in amazement, she managed to flop her hand back and forth a few times. It was a clumsy wave, but the achievement made her feel she'd been released from irons.

"Well, look at you," declared the nurse as if she was encouraging an infant who'd just learned how to shake a baby rattle.

Kathleen's sense of triumph vanished, driven off by the woman's patronizing tone. Her mood swung to the opposite extreme as it often did these last few days. A bottomless despair for her future loomed so black and large in her head, it crowded out everything else—the bed, the ICU, the walls of the hospital. It left her to float in a night empty of hope and as vast as space.

Don't you know I'm damn near forty, have a grown daughter, and am a geneticist, you idiot, she wanted to scream at the faceless smile. *Do you even have a clue what it is to lose what I've lost, to feel condemned to being a baby again? To know if I live, all I've got ahead of me is absolute helplessness, unless I relearn every move, every action, every simple feat that I haven't thought twice about doing since I was three years old. Have you the slightest inkling what it's like to have no guarantee I'll ever get any of it back, no matter how hard I try? Because if you did, you'd spare me your goo-goo, gaga routine and save it for the nursery.*

But she figured it would lose something in the translation, gasping all that out in three- and four-word phrases.

She tried to move her forearm, but it still wouldn't respond. A quick inventory on the other side revealed she'd no improvement over the finger movements she'd fallen asleep with. But when she tried her feet, both sets of toes wiggled, brushing against the weight of the sheets, the right more than the left.

So she'd a live hand stranded on a dead stick, and could mess up the bedding at the foot of the mattress. All in all, not much, but she'd take it.

At least her newfound skills with her wrist allowed her to grab the tube in her neck. She couldn't disconnect it from the respirator, but a few tugs on it got rid of her minder's frosty smile.

"Whoa there," she said, slapping Kathleen's hand away and giving her a cross look. "That's for me to do, not you."

Then get to it and let me speak.

The annoying woman did everything else but, adjusting the IV, checking the monitors, recording her vitals, even adjusting the head of her bed.

Damn it to hell! Kathleen seethed. She wanted Richard. She wanted Detective McKnight and the whole bloody NYPD. Not her pillows fluffed.

Richard quietly got a foothold on the edge of a nearby shelf, hoisted himself off the floor, then felt around above him for the overhead pipes. Probing the darkness with his fingers and feeling nothing, he knew he'd have to go higher. Another step up did it, and his hand slid over a plexus of conduits until it found one that felt as big as a log. After looping his arms around its iron surface, he swung his legs to the top of the lengthy filing case he'd just climbed and hooked it between his heels. Quietly, he pushed and pulled against it, enough to feel it teeter, but not fall over. He was ready.

"Who are you?" he called. "What do you want?"

Only the whispers of the vents spewing out their cold by his head made a sound. He began to worry he wouldn't hear the man approaching.

"I said, who are you? Why are you after me?"

What if the man didn't take the bait, remained too wary, simply waited at a distance? Richard wouldn't be able to hang there forever. Maybe he could bluff the creep into rushing him.

"Hello, police? This is Dr. Richard Steele," he said, doing his best to mimic a panicky call to the cops. "I'm on my cellular, and there's a man who has me trapped in the basement of New York City Hospital. He's threatening to kill me. . . . Yes, I'm sure. . . . He may even be the the person who murdered Doctors Tony Hamlin and Matt Lockman. . . .Where am I exactly? In the Medical Records Department—"

"Damn you!" a high-pitched voice shrieked from some distance. Dull footfalls on the carpeted floors machine-gunned in his direction.

Holy shit! thought Richard, caught off guard by the outburst, and he strained his legs against the heavy cabinet, shoving it away from him to the brink of going over.

"You will not thwart me," his attacker screamed as he thudded into the aisle below.

Richard rocked the shelves back toward him.

"I will avenge your wrongs against God's works!"

This guy's nuts, he thought, getting the wall of metal and paper moving nicely to and fro a few times, until one final tug sent the entire structure and all its contents crashing onto the man underneath.

His howls of pain and rage trebled.

For good measure Richard dropped his own one-ninety pounds onto the back of the toppled cabinet, giving his human sandwich a final whack.

Then all was silent.

Too silent.

Christ, had he killed the lunatic?

As he scrambled over the slippery surface, he felt the slope of it under his feet, presumably because the man's body lay wedged between it and the floor. When he reached its end he knelt down and listened at the opening to the space it had created, hoping to hear the guy's breathing.

At first there was absolute silence. Then a soft brushing sound came toward him.

He was alive. Time to get out of here. But the man had answers that might save Kathleen.

"Are you all right?"

The movement continued, then stopped.

Maybe he was hurt and couldn't answer.

Richard got back to his feet, slipped his fingers around the edge of the top shelf and gave a heave. He couldn't lift it. Maybe it had pinned the guy and was crushing the air out of his lungs, he thought, his alarm growing. Feeling around he could tell the heavy structure was at least partially hung up on the cabinet in front of it. Not all the weight was on the trapped man.

Still, if he had knocked him out, the man could have swallowed his tongue and be having trouble breathing. Shit! The sounds Richard had heard could even be him seizing.

Or he could be playing possum.

Richard hovered, thinking of Kathleen. If the man died, so did his best chance to find out what Hamlin did to her.

Goddamn it! Better check him, he decided, yielding to his ER reflexes.

He lay flat on his stomach and slithered into the tiny space, his slim frame finding clearance without much difficulty. "Answer me if you can. Are you able to get your breath?"

Nothing.

He inched ahead, unable to see anything. Every two feet he stopped and listened. Not even the sound of the air-conditioning penetrated in here.

Before Richard heard him, he smelled him, a sour aroma of sweat and the biting perfume of aftershave subtle as toilet bowl deodorizer in a gas station restroom.

Squirming forward a few more inches, Richard caught the rise and fall of the man's respirations, quiet and regular, not at all labored.

Too regular for someone in distress.

He instinctively pulled up, just as a handful of fingers swept by the front of his throat and another clutched at his neck but missed.

"Shit!" he screamed, writhing backward as fast as he could. The man crawled after him, grunting and huffing as he came. Richard continued to propel himself feetfirst toward the opening with his elbows and knees, burning the skin off them as he went. At first, the man's hands brushed his face as they kept grabbing and reaching for him, and puffs of the guy's breath blew hot against the backs of his own hands. Richard sped up, easily increasing the distance between them.

The creep must be fatter than me, he thought.

Seconds later Richard was out from under the cabinet and heading for the door, his own breathing quick and burning. He'd need help; he was too spent to fight. As he raced away, he heard a plaintive wail.

"You can't escape me. For I am a soldier in the Legion of the Lord," the man bellowed.

What was it with all the God stuff?

"And as I do His work, He is at my side!"

The creep really must be loony.

"You hear me! As an enemy of His plan you shall perish! As a destroyer of His seed you will receive the Almighty's just punishment."

Oh shit! Richard thought of all the times he'd treated psychotics in ER who sounded like that when they were in the throws of some religious delirium. What if he was some escaped psychiatric patient who'd wandered off the floor and had nothing to do with the killings?

Increasingly uneasy that he might have made a terrible mistake, Richard ran faster.

"Hey!" yelled the man. "Stop!"

Visions of litigation for assaulting a patient danced through his head.

"Hang on, I'm going to get some people to help you," he called back, figuring about six orderlies and a syringeful of Haldol ought to do it. The door couldn't be too much farther.

Sounds of running joined his own.

Christ, the son of a bitch was after him again.

This must be in the reception area, he thought, and sprinted for where the way out ought to be.

"You are damned to hell!" screeched the man descending on him.

Yeah, right. Slamming into the wall he immediately felt along it for the handle, the frame, anything. His lead couldn't be more than ten seconds. His hand closed over the latch. He yanked it open, bringing the light from the hallway flooding in, practically blinding him. Out he ran, and made a beeline for the stairs.

"You're agents of the Devil!" the man screamed from inside the room. "His vengeance will destroy you both."

Both? Now he was seeing double, Richard thought.

Before starting up, he looked back, hoping to catch a glimpse of his pursuer.

No one followed.

"Where are you now?" McKnight said.

"At the front entrance, with the security guards."

"Can they block all the exits?"

"Not likely. This time of night there's only a skeleton staff. But we've got men here and at the ER doors."

"And there was no sign of this guy when you returned with the orderlies?"

"None."

"So where is he?"

"We figured he slipped out a fire exit."

"Shit! Can you describe him at all."

"He's got bad breath and wears lousy cologne."

"That's it?"

"Hey, I never saw him. The lights were out, and once I reached the corridor, he stayed out of sight."

"None of the floors are missing a psych patient?"

"No."

"Jesus Christ! We'll have to search the whole fucking hospital, just to be sure he's not still hanging around. Look, I'm on my way, and I'll dispatch a couple patrol cars—"

"There's more. I'm sure this guy's tied in with whatever Hamlin and Lockman did to Kathleen."

"And how do you figure that?"

"Because she just told me a man dressed as a cleaner tried to inject her with something a few hours earlier."

"What!"

"That's what set her off."

"Holy shit! Is she all right?"

"Yeah. The dragon lady who drugged her happened to be in the right place at the right time for once and, without even realizing it, interrupted him before he could do anything. The man came within seconds of taking Kathleen's life." Richard kept his voice icy calm, his feelings deep-frozen for the moment.

"But wait a minute," McKnight said. "How do you know it was the same guy as in the basement? You said you couldn't see down there."

"Because we both smelled him."

5:07 A.M.

"Fasten your seat belts. It's going to be a bumpy night . . ."

Jim Norris woke with a start to hear Bette Davis's voice blend with the sound of a bell ringing. He lurched out of his easy chair and stumbled toward the phone. He found it by the silvery glow of his television set that he kept permanently tuned to the classic movie channel. Having the likes of Gary, Humphrey, and Clark around for a while was the only way he could get any sleep these nights, their familiar voices in the distance as comforting as if they were old friends in the next room watching over him.

The ringing didn't stop even after he picked up the receiver, and he stood staring at it, the buzzing dial tone puzzling him even more. Urgent tapping replaced the bell, and a woman's voice, not Bette Davis's and barely above a whisper, said, "Norris, wake up, I know you're in there."

He pulled his housecoat around his lean, well-creased body and did up the tie, having nothing on underneath. After dispatching the TV with his remote, he shuffled over to the door. "Francesca?" he said.

"Let me in, Jimmy."

Norris drew a breath and held it. "Are you alone?"

"Of course I am. Let me in. We have to talk."

"The way you've been chatting it up with Laurel and Hardy," he said, resorting to the label he'd once jokingly given tiny Adele Blaine and the corpulent Paul Edwards, "I wouldn't think there'd be much left over you could say to me."

"Those two disgust me."

"Then why go running to them every time they call?"

"I'll tell you inside, Jimmy. I'm asking nicely."

"You're waking my neighbors, is what you're doing."

"Please, Jimmy, let's just stop hurting each other. I've got a way out of this for both of us."

He opened the door leaving the chain on. The grim face that greeted him seemed so sucked-in on itself he thought it would fit through the inch-wide crack between them. The dark rings under her eyes matched his own.

What the hell, he thought, flicking the metal clip free of its slot. He stepped back and waved her into his living room. "I guess misery really does love company."

She walked in and stood hugging her raincoat around her. The gray of first light through the windows tinted her blond hair and pale skin the color of ashes.

Like a lot of apartments on the upper West Side, his had a large, high-ceilinged, living-dining area, a small pair of bedrooms placed like apostrophe's about an even smaller kitchen, and a closet for a bathroom. When they'd first started dating eighteen months ago, she had him make love to her in every conceivable nook and cranny, to "make the place ours" as she put it. He got the impression she was exorcising all his previous women. He even welcomed her erasing those ghosts. There were a lifetime's worth, his easygoing charm and rugged looks having lured them in over the years. Once they realized that the best they could expect was to be second to his lab, they all left quickly enough. The system suited him. There was always another resident, technician, or nurse eager to test his reputation in bed.

As he'd anticipated, Francesca was different, because she was as smart, tough, and passionate about her career as he was.

She looked around, her expression pained. He wondered if she was taking inventory of their time together, and if her memories of what they'd done to each other seared her as cruelly as his did him. He'd been so confident back then, on fire about how the six of them would turn medicine on its ear, his lifetime in the lab about to pay off. The shambles of that pipe dream tasted dry as dust now. "Should I put on some coffee?" he said, desperately needing a diversion from the awkwardness he felt.

"Yes, that would be nice."

He retrieved his espresso maker from where it had been sitting on a shelf since she left over six months ago. Spooning in enough fresh grounds for two, he recalled how weeks afterward he'd still absently take a pair of cups down in the morning, then remember she was gone. That's when he had switched to tea.

She was so frail looking, he thought, watching her through the doorway, waiting for the brewing cycle to finish gurgling and growling. Yet he knew the strength of will that lay beneath her slight exterior, having felt its full, bruising impact once she'd decided to shut him out. Not hurt each other? That was a laugh. Both of them were too expert at it to quit.

"So what do you want?" he said minutes later, standing a few feet behind her with the mugs on a tray.

She gave a start, her mind clearly elsewhere, and turned to look at him. His being nude under the robe made him feel self-conscious.

"Right!" She sat on the edge of his couch, her hands in her pockets. Leaning forward, she seemed about to get up and leave at any second. As he placed her cup in front of her, she looked him in the eye and said, "Lockman's dead. Murdered. I was called into ER for a case tonight and word was all over the hospital."

She was studying him for a reaction, he thought. But he was ready for her. "I know. One of my lab technicians heard it on the news. She called me around midnight."

"Really?"

The question hung there, suggestive as a striptease.

"Yeah, really." He took a seat in an easy chair opposite her, and clasped his own hot drink between his palms. "You know how they like to keep a radio on down there, to take the edge off being alone in the depths of the hospital."

"You heard as well that Sullivan got Steele, along with a detective in the NYPD, to believe her story about Hamlin and Lockman?"

"Yeah."

"Damn it, Jimmy. How can you just sit there? Didn't your lab tech tell you what else they're saying about the murder tonight?" Her tone of voice was scalpel sharp.

"Yeah. Somebody took the trouble to cut Matt's heart out."

She shivered, and seemed to retreat deeper into the folds of her coat but kept her eyes welded to his. "You seem mighty cold about it."

"Is that why you're here, Francesca?" he said. "To see my reaction?"

"Jimmy, please, don't."

"You want to know if I killed him? And Hamlin?"

"I didn't say that."

"If my cutting out Lockman's heart was a special message to you?"

"Please, you're frightening me."

"Or maybe you think I had them killed?"

"Jimmy. Listen to me—"

"Well, here's one right back at you, Francesca, just so you know we're on an equal footing in the *who's got good reason to distrust who* department. You're the one who could benefit most from Hamlin and Lockman being dead. Hell, maybe with the lot of us knocked off you'd be free and clear to take your work public and reap the fame, along with the fortune that's bound to come with it. But of course in the meantime, if you arranged the first two deaths, you'd have to pretend to be suspicious of me and the others. And taking out a heart, that's just the thing to make it look as if the killer's sending you a specific warning. 'Poor Francesca! Maybe she's next,' the rest of us are meant to say, thereby diverting suspicions away from you."

"Why that's preposterous—"

"Really?" It was his turn to let the word drip insinuations into the air.

She studied him in silence. "Look, Jimmy," she said after a few seconds, "I'm scared." She stood up, came over, and took the cup from his hands placing it on the end table. "Come here," she added, tugging on his arms. "I don't think you killed them. I know you too well. You're a dreamer, not a murderer. I think it was Adele or Edwards, hell maybe even both of them, trying to save their own skins," her voice was as soft as the approach of daylight.

"Don't play games with me, Francesca—"

"Just stand up."

He rose to his feet.

"Now put your arms around me."

"No. You fucked me up when you left—"

She silenced him with a finger to his lips. "I know. I know. I hated you. Felt you'd seduced me, my career, my whole life into a disaster. But I've missed you more than I can bear. And you're right. With Hamlin and Lockman dead, I can go public and get out of this. But I want you with me."

Her candor appeased him.

"For my work?"

She gently clasped his bearded face between her palms. "I want more than just your work, Jimmy, much more."

"What about Blaine and Edwards?"

"We don't need them, and they won't dare talk."

"How can you be so sure?"

"They'll be too scared, Jimmy. Of cops, of us, of each other. After all, they've got more to lose than I do if they get caught. It gives me an edge over them."

"Over me as well. Why shouldn't I be scared of you?"

"I already told you. Because I tried living without you and was miserable. Because I've got so damn much more to win by keeping my mouth shut and just getting on with the work. Because you're brilliant and I need you in the lab. What you set out to do was a noble and beautiful thing, Jimmy, still is, and it's not too late for us to make it happen. Now are you with me?"

He hesitantly let her guide his arms around her waist and didn't resist when she undid the tie to his robe. As her fingers slid inside its folds and she drew him to her, he inhaled the aroma of her hair and felt the iron-hard hurt he'd carried for the last six months release its grip. For the first time in ages he seemed able to breathe freely. Because much as he desired her, equally intoxicating was the possibility she'd help him finish what he'd started, bring it to fruition in a way that would make it noble in the eyes of the world. The hope they could bury forever its association with Hamlin and Lockman made him feel ready to dare again and be the warrior he always imaged himself. Providing of course Blaine and Edwards kept their mouths closed. And Francesca didn't betray him afterward. Doubts flooded in on his desire.

The only part of what she'd said that he believed for certain was it being in her own best interests to shut up and get on with their work. Whether she wanted him back again just for his skills, or for "much more" as she'd claimed, he couldn't tell. Neither could he read her protesting her own innocence. Maybe she really did suspect that he'd done the killings and wanted him back anyway. Whatever her reasons, she seemed able to overcome her doubts about him, just as the promise of sex, his loneliness, and the prospect of becoming a scientific celebrity made it easier for him to ignore his own worst fears about her, for now.

At least that's what he told himself, yielding to the tumble of the moment.

But who was conning who this time? said a little voice from somewhere off to the side.

Probably it was mutual, he conceded, ready to believe anything in his rush to slip off her raincoat, glide his hands under her OR top, lift it over her upstretched arms, and escape his solitude by losing himself between her breasts, even if it was just for the next few hours.

11

Richard watched as the police artist put the finishing shading on the composite created with his laptop computer from Kathleen's instructions.

"Is that him?" McKnight said.

She studied the image of a clean-shaven, broad-faced man with blue eyes and very closely cropped hair who might have been anywhere in that no-man's-land of age between the mid-twenties and early thirties. At least Richard, peering over her shoulder from the opposite side of the bed, couldn't peg it any closer.

Kathleen took a breath and, able to use her right hand to block her tracheal tube, said, "Yes." She could also turn her head slightly to that side, enough to look at the detective and back to the young officer who'd done the portrait.

"What about you, Doc? Is that the guy you ran into on your way out of ICU?" McKnight asked.

"It could be. But as I said, I hardly paid him any attention at the time. If it was, I was by him so fast I don't even remember getting a whiff of that awful aftershave he wears."

McKnight glanced up at the wall clock, which read 6:51 A.M. "Before the night shift goes off at seven, ask them to take a look as well," he said to the young policeman who was making backup disks of his work.

"Right, sir."

The man closed his case, shouldered it, and wandered off toward the nursing station. Soon he was surrounded by women who seemed as interested in him as his sketch. Richard's nemesis with the spiky hairdo and aquamarine eyes arrived and appeared particularly fascinated by him. Richard wondered if the cop would end up drawing her, in private. "Look out for sharp teeth if you do," he said under his breath.

". . . as many witnesses as possible usually gives us the best likeness," McKnight was explaining to Kathleen. "Then we'll e-mail copies all over the hospital and to the media, to see if anyone recognizes the creep. Now, we'll also check the cleaning cart and around this cubicle for prints, plus medical records, especially the shelf unit your Doc toppled on him to see if we get a match for all three areas, but with everything so public—"

"He wore . . . latex gloves . . . when he was . . . in here," interrupted Kathleen.

"And I wouldn't be surprised if he kept them on the whole time," continued McKnight. "No, it'll be the picture of him that'll help us. That and the fact the motive here seems pretty obvious."

Something uneasy stirred within Richard. "You know, the way the guy was screaming about 'the Almighty's just punishment' and killing me off as an 'agent of the devil,' a rational motive may not exactly be the guy's strong suit."

"What are you talking about? It's clear this creep was trying to kill Dr. Sullivan before she could convince anyone that Hamlin and Lockman had done something to her. He obviously didn't know she had managed to communicate with us. And he probably went after you because he realized you were going through the charts and was afraid you'd finally figure out whatever is the secret of Hamlin's DOAs."

"So all the Jesus talk and the trouble he went to carving up Lockman, not to mention his leaving a twig at both murder scenes, it was solely to throw you off and make you think he was a crazy?"

"Why not?"

"Because the man I heard wasn't that coldly logical."

"You're not . . . suggesting . . . this psychotic . . . singled out . . . you and me . . . by chance, Richard."

"Of course not."

"Good . . . because our . . . linking . . . the attacks . . . with the murders . . . of Hamlin and Lockman . . . is the . . . only way . . . everything . . . adds up . . . in a sick way."

"I can't see it being otherwise," McKnight chimed in. "There's too much method in this guy's madness."

Her eyes skipped from Richard to the detective as lightly as if she were changing dance partners. "Exactly . . . it's the timing." Her face, until now a death mask, flickered to life, tiny movements that weren't there before appearing at the corners of her mouth. "Especially if . . . we consider . . . what he . . . would have accomplished . . . had he killed me . . . last night . . . before I could . . . tell you or anyone . . . about . . . Hamlin and Lockman."

McKnight nodded in enthusiastic agreement. "Precisely!"

"Had he succeeded . . . in sending my secret . . . to the grave . . . the investigation . . . into Hamlin's murder . . . and Lockman's . . . would have played out . . . very differently . . . with you and your colleagues."

The detective beamed at her. "My figuring exactly. We would never have known the two men were linked in some nasty business together, nor have had cause to think their murders might have been to silence them. In all likelihood we'd have figured some psycho was slaughtering doctors from New York City Hospital for a lunatic reason that had to do with the twig he left at the scene, just the way Dr. Steele suggested."

"In effect . . . a perfect . . . cover-up."

"You got that right," said McKnight, shaking his head at the dire possibility.

"All . . . but for the fluke . . . of my getting Richard . . . to bring you in . . . Detective McKnight."

Richard wasn't sure whether he saw a tinge of crimson spreading over the big man's ebony cheeks, but there was no mistaking his delight with Kathleen or his enjoyment of their bouncing ideas off each other. "What d'ya think, Doc?" he said, turning toward him and breaking into the kind of goofy grin a man wears when he's found a beautiful woman who agrees with him. "Is all this motive enough for you or what?"

What Richard wanted to say was that the love of his life was flirting, which probably meant she had something in mind she knew he wouldn't go for and intended to pursue it through McKnight. Instead he replied, "I don't know, it's just that the more I think about what I heard down there, the more it seems . . ." Richard cast around for a word.

"Crazy?" offered Kathleen, the ends of her lips twitching to give a hint of a grin. "What else . . . would he . . . make himself . . . sound like . . . silly. . . . It was . . . the whole point."

McKnight turned to her and let out a deep chuckle. "Hey, that's a good one."

"Why, thank you."

Why didn't she just bat her eyelashes at him, thought Richard, still wondering what she was up to.

A second later, she did exactly that.

Oh, Jesus, he thought, smiling in spite of everything. "Maybe you two can stop congratulating each other and explain why this guy would bother pretending he was nuts if he was going to kill me anyway."

"Who knows? Maybe he's into Method acting and stays in character," said McKnight. "Now, Doc, what's your best guess was in the syringe? For him to complete his cover-up, I figure he'd have had to make her death appear to be from natural causes, so as not to suggest any link with the other murders . . ."

As the detective talked, Richard kept his eyes on Kathleen, wondering if she should take a break, since she'd been off the respirator much longer than she was used to. Yet the color suffusing her cheeks wasn't the blue of cyanosis but a flush of excitement, something totally absent since the stroke felled her two weeks ago. As bizarre as it seemed, her playing intellectual leapfrog with McKnight in pursuit of the creep who had tried to murder her appeared to be bringing her even more alive. Maybe the prospect of soon closing in on him gave her back some sense of control.

". . . and it would have to be something nobody could trace."

"Potassium chloride," answered Richard, having already mulled this one through. "Are you sure you want to hear this?" He squeezed Kathleen's hand. "It scares the hell out of me, how close a call it was."

"Don't think . . . I haven't already . . . figured that out."

"Okay then." He fixed his gaze on McKnight, finding it less disconcerting to describe Kathleen's near death by not looking at her. "A bolus of it directly into the IV would have been his logical choice. It would have taken seconds to administer with a syringe while he was cleaning near her bed. The heart would be rendered useless within a minute, enough time for him to walk out of ICU with no one even having taken much notice that he was ever there. And a cardiac arrest from massive hyperkalemia can be difficult to treat. . . ."

As he talked, his voice seemed to distance itself from him, as if someone else was speaking and referring to a poor woman other than Kathleen. Yet he couldn't keep himself from imagining what might have happened, her body bluish-white from death surrounded by strangers sticking her with needles and pounding on her chest, her limbs convulsively jerking then flopping back lifeless after each countershock from the defibrillator, her eyes, still alive, staring straight at him.

". . . the high potassium would have been noted," he continued, struggling to keep his words layered in calm by imagining he was stressing a teaching point with his residents, "but there'd be a number of explanations offered, from unexpected renal failure to a nursing error, none of them satisfying. Yet throughout it all there'd still be no cause to suspect a deliberate act, providing, as you both said, the killer succeeded before Kathleen made it clear someone had a motive for wanting her dead."

"But for dumb luck," muttered McKnight.

"I feel . . . I just attended . . . my own autopsy," said Kathleen.

Richard squeezed her hand again and gave her a kiss beside her ear. "You know you're getting your smile back," he whispered.

Her face brightened. "I thought . . . I felt it . . . and look at this," she said, making her foot move her covers as if a nest of mice were scurrying underneath.

Richard chuckled with genuine delight. "When did that happen?"

"Last night. . . . And how long . . . have I been off . . . the respirator this morning?" she asked, the whispering quality of her speaking not able to hide the note of triumph.

"A little over an hour and a half," he said, glancing at the oxygen saturation monitor. He couldn't believe what he saw. "It's ninety-five percent?"

"What's that mean?" said McKnight.

Richard swallowed. "It's nearly normal."

"And I don't . . . feel tired."

"It's amazing, Kathleen. In fact it's wonderful." He felt ecstatic at what all at once seemed to be a leap of progress, until his own words fell like a shroud. *It makes them do incredibly well, then kills them.*

"Uh, excuse me, I've only got a few more questions, then I'll leave you two," said McKnight, obviously embarrassed by the intimate little exchange. "Uh, Doc, about Hamlin's charts, you didn't tell us the stuff you found. Did any of it give you an idea what he was doing to his patients?"

"No," he lied, not wanting to get into the details of DOAs, rebleeds, and what the records suggested was in store for her even if she did recover. She had to be frightened enough about what was ahead without him adding stuff like that. All he'd told her while waiting for McKnight was about Hamlin's patients going to Adele Blaine's rehabilitation institute. He also suggested it was better they didn't mention Blaine's possible involvement to McKnight just yet, explaining how it would be wiser not to put the woman on the defensive by sending in the cops since he intended to con her into showing him the files he still wanted to see.

But McKnight wasn't to be deterred, his eyebrows giving a skeptical salute. "Nothing at all?"

Richard immediately felt guilty. "Hey, the guy interrupted me before I got anywhere," he said, thinking the explanation would make the detective back off. He'd fill him in later, out of earshot of Kathleen, at least the parts not involving Blaine.

His manner only grew more incredulous. "You're sure?"

"Not even . . . with the DOAs?" joined in Kathleen. "Hamlin himself . . . seemed certain . . . you'd catch on . . . if you took a . . . good look . . . at those."

"Yeah, Doc," McKnight continued to press, "and the guy who attacked you probably figured you'd not only see their secret, you'd see it pretty fast. Why else would he have broken off his attempt on Dr. Sullivan?"

"He said it was because I'd wronged God's works."

McKnight's eyebrows shot up another inch. He hadn't appreciated the wiseass remark. "What's your point?"

Jesus, McKnight's cop instincts were in overdrive and he seemed to be getting pissed that Richard was holding out. Yet Richard would be damned if he'd upset Kathleen. "My point is the same as before. The man didn't seem to be pretending he was crazy. I've heard enough religious manias in ER to know." Richard heard his own voice growing testy. "There's definitely something screwy about your idea the killer's putting on an act that he's insane and what I heard him say down there was just for show. Believe me, it sounded like the real thing."

"So what are you inferring? The guy's a bona fide madman, the attack on you wasn't part of an elaborate cover-up and isn't connected to the murders—"

"No, no, not at all," said Richard, still marveling at how a ridiculous spat could grow so heated. All he wanted was to get McKnight off the subject of charts. "And I agree it's important I keep looking through the charts, okay?" He'd set things straight with McKnight outside. "I presume your investigators will be finished in medical records soon."

"I'll tell them to let you in even if they're not."

"Great. Anything else?"

"Yeah. Do you have any idea who the other people Lockman referred to might be?"

Richard instantly thought of Francesca Downs and Paul Edwards as well as Adele Blaine, but stuck with his decision to say nothing.

The air between him and the detective went polar.

"Excuse me . . . both of you," cut in Kathleen. "Detective McKnight . . . I'm sure what . . . Richard's so blatantly . . . trying to avoid saying . . . is something . . . he probably fears . . . would frighten me."

"I didn't avoid anything," said Richard.

McKnight clamped a cop stare on him, but didn't utter a word.

"Richard, tell him. . . . Nothing you could say . . . is as bad as . . . what I've already . . . imagined . . . is in store for me."

Richard ripped free of the spell McKnight's eyes had cast on him and looked down at her. Seeing the brave effort she was making to smile even with what little movement she had, he knew she was right. He couldn't protect her from any of this. "Okay," he said, stroking the side of her face, and he told McKnight everything he hadn't wanted Kathleen to hear. She then insisted he also confide the need to get at the records in Blaine's rehab center without putting the woman on the defensive.

"If she is guilty, I doubt you'll con her into showing you anything," said the detective, after hearing his concerns. "But we'll think of a way to get a look at them."

"I already have," said Kathleen.

The two men looked at her.

"You send me there . . . as a patient."

"The place is crawling with cops," Paul Edwards said into his private phone a few floors above, his voice so squeezed into a higher pitch it sounded as if someone had him by the neck. "I'm not even sure where Francesca Downs keeps records of her protocols and test results, but it sure as hell isn't the time to go sneaking through her office."

"Why not hack them off her hard drive?"

"I tried. Too many passwords protecting it."

"Are the police onto her?"

"I don't think so."

"And what about Hamlin's research. Are the detectives investigating his death likely to turn it up?"

"No. Thank God he kept his stuff off the premises, with Adele Blaine, for safekeeping. As long as they don't have cause to go snooping around her rehab center, they'll be safe."

"So you can get at those?"

"I hope so. But, none of us are exactly buddy-buddy with each other these days, and she's an even bigger genius than Francesca when it comes to computers."

"And Norris's work? There's no deal without that."

"Again, I'm sure it's in his lab, but I'll need time to get at it."

"You don't have time, my friend. My backers want the material now, while it's still confidential. And I remind you, the price we discussed presumes the data will give them at least a two year head start on the rest of the world. That means you must guarantee the silence of your colleagues. If any one of them goes public, or the homicide investigation gets too close and the story's liable to end up on the evening news, the deal's off. After all, no one's going to pay four million for something they'd be able to get off the Internet a few weeks from now."

"Don't worry. I'll handle everything," said Edwards, trying to sound confident while feeling anything but. He caught a glimpse of his appearance in a gilded mirror that matched a set of Louis XIV chairs arranged invitingly in a corner. His face looked a size too loose, hanging off him as if it were about to slough onto the floor. He gave the impression of a man who couldn't handle a trip to the bathroom without pissing himself, he thought, and felt relieved his caller couldn't see him.

After hanging up, he eyed the tray of croissants his secretary had left him and shoved it away, his stomach one huge, swollen bubble of acid.

A needle of morning light came through the window at the far end of the long narrow room and pierced him as if singling him out and pinning him to the wall. He made no attempt to avoid the pain, knowing he deserved it. Let the movement of the heavens decide when he'd paid sufficient penance, he declared, going over and over where he'd gone wrong.

He'd felt such a surge of confidence when Steele had appeared. He'd been so certain that a divine power had intervened to redirect the mission, that he would dispatch two agents of Satan back to Hell where they belonged, and what a night it would have been for the Legion of the Lord!

Yet the Devil had triumphed.

Because I surrendered to the sin of willfulness and didn't follow orders.

He had crept up the stairs to his lair, closed the door behind him, and sunk to the floor an hour ago. The high ceiling over him reminded him of a coffin lid. His skin, already clammy from his hasty retreat through the streets, released a sour odor that disgusted him. It mingled with the other smells permeating the stale air, the stench of urine from the wooden boards under him that persisted no matter how much he'd scrubbed them, and a constant fragrance of cabbage that always seemed to fill the entire building.

"Forgive me my disappointing you, oh Lord," he whispered, over and over, seeking comfort from the words as he would from a catechism. But no solace came.

He got up and began to pace, passing a triangular countertop wedged into a corner beside a blackened sink. The tiny area served as his kitchen, but barely held a toaster oven and a single place setting of dishes. A few pans and a coffeepot filled a shelf underneath. The mere thought of food evoked an angry growl from the pit of his gut.

After a few turns he flopped onto a mattress, its well-worn sheets gray from washing and stained by his lapses with the Lord's seed. An aroma that soap and water could no longer remove clung to the disheveled bedding, a tangy scent of ammonia that made him ashamed of his own weakness. Sometimes, on particularly damp days, it seemed to override the stink of pee and sauerkraut.

Glancing at his watch, he rolled over and flicked on a small portable TV with a built-in VCR that stood on one of the few chairs he owned. Wanting to see if his attempts to kill Sullivan and Steele had made the local news yet, he turned the dial to the *Good Day NY* program.

He waited through reports of Israelis and Arabs killing each other, a shampoo commercial, and an update on the mayor's progress with a union problem. Then:

"*. . . there are more revelations at New York City Hospital about the murder of a second physician, a radiologist, Dr. Matt Lockman, found last night in his home. According to anonymous sources, the body was severely mutilated. Police refused to speculate as to any connection between this killing and the shooting death of another NYCH physician the night before, neurologist Dr. Tony Hamlin. However, nurses who refused to be identified state that Hamlin and Lockman may have been involved in committing irregular practices on some of their patients. Even more intriguing are rumors of an attempt made on the life of one of these patients just before midnight last night, followed by the alleged attacker going after yet another person. This one was a hospital physician who was alone in medical records investigating the files of Hamlin and Lockman. Again, police would not confirm these allegations.*

*But authorities are looking for this man in connection with these unusual
events. Anyone with information of his whereabouts is asked to contact . . ."*

He stared in disbelief at the picture.

At first he tried to convince himself that it hardly looked like him.

But rage soon consumed any such false assurance. It must have been
the Sullivan bitch who had described him.

He'd have to hide, and there were things he must take with him.

He turned to his prize possession, a computer, keyboard, and printer
mounted on a melamine desk beside the window. The screen, adjacent to
a view of the tawdry, glitzy wares for sale on the street below offered him
a world that outshone everything down there, including the prostitutes.
It stood like a beige shrine midst the gloomy interior and the grimy dark
wood underfoot, serving as his intelligence center, his connection to his
chosen family, his link to the others who'd dedicated their lives to stop the
slaughter. It was also where he reconnoitered whatever he needed for their
mutual cause.

This morning he required sanctuary.

Within minutes he'd contacted his network and alerted them to his
plight. Though their's was an organization with no hierarchy, head-
quarters, or membership lists, all of which made them hard to find and
defeat, fellow soldiers could mobilize on behalf of each other at a moment's notice. Someone would be at his door with transportation in less
than an hour.

He quickly found a screwdriver and, shoving aside the mattress, exposed the floorboards that he'd pried up creating a hiding spot he could
easily access. After undoing the screws, he lifted a half dozen four-foot
planks. His weapons stash lay inside.

A buzz of flies along with a whiff of rot came from within a small
bundled sheet placed back in the deeper shadows. When he lifted it up,
the contents clanked together, and the insects whined angrily, to the
point he could feel the vibration of their wings beneath the thin material.
He also took out the M-4 carbine he'd used to shoot Hamlin. He'd
bought it years ago in a hunting store north of Buffalo in Niagara county.
Beside it was the most precious of all—a pair of Walther PPK handguns
that had once belonged to a set of three. He'd escaped with them out a

back window in a Rochester motel, his father having tossed them down to him while keeping the third to hold off the police. The pain of that day had hardened him the way scar tissue hardens skin, destroying all feeling for anything soft. But whenever he slid his palms around the grips of those guns, he felt as if the man who'd held them minutes before dying a soldier's death once more was taking him by the hand.

Next came boxes of ammunition, his collection of hammers, and the signature pieces of his organization, pipes loaded with plastic explosives and nails. These were ready for detonation by timers or remotes, the latter kit-bashed from devices used to activate door locks on cars at distances up to a hundred and fifty feet. He picked up the vials of medication that he'd pilfered over the years, then stuffed them between pairs of socks in a small box so as to adequately buffer them against breakage during the move. Finally came the pamphlets they didn't dare print on their Web sites, training manuals for would-be recruits into the Legion of the Lord, including instructions on how to make and deploy bombs using dynamite, plastics, or ammonium nitrate.

He'd take all this along, including the computer, to wherever his comrades would hide him. To finish his current job he'd have to move fast, launching his attacks one on top of the other. And he'd have to abandon the order he'd been told to follow. Sticking to it meant additional risks. He could no longer afford to wait around for the right circumstances to gel in sequence. Instead he'd have to pick off whoever gave him the opportunity first. With his likeness plastered all over TV and probably soon to appear in every city newspaper, it would only be a matter of time before he'd be spotted, and stopped.

The more he thought, the more he feared that he'd ultimately fail in his mission. He tried to reassure himself his battle was not with the police or the secular forces massing against him. Live or die, his life would be in God's hands, and the war was against Satan.

He changed into a jogging outfit with a hood, packed up the rest of his clothes, and popped a few acetaminophen into his mouth to kill the muscle aches that the night's activity had caused. Emptying the pockets of the cleaner's uniform he'd worn, he retrieved what he found in Medical

Records. Staring at it, he began to think how it could be useful in salvaging what he'd bungled.

Once more he turned to his keyboard, this time summoning up those in his network who could supply him with the other special items he'd need to complete his assignment. He asked for a machete, a loose-fitting jacket with the case for the blade of the machete stitched into the lining, a bicycle, a theatrical makeup kit with material for making beards, and a selection of wigs.

He was ready. In training he'd gone seventy-two hours without sleep. With any luck, he'd have completed the Lord's work and be through the list within that amount of time now. But no matter how long it took, he wouldn't quit. No way.

As he waited for his friends to arrive, he removed a faded photo from his wallet. Cracked and creased, it showed a blond man and a fair-haired boy standing in front of a tent pitched by a lake. Both were holding up fish on a line, displaying them to the person taking the picture. But while the youth who appeared to be about ten wore a wide grin, the man's features looked wooden, the lines of his smile chiseled into skin the color of wax, his eyes gouged-out hollows.

12

Monitors surrounded him; catheters threaded through his arteries, veins, and viscous organs like weedy roots; his every heartbeat, breath, and change in pressure sent out streams of digital readings, fluorescent green squiggles, and eternal beepings.

Francesca Downs swept into her patient's room and up to his bed, her white coat floating behind her. Norris followed.

"Meet Mr. Ralph Coady," Downs said.

"Hi." Norris held out his hand.

Coady, propped upright on pillows, his plump skin a bluish shade of white, eyed the outstretched hand as if it might slap him. "How'd you get to stay so skinny," he moaned. "I wouldn't be in this mess if I could get thin like you."

Norris smiled.

"I got the damn heart attack because my girlfriend, Bunny, suggested we take up line dancing to help me lose weight."

"Mr. Coady's recovering from my having dilated two of his major vessels last night," Downs elaborated.

Coady's mouth turned down in disgust. "You Roto-Rootered me."

"How's your breathing today?"

"Rotten! Just like the rest of me."

"Lean forward and take deep breaths," Downs said, hooking her stethoscope into her ears and plopping its head onto the base of the right side of his chest. Listening attentively, she marched the stethoscope toward the left like an attacking rook on a chessboard. "Most of the water's out, but there's still some in there," she finally pronounced.

She freed the ear pieces, letting them cling around her slender neck, and sat down on the side of the bed. "You've had quite a bit of damage to the left ventricle, and are experiencing what we call heart failure, but the medication's getting rid of the fluid buildup."

"You mean that's why I got to piss so damn much? It's those injections and pills you keep giving me?"

Downs put a hand on his shoulder and gave him a warm smile. "Yep," she said. "They're meant to flush you out."

Norris found himself staring at her, marveling at how beautiful she was, her skin still flushed with a soft glow from their lovemaking. What a life force she could be, her fierce confidence infusing hope even to those near death.

"Well, that's a relief," said Coady, "I guess. For a while I was beginning to think either I had a touch of the clap or my prostate was acting up again. But will I always need shots and horse pills?"

"Not shots, but oral meds, yeah. I won't know the full extent of the injury to the heart wall until we get an echocardiogram, but for sure it won't have the same strength as before."

He gave a thin little grin. "You mean I get to give up line dancing?"

"Not unless you want me to tell you to. Exercise, in moderation, is a good part of living well."

"I prefer slow dancing. It's sexier."

Downs gave him a string-of-pearls smile. "I do, too."

He swallowed a few times, cleared his throat, and asked, "And what about sex?"

"I think it's a little early to worry about that, Ralph. Normally we suggest a gradual return to regular sexual activity in about three months."

He looked alarmed. "Three months? Jesus, Bunny and I hardly can go without it for three days."

Downs giggled. "Lucky Bunny."

He did some more swallowing, and cleared his throat again. "And will I be able to, you know, do it the same?"

"Probably. Again, you're way ahead of yourself. We'll be doing tests to determine the workload your heart can take in the coming weeks."

"Probably?" he repeated, as if he hadn't heard the rest of what she'd said.

"Relax, Ralph. Hey, these days, it's the lady on top. I'm sure you'll still enjoy yourself."

More swallowing, more clearing of his throat. "What about flying."

Downs grimaced. "Ouch! Well, there the news isn't so good. But I don't have to tell you the national aviation rules, do I?"

He said nothing and ran his fingers through well-groomed but thinning salt-and-pepper hair.

Norris, standing at the foot of the bed, saw a glistening in the man's eyes that wasn't there a few minutes before.

"I can't change commercial airline regulations, Ralph," continued Downs, reaching out and giving his shoulder a squeeze. "What can I say?"

"Doc, tell me there's hope. Some chance. Something you can do for me. The nurses said you do research in experimental surgery. Isn't there anything for me? I'll volunteer. I don't care what the risks are. Hell, I'm only forty-five, and flying's the one thing I have that's special. It's my life. It gives me my place in the world. It's what makes me matter. Goddamn it, I'm the one they call to teach the rookies. How the hell am I going to replace all that?"

"I'm sure your family and Bunny will continue to love you even if you're not a flyer—"

"What family? My first wife left me because I was away all the time, and I don't have kids. As for Bunny, she won't want to be around me if I'm grounded."

"That's ridiculous. It's obvious she adores you—"

"You make her live under the same roof as me if I'm grounded, and she'll be gone in six months."

Downs said nothing.

He's perfect, Norris thought—the right age, his way of life wrecked at the peak of his career, and, just as Francesca had predicted, desperate.

"What about a heart transplant?" Coady said, "Give me a new one. I hear about them all the time."

Downs shook her head, her lips drawn in a straight line. "You're still better off with the one you have. Transplants aren't magic, and we only use them on terminal cardiacs."

"Well, I feel terminated. Doesn't that count?"

"Afraid not."

"But you must know what's new. Stuff over the horizon that hasn't been tried. If money's the problem, I can afford it. I'm well-off, and Bunny's got her own computer business. . . ." His voice trailed off, the glistening in his eyes swelling into tears, and his pale features crumpled like ruined tissue paper. Yet he didn't utter a sound, his shoulders shaking in silence, as if by sheer willpower he kept the sobs bottled up in his chest alongside his failing heart.

Downs remained sitting, her hand sliding up and down his arm the way one might try and comfort a child who'd fallen.

Yet some falls were from heights that couldn't be survived, thought Norris, shuddering at how he'd feel at being so suddenly and completely sidelined. When Downs looked up at him, he nodded, giving her his agreement that she should go ahead.

"Ralph, I don't want to give you any false hopes, but neither do I want you to despair. Dr. Norris is a fellow researcher, and we have been working on something that's as close to a medical miracle as you or I will ever see in our lifetime."

He mustn't have heard her at first, continuing to shudder convulsively with absolute quiet, his head between his hands. But when he did look up, his gaze darted from her to Norris, his expression suspended between a twist of agony and slack-jawed disbelief. "Pardon?"

"But we must insist you keep what I'm about to tell you confidential," she went on without pause, "or there'll be no more discussions about it, period. Is that agreed?"

"What is it?"

"And we would tell you about this only in general terms. As you can understand, since this is our original work, we must keep it secret, so that no one can plagiarize what we're doing before we publish. You'd also have to agree that we can make your case public, announce it in a press conference and put it in the media, because the procedure we are about to do will make you an even bigger sensation than the first heart transplant case."

"Yes, yes. But tell me what is it?"

"Understand you will have to cover all expenses beyond what your insurance will pay for conventional treatment," Norris added, "including the lab costs. Dr. Downs and I will give you a breakdown, and we would require you to sign a nondisclosure contract subjecting you to heavy, and I stress heavy, financial penalty, should you reveal anything about our work or not comply with all steps of our protocol once we start."

"Yes, yes, yes. Now explain the miracle."

"Ralph, we can do better than that," said Downs. "Later today the nurses will begin sitting you up at the bedside for ten minutes at a time. If that goes well, I'm going to give you a special treat and whisk you in a wheelchair down to Dr. Norris's lab. By then we'll have the papers of our agreement drawn up, and on your signing them, we are going to let you peek in a microscope and see what you will not believe."

So we're on our way, Norris thought, leaving the ward a half hour later after Francesca had shown him a few other possible candidates. A million Americans a year had heart attacks, a half million died of heart disease, and he and Francesca were going to show the world they could change all that. Coady was perfect. Whether the guy would ever fly again, who knew, but someone like him, with so much to lose and everything to gain, could offer hope to millions and create a demand for the technique no one could stop. Jesus, they were liable to get the fucking Nobel Prize. All this, plus he was back with Francesca. God! It was like a reprieve from the dead.

No sooner had he gotten to the elevator than the doors opened and a half dozen police officers brushed by him, fanning out to the various nursing stations, pads of paper and small tape recorders at the ready.

"... you show them the composite. I'll interview anyone who even thinks they recognize the man ..."

"... who's got the list of staff who worked with Hamlin's patients ..."

"... I'll take the doctors ..."

The ride down stopped at a half dozen floors, each pause long enough to reveal small groups of NYPD blue midst the various pastels and blazing whites of orderlies, nurses, residents, and staff doctors. They were all huddled in circles looking at something.

Intrigued, he stepped off at the next stop and approached the periphery of a dozen people surrounding a tiny blond woman on whom the dark uniform and heavy gun belt of a police officer seemed overly bulky, making her appear particularly vulnerable. Her voice became audible as he drew closer.

"... so if any of you have seen this man, or think that you may have witnessed something suspicious that Doctors Hamlin or Lockman may have been doing to patients over the last few years ..."

It wasn't that he hadn't expected the authorities to come snooping. But to hear with his own ears how close they were to his secret, especially with such a massive police presence throughout the hospital, sucked the euphoria right out of him. A clammy fear crept right down to his marrow, and the shiny new life he'd imagined for himself became a taunt, a tease, a glimpse held out of what he would never have.

His mind ran amok playing scenarios, every one of them hurtling down a dark road to his own destruction. The police would find the reason behind the murders, and that would certainly bring them to him. Would Adele Blaine and Paul Edwards keep their mouths shut then? Hardly. For all he knew, they could be turning him over to the cops right now. Those meetings they'd been having together lately! He could imagine them setting him up to take the fall over drinks and dinner. And what of Francesca? Once again his darkest thoughts about her emerged. Had she, too, conspired with them? Were the three of them engineering his downfall together? He gave a bitter laugh. After all, why should that prevent her from making use of his skills in the meantime to assure her success with Coady.

He abruptly reigned himself in.

God, how could he be so infatuated with a woman and trust her so little? He felt disgusted by his own paranoia. He spent the next few minutes trying to reassure himself that the woman who had given herself to him so completely a few hours before couldn't be capable of such treachery. The woman whose dream of restoring a normal life to the Ralph Coady's of the world burned as fiercely as his own.

The uniformed officer seemed to be winding up.

". . . your statements will be kept confidential, and you may call me later to set up a private meeting away from the hospital . . ."

He sidled up for a closer look at the picture she was holding and saw a broad-faced man who seemed a complete stranger to him. "Who is this guy?" he whispered to the woman standing next to him.

"Didn't you see the morning news?"

"No, I was . . ." The image of Francesca bent over him, urging, offering herself to be entered, ran through him like a flash fire.

"That's who the police are looking for. He's the one they think killed doctors Hamlin and Lockman."

"Really?" he asked, still reasonably sure he'd never seen the person before. "What's his name?"

"Nobody knows. That's why they circulated the composite, in case anyone here might recognize him."

"Any luck?"

"Not so far. At least nobody here can pinpoint him."

Norris continued to stare at the suspect's features. As he concentrated on the man's eyes, some familiar stirrings at the base of his skull tried to tell him something but failed to congeal into anything specific that he could decipher.

"Do you recognize him?" the nurse asked.

"No, I don't think so. For a second there I thought he looked familiar, but I must be wrong. How did the police get this likeness anyway?"

"Boy, you really are out of the rumor loop. He's the one who tried to slip an IV dose of something to Dr. Kathleen Sullivan in ICU last night."

Norris felt ice run up his spine. "What?"

"Yeah, and they also are pretty sure he's the one who attacked Dr. Steele in medical records?"

"Steele?"

"Right. He was going through charts to see if he could find out what it is that Hamlin and Lockman did to Dr. Sullivan."

"I see," he said, trying to appear simply as curious as any other innocent bystander. Inside he was panicking—not just about Steele being well on his way to finding him out, but because he had absolutely no idea what was going on.

10:30 A.M.

"Dr. Sullivan, I'm Dr. Adele Blaine. Josephine O'Brien told me about your case."

Kathleen snapped her eyes open. The diminutive, trim woman standing at the foot of the bed ran counter to what she'd been expecting, though she wasn't too clear what that had been. Her being African-American hadn't anything to do with her surprise. It was, perhaps, more the woman's lack of size. Kathleen had been expecting someone big. Even forbidding? Instead the woman's short, coiffed dark hair, beige business suit under a loose-fitting lab coat, and triple strands of gold around her neck made her appear as an expensive mahogany figurine half-covered by a white drop cloth. "Thank you for coming . . . Dr. Blaine."

"Did Richard also recommend me?"

"Ah, well, he said . . . you were . . . an excellent choice . . . when I asked him. . . . The poor man's . . . been so distracted . . . by all that's happened. . . . I don't think he . . . even thought far enough ahead . . . to consider rehab. . . . Everyone, including him . . . seems surprised . . . that I'm going to be ready . . . for it so soon. . . . I think he's . . . mainly relieved . . . I'll be getting out of here . . . and to someplace safe . . . as quickly as possible."

In reality Richard had railed about her going. "You could still be a

185

target if she's involved and finds you sneaking into her files on Hamlin's patients."

"The same . . . goes for you . . . Mr. Chart Snooper," she'd fired back. "The woman . . . won't buy . . . your 'I'm doing . . . an audit' line."

McKnight had settled the problem by promising a police woman would be at Kathleen's side day and night. "And as an officer of the law, I'm certainly not going to recommend anyone break into medical files," he cautioned them both. "But people chat—secretaries, nurses, orderlies, therapists. Whoever works there might let something slip, Dr. Sullivan, with your encouragement. We could end up knowing more about what's going on than we do now. You said yourself, Richard, we can't go in there with sirens blaring and expect to learn anything."

Kathleen had liked how McKnight called Richard by his first name like a brother giving advice, rather than a cop giving orders.

After that Richard hadn't so much agreed as run out of arguments. He did suggest they recruit Jo O'Brien to set it up. "Blaine has a habit of dropping by ER and doing wallet biopsies, looking for affluent patients in need of her services. It borders on ambulance chasing. A word from a veteran nurse," he explained, "suggesting Kathleen as a prospective client wouldn't seem out of the ordinary. Even if Blaine suspects we're on to her or is nervous about you coming to the center, she won't be likely to refuse. Saying no in the face of trying to scrounge up new business would so fly in the face of her usual eagerness to take on well-off, high-profile people, it would seem too odd, suspicious even."

Now, Blaine pulled a chair close to the bed and sat down. "Jo told me about the attacks on you and Dr. Steele last night. How horrible!"

Her alarm seemed genuine enough, Kathleen thought. But there was a practiced opacity to her gaze, the kind that kept outsiders from peering in. She also noticed the slightest delay in Kathleen's reply, the instant it took for her fast mind to calculate a safe response. She was studying Kathleen as carefully as Kathleen was studying her. "Yes, it was hideous. . . . I don't even want . . . to think about it right now. . . . Thank you for . . . seeing me . . . so quickly. . . . As you can understand . . . I'm eager to learn . . . what I can still do."

"Of course you are, honey."

The ridges of Blaine's rather guarded expression smoothed themselves out a little, and her eyes became less guarded, revealing the usual transparent sadness most older physicians carry from having witnessed so much loss and suffering. Were the ruins of something personal there as well, Kathleen wondered. "Believe me," Blaine continued, "I know how sandbagged you must feel. Strokes are so nasty. They rob you of so much, especially when you're young. But I've looked at your file, and trust me, you've already shown remarkable progress."

Kathleen felt a flash of genuine anger.

"Really? . . . Wiggling my toes . . . flapping my hands . . . is progress? Maybe . . . in your book . . . but not in mine."

The sadness in Blaine's eyes deepened. "You're right, girl. It's tough."

"Tough doesn't . . . begin to cut it . . . and I'm tired . . . of people telling me . . . they 'know' how it is. . . . Hell . . . I pee in a bag . . . and shit in a pan. . . . You don't. . . . These fingers," she motioned with her left hand, curling it into a claw, "once capable of . . . the most delicate work . . . under a microscope . . . couldn't manipulate . . . a knife and fork. . . . I bet you've . . . got a dinner date tonight. . . . I sure as hell haven't. . . . Worst of all . . . I look at the man I love . . . and wonder if the best . . . I'll ever offer him again . . . as a woman . . . is to be his inflatable doll—"

"Dr. Sullivan," interrupted Blaine, standing up and bending close enough to grasp Kathleen's face firmly between her hands. There was nothing tender about the grip, and, mingled with the scent of a very tasteful perfume, a sour whiff of stale alcohol came off her breath. "Listen, honey. I'm not going to make promises I can't keep, but you've every hope of feeding yourself, having sex, and maybe even walking again. But it'll take work, unbelievable patience, and time." She let go and took both Kathleen's hands in hers. "Squeeze my fingers."

"What's the point? . . . The nurses . . . are asking me . . . to do that . . . all the time. . . . My grip's pathetic."

"Squeeze!"

She obliged.

"Hang tight!"

Blaine abruptly pulled the still-paralyzed arms up in the air. The movement sent the flexor muscles flying into spasm, curling Kathleen's fingers, wrists, and elbows in on themselves with a contraction so powerful it lifted her trunk right off the bed and caused Blaine to stagger trying to support the weight.

"Okay, honey, now try and relax it out," Blaine said, leaning forward and gently lowering Kathleen back down by carefully reextending her arms. "See?" she added once the limbs had loosened up. "There's no problem with your strength, just your control. That will improve by the day. If the hard wiring is still there, I could have you sitting by three weeks and walking by twelve."

Kathleen felt astonished by what Blaine's brutal maneuver had elicited from her body, then resentment at being treated so roughly. Stunned, yet not sure whether to be angry, all at once she became genuinely intrigued by what this severe woman could do for her. The bold prediction, *sitting by three, walking by twelve,* had sounded a bugle cry of hope.

"Will you work . . . with me . . . take me as a patient?" she finally said.

Immediately the glaze came over Blaine's eyes again, and a beat—a fraction of a second—passed between them, not enough even to be noticed by anyone not paying particular attention. "Of course I will, Dr. Sullivan. Don't worry about a thing," she replied, her voice smooth as cold glass. "I'll make all the arrangements. We'll aim to make the transfer in forty-eight hours, as long as all continues to go well here."

"Forty-eight hours," said Kathleen, immediately alarmed. She'd been expecting this would happen sometime next week.

"Sure. Your O_2 sat is ninety-five percent. They'll have you weaned off this wheeze box by then. And my nursing staff are good as any here, better even. I hire only veterans who can handle patients directly from ICU so as to start therapy as soon as possible. Believe me, every day you don't use a muscle, it takes twice as long to get it back." She gave Kathleen a reassuring pat on the shoulder. "And for starters, this morning I'm going to order the nurses to begin putting you in a chair ten minutes at a time, safely harnessed of course, to check out how your trunk muscles are coming."

Remarkable woman, thought Kathleen, and hard to read. But she liked her, instinctively . . . even though she *knew* she shouldn't.

"Dr. Blaine . . . you're a very tough cookie . . . but a good one."

Blaine chuckled, a rich throaty sound of pure pleasure. "You got that right, honey; I'm not just good. I am the best!"

No hesitation in her reply this time, Kathleen noticed. The hint of candor emboldened her to ask, "And you care . . . don't you?"

"More than you'll ever know."

Kathleen eyed her, and under her steady gaze, something in Adele Blaine seemed to give way. Suddenly she cleared her throat and leaned close.

"I'll tell you why I care so much about rehab," Blaine said.

"Why?"

"Because of my mother."

"Your mother?"

"Because she had a stroke."

"Oh, I'm sorry."

"I was only three."

"Look, I—"

"We lived in rural Tennessee. The bastards at the hospital there just shoved her out the door in a wheelchair once it was clear she wasn't going to die. Said she ought to be grateful simply for being alive. The fact she couldn't talk, eat, or walk didn't matter at all to them. I spent so much time with her, I could see her trying to say words, chew her food, even move her legs. I felt sure she could do more, but hadn't a clue how to help her. But I taught her how to roll her wheelchair."

"Jesus . . . I see why . . . you're so committed—"

"No you don't. What could you know about being a poor black woman trying to raise a family—"

"Something . . . I think."

"Maybe you do. Well, lady, she used the skills I taught her through the years to finally roll herself in front of a bus."

"Oh, my God." Kathleen felt tears well in her eyes. If only she were able she would hug this "tough," diminutive woman.

"So that's that," Blaine said. "I'll see you in a day or so. Toodle-oo." Her sleek figure cut through the curtains so cleanly they hardly seemed to part.

"You know . . . I hope she's innocent," Kathleen confided to Jo O'Brien when the nurse dropped by later to see how the encounter had gone. "She's one strong-minded therapist. . . . And that's what I need. A mean-minded gal . . . like me . . . who'll kick my ass . . . until I can walk, work, and fuck as good as before."

Yet she remained uneasy. Why hadn't there been more resistance? she wondered. Blaine's eagerness to get her into the center so quickly wasn't at all what she had expected. And the woman drank, but it wasn't as if she needed a steady hand like a surgeon. More, though, that story about her mother—could it all be a lie?

11:00 A.M.
Medical Records Department

"How dare you presume to bad-mouth poor Dr. Hamlin after he helped my father so much. And don't you phone here again. You've got my mother in tears with your talk about digging up her husband and doing an autopsy after all this time."

"I'm sorry, ma'am, I certainly didn't mean to upset—"

"Well what the hell did you expect would be her response, you idiot?"

"I know, I didn't phrase it right—"

"Phrase it right? She's still grieving, for Christ's sake, and out of the blue you tell her maybe Hamlin put something in her husband's brain that killed him. Why, I ought to report you to the hospital. In fact, I will. Bothering widows like this."

"Yes, it was stupid of me, I know; it's just, I'm desperate to find out what he did to a friend of mine—"

"What's that got to do with us?"

"Can you just tell me if your late father suffered from hypertension?"

"Who's your supervisor?"

"Uh, well, actually I am, in ER, where your father was first seen after both strokes—"

She hung up on him.

Christ! That's all he needed, another complaint to Ingram about him. And this time it would be for frightening a helpless old lady.

He'd been in medical records all morning, seated at the same desk where he'd worked last night, crawling up one blind alley after another.

His previous call hadn't been any more successful, the husband of the woman who'd been DOA also suggesting Richard was straying way beyond the bounds of propriety. But instead of threatening to take his complaint through channels, the man offered to reprimand him using a baseball bat, "if anyone with a shovel so much as goes near my wife's grave." At least, though, he had denied she'd ever had high blood pressure—before demanding to know what business it was of Richard's anyway.

McKnight had warned him that he hadn't much hope of convincing the next of kin to request exhumation orders. "People generally don't like the idea of pulling their dead back up out of the ground and cutting them into pieces," was how the detective had put it.

Richard also had attempted contacting the private physicians of the deceased, but they, too, wouldn't discuss anything, both citing confidentiality.

"Look, doesn't it bother you that there's no explanation of the second bleed?" he said to the physician who had taken care of the woman. "It happened eighteen months after the removal of a congenital malformation, there was no evidence of a second defect being present at the time of the initial surgery, and, according to her husband, she never had hypertension to make her at risk for another hemorrhage."

"Not enough to get sued, it doesn't," the doctor had replied, her voice clipped and impatient. "Besides, out here in the real world, as opposed to ivory towers, we see enough to know bad things just happen sometimes without risk factors to explain them away and help doctors feel better about it. There's more to medicine than trying to tie everything up into tidy little knots for your residents."

The woman's resentment had hummed over the line as Richard scrambled to think of a way to win her cooperation. He could picture her, stranded amidst a waiting room full of patients with too little time to see them all. Then, too, she probably was so far removed from the milieu of academic medicine she felt threatened by anyone from that world who challenged her.

"Nevertheless, Doctor," he'd said, "would you raise the question with her husband for me?" He intended to flatter her into helping by playing the university-coddled, hapless person she already thought him to be. "You obviously would know better than me how to handle him. Seems I said all the wrong things and pissed him off."

"Me? You've got to be kidding. He already phoned a few minutes before you did warning that some ER doctor might call. Threatened to redecorate my office with a baseball bat if I said anything that led to anyone disturbing his wife's remains."

So much for his people skills.

Nor had Hamlin's old charts helped any. Even after a few hours going through them, he could no more tell what the neurosurgeon had started doing differently two years ago than he could decipher hieroglyphics.

Should he start phoning all the surviving patients Hamlin had operated on in recent years? Suggest their surgeon, who'd just been murdered, might have put something in their brains that would kill them suddenly? Promise that if they would let him see their charts in rehab, or come in and let him test the hell out of them, he might find what it was in time to save their own lives?

Yeah, right!

Even if he did it—CTing them, MRIing them, reangiograming them, in itself not a harmless procedure, PET scanning them, not to mention scaring them all to death—Jesus, what a mess that would be.

Because testing them blindly without the least idea of what to look for, he might still miss the very thing he was after.

He slammed his list of names and chart numbers down on the table, startling the uniformed policeman positioned just inside the door.

"Is everything all right, Doc?" he called.

"Sorry," said Richard, staring at the smudges left on the paper from the ink they'd used to fingerprint him and listening to the chatter of a half dozen men and women prowling the stacks. They were leaving big splotches of brushed-on dust wherever they went. "Have your technicians had any luck?"

"We got a partial superimposed overtop of yours on the inside handle of the door here. Also there were a few shreds of latex on a seam of that metal cabinet you toppled onto him, so we figure he tore his glove, and didn't realize it in the dark. We may get more if he was feeling his way along the way you were."

"Any on the circuit breakers for the lights in here?"

"No, sir. Can I get you another coffee?" The man had studiously kept Richard well supplied in caffeine all morning after initially taking a detailed statement from him regarding the attacker and what he'd said. That the creep had yelled "I am a soldier in the Legion of the Lord" seemed particularly to interest him, though he wouldn't say why. Following the interview the officer also managed to deal with the dozens of secretaries who'd been attempting to do their usual job of retrieving the hundreds of patient records needed upstairs. While trying to oblige them, he had to prevent their contaminating the crime scene. This meant limited access, missing files, and ultimately angry doctors showing up demanding their patients' records.

Since the rumor mill had already placed Richard at the center of everything that had happened overnight, he found himself the recipient of numerous sour looks whenever the door opened a crack and yet another furious supplicant demanding yet more records spotted him sitting there amidst piles of charts. "Hey," he felt like saying, "I'm not to blame for your troubles." Soon, though, the parade of tightly pursed faces so resembled one another, he found them ridiculous. He took to raising his cup in a toast and grinning at his accusers instead.

But the young officer had handled them all with courteous aplomb, his composure as impeccable as his perfectly groomed appearance.

"They don't pay you enough," Richard told him.

"Pardon, sir?"

"Never mind. Sure, I'll have another coffee. To go." He already felt rewired and jump-started having drunk far too many cups. But after no sleep for over twenty-four hours, why the hell not? Getting to his feet, he remembered a bit of unfinished business. "By the way, did any of your people find my cell phone?"

"Not so far," the policeman answered from where he was boiling a kettle of water and opening up his jar of instant.

"How about you let me in there to have a look around myself?"

"Sorry, you know I can't do that until the crime lab people are done."

"But I'm finished with my work here, and I need it back."

"We'll get it eventually."

Richard's temper, always kept on a tight spring at the best of times, lurched up a notch. "Detective McKnight assured me I'd have access to Medical Records—"

"Which is exactly what you've had, sir, for the last three hours, all the records you requested from your list." The young man handed him a fresh Styrofoam cup, its black contents sending up entrails of steam.

"But I want to look for my cell phone—"

"We found no phone, sir."

"Jesus Christ," he muttered, marching over to the nearest desk extension, setting down his drink, and punching in the cellular's number. "Son, when you hear it ringing, follow the noise, and just bring the damn thing to me, will you."

"Yessir. Glad to be of help, sir."

Richard studied the young face for any hint of sarcasm as he waited for the call to connect. Christ, the boy was so sincere, he thought, unable to detect even the flicker of a smirk. Either that or he was a hell of a straight man.

From the receiver he heard the repeating one-second buzz that meant his portable should be beeping, but no such signal came from anywhere in the room, not even faintly. "Look, can you just walk around in there toward the back. The noise of the air-conditioning may be masking the sound."

"Sure, Doc," he said, as pleasantly as always, and headed into the stacks.

Jesus, he was so polite it was eerie.

About thirty seconds later a voice came through the receiver. "Hello?"

"Hey, you found it. Thanks a lot," Richard said into the mouthpiece. There was no reply.

Thinking the policeman had already hung up, he started to ring off, when he heard, "Well, well, I was wondering when you'd call." It was a high-strung voice, not anything like the young cop's.

"Who's this?"

"The issue is who you are, Dr. Steele, as you account to the Lord for desecrating His Holy plan."

Richard's pulse slowed, his breathing went still. He looked around for one of the other officers, but they were all in the stacks. "You want to speak to me?" he said, keeping his voice smooth as he slipped into the same cool, clinical state of mind he adopted when addressing a violent patient.

"God wants to speak with you and your kind. I'm only His messenger."

"What's my kind?" He still couldn't see any cops.

"You would murder His seed."

"How do I do that?"

"Do you know what it feels like to have your seed murdered?"

The thin, high voice made him want to hold the receiver from his ear. "I don't know what you mean, uh, can you tell me your name?"

"Don't insult me, Steele. I'm not one of your crazies you can con."

"Of course you're not." Don't confront, don't antagonize, don't patronize, he taught the residents when they encountered agitated psychotics. It took seconds to say, years to learn. And the hardest lesson of all to master—no matter how off-the-wall, disgusting, or outright terrifying the person you're dealing with is—be sympathetic, never judgmental. "You sound like a very determined man."

"You haven't seen anything yet."

"Tell me."

A high-pitched laugh rattled over the line. "I'm not sure you want to hear this, Doctor."

"Sure I do."

"You know where I'm sitting?"

All at once a crescendo of traffic noises came from the background.

He must be holding the receiver toward the street, Richard thought. "Could be anywhere in any big city. Still in New York."

"Smart. Let me narrow it down for you. I'm at the corner of Lexington and Thirty-sixth."

Richard's mouth went dry.

"Cat got your tongue, Doctor? Better get it back, 'cause I've gotten lots of calls for you that you should return. It's been fun being your secretary."

"Calls?" The creep couldn't be where he said he was, couldn't be at his house. He prayed the man had just picked the location to rattle him simply because it was so near the hospital.

"Yeah, call ER. Call ER. Call ER. You don't get much variety in your phone life, do you."

"Tell me about it."

"Your son sounds nice though."

Oh, Jesus. "What do you mean?"

"He called to see how Dr. Sullivan is."

Icy fingers touched his heart. Chet didn't usually call him during the day. This creep had to be lying. Had to be! But he couldn't convince himself and fear suddenly smashed through his armor of professionalism. He jabbed the speaker button, then let loose. "Listen, you sick fuck, you stay away from my son—"

"You who would murder the Lord's seed expect Him to bless yours?" The high-pitch laugh revved up again and filled the room.

The young officer came running out of the stacks, a puzzled look on his face. A couple of his colleagues followed. Richard furiously beckoned them closer, then, whipping out his pen, scribbled one-handed on a nearby chart. *It's him! He may be at my house. Lexington and Thirty-sixth. Send cars.* "I don't know what you mean—"

"Oh yes you do. What I bet you are wondering is why your son phoned to inquire about Dr. Sullivan. Why would he interrupt his busy Daddy about stuff like that, especially since the bitch is doing so well?"

Waving his scribbled message before the startled officers, Richard kept his breathing steady, his voice under tight control. "Why don't you tell me?"

"But you won't want to hear this."

The expressions on the faces of the policemen went wide with surprise. The young one strode quickly out of earshot and started snapping orders into his handheld radio. Another ran to a bank of phones on a nearby desk and punched in a number. A third said, "I'll get McKnight," and headed out the door.

"I called his school, Lexington High," the man continued. "Left a message with his principal that he was to contact you right away, on you're cellular. A family emergency . . ."

The man's words ripped deep into Richard's chest and took his breath away. How could he know all this about Chet?

". . . When he called me back, he was so concerned. Seems he thought something had happened to Dr. Sullivan. 'Yes,' I said, 'She's had another hemorrhage. I've got your father's cellular because he's in working on her. But don't come here. Your dad wants you to go home and keep Lisa company. She's in a terrible state about this, and can't stand being in the hospital while waiting for news,' I said it all breathless and earnest like. 'She needs you Chet. Hurry. It looks bad for her mother.' Bullshit like that. Anyway, he bought it—"

"You son of a bitch! Have you got my son? And how do you know about Lisa?"

The young policeman, still speaking into his radio, stared incredulously at the speakerphone as if he couldn't believe what he'd just heard. A few of the other officers who'd been listening with increasingly horrified looks on their faces immediately got on their walkie-talkies. Richard, his hand trembling, scrawled *Call Lexington High. See if Chet Steele is still there,* and showed it to the young cop.

He quickly nodded, moved off a few steps, and began speaking again into his radio.

"Nice house, Steele. The red tint to the stone is attractive."

"Where's my son, you bastard?"

"Inside, waiting for you. See, I had this syringe of potassium chloride I never got to use—"

"No! Don't, please." He started to pace, wheeling in circles, a hundred choices avalanching through his head. Race to the house. Get to Chet. But what if the man were lying? He might not even have him. Or if he had, he could be holding him somewhere else.

"Your seed for the Lord's seed, Steele."

The cops were on the way. He'd keep the guy on the line until they got there. "Why are you doing this?" he yelled, his voice cracking.

"You and your geneticist friend are killing the Lord's innocents."

"We're what?"

The policeman stepped up and whispered, "I'm dispatched through to the principal's office at Lexington High School. You're son's not there."

The cold fingers that had been playing havoc with Richard's innards closed a fist around his throat.

"Hey, who else is with you, Steele?" said the voice. "Am I on a speaker-phone? Is someone calling the school to make sure my story checks out?" The screeching laugh once more reverberated through the room.

Richard reached out to take the policeman's radio. "Can I speak to them through this?"

He nodded, unplugging an earphone he'd been using to keep his conversation quiet, and the portable unit crackled to life.

"What do you mean my son's not there," said Richard.

"Dr. Steele?" a woman's voice answered, her fright amplified into the room as clearly as her words. "We got an urgent message from one of your residents, saying for Chet to reach you on your cellular, that there'd been a family emergency."

Richard clutched the radio so tightly he heard the plastic seams crack. "You let Chet go?"

"Yes, sir, the situation seemed so urgent. When we got him to the office so he could use a phone, your resident answered, and said Dr. Sullivan had had another stroke. I know how close Chet has grown to her—we met when she came to one of his parent-teacher nights—"

"What the hell did you do with Chet?" said Richard, cutting off the woman's babble.

"Well, since the young doctor who called had privy to your cell phone, it never crossed my mind he wasn't authentic. So I put Chet in a cab, and sent him home to be with Lisa. But that was an hour ago. Please, tell me what's going on."

"Please, tell me, what's going on," mocked the piercing thin voice of the man on the other end of the speakerphone. "Better get here, Dad, and see what I've done to your seed."

The taunt shredded whatever remnants of self-control Richard had left. He pushed away from the young cop, leaving him the walkie-talkie, and bolted for the door. "Damn you to hell," he roared over his shoulder.

A loud click followed by a buzzing dial tone was the response.

"No, he didn't mean you, ma'am," said the young policeman into the handheld unit.

"Are your cops at my house yet?" Richard shouted at him while sprinting through the exit.

"Excuse me ma'am, gotta go," he said, starting to follow, twirling a dial to change channels.

"I called them in," said one of the other officers.

"An ambulance is on the way as well," yelled another.

"The rest of us better stay here and keep this scene secure," added a third.

"Any respondent to Lexington and Thirty-sixth?" the young cop said into his receiver as he ran into the hallway a step behind Richard.

"That's a roger," rasped a man's voice through the hiss and spit of the unit's speaker. "But there's no answer at the address you gave us. Do we go in?"

"Yes!" said Richard, reaching the stairs and starting up two at a time. "Tell them there's a key on a magnet behind the street numbers. One of them is loose. But for God's sake, remember my son's inside."

"That's a roger," said the voice on the radio.

13

Gridlock imprisoned the midday traffic that filled the streets outside the hospital exit closest to Second Avenue.

The young cop at his heels, Richard sprinted toward Thirty-fourth Street. He was across it and halfway to Thirty-fifth in twenty seconds, the crowds of people on the sidewalk regarding him queerly and parting readily in his path. Then he realized he looked like a fugitive in a white coat being chased by the police. He used the misleading impression to pour on even greater speed.

On the other side of the street, a man with a broad face wearing a loose-fitting jacket over a jogging outfit stepped out the doorway of a deli. He unlocked a bicycle chained to a meter, and began peddling in the same direction Richard ran full-out. Although it was overcast he wore sunglasses, and even though it was late June and very warm, he'd pulled up his hood. He allowed Richard and the cop to stay a little ahead of him.

He hadn't expected the cop.

He took only occasional glances at the running men as he trailed them, keeping his face averted the rest of the time. With his picture having been all over local TV, the bike was the perfect vehicle for a quick getaway with so much traffic, in case someone recognized who he was and came after him. He'd be safer once he mastered the application of beards and wigs so they would pass muster up close.

Overpowering the boy had been easy. A knock on the door after the kid arrived home was all it took to get inside. The rest simply flowed from there.

And now he'd succeeded in sending Steele racing home in a state of panic and thinking only of his child. It should have been easy to come up on him from behind with the bike, draw the machete, and hack halfway through the back of his neck with a single stroke.

But the fucking cop changed all that.

In front of him the two men tore across Second Avenue and along Thirty-sixth. By the time he swung into the street after them, they were a quarter of the way up the block. They would have to cross Third Avenue, then Lexington, before reaching Steel's home.

He peddled faster, quickly closing the gap. He'd planned his attack for the next intersection, intending to sweep in on his quarry, strike, and race away. A very public, very fitting execution.

But what about the cop?

Could he take him out first? Surely a bystander would scream. Then Steele would stop and turn around. In that instant he could get in another swipe that would get the Doc. He grinned. Good plan.

Steele and the policeman were about thirty seconds away from the street corner.

He accelerated, closing in on them, threading the space between the oncoming traffic that jammed the center of the street and the line of cars parked along the curb, yet staying just outside their range of vision. A cacophony of horns continuously shredded the air, the gridlock seeming to have primed every motorist within blocks to within a hair of road rage. Continuing to steer with his left hand, he reached inside the coat for his weapon. Locking his fingers around the grip, he peddled just a little faster, inching abreast of the two men.

Fifteen seconds, he estimated, until they reached the crossing.

He got ready, and started to draw the blade.

He saw Steele glance south, checking the crush of vehicles coming from that direction.

Ten yards to go.

He didn't hear the click ahead of him because of all the surrounding noise. The door of a car parked almost at the intersection opened without warning. He saw it in time to swerve partially out of its way, but his knee smashed into it, and he crashed to the pavement.

An old man with a cigar in his mouth got out and gaped at him.

"Jesus, don't you damn cyclists ever watch what you're doing?" he said, and started to check the paint on his car door.

His hands and knees stinging from the scraping they'd gotten on the asphalt, he realized how lucky he had been not to have got the blade out fully. Managing to resheath it, with no one the wiser, and groaning, he got to his feet and limped over to the bike. No breaks. He could move easily. He wasn't able to say the same for the front wheel of his bike. It was folded over on itself, like a piece of pita.

His prey, he saw, was already well past Third Avenue. Thanks be to God for His having given him the sense to provide a backup plan, he thought, lurching after them on foot. Feeling in his pocket, he made sure the remote hadn't dropped out during his spill.

Three white-and-blue NYPD cars stood at crazy angles to the curb, their doors ajar. The other end of the street pulsed red where a solitary unit had blocked off the traffic. A uniformed woman stood on the steps before the open front door of Richard's house. She spoke quickly into her radio, and the alarm in her eyes along with the strained look on her face made Richard's gut contract with fear.

"Have you found him?" he called as he raced up to her.

She immediately broke off her radio communication. "Are you the father?"

Oh, God, no! he thought, pushing past her as he sensed she just used the question to gain a few seconds because the news was bad, the way he'd done so often when a frantic parent rushed into ER. He'd always taken that pause instinctively, caught in the grip of a crazy feeling that as long as he delayed the verdict, a mother's or father's last moments of hope for their child's life lived on. But the doctor in him would regain control and, as with a held breath, he'd have to let the moment go, tell them what they most feared, then watch their faces crumple, his words suctioning the life out of them.

He wouldn't let her do that to him.

"Wait! Sir! Don't go in there!" She made a grab for his shoulder but he eluded her and raced down the center hallway.

"Chet!" he screamed, beside himself with fear.

Two uniformed policemen had just raced out the door to the basement and were running through the passage toward the back of the house. One of them turned in his tracks. "I've got him," he said, and started to approach Richard. The other continued to dart away, flying through the swinging door that led to the kitchen. Before it swung shut again, Richard could see that the cop was out the rear entrance.

"Where's he going? What's happened?" cried Richard as the officer who'd remained behind motioned palms downward, the way he would attempt to settle a wild dog. "Calm down, sir. Come on out to the street with me—"

"Where's Chet?"

"Just let's go outside, Dr. Steele," the man added, reaching for Richard.

"Where is he!" Richard shoved him aside, only to be grabbed from behind by the policewoman he'd initially evaded and the young cop who'd accompanied him.

"Sir, stop it!" she yelled. "We haven't found him yet. Are you sure he's here?"

"You mean that bastard took him?"

"We don't know anything yet. We've looked upstairs and are searching the basement, but so far there's no sign he's even been here. Are there any cubbyholes, attic access, storage areas that we might have missed?"

Richard's thinking seemed frozen solid. "No, I don't think so."

"Your son may have come and gone," she continued. "Why don't you phone the school and see if he went back there. Now are you going to behave?"

"But that maniac may have kidnapped him—"

"First check the school," she cut in.

Richard nodded, and the arms around him immediately released their grip. In two strides he made it to the phone sitting on a little table by the front entrance, willing to clutch at any pretense not to think the worst. *Please, oh, God, please let him be safe,* he prayed as he dialed. But as he listened to the ring, he knew this was just another cop trick, a way to manage him while they continued to search for what they already knew to be inevitable—that Chet was dead. The howl of an approaching ambulance vibrated up and down the length of his spine.

"Yes, it's Dr. Steele calling from home. My son doesn't seem to be here." He forced himself to sound calm, as if treating Chet's absence as something with an innocent explanation would change the reality, would prevent the nightmare. "Has he showed up back at school, by any chance?" But his voice cracked, and it was all he could do to keep from sobbing.

"No, Dr. Steele, he's not here," the principal said.

Richard couldn't remember his name, only that he was bald, wore large wire-rimmed spectacles, and seemed prone to making overly long speeches at parent-teacher nights.

"But we'll call you, Dr. Steele, the second he turns up."

"Yes please, the second he arrives. And thank you—"

Richard went absolutely still. His blood turned to ice water.

Hanging on a coat rack in front of him was a battered knapsack, the one in which Chet carried his books. "Oh, my God, no!" he murmured and dropped the phone.

"Dr. Steele? Dr. Steele!" the principal's voice called from the receiver somewhere near the floor.

"He's been here," Richard said. He grabbed the bag off the hook and tore it open. "This is his. It's all his school stuff. He never would have gone back without taking everything here with him."

The woman cop's radio crackled to life. "Captain, get down here fast."

"You found him?"

"Yeah, and we need help. He's stuffed in a coal chute."

"No!" Richard screamed, and he bolted for the stairs.

A chorus of shouts broke out behind him.

"Wait!"

"Stop!"

"Hold it!"

He beat them to the landing and raced down. The normal coolness had a damp bite to it and the familiar musty smell seemed even stronger than usual. He started for the end of the unfinished room where a huddle of policemen were gathered in a semicircle using flashlights to peer up a two-foot opening in the middle of a brick wall. It had been there when Richard bought the house, a remnant that predated electric heating. Apart from padlocking the outside door and shoving a wad of insulation up it, he'd paid it no mind. Now it gaped at him, menacing as a massive bullet hole, the black orifice filling his vision as he approached. He saw the mouths of the policemen moving but didn't hear their words. He barely even sensed their hands pawing at him as he barged through. He felt as if he were running underwater, impeded, struggling to reach what the police looked at.

He plunged up the dark cavity, his arms outstretched the way he might surface from the depths of a pool. Sounds of someone hammering on the far end of the metal tube reverberated around him.

His hands closed around a pair of stockinged feet.

"Chet!" he sobbed. "My poor little Chet."

The soles all at once pressed down against his palms, frantically but firmly delivering a quick succession of beats. A flurry of muffled, urgent moaning noises filled the chamber. From behind him he began to hear the cries of what the police had been trying to tell him.

"He's alive!"

"As far as we can tell he's okay."

"But we want to check him from the other end of the chute first, before pulling him out."

With a loud clang, the distant metal cover sprung partially open, and a flood of light cascaded into the tiny space.

"He's gagged," yelled one of the men who had opened the hatch.

The tearing noise, the sound of tape being stripped filled the air.

"Don't move me!" Chet cried, his voice stretched taut and high with terror. "He said I'm attached to a bomb that goes off if I even budge."

Voices erupted from everywhere.

"Jesus!"

"Get the explosives squad."

"Do you see anything?"

Richard, already whiplashed from absolute despair to incredulous relief, plummeted back into free fall. "Chet, we're going to get you out," he managed to say, the words sounding as hollow as his hopes.

"Dad! Don't move me."

"No, we won't, we won't, not until we're sure it's safe."

"We don't see anything up here," yelled one of the men above. "No wires, no device, nothing. Just a little pile of goddamn sticks."

Cold dread gripped Richard's chest, then a pair of hands was on his back pulling him out. "Sir, I have to take a look," said the young cop, his manner as polite as ever, but his firm touch brooking no resistance. "Chet, my name's Ted Mallory," he called loudly, "and I'm coming in, just to feel around your legs and trunk. Did he stick something in your clothing? Or did you feel him shove in anything else after he jammed you up there?"

"He tied my hands to a pipe, then told me if I moved, I'd blow up."

"Are your hands behind your back?" Mallory asked as he slid up below Chet, checking every inch of the way with a bright but small flashlight.

"Yeah, and they hurt. My ankles, too."

"Okay, that's me you feel at your feet. Hope you're not ticklish."

"No," said Chet, his voice a shade lower. Mallory's chatter was having a calming effect.

"Good, because I don't want a foot in the face."

Richard felt someone slip up behind and take him by the elbow. "You better come outside," whispered the policewoman.

Richard only then realized the rest of the cops were no longer in the room. "No. I stay here!"

She swallowed, nodded, and gave him a wan smile. "I understand." she left quickly then.

As he turned back to watch Mallory, Richard had a new appreciation of the cop's courage. The man could have waited until the bomb squad arrived. Instead he stood with the upper half of his body enclosed in what could be a torpedo tube primed to go off any second, and soothed a frightened teenager.

"Now, Chet, there doesn't seem to be anything by your legs," he said, his voice sounding piped-in. "I'm going to cut the tape around your ankles, but don't move."

Richard saw him reach down and take a small exacto knife from his utility belt. "There, does that feel better?" he heard Mallory ask after a few seconds.

"I'll say."

"Now let me try and get your wrists. Doctor Steele, can you find me a box or something to stand on? About a foot high ought to do it." Mallory sounded as casual as if he was fixing the furnace.

Richard got him what he needed.

After a few seconds more, Mallory said, "Now I'm at your hands—oh, shit!"

Richard stopped breathing.

"What's happening?" cried Chet, his voice shooting into the upper registers again.

"Nothing," said Mallory with the same phony *all is well* smoothness that Richard adopted when a case was going from bad to worse in a hurry. "It's just that the guy taped a pipe to your wrists, probably to twist them tighter. I'll have it off in a second, but I need something better to cut it free."

He ducked out of the chute and led Richard a few feet away. "If that's what I think it is, we have to get him out of here now."

"But—"

"I haven't time to explain—except I'm pretty sure I know who's doing this. I haven't a clue why they'd be after you, but if I'm right, that's a pipe bomb. It'll have the works from an automatic car lock attached to it, and a simple remote can detonate it. Now get the hell around to the guys on the other end and tell them quietly what I said, so as not to alarm Chet. But I'm going to cut the thing away from him, and when I say pull, you yank him out and run like hell!"

"No, I won't leave—"

"Go, damn it. The bastard could be anywhere within fifty yards of us right now and getting ready to set this thing off!"

"But!—"

"That bomb's for you. He lured you here, and for sure he'll blow it up. This bunch doesn't care who else they take." His terse whispers sounded like fabric tearing.

"Who—"

"Move!" Mallory skinnied back up the chute. "Okay, Chet, your dad's gone round to help pull you out as soon as I free your arms."

"No! He said if I moved the bomb—"

"He lied, Chet, to frighten you into staying put. Now you'll feel me cut away the duct tape he used on your arms. . . ."

His cool voice faded in the distance as Richard ran up the stairs. He raced through the kitchen and burst out the back door, startling the two officers who were peering down into the darkness at the mouth of the chute. They had both put on what looked like hunting vests but what Richard figured was Kevlar. If the bomb did go off, he knew it wouldn't protect them. Kneeling by their sides, he looked in. Chet was about three feet below, attempting to give his dad a brave smile.

"Hi, Dad."

Richard forced himself to grin. "And to think of all the times I told you not to play in there."

"What's going on?" one of the cops whispered.

There was no way for Richard to answer fully without Chet hearing. "When Mallory says pull, we yank him out." Under his breath he added, "And run like hell, if you know what I mean."

The cop looked at him sideways, his lips drawing a little tighter, but he said nothing. Instead he nodded to indicate that he understood. The grim expression on his partner's face showed that he'd gotten the message as well.

"Are you sure it's all right, Dad?"

Chet's voice sounded small, its reediness almost a man's, yet the tenor tones betrayed his closeness still to boyhood. He seemed so vulnerable, Richard felt himself wince.

"It'll be fine, Chet. Just get ready to come out of there." He reached down and gave his son's dark tousled hair a rub. Then he got a grip on Chet's shoulders.

"How's it coming Mallory?" the cop beside him called.

"A few snips more should do it," came the voice from below.

"You guys hold Chet, I'll haul back on you," said the officer behind them.

"Now!" cried Mallory.

Richard and the man at his side strained as hard as they could, barely budging the boy.

"That hurts!" Chet yelled.

"Push against my shoulders, Chet, with your feet," Richard heard Mallory say from below.

Then up Chet came, all at once, the way a baby finally tumbles out of a womb.

"Let's move," said the cop who'd been pulling on Richard's back.

With Chet supported between them they ran toward the neighbor's fence. We can climb over here," Richard yelled. "Then go through—"

A roar exploded out the mouth of the chute behind him.

He swung around in time to see a volley of tiny silver missiles streak through the air and shred the leaves of the trees overhead. They peppered the walls of the house behind his with a single loud thwack. The initial crack of shattering glass in the windows gave way to the tinkle of pieces falling to the ground. Larger shards clattered after them.

But the worst came in the silence that followed.

The cry started low, almost tenuous at first, as if the agony behind it wasn't making itself fully felt just yet. Then it grew in volume, leaving Richard no doubt that Mallory's pain was taking hold and the momentary shock, the few seconds when he wouldn't grasp what had happened, was lifting. The sounds continued to crescendo, in keeping with a growing horror as he must have recognized what was missing and what remained, however shredded. Coming out of the chute his screams seemed to be from the bowels of hell itself.

14

Richard was the first into the room.

Fumes from the explosion filled the air, but there was surprisingly little smoke, and there was very little structural damage, though chips of concrete lay everywhere. The floor was pockmarked where the nails flying out of the chute had first hit the cement, then ricocheted up to carry out their real purpose, the rending of flesh.

From the waist down Mallory was a mass of gelatinous twitching muscle embedded with spikes. Torn cloth entwined with strips of skin trailed off him, ending in two smears of blood stretching several yards along the floor where he'd tried to drag himself away from his own carnage. Quivering with shock but still conscious, he lay propped up against the wall, his eyes bulging in disbelief as he stared down at what little was left of him.

"No! Not that! Not my legs!" he sobbed, between howls of gibberish and screeches of agony that had every cop who came into the room cringing or cowering away.

"Ted, can you hear me?" said Richard, kneeling by him, the cloying stench of seared tissue filling his nostrils.

". . . oh, God! Help me! Help me! Help meeeeeeeeee . . ."

The shriek pierced to the bone. "Get the medics in here," Richard snapped over his shoulder, already planning how they'd lift Mallory's mangled limbs without pieces of muscle sliding off his tibia or falling away from the femur. "Tell them to bring their drug kit, and sterile blankets. Then you guys clear the road to the hospital!" IV's, airways, oxygen, and painkillers—what they could give him here—weren't enough.

". . . give me something, oh God, something for the pain . . ."

Richard gently took Mallory's face between his hands. "Just seconds now, Ted. They're bringing it now. Just seconds more, then I'll make the pain go. After that I'll get you to emergency. We're minutes away, and you're going to be okay, hear me? Okay!"

Mallory didn't seem to understand and frantically strained to peer around Richard as if he dared not let his lower body out of sight.

". . . where are my legs? Let me see them . . ."

"They're there, Ted. Your legs are there."

". . . don't let the doctors take them. Give me something, do something, oh God, get my legs—"

"Ted, hang on. We'll make this right," he said, trying to coax the young man's stare back to his own, knowing full well no one could make that much damage "right" ever again. But his years in ER had taught him to lie. The issue wasn't Ted's legs. It was his life. And Ted might be mad with pain, but he could cling to an offer of hope, albeit a false one. Death was coming fast. Even if he told Ted, the young man would find it impossible to prepare for. Hearing a promise that he could still be made whole—that someone would undo the hurt, stop the hemorrhage, repair the mashed limbs—gave comfort. Damn what the textbooks said about doctors always telling the truth.

"Look at me, Ted," Richard continued. "Hear what I'm saying. Hang on and you'll be fine."

Mallory started to sob again. For an instant his eyes focused on Richard. "Just hold my hand," he cried, his teeth chattering. "Don't let go of my hand."

Richard clutched the outstretched fingers. They were trembling and felt as clammy as if Mallory were already dead.

Two medics clattered down the steps bearing their stretcher, an equipment case teetering precariously on top.

Finally!

Richard flipped open the case, found a ten-milligram vial of morphine, and drew it into a syringe. "Here we are, Ted. Sweet relief."

"Oh, Jesus, yes."

Pulling up a sleeve and finding a vein, Richard slowly injected half the contents keeping an eye on the man's breathing. Within seconds Mallory started to whisper. "Yes. Yes, oh thank you, God. Oh, Jesus, thank you." A few seconds later he murmured, "Doc, shoot it in, all of it. Take me out. I don't want to live like this."

Richard ignored the plea. "We'll slide a sheet under him, then lift," he told the attendants as he withdrew the needle.

"No, Doc, please."

"Enough of that talk, Ted. You're going to make it, and in one piece. Are you married?"

"Engaged."

"What's her name?"

"Cathy."

"Well, you just think of Cathy, and how proud she'll be of you when I tell her how you saved my son." Shifting to get in a better position to move him, Richard felt his shoes stick to the floor. Looking down he saw a rapidly spreading pool of bright blood pouring out from behind Mallory's buttocks. "Damn it," he muttered and moved to grab a pair of gloves from the open case. He snapped them on.

"Hold my hand again," Mallory said, his words slurred and his voice much weaker than before.

"I have to check where you're bleeding, Ted," he said, carefully probing with his fingers through the bloody mess that had been the man's groin.

"Noooo! Don't touch me. . . ." The young man writhed as if he'd never had any morphine at all.

Richard felt the tip of a nail pulsing like a jackhammer. It had speared his femoral artery. It probably had gone through, and the blood was coming out the other side.

Diving back into the equipment case, he grabbed a pack of gauze pads and jammed all of them into the site.

"You bastaaaard . . ." Mallory roared, trying to hump away from him.

Richard gave more morphine, the medics got a sheet underneath Mallory, and they hoisted him onto the stretcher.

His screams trebled in volume. Blood pulsed in a crimson arch across the room. Richard bunched up yet more wads of gauze pads, but the protruding nail prevented him from compressing the vessel properly. In the process of trying, he disturbed a cluster of other spikes, adding more pumpers to the flow. He needed to close off the main supply, the femoral, but that required scalpels and a special clamp called a Kelly, routine equipment for an ER. The kid would bleed out before they ever got there. Time for a Hail Mary.

As they moved toward the steps leading to the ground floor, he grabbed the first nail with his fingers and pulled.

Mallory's screams were almost impossible to bear.

The nail was so embedded into the bone of the underlying femur that Richard couldn't budge it. Jets of blood continued to shoot up around his fingers.

"Hold it a second," he said to the technicians before they started upstairs, and ran to what was left of his workbench. Rifling through a tool kit, he grabbed a pair of vice grips and returned to the stretcher. He'd given Mallory all the morphine he dared without putting him into a respiratory arrest. This was going to hurt. "Hold him," he ordered.

One of the medics gripped his arms and upper body, the other used the sterile sheets to protect his abraded legs and pinned him above the knees.

It was as hard as pulling a nail out of wood. Blood flew everywhere, coating his latex gloves and making it difficult to get a grip. Mallory's shrieks reached new levels that nearly made Richard stop. A familiar cold gnawed at the pit of his stomach, making it feel empty as a waiting grave. But with a third yank, the spike gave.

Immediately a hose of blood sprayed him and half the room. He cleared away a few more of the nails, then pressed another wad of gauze hard onto the artery. With nothing obstructing him, he finally stanched much of the flow.

"Let's go," he ordered.

When they got to the street he saw Chet turn white and recoil from the blood-drenched procession as they raced by him on the way to the ambulance. The policewoman at his side slid a protective arm around his thin shoulders.

"Chet, you ride to the hospital with one of the officers," Richard called over to him, "and get to Kathleen. You'll be safe there."

The officer who'd taken the boy under her wing pulled him closer. "I'll drive him myself."

His youthful eyes grew darker. "What about Ted?"

"I've got him. He'll be all right," Richard said. He helped load the stretcher into the rear of the ambulance and climbed in with one of the techs. He caught a last glimpse of Chet's anxious face as the doors closed behind them, and the vehicle took off, its siren wailing at full blast.

As they rocketed down Thirty-sixth and reeled around the corner at Second Avenue, the movement must have widened the arterial tears around the many remaining nails because the bleeding got worse. Richard and the attendant hadn't enough hands to compress all the jets of red that rose from the glistening remnants of Mallory's limbs, soaking the sheets and spattering the racks of supplies along the walls. They'd no time to start IVs or hook him to a monitor.

"I'm going," Mallory said, his voice barely audible above the roar of the motor.

"Not if I can help it," said Richard, scrambling to find and staunch yet another pumper.

"Tell McKnight it's the Legion of the Lord."

"Are you Catholic?" asked Richard. "A priest will be at the hospital, if you want me to call him."

"No! Tell McKnight it's the Legion of the Lord!"

Shit, he must be getting delirious, thought Richard, recognizing the phrase Mallory had kept asking about this morning. "Don't worry, Ted, you'll soon be able to tell him yourself."

Mallory grabbed him by the arm, and squeezed hard. "Tell him!" he yelled, half sitting, his voice suddenly loud again. "And quit fuckin' lying to me!" His black eyes held Richard's for a few seconds, then seemed to wobble, and he flopped back on the stretcher, muttering incoherently. Being upright, even for just those few moments, had drained off the little blood his brain had left.

No sooner had they wheeled him through the ER doors than Steele's team had two central lines in him and a pair of large-bore IVs. A minute later blood infusions were up and running, catheters and monitors in place.

But nothing brought his pressure back.

"Too many fucking holes," Richard muttered.

As his team worked to keep him alive and vascular surgeons heroi-cally cut down to the mangled arteries, clamping them off as they went, Richard was reduced to once again holding the man's hand. He stayed crouched over his head, and talked constantly to him. He knew from all the others who he'd watched slip away that hearing would be the last to go. "Okay, Ted, no more bullshit. Whoever is dear to you, I'll personally help them through this, because you gave me back my son, who's so dear to me. And I'll tell Cathy how magnificently brave you were, that you spoke her name."

His pressure fell until it became undetectable, his pulse vanished al-together, and shock quickly carried him off, his cries fading to a mere murmur.

". . . Legion of the Lord . . . Legion of the Lord . . . Legion of the Lord" he muttered until he died.

One of the doctors made a last-ditch effort, cutting into his chest and massaging his heart with her hand.

Richard walked out, knowing it was over.

"What about his fiancée?"

"She's in L.A., on a business trip," McKnight said.

"Did he have anyone else?"

"A father. He's already on the way in."

"Did anyone tell him yet?"

"No. Mallory was still alive when we reached him."

Richard sat in his office staring at an untouched cup of coffee. Half an hour ago it had been he who'd been rushing to what he feared would be the worst of all possible news. Now it was another father who'd been summoned to meet that fate. He shuddered, a free-for-all of relief, guilt, grief, and gratitude careening through him. "I'll tell him," he said.

McKnight, sitting across the desk from him, his eyes leaden as pewter saucers, didn't say a word.

Richard pulled the chaos in his head to order. "Ted Mallory told me before the explosion went off that he thought he knew who'd planted the bomb, but he didn't have time to explain. He also seemed to realize right away that it was a pipe bomb and would be detonated by a remote, not Chet's movement."

"A remote?"

"Yeah. One that triggers an automatic car lock."

The detective snapped forward. "Did he say anything else?"

"Not really. After the blast, he seemed to be talking gibberish. Going on about 'Legion of the Lord.' "

"What?"

"They were his next to last words to you as well. 'Tell McKnight it was the Legion of the Lord,' he told me. He'd been dwelling on the phrase a few hours earlier while taking my statement."

"How do you mean?"

"When he took my statement about how the attacker ranted at me last night. At one point I said that the creep hollered, 'I am a soldier in the Legion of the Lord,' and it grabbed Mallory's attention. He kept asking me was I certain the man used those exact words."

"Holy shit!" McKnight muttered, his pupils igniting and burning off the fatigue that had been there seconds before.

"Why? Does it mean something to you? It sure didn't seem any different to me from the other ravings that maniac was spouting off."

"Yes! But it doesn't make any sense," said McKnight, wearing the intent stare of someone traveling through their own thoughts at a thousand miles an hour.

Before he could say more, Jo O'Brien knocked and opened the door. "Mr. Mallory's here," she said and showed in a slender, wiry man with a stubble of white hair that occupied only the back half of his gleaming scalp.

"Is Ted all right?" he asked, his eyes darting desperately from Richard to McKnight and back again.

The moment Richard dreaded more than any other in medicine hung between them—the held breath waiting to be expelled.

"Mr. Mallory, sit down, please. I'm afraid I have very bad news."

It was two o'clock that afternoon when, after making sure the nurses had cleaned up the body and covered the mangled legs with a sheet, he led the father to view his son. Trembling, the old man walked hesitantly between him and Jo O'Brien as they supported him by each elbow. McKnight followed closely behind. When the elderly man gazed down at the slack youthful features, blanched by the loss of blood, his face folded in on itself and he let out a bellow of grief stripped so raw, the sound ripped through every corner of ER, casting anyone who heard it into silence.

McKnight then guided the broken figure to the waiting room where a gathering of men and women in dark blue gently engulfed him. Murmured words of solace filled the air, somber and solemn as chanting in a church.

Richard watched and wondered should he say something now to Mallory Senior. Tell him who Ted had saved? But he checked himself, imagining what it would feel like were the situation reversed. How would he feel if he had to endure condolences from the father whose son had been spared, the death of his son having been the price? He might know in his head it hadn't been an either-or pick, but he'd be raging at the unfairness of the choice in his gut, and loathing himself for it. No, better he say nothing that might unleash all that now, and spare the old man the added anguish. There would be a time later, when his grief was less fresh. Then Chet himself might offer comfort, if there was such a thing in the face of losing a child.

His sadness deepened. Part of him wondered if he hadn't copped out just now. Was he really protecting Ted Mallory's father, or himself? Was he hiding out rather than facing the man's wrath over whose son had lived and whose had died? After all, he had a flaw when it came to facing feelings that cut to the bone. And the trouble with having run once, bullshitting himself every step of the way, was that he couldn't be sure he wasn't doing it again.

He slapped himself out of such morbid thinking. Enough, damn it. Hell, if he was feeling so torn up over Ted Mallory's death, how would

Chet take it? He didn't know yet. Better he got the news from his own dad before he simply overheard the nurses talking about it. He'd be damned if he'd let Chet slide into some sort of survivor's guilt.

McKnight didn't look as though he'd be leaving Mallory Senior's side anytime soon. Finding out from him what the Legion of the Lord was all about would have to wait. Richard signaled to the detective that he'd phone him later. Rather than wait for the elevator, he took the stairs and reached the floor in a matter of minutes, entering through the sliding doors to ICU.

Chet looked up from where he sat, his hand in Kathleen's. Some of his color had returned, but his eyes were red from crying. Behind him stood Lisa, her slender arms around his shoulders, her green eyes also red. A policeman hovered at the entrance to the cubicle.

"You told me he'd be all right, that you'd save him," Chet said as Richard approached. There was no recrimination in his voice, just incredulity, as if he'd still believed his father was infallible, at least in ER.

Kathleen, the tiny movements of her face making a white mask brimming with sadness, held her good hand out to Richard while still holding onto Chet's with the other. He walked over, clasped them both, and slid his arm far enough around Chet's narrow shoulders that he reached Lisa. Infused with grief for Ted Mallory and gathering all that was precious to him in a single small circle, he feared for the three lives in his embrace. Would the police be able to protect them? Obviously this monster didn't care who he killed, and whatever his purpose, he might very well try to use both Chet and Lisa as bait again.

"Who did this, Dad? And why?" Chet asked, his voice quivering.

Not since Luana died had Richard seen such anguish on his son's face. Lisa seemed just as lost, her skin the pallor of paste. "I don't know," he said, realizing neither of them knew all that had happened in the last twenty-four hours. He quickly added, "But until we get some answers and catch this guy, the police will be guarding us all better than Fort Knox." As he launched into talk of police protection, he watched for the tight folds at the corners of Chet's mouth and the pinched lines adjacent to Lisa's eyes to flatten, his barometer of how well he was reassuring them. He could explain later about the other attacks and their tie to the murders. It would only raise more disturbing questions than provide satisfy-ing answers—such as why was this shit still coming at him now that the cat was out of the bag? It wasn't as if by getting rid of him at this point the killer could prevent anyone else from investigating the hell out of Ham-lin's former patients and finding what had been done to them.

He shuddered. This last attack seemed all the more vicious because it made no sense. What if the game had become something different? Like an attempt to kill Richard to make sure he didn't come after the killer. But why? Was it because he might see something the cops wouldn't? What? Richard couldn't even guess. Unless of course it was medical. Well, if that bastard thought he'd frightened him off, he had to think again. Whoever he was and whatever he was up to, he messed with the people Richard loved. One way or the other, he was going to track that creep down for sure, and when he did, if the law wouldn't put him away, Richard would.

He wanted to talk to McKnight and find out about the Legion of the Lord. He resisted the urge to pull away and get to a phone, because every-thing in Chet's expression pleaded, *Don't leave.*

"Where will we live, Dad?" he said after a few moments. His voice still had a quaver or two, but was less shaky than before. "I don't want to go back home."

"Don't worry. We're not going back there anytime soon."

"But I can't stop thinking about Ted, of what happened to him down there. All that blood, and I keep hearing his screams. . . ." His voice trailed off as tears made a path down his freckled cheeks.

Richard hugged him harder. "Shhh. I know it seems impossible, Chet, but that will pass—"

"What if it doesn't?" The boy's stare appeared so wide with fright it was as if everything he'd witnessed had reappeared before him, an appari-tion the rest of them couldn't see.

"It's okay, Chet," said Lisa, running her fingers through his wild black curls. Kathleen reached up to touch the boy's face, but couldn't quite ex-tend her arm far enough. Richard looked helplessly on, then said, "Chet, maybe it's time all of us, you, me, Lisa, and Kathleen, thought about con-solidating our little band under one roof."

The two teenagers gaped at him, and Kathleen's pupils narrowed to pinpoints.

"You mean we move into their apartment?" Chet asked. A momentary look of wonder swept aside the tight creases around his mouth.

"Cool!" Lisa added. "But it would be crowded as hell."

Kathleen said nothing, her gaze all at once more blank than the rest of her face.

"I mean we find a new house for the bunch of us," Richard said. "You three are as dear to me as life itself, and I want you around me forever."

Lisa at least grinned. "Hey, Chet. My mother, your dad, living in sin. That'd make us a common-law brother and sister. Scandalous!"

Chet gave her a tenuous smile, then looked up at him. "For real, Dad?"

"If Kathleen will have us," he answered, turning to look at her and expecting to see some show of delighted surprise.

Instead she looked away.

He hadn't risked waiting around to see the outcome of the explosion, immediately retreating to his new hidey-hole, a gray, unlit coffin on Wooster Street little different from the one he'd evacuated that morning. He spent the next few hours perfecting the application of a small mustache to match the curly wig of black hair he'd been provided. By the time he satisfied himself that the effect would disguise him, not draw attention, the radio was breaking the story.

"... one dead, the identity being withheld pending notification ..."

He began to fret that he'd messed up again. "Settle down," he kept repeating into the noise of jackhammers from the street. He'd know soon enough how he'd done and there was nothing more he could do about it now anyway. If he got Steele, only three more on the list to go, and best he remain focused on them.

He changed into the greens of an OR orderly, pulled on his jacket, and set out.

Despite all the cops being around, he had little difficulty in slipping back into the hospital. The cops were concentrated around the main entrances, checking credentials of staff at shift change and visitors at all hours. But he knew other ways to come and go, and was familiar with the routines that could be put to his advantage.

The laundry. Pickup at seven, delivery at five. The truck would back down into a basement loading dock that was still a popular hangout for the hard-core smokers—the ones who couldn't make it through to their scheduled breaks without sneaking out for a few desperate drags. They'd be looking out for their supervisors rather than paying attention to him.

A few minutes before five, standing on Thirty-third, he lit his own cigarette and watched the laundry truck reverse down a ramp outside the big corrugated metal doors. When the driver honked and the doors rattled open, he simply stepped through. The sallow-faced gang of puffers inside scrambled like startled mice to get clear as the vehicle lurched back into the loading bay. Nobody so much as glanced at him.

"My, God! You're sitting up." McKnight walked into the cubicle and saw Kathleen in a chair.

She gave him her faint sketch of a smile. Gravity accented her weight loss from the tube feedings by pulling the loose skin down over her cheekbones.

Richard stood behind her, aware that she wasn't so much sitting up as strapped in, and that it was her third ten-minute session that day. He'd seen the nurses put her there and knew the cost—her back muscles coiling into spasms until they stood out like ropes. Sobs of air exploded out the tube in her throat, and her face twitched in extreme agony. Throughout the ordeal she steadfastly kept her eyes on him until he felt he was under a microscope. She was studying his reactions, seeing if he could take it, watching for his flaw to reappear and send him running again. Lord knew, with his record, she's had cause.

Appearing exhausted, she still lifted her right hand vertically from her lap and closed the hole in her trachea without help. It was a far more demanding feat than the horizontal maneuvers she'd been accomplishing in bed, but Richard's move to assist her received a sharp shake of her head. "I'm to put . . . my muscles . . . to use," she told him, sounding cross. "If I have any."

McKnight gave a soft whistle of appreciation. "Boy, you're one tough woman." He pulled a chair into the cubicle and drew the white curtains closed, as if that would keep their conversation private. "Where are the kids? And come to think of it," he added, glancing around, "where's my officer?"

"She took Chet and Lisa down to the cafeteria for supper," Richard said.

"But I ordered her not to leave Dr. Sullivan—"

"And I made her go with them, so blame me. Now what about this Legion of the Lord?" He wasn't in any mood for more delays.

His bluntness seemed to catch the detective by surprise. McKnight cocked his head, and gave Richard a *who do you think you're talking to?* look. It lasted but a second, then vanished as he leaned in close toward the two of them. "First I have to ask you both a personal question," he whispered.

Richard couldn't remember any other time the big man spoke so quietly. Normally he projected across whatever room he was in. "Okay," Richard replied. "Try me first."

"Have you ever been involved in giving abortions?"

"What?"

"Keep it down," said McKnight, putting a finger to his lips.

"You mean therapeutic abortions? Terminations?"

McKnight nodded.

"No, at least not since I assisted in a few as a resident twenty years ago. Why?"

"Have you been a vocal advocate for the pro-choice movement, speaking out about it, participating in marches, that kind of thing."

"Not really."

"Would you say you're more outspoken on the topic than other doctors in ER?"

"No, except as chief I have a higher profile. I sure as hell have made my opinions known to the residents though."

"And that opinion would be?"

"That the issue should remain a medical matter between a woman and her doctor. What the hell has this to do with all that's happened?"

"Humor me for a minute." He turned to Kathleen. "How about you, Dr. Sullivan? Has your name ever been associated with abortion clinics or causes."

"Not as a spokesperson . . . or in any official capacity. . . . I certainly agree . . . with Richard . . . about a woman . . . with an unwanted pregnancy . . . having a right . . . to safe options. . . . But I don't . . . go out of my way . . . to preach it."

McKnight leaned back and rubbed his forehead. "This doesn't make sense." He had mumbled, but whether to himself or to them, Richard couldn't decide.

"Please, tell us what's going on, Detective," he said, ready to scream if the man resumed the Q&A routine.

McKnight leaned forward again, this time perched on the very edge of his chair. "Do both of you remember that abortion clinic in the East Village that got blown up two years ago?"

"Oh, my God, yes," Richard said, completely caught off guard by McKnight's bringing up such a horrible incident out of the blue. The blast had gone off at night, and there was one victim—a cleaning lady who'd been working in the building after hours. They brought what was left of her to his ER. She was a grandmother, and her son kept telling everyone how she'd had nothing to do with the politics of abortion, didn't even believe married couples should use birth control, as if that should have protected her. She'd been nearly skinned alive because the bastards had used nails, yet she lived three more days. They practically had to anesthetize her to stop the screaming. "You're not telling me . . ." A sickening coldness congealed in his throat.

"I'm afraid so. Whoever did that job chose a pipe packed with nails and plastic explosives, then triggered it with a device made from an electronic car lock using a remote key. Mallory knew about it because he worked on the case. Hell, a hundred of us did, because we were afraid the attack was the start of a terrorist campaign. Similar explosions were going off in Boston, Seattle, and L.A. at the time. No one claimed responsibility for them, though the reasons were obvious. It was only later when the ramblings of a group calling themselves the Legion of the Lord began to appear on the Internet advocating violent actions against abortion clinics and touting the same type of bomb that we realized who we were up against."

"Jesus," said Kathleen. "I saw a . . . documentary on them . . . last year. . . . They're hideous . . . righteous control freaks . . . who've got a . . . real problem . . . with women's independence . . . and no problem . . . with killing."

"You're saying the guy who attacked us was part of all that?"

"We have to consider it. The particular piece of shit who planted the package in the village was never caught, and I just got a preliminary lab report confirming the creep who did your house stuffed his little present with nails identical to the ones we found at the clinic—four-inch spirals."

"But why would an antiabortion nut come after me?"

"Or me?" Kathleen said.

"Or Hamlin and Lockman?" Richard added.

"As I said, it doesn't make sense for you two. And unless Hamlin and Lockman were secret abortionists, it doesn't add up for them either. This bunch doesn't target doctors who aren't somehow directly involved. Mind you, it wouldn't have to be big time. There was a woman gynecologist in Rochester they shot to death a few years ago who hardly did any abortions at all, performing them only occasionally and in a hospital as part of her obstetrics practice." He shrugged. "So you never know."

"Wait a minute," Richard said. "This same group did that?" The case had made headlines across the country and resulted in gynecologists everywhere wearing Kevlar.

"It's real tough to get a handle on these types. They don't have designated leaders, no membership lists, and they only meet on the Internet. It seems that nobody even gives an order to make a hit. They simply encourage individuals filled with like-minded poison to launch campaigns as they see fit. 'Soldiers' they call themselves. To me, they're cowards by any name. In practice they're more like urban guerrillas. That's what makes them so damn elusive."

Kathleen raised her hand to cover her tube. "Could their . . . targeting us . . . be a mistake?"

"I'd say the deliberateness of this guy and his coming after Dr. Steele a second time makes that seem pretty unlikely. He wants you two, no doubt about it."

"Could whoever he is . . . have copied the bomb . . . yet have nothing . . . to do with . . . Legion of the Lord?"

"Possible, but unlikely. For obvious reasons none of the police departments involved with the cases published much detail about the mechanism, and the type of nails they used wasn't listed on the Internet. I figure it's more probable he was once part of them, or at the very least knew someone who was."

"Now I understand why this nut kept talking about 'destroyers of the Lord's seed' and 'killers of the Lord's innocents,' " Richard said.

"But what's he after then?" McKnight asked. "Why has he gone off on some tangent that doesn't fit the group's usual antiabortion agenda and gotten himself entwined in whatever Hamlin and Lockman stirred up?"

Richard flashed back to a tableau of angry faces staring at Hamlin, and focused on one in particular. "Paul Edwards," he said out loud.

The heavy lines of McKnight's forehead deepened. "Who?"

Richard's mind was already miles ahead. "Hell," he muttered, all at once realizing what that odd group might have in common. What they might have done to Kathleen. What could cause miraculous recoveries and why the Legion of the Lord would want to kill them for it. "I think I got it," he said, still incredulous at having stumbled onto a common thread that seemed to pull the nefarious parts of the puzzle together. He even thought he knew what those little branches the killer left were supposed to mean.

"Pardon?" McKnight asked. His expression had grown more quizzical by the second.

Kathleen was also eyeing Richard strangely.

But he remained lost in thought, quickly testing his idea to verify if it held up—checking it against Hamlin's actions, seeing if it jibed with what was in the patients's charts, racing through scenarios that might profit a cardiac surgeon, a rehabilitation specialist, and a chief of gynecology with a reproductive center at his disposal. Everything just kept flying together, piece after piece. It all fit!

But how to get proof? What would convince others to take his hypothesis seriously?

That eluded him.

The only thing he came up with was yet another way to test his theory.

It wouldn't sway McKnight to take police action, but it might help get someone at the hospital at least to consider the possibility that had brought his brain to such a boil. And he had just the person in mind.

"Stay here!" he said. "I've got to check something out."

"Wait a minute. Shouldn't I come along?" McKnight called.

"No!" he shouted over his shoulder. "This is doctor to doctor stuff." And he rushed from the room, leaving McKnight and Kathleen staring after him.

15

Paul Edwards sat staring at a mahogany statue of a pregnant woman. He'd received it nearly twenty-three years ago from a patient's husband. Prillo was the man's name, and the couple had been trying to conceive for ten years. The fertility drugs of the time didn't work, and in vitro fertilization techniques were still in the experimental stages, yet the man begged for something new to be tried on his wife, sliding an envelope with ten thousand dollars in it across the desk as he spoke.

The guy's promises of more to come had made it seem worthwhile to explore the idea, and a few phone calls led to a young researcher who'd been working on surgically extracting eggs from an ovary. Several months later, James Norris helped him successfully fertilize Mrs. Prillo's egg with Mr. Prillo's sperm and implant it back into her uterus. For his trouble the "more to come" turned out to be the statue, but since the future proud father, along with a few of the new baby's uncles, showed up to express their appreciation driving black limos and dressed like the cast of *Guys and Dolls*, Edwards decided to keep any complaints he had about remuneration to himself.

Mr. Prillo had sensed his disappointment. "The way I see it, Doc," he said, leaning over the desk between them, supporting his weight on as big a set of hairy knuckles that Edwards had ever seen, "this fertility racket I got you started on is going to pay off big."

And it had.

Until HMOs started to rewrite the financial rules in the nineties, declaring war on doctors in general and fertility superstars in particular. Fees plummeted or weren't covered at all. No matter how many hospital endowments he brought in, research grants he won, or office perks NYCH awarded him in recognition, it didn't keep his personal income in the stratosphere he'd gotten used to. So he'd expanded the range of his work with Jimmy Norris, and was so close to what could be the biggest payoff in the history of medicine.

Except now he was about to run away from it all. Tonight.

Five-thirty that afternoon Mabel Brown, his secretary, had rushed into his office, "Paul," she said, "did you hear the latest rumors?" The woman, habitually dressed in gaily colored jumpsuit outfits that resembled haute couture battle fatigues, had been a lieutenant in the army before joining the health care ranks, and seemed to be in a perpetual crisis mode. She announced even the most mundane pieces of news as if they were "Incoming!" But they were rarely harbingers of anything important, so he wasn't prepared for what indeed would be the equivalent of a mortar shell going off. "The police think the attacks on Dr. Steele are by that antiabortion group that goes around blowing up clinics."

A tightness gripped his ample gut. "What!"

"The LOTL, they called them. Something about 'Legion of the Lord.' The cops are saying they're behind the murders of Lockman and Hamlin as well."

"But that doesn't make sense," he'd protested, trying to cover up his horror at how much terrible sense it did make. "Steele doesn't have anything to do with abortions. Neither did the other two."

"Maybe this bunch thought they did. Their blowing up those clinics certainly was crazy. Why should people like that be logical? Hell, what with all the frozen embryos you keep down in the fertility clinic, it's a wonder one of them hasn't already come in and started shooting at us."

"What do you mean?" he'd snapped, all at once fearing she'd discovered what he'd been doing.

"Oh, I know those kinds of people are supposed to think we're the good guys, that we make babies here, not destroy them, but the way they're also going on these days about embryos being used in research—"

"What research?" The instant he'd blurted out the question he wanted to take it back. He was overreacting. She couldn't know about his supplying Norris.

"Oh, come on now. All the public controversy over using embryos to get stem cells, and nutty assholes like the LOTL running around? Who knows what one of them might do?"

Oh, my God, she'd figured it out. But how could she have? "We're not doing any research with embryos," he had said lamely, trying to keep his voice steady.

"You and I know that, but the whole world is aware that fertility clinics routinely supply labs with embryos otherwise slated for destruction. Just because we don't, do you think that's going to stop one of those wackos from using us to make a statement? All they're liable to see is that the potential of using fetal tissue to harvest stem cells is here. Why wouldn't they be as likely to blow us up as anyplace else."

That was twenty minutes ago. She had left him sitting alone in his office, pinpoints of perspiration welding his shirt to his back as he considered his options. If the cop rumors turned out to be true he was a dead man, because the only way a bunch of fanatics like the LOTL could have found out about Hamlin and Lockman would be if someone fed them the information.

Who? That bitch Downs of course. Instead of making a side deal with the cops as she'd threatened to do, she was using that pack of mad dogs to wipe them out. She probably figured they wouldn't go after her because she was no longer using embryos.

"Vicious murdering cunt!" He picked up his private phone and dialed an eleven-digit number he knew by heart. An hour later he'd concluded the terms of a radically altered deal with Fountainhead Pharmaceuticals. Hanging up the phone he looked at his watch. Seven P.M. What remained was to steal Norris and Downs's backup records from their office in the basement, if they hadn't already moved them. He wrote off Hamlin's files, having convinced his new partners at Fountainhead they didn't need them because the late neurosurgeon's technique was too wonky for anyone else to try.

Then it would be home to pack and an early flight to the offshore island he and his contacts had agreed upon, a place where U.S. cops, internal revenue agents, and rabid bombers wouldn't find him.

His own staff, including Mabel, were long gone for the day, but he thought it better to wait another couple of hours, since researchers often hung around into the night, tending to their experiments the way some parents doted on their children. In the meantime he slipped out to the parking lot and got a tire iron out of his trunk, figuring he'd be doing a fair bit of breaking locks tonight.

7:30 P.M.
NYCH Department of Cellular Research

Ralph Coady squinted into the binocular eyepiece of the microscope. Eventually he got the knack of how to focus, merging the two round images into one, and saw what looked like a mat made from tiny red strips of meat. Except it pulsed, contracting and expanding as regularly as a heartbeat. "What is it?" he asked, looking up at Francesca Downs.

"You tell him, Jimmy."

The researcher flipped a switch, and the image from the microscope filled a screen mounted behind it. "This is functioning human heart tissue, Ralph, brand new, and grown in a petrie dish," he said, his voice sounding rather flat compared to the enthusiasm he'd shown during their first conversation together. "Have you ever heard of stem cells?"

"I'm not sure. It sounds familiar."

"They're the cells in an embryo that hold the potential to become every type of tissue there is in the human body—heart, brain, liver, lung, blood, bone—you name it, these cells can transform into it."

"Yeah, I remember now," said Coady. "It's in all the papers. Talk of growing new organs, never having to wear out or get old." A wild surge of excitement flew through him. "Holy shit! Can you grow me a new heart?"

Norris, pretty grim-faced up to now, gave a chuckle. "No, we can't do that yet, but the same way we grew these cells in a culture, we can grow new myocardial muscle in your heart."

"You see, Ralph," Downs said, "a heart attack blocks the blood flow to a portion of the heart muscle, killing it off and leaving rigid scar tissue in its place. Damage enough of the heart wall that way, it no longer functions as a pump. That's why your lung filled up with fluid."

"You mean how the basement floods if the sump quits."

She smiled. "Exactly. Except in your case, I can give you an infusion of stem cells into that scar tissue, and new tissue will fuse with the old to work in sync with the rest of your heart. Your failure will be significantly reduced, if not eliminated."

"You're kidding," Coady said. He looked from Downs to Norris, and back again.

"No I'm not. I've already done it, experimentally, of course, on mice. You'd be my first official human subject. But believe me, I know what I'm doing."

"Is it an operation?"

"It's nothing you haven't already endured. Without getting involved in arcane technical details, we basically go in with an angiocath, the long arterial line I used when we Roto-Rootered you. Except this time, guided by X ray, I deposit an infusion of stem cells around the edge of the scarred area, injecting them through a set of microscopic needles."

"But how does it work? You said these cells can become anything. What's to keep them from turning into a hunk of bone or growing a foot in the middle of my chest?"

Downs's smile sparkled brighter than ever and her eyes practically danced with delight. "This is the miracle of stem cells, Ralph. They seem to know exactly where to go and what to do."

"But how?"

"There's a few theories, but let me explain it this way. Remember all the hoopla a year ago when they completed the human genome study."

Coady felt his spirits drop. "Yeah, they were promising great medical breakthroughs from it, then came the other shoe. It may take decades before any real benefits are actually on the market. You're not going to tell me this stem cell stuff will be disappointing like that? Not after getting my hopes up."

"No, Ralph. But to understand how stem cells know what to do, you have to look at one of the big surprises from the genome project—that there are only about thirty thousand genes in the human body."

"Yeah, I remember them talking about that, too. But so what?"

"It's too few."

"Come again?"

"Every cell in your body has the same genetic structure. Yet some cells know to become heart tissue, some bone, some skin, just as we said. But the exact instructions with every detail of how to make a heart muscle cell, a brain cell, a kidney cell are so complex they couldn't all be contained in the mere thirty thousand genes that we have. So this information must be coming from somewhere else. We think it's in messages sent by cells already in the immediate neighborhood."

"Say what?"

"Heart muscle cells tell stems in their midst to become new heart muscle. Brain tissue says to the ones that happen to arrive in their vicinity to become brain. Not only that, these messages seem to be carried in the chemicals released by cells when they're injured. We think they also send out a distress signal that attracts the new cells to the site where the repairs are most needed. Hence, they know 'where to go and what to do.' In effect the whole process is an inherent mechanism the body has to repair itself, and all we're doing is harnessing it."

"My God," Coady said. He couldn't believe what he'd just heard. The dread he'd been carrying since he'd felt those first terrible chest pains released its hold. He tried to speak, but felt so overcome by relief that he burst into tears. "I'm sorry," he said a few moments later, "but the idea that part of my heart had died made me think I was already part corpse. To hear now that I can completely beat this thing, be whole again, that's like damn well turning back the clock, becoming young." He wiped his eyes clear of tears. "So when do we do it?"

"Well, here's the rub," Downs said. "We have to wait until your own inflammatory response dies down and is no longer cleaning away the dead tissue left over from your heart attack. Otherwise your macrophages, a type of white cell that acts as a vacuum cleaner to sweep up organic debris, would gobble up the stem cells as well and carry them off."

"How long?"

"About three months ought to do it."

His spirits once more plummeted. "Shit." He didn't say anything else right away, feeling himself shrink into the wheelchair. "Still, considering what you've offered me, it's a deal." He held out his hand to close the transaction.

"You haven't heard it all yet," Norris said. "I'll need to see you in about six weeks to take a bone marrow sample from your femur."

"What?"

"That's where we're going to get the stem cells that we'll use. I'll then culture them through several generations, in order to get a sufficient number by the time Dr. Downs is ready to proceed."

"But I thought you said the stem cells came from embryos."

"In the first trials they did, but not anymore, at least for our purposes here they don't have to. We now use a special type called stromal cells that all adults carry in their femoral marrow. It works just fine."

"On mice maybe. How do you know it'll be okay in humans?"

"Trust us," said Downs, giving him a wink and a flash of that smile that he would follow through hell and back. "We know."

"You're sure about going ahead?" Norris asked her after she had returned Coady to CCU. "This maniac from the Legion of the Lord just might come after you or me next." Since word of the second attack on Steele had swept through the hospital this afternoon and the cops started telling the nurses that the killer might be part of the fanatical antiabortion group, he hadn't been able to think of anything else.

"Relax, Jimmy. We talked about this," she said, keeping her voice low as they walked to his research labs.

"But don't you see? Whoever the guy is, he's on to us. Why else would one of these fanatics kill Hamlin and Lockman? And how did he find out? I'd say Edwards or Blaine is using him to clean house and get rid of witnesses. It wouldn't be hard. These kinds of nuts are already foaming at the mouth over stem cell research as much as they ever did about abortion. They're just chomping at the bit to terrorize researchers the way they have doctors."

"All the more reason for us to go public about doing Coady, Jimmy, tell the world we aren't using fetal tissue. Then this creep and his buddies ought to love us."

"We might not have ten hours, let alone ten weeks if whoever sicked him on Hamlin and the others also pointed him at us."

"So we preannounce. Hold a press conference about the advantages of stromal cells and say human trials are imminent, but we withhold Coady's name, stating patient confidentiality. That'll keep the press off his back until he's well and everything's over. And we stress how noncontroversial the process is since all we're doing is giving him back his own cells and avoiding the whole issue of embryonic tissue. Hell, as far as the actual technique goes, we can make it sound almost as if we're carrying out nothing new—autotransfusion, coronary arterial catheterization, insertion of microneedles into myocardium—claim none of it even needs FDA approval because it's old hat. Just a new application."

Norris once again felt himself giving in to her soothing reassurances. God, she could cast a spell on him, he thought, but all he said was, "We'll need to show them some data."

"Fine. I'll get my unpublished papers for the animal research together, you do the same. We'll look closely at the dates to see what we have to fudge to make some of the research seem recent. Let me know when you're ready." She gave him a quick kiss and went on her way down the hall toward her own office and animal lab.

So sure of herself, he thought, watching her stride away, her head leading and hips sliding freely under her OR greens.

It was so easy for him to submit to her, so easy to let her take charge—in or out of bed. His cheeks burned at the admission. After decades of being adrift with women who could never stand up to him she was a life force, capable of getting astride him and driving them both straight as an arrow to the limits of what they could do. He loved her for it. She carried him free of a becalmed dreariness he'd been wallowing in for most of his life, and he never felt more liberated than when he was under her control—except when he was alone. Then his old doubts surged to the fore. Was he fooling himself into believing he could trust her? He hadn't gone a dozen steps when he began to think the unthinkable: she could have rock-steady nerve because she controlled the killer. She could have set him in motion to free herself from anyone who was able to testify against her.

And, he reassured himself, he would be okay, too. As long as he was useful, or she didn't see him as a hostile witness.

Richard's heart was pounding with excitement. He was once again in medical records, looking now at Downs's morbidity-mortality numbers.

He knew that research with mice the world over had demonstrated how stem cells could do everything from repairing damage in experimentally induced strokes to regenerating myocardium lost to simulated heart attacks. The marked improvements in Hamlin's patients, at least initially, could mean he'd illegally used stem cells. It had never been tried with humans in any authorized experiments, and no one could explain for certain why it worked in mice. Scientists studying the brain hypothesized the stem cells might induce regeneration of existing tissue by serving as a supply house for substances known to stimulate recovery such as growth factors or cytokines. Researchers who had successfully demonstrated how stem cells could actually form new myocardium to replace the old tended to think it was the surrounding normal tissue that directed the process.

Back in ICU, he'd realized that if Downs had been implanting stem cells and it had worked, her outcome statistics might show the same abrupt improvement as Hamlin's.

And they did.

Her overall numbers appeared too good to be true, the incidence of subsequent heart failure being half the average for the country. But how did she do it? "Francesca, you've got some 'splainin' to do," Richard muttered.

Richard knew he was on the right track, but to be prudent he first had to make sure there weren't other explanations for Downs's success rate. After all, new drug regimens were being tried all the time. He'd better look at the charts, the way he had with Hamlin's cases.

But cardiac surgeons could ream out or bypass clogged arteries a lot faster than neurosurgeons could dissect out vascular malformations. And the incidence of heart attacks was about a thousand times that of hemorrhagic strokes from capsular hemangiomas. Compared to the 18 dossiers of Hamlin's that he'd looked at, Downs had 503.

"Jesus," he said under his breath. What a job. But he set out through the stacks to retrieve the files, just as he had the previous night. He might have felt déjà-anxious if it hadn't been for the armed policeman standing guard at the door—and a sense he'd found the hot trail that just might save Kathleen's life.

He awoke with a start in complete darkness. It took him a few seconds to realize where he was.

After entering the hospital, he'd gone directly to the basement wing that housed the Department of Cellular Research, a sprawling maul of large, low-ceilinged laboratories interspersed with warrens of small offices. As he had passed the many open doors, he saw researchers in white coats hunched over their benches or desks, each dwarfed by the massive amounts of scientific equipment surrounding them. No one looked up when he walked by.

It had changed some in the two years he'd been away, but he'd been able to guess what went on in each room by what he saw. Outside one, a wall of cages lined the hallway, some containing white rats, a few of which stood on their hind legs and watched him pass, their pink noses twitching busily through the wire mesh. A few feet farther on was a steel table on wheels loaded with bottles of clear liquid marked chloroform and a big glass jar surrounded by piles of cotton balls.

Death chamber, he concluded.

Next came a lab in which he saw what looked like a kid's chemistry set, flasks connected to one another with coiled plastic tubing and dark red fluid coursing through it. At its center, suspended like a fly caught in a web, was another lab rat, but with a pair of needles in its chest. The lower of the two carried dusky maroon blood to a set of cube-shaped machines. Bright crimson plasma returned to the site below the creature's neck where the root of the aorta and circulatory system would be. The equivalent of a heart-lung machine, he thought.

Through another door he saw rows of benches where there were microscopes with overhead viewing screens, semicircles of scalpels arranged on an assortment of instrument trays, and dissecting basins set in the stainless steel countertops. Self-explanatory.

The adjacent room had a centrifuge the size of an oil drum, racks of automated pipettes dipping repeatedly into trays of sample wells, and more spirals of plastic tubing, these carrying a variety of colored fluids to automated analyzers. This was the end of the line where the remnants of the rodents, reduced to body juices, yielded up their secrets, and their truths would spew over broad sheets of digital printouts enumerating the chemical contents.

Through a set of swinging doors he came to a separate suite of facilities for humans. A small OR, an examining table parked beneath an overhead silver surgical lamp, and the equipment trays lining the stainless steel countertops here covered by sterile green towels. Beside them were open racks of test tubes with red, orange, or blue stoppers. Clear specimen containers filled the glass cabinets mounted on the wall. Ventilation hoods ran the length of the room, stacks of small culture dishes the diameter of poker chips piled within it. What looked like the doors to a half dozen freezer lockers all in a row lined the other side of the hallway. He could feel the chill off them as he passed.

The administrative offices at the end of the corridor looked the same as always. Using his knowledge of the nooks and crannies in the place, he had found an unlocked storage closet opposite Norris's office where he could settle down to wait for his next quarry.

But he had had trouble keeping his eyes open since he hadn't slept for two and a half days. Despite his best efforts, he kept nodding off as he sat in the dark little cubbyhole.

Wide awake now, he snapped on his pen light and stared at his watch in disbelief. It read 8:50 P.M. He'd been asleep over three hours.

Oh, God, he prayed. *Forgive me! Let it not be too late.*

But he knew it likely was. Norris had a reputation for spending every waking hour in the lab, still he'd probably gone home by now. He'd wait a while longer, he decided. God might still deliver Norris to him.

———

Around nine o'clock Edwards decided it was time.

Still raging at Downs, he hurled the statue that had sat on his desk since 1978 against the dark wood paneling beside his bookcase. It hit with the sharp crack of a baseball bat, denting the smooth surface before landing on the carpet with a dull thud.

After taking a last look at the domain he was abandoning, he decided the foot-high figure was probably the only thing he wanted to bring with him anyway. He retrieved it from where it lay and dropped it into his briefcase. Then he slipped out of his office and into the nearest stairwell. At this hour he'd be less likely to meet anyone here than in the elevators.

Reaching the landing for the subbasement, he poked his head through the doorway into the hall.

Nobody.

He stepped into the dimly lit corridor and made his way toward the lab complex where Downs's office was located. His steps echoed loudly along the length of the deserted passageway, but hearing no other footfalls, he figured there wasn't a soul nearby and didn't bother to tiptoe.

On the way he passed the closed doors of many other investigative divisions—virology, bacteriology, pathology—all of which were shut down for the night. Approaching the entrance to the autopsy rooms he accelerated his pace and scooted by, the aroma of formaldehyde tickling the inside of his nose and almost, but not quite, obliterating the sweet odors of decay emanating from the morgue.

He reached the entrance to the area marked DEPARTMENT OF CELLULAR RESEARCH and used the pass card that Norris had issued him in happier, more trusting times to let himself in. "That way you can come and go at all hours of the night," the lanky researcher had told him. "It'll make it easier for you to sneak in as many stolen embryos from your fertility center as you can."

And so he had, slipping down here all hours of the night and secreting frozen alliquots of life from his own liquid nitrogen freezers into Norris's. Babies seemed to want to be born in the wee hours. Since he was so often in the hospital between midnight and dawn doing deliveries, it was easy to carry out these surreptitious side trips without drawing attention to himself. In return, Norris grew the samples through multiple generations, thereby keeping Hamlin and Downs well supplied in pluripotent stem cells. The experience Norris gained culturing them made it possible for him to start harvesting stromal cells, once reports of their unique potential began to appear in scientific journals. The initial patients post-op at Blaine's institute achieved results way beyond expectations, and most returned home, thanks to her aggressive rehab techniques. It had promised to be so perfect, the six of them preparing to make medical history together, yet it had all turned to shit.

Edward's bitterness at the shambles they'd made of their big chance hit him with renewed force.

Well, at least he'd come up with a way to profit from the mess.

He walked by the liquid nitrogen freezers to which he'd brought so many offerings, their chill making him shiver.

Arriving at Downs's office door he tried the handle.

Locked, as expected, and his pass card wouldn't work here.

Taking off his lab coat, he balled it around his hand, then smashed the window with the tire iron. The glass splintered and the shards shattered onto the linoleum floor.

He reached in and turned the handle.

The room was as severe and ascetic as the woman herself. Lining three of the walls were meticulously ordered bookshelves with glass doors where not so much as a pamphlet dared stand at anything less than attention. Several yards of locked filing cabinets bracketed the entrance in which he stood. Her computer sat on an otherwise bare metal desktop, and the only other furniture in the room was a pair of spartan metal chairs opposite her own, a modest swivel back covered in black cloth.

He was looking for a set of compact discs outlining in detail the techniques she'd used to infuse pluripotent and stromal stem cells into her patients. He'd seen these records when she'd presented her data to the group, and knew they were in containers labeled REGENERATION. He went to work on the nearest metal drawer and pried it open.

Lots of paper, but no CDs.

One after the other, he forced his way in, the locks giving with a loud pop each time, but still he found nothing.

He was halfway through when he heard the crunch of someone stepping on glass behind him.

He spun around in time to see a dark-haired man with a broad face and a small mustache stride into the room. He gasped. The man held a machete over his head.

"Doctor Edwards," said the approaching figure, a smile breaking out and making his features appear even wider. "What a surprise to see you here. It saves me the trouble of finding you later."

Edwards heard his own scream as if it came from someone else. The cry quickly diminished to a whimpering noise as he reeled backward, crashing up against a bookcase. Instinctively he raised the tire iron to defend himself, but cowed before his attacker.

He knew that voice, he managed to think before the blade descended. He stared down, unable to believe what he saw until a searing pain roared into his brain and brought his reluctant eyes to focus on the oval void at the end of his forearm. Its opening overflowed with dark red and sent streamers of brilliant crimson arching through the air.

He began to scream. Scarlet patterns sprayed across the walls and ceiling. Out the corner of his eye he saw the man raise the weapon again and sweep it toward the side of his neck. He tried to lean away from the flashing edge, but an explosion of white went off inside his skull and a dizzying blow struck him somewhere under his jaw. It didn't feel like a cut, he thought, relief flooding in. The man must have smacked him with the flat of the blade. And he wasn't yelling anymore. He opened his mouth to beg for his life. Even though he could feel his lips moving, no sound came. That was strange, he told himself as the white light quickly subsided toward black. For an instant he could see the room again—except he was lying on the floor looking up at a body with no head.

16

No matter how often the nurses turned her, she hurt where she lay. By marshaling the minuscule movements she was able to make with her arms and lower limbs she could shift the pressure slightly, but it did little to reduce her pain. A captive to her body and other people's schedules, she wanted to scream. She would have, too, except by the time she raised her hand to her throat, took a breath, and covered the opening, her howl of outrage had been robbed of its spontaneity. What was the point then?

Frustration and anger. Anguish and rage. They kept her adrenaline pumping. And adrenaline kept her up. In Blaine's presence she had felt supremely optimistic. Without her, Kathleen felt deflated.

And Richard only made everything worse. He was pushing her to a place she didn't want to go with all his blather about living together. Playing happy family, she thought scornfully. It would be playing all right, because Kathleen the mom couldn't feed herself, go to the bathroom alone, or even talk properly. Kathleen the lover couldn't even—what? Maybe couldn't even feel?

Her eyes welled with tears that she fought back. Her emotions were on a roller-coaster ride, but the dips kept taking her closer and closer to an abyss, deep, perhaps bottomless, and black. Hopelessness and helplessness lived there. Better to be angry than feel such despair.

She *did* feel angry with Richard. He was a doctor, but still he couldn't have any idea how he'd react to taking care of an invalid. It would be

241

worse than his wife's dying, because there would be no end to it. He was so damned determined to do the right thing he couldn't see the reality, refused to see it. If she tried to send him away he would dig in his big stubborn heels and be more determined to stick than ever. But how to set Richard free in a way he would accept? It was a question she was pondering and crying over as she saw the white curtains enclosing her move slightly, stirred by staff rushing about their business. She kept an ear out for anyone approaching her cubicle, but only the usual noises of ICU sounded from beyond her dimly lit space, the quiet chirp of monitors now as familiar to her as birdsong. At least the nurses wouldn't know she cried. She figured they'd put down the wet spot on the pillow to drooling.

Then she heard the woosh of the main door opening and his unmistakable step as he strode up to the cubicle. Richard identified himself to the policewoman stationed outside, the curtains opened, and he walked in, his face sagging with fatigue. "I think I know what Hamlin did to you," he told her straight off. He took her hand and pulled up a chair. As tired as he looked, his dark eyes sparkled with excitement. "It's stem cells."

"What?"

"He used stem cells on you."

She was incredulous. "Stem cells?"

"He injected them into your brain. An infusion of stem cells. And that's why you're making such rapid progress."

She scarcely noticed his assertion of progress that usually riled her so much. "Stem cells? As . . . from embryos?"

"It's what this whole business is about. Only it wasn't just Hamlin and Lockman. Paul Edwards, our chief of gynecology, has probably been supplying the embryonic tissue these cells came from, and Francesca Downs, one of the cardiac surgeons, has been using them on patients as well, but she's been entirely successful as far as I can see."

"Slow down . . . and start at the beginning."

He leaned close to her, his voice low. "After going through only fifty of her files I already see a pattern. Any patients of hers who suffered heart failure after their heart attacks received a repeat angiogram about three months post-op, the same procedure you had the night of your admission—except the catheter passes into the coronary arteries and they inject dye to see if there are any blockages—common stuff when it comes to cardiac cases. But usually cardiologists only do them if the person shows symptoms of a recurrent obstruction, such as increasing symptoms of angina, or chest pains. From the clinical notes, I gather that many of the people she cathed had no pain at all, or what pain they had remained unchanged and stable."

"So?"

"She's been performing unnecessary procedures, and probably for free. No HMO would pay her for 'just taking a look.' Yet when her patients came back after another three months, in more than half the cases their echocardiograms showed a marked improvement in the contractile strength of the affected myocardium."

"Say what?"

"They had no more heart failure! The second cath could be where she slips in stem cells, and *they* repaired the injured heart wall."

"They can do that?"

"It sure looks like it."

"And let me guess . . . Lockman was the radiologist."

"You got it."

"So that's what . . . they infused . . . into my brain."

"I'm certain of it."

"But why the delay . . . for the cardiac patients? . . . Hamlin did me . . . right away."

"I don't know. I flipped through as many of her charts as I could trying to find the answer to that one, but no luck. What I did turn up was another player in their game."

"Who?"

"A cell researcher named Jimmy Norris. The man's an outsider and a bit of a roué, but in the world of microbiology, he's on the cutting edge in the field of tissue cultures. Who better to hook up with for messing around with stem cells? It's common knowledge around here that he and Downs have been lovers on and off, so it makes for a particularly cozy relationship. What I saw tonight was that his name kept showing up in the charts of patients whom Downs operated on in the last year. He visited nearly all of them. Not in any official capacity. There were no requests for formal consults with any of these people and no explanations as to why he'd have a clinical reason to be interested in them. But I found a couple of notes made by ward clerks that he'd dropped by a patient's room. And two or three nurses reported patients saying that they would be seeing Dr. Norris in his lab about six weeks after discharge for some 'testing' Dr. Downs wanted done. In the records for patients from the previous year there was no documentation of any visits with Norris at all."

"What do you . . . make of it?"

"I've no idea yet, but whatever it is, I'll bet it has to do with his supplying her with the cells she's been using."

"Why not charge . . . all three . . . Edwards, Norris, Downs. . . . Accuse them of . . . performing experimental treatments . . . without official approval . . . or patient consent?"

"I can't. Just because her charts are consistent with the idea, doesn't mean it's proof. Francesca Downs could simply say she hasn't a clue what I'm talking about, and since when is excellence a crime. After all, she'd be on safe ground. There's no records of suspicious DOAs arriving in ER on her list. It's not likely her patients will complain even if we asked them. They're all doing great. So if she and her buddies keep their mouths shut, nobody can touch them except maybe the killer. Obviously the Legion of the Lord crowd aren't hot on anyone doing stem cell work."

Head reeling from all she'd heard, still she was able to seize on what he'd overlooked. "Not if Francesca Downs . . . this guy Norris . . . and the others you mentioned . . . are the ones . . . controlling him."

"What?"

"Why would . . . a fanatic on a rampage . . . against stem cell use . . . try and kill me . . . in a way . . . that would have . . . covered up the whole scam. . . . Or why would . . . that same nut . . . be trying to eliminate you . . . who's on the trail . . . of those using stem cells. . . . It's Downs . . . and her buddies . . . who'd have reason . . . to want us dead . . . before I talked . . . or you found them out . . . not a publicity-craving . . . terrorist. . . . Well . . . tell them for me . . . 'You're too late . . . assholes.' "

She fell silent then, nursing her fury at Hamlin's arrogance, barely listening as Richard pondered aloud what they should do next. Yet the power of what the neurosurgeon had been trying to do filled her with wonder, and in a bizarre way, hope. When Richard finished speaking, he all at once slid his arms around her, kissing her on the mouth for the first time in weeks. It felt sweet, magnificent even, taking her completely by surprise. To her astonishment, she welcomed it, too stunned to do otherwise, and she began to feel what she thought was dead forever. Desire. She wanted him, wanted to move against him, feel his hands touch her as they had before. It terrified her. A thousand questions raced through her head along with a flood of irrational hopes, until, pushing him away, she forced herself to shut everything out—the emotions, the tumult of thoughts—and return to reality. "Please Richard . . . I've got to sleep now. . . . this is all a pretty big shock."

"Don't worry, Kathleen. For the present, whatever cells you received are probably helping you. If Hamlin's other cases are any example, there's an excellent chance you'll have as good a recovery as they did."

It wasn't lost on her how he skated around the DOAs. Maybe it was the sum of all her frustrations, but she wasn't about to let him get away with it. In fact, she damn well wasn't going to let him get away with everything that had eaten away at her since the stroke first hit.

"What good progress?" she demanded. "You call . . . what you see here . . . good progress? Would you be willing . . . to live this way? More to the point . . . if you were like me . . . would you let . . . anyone else near you? And what'll be your reaction . . . waiting for the hammer to fall . . . Watching for me . . . to end up . . . DOA? Will you run?"

His color drained. "Kathleen, I swear, I won't desert you—"

"*I swear . . . I won't desert you,*" she mimicked. "Gimme a break Richard. . . . Who knows what . . . you're going to feel . . . about me . . . years from now? So why should I . . . count on anything?"

"Kathleen, don't."

"Why not? This is the reality . . . chum."

He looked poleaxed.

She watched him swallow a couple of times, and knew she'd really gut-punched him.

Finally he said, "But we've got time to find out why his patients died. Maybe do something about it. What's the matter with hoping for that?"

"Open your eyes, Richard. . . . I'm what's the matter. . . . I couldn't handle . . . your fear . . . your hanging around . . . like a deathwatch." She hadn't meant to lash out, yet something propelled her.

"But—"

"Please! Let me sleep."

His face sagged in the half light, his features reduced to shadowy grooves and gently lit folds.

She wanted to reach up and smooth them away except she hadn't the strength to raise her arm that far. Might never be able to. Before he could utter another word she added, "Go be with the . . . children, Richard. . . . They need you tonight. . . . The police took them . . . to a hotel. Do . . . that for me. . . . And McKnight said . . . he'd drive you. . . . You're to call him. . . . But don't let him . . . question you too long . . . about all this. . . . Chet and Lisa are . . . the priority."

Confused, he studied her. "Of course," he said, and kissed her gently on the side of her face.

She made no attempt to respond. It had to be this way, she told herself. She couldn't harbor false dreams. They would end up tearing her apart.

He'd screwed up again.

He hadn't noticed the name on the door as he'd entered after Edwards. But on the way out he had.

Dr. Francesca Downs was the one person his orders had insisted he spare. He'd no idea why, but the instructions were clear. *Don't harm her; leave her offices untouched; avoid implicating her.*

And now he'd beheaded one of their targets in her office.

Christ! He'd have to move the corpse and clean up the mess.

He glanced at his watch.

It would take most of the night, but he had time. Good thing he'd been an orderly so he knew how to clean up bodily fluids, especially blood. And from his years of working here he had an idea where he could hide a body so it wouldn't be found until at least early next week.

He got to work.

Thursday Morning, June 28

The ringing woke Norris, as usual asleep in a chair in front of the television.

". . . Badges? We ain't got no badges. We don't need no badges. I don't have to show you no stinkin' badges," a big man who wore a sombrero and a cartridge belt across his chest was saying to a grizzled Humphrey Bogart.

Ignoring the movie, he fumbled the receiver to his ear.

"Jimmy, get down to my office."

Downs's voice sounded frightened, even over the phone. He glanced at the clock on top of the TV. It read 7:10. "Why? What's the matter?"

"Just get here."

It took him less than fifteen minutes to reach the hospital, driving across town through only half-jammed streets, shielding his eyes from a blazing sun rising over Queens on the other side of the East River.

He entered the department. Initially, he saw nothing out of order. Some of his staff was already at work in their labs, but as he approached Downs's office he noticed the broken pane in her door and a large sheet of white paper pasted over it. Immediately he thought of all the secret data they kept in her computer and locked away in the cabinets.

When he got closer, his feet crunched on small particles of glass. Someone must have hastily cleaned up the breakage, but hadn't had time to get the gritty pieces.

"Who is it?" Downs demanded before he had a chance to knock, her voice tremulous.

"It's me."

He heard the lock click and the door opened a crack, enough for him to see a pair of brown eyes surrounded by a pasty shade of white as Downs peeked out at him. "Quickly, come inside."

A heavy aroma of rubbing alcohol bit into his nostrils as soon as he entered, and he saw a row of filing cabinet drawers partially opened, their locks bent out of shape. His fears about a break-in were confirmed. What struck him most was the strain in Downs's face. Her lips and cheeks were so tense they appeared to be in rictus. "Don't tell me someone's taken all our records."

"No, I don't think so. Whoever it was only opened a few drawers, and I can't find anything missing. Besides, our stuff's so well encrypted I doubt anyone could crack it."

"There's a way to crack anything," he said, her naive reassurance to the contrary fanning his alarm. Rushing over to one of the drawers and pulling it open, he added, "We've got to make sure nothing's gone. Why would anybody break into your office if they didn't want our research reports? I'll bet it was Edwards or Blaine intending to grab our work and cash in on it." He saw only files of papers and pulled out another drawer.

"Trust me, the CDs are safe. Something else happened here, Jimmy. Something much worse. You smell all that isopropyl alcohol?"

He stopped his search. "Yeah. It hit me as I came in. You been sterilizing your office?"

"Someone has, but not completely. I swear there's a spray of blood on the underside of my desk. There's also spots of it on the walls, in corners, between cracks in the tiles—everywhere. Jimmy, I think there's been a bloodbath in here."

"A bloodbath," he said, astonished.

"See for yourself, damn it!" She pointed toward her desk.

The rawness in her voice grated. He knelt down to inspect the two gray pedestals that served as legs for the cumbersome piece of furniture. He could see streak marks where they had been washed, but sure enough, along the overhang of the desktop itself was a spatter of dark maroon spots. And at his knees he saw a similar discoloration along the seams between the black-and-white squares of linoleum. He got up and went over to the glass doors in one of the bookcases. He found the same reddish grunge filling the grooves in the hinges beside more faint streaks of a recent washing. On the other two cabinets he discovered similar marks and material.

"You're sure it's blood?" he asked, finding it hard to swallow.

"Yeah. I put a scraping under a microscope."

"Human?"

"Sure looks like it. I'm not about to submit it to a hematologist and get a DNA analysis."

"What do you think happened?"

"I don't know. But I'll bet you the maniac who killed Hamlin and Lockman is behind it."

"You think he went after you and got someone else, by mistake?"

"Maybe. Or lured one of his other targets down here, then cleaned it up, leaving enough traces so the police would think I did it."

"Oh?"

"Sure. It makes sense, Edwards or Blaine. One of them's trying to set me up as the mastermind controlling this psycho."

"And you think the blood belongs to the other one?"

"Yes."

"Jesus." He shuddered. "So where's the body?"

"Goddamn it, will you can the questions. I haven't all the answers. For all I know our murderer could have rolled it out of here on a stretcher, loaded it into the trunk of a car, and thrown it into the East River. Do your own figuring for a change and stop acting like a passive wienie."

There were nurses and residents all over the hospital who'd been scorched by her acid tongue. It was part of hospital lore, resented but endured because of her exceptional skills as a surgeon. Until now he'd escaped its heat. His dread that she'd dump him in a heartbeat if it came to saving her own skin resurfaced full force.

"But we'll know which of the two it is if one of them doesn't show up for work today, won't we?" she added, her pale lips pulling into a taut line.

"You're just going to sit around and wait to see who's missing?" he said, his voice as cold as the empty feeling in his gut.

"No. You and I are going to get some toothbrushes and a gallon of isopropyl, then give this place a proper cleaning so not even the cops could find a trace of whoever's blood it is."

Her bossing him around like this no longer felt good. "You think so, Francesca? You should read more of the lab journals. Cops have chemicals that can make even the slightest amounts of blood fluoresce. And you know as well as I that once they find it, it takes little more than a few cells to do DNA testing. If they ever do find a body, tracing it to this office will be a snap."

She went completely still, the way a snake poises before it strikes, and studied him. "Then you better shut up and get busy."

He wanted to walk out on her, but the rage he sensed was smoldering beneath her smirk made him wary. "Okay, Francesca," he said, deciding it best to acquiesce for the moment. He was about to go fetch what they'd need when he heard the sound of approaching footsteps, followed by a sharp knock at the door.

"Yes!" she replied.

"Francesca, it's Richard Steele. I'm here with Homicide Detective George McKnight, and we need to talk with you."

Norris's heart kicked in to triple digit beats. If there was another way out, even a window, he would have bolted. Feeling as trapped as he ever had in his life, he looked to Downs.

She stood stark still. He saw her lower her hands to her sides, take several deep breaths, and swallow once. He'd seen her steady herself in their OR this way, whenever the shit hit the fan and only raw nerve could see her through. "Yes," she replied, her voice instantly coated with several layers of cool civility despite her wildly gesturing at him to keep his mouth shut before unlocking the door.

Steele and the large detective he'd seen around the hospital these last few days stood at the entrance like grim reapers, their faces as drawn as Downs's. He dared not think what his own expression must look like.

"Come in, and be careful of the glass on the floor. Someone broke in here last night and pried open a few of my filing cabinets," she said, managing a smile with a smoothness that took his breath away. "Luckily whoever it was must have been scared off. Nothing's missing, thank God."

The two men entered the modest office making it feel instantly over-crowded. "Well, if you're finished with me, I'll be going, Francesca," he managed to say, knowing he couldn't come close to matching her outer calm. "I'll get maintenance to do the repairs, and have security check how anyone could have gotten in here—"

"Actually, this involves you, too, Jimmy," Richard said, moving to bar his way. "Have you both met Detective McKnight?"

"Involves me?" he croaked, instantly unsure how even to greet the policeman. He held out his hand, but the big man kept his pocketed in an overcoat the size of a circus tent.

"I'm sorry I don't have enough chairs," Downs said. She sounded as if she had a pair of unexpected guests for tea.

"I'll stand," McKnight said, leaning against the broken filing cabinets and eyeing the bent metal around the locks. "I'm just here to provide Dr. Steele with police protection. As you probably know, there already have been two attempts on his life. Why don't the rest of you sit down?"

Nobody took a chair.

"Yes, Richard, I heard. Let me say how shocked—"

"Listen, Francesca, after the attacks on Kathleen and my son, I'm in no mood to be delicate, so I'll get right to the point. I think I've discovered the reason Hamlin and Lockman were murdered, and I think you know it, too. They were playing around with stem cells, weren't they? Infusing them into stroke patients illegally."

Norris thought he would faint. He glanced over at Downs and saw her standing with her mouth open, not uttering a sound. The seconds seemed to slow and elongate. He slumped backward, letting one of the bookcases support his weight.

The movement caught Richard's attention, and like a tiger drawn to the weakest in a herd he swung his headlamp gaze to him. "You must have been supplying them, Jimmy," he said. "I can't imagine anyone else around here with the smarts to culture up the quantities they'd need for two years' worth of work."

Norris felt his face grow flushed. "I . . . I . . . I . . . swear I don't know what you're talking about."

"Then why so flustered, Jimmy?"

"Dr. Steele!" Downs broke in. "We're both 'flustered' because what you claim is just so . . . so . . . unbelievable. And even if your accusations about poor Tony and Matt are true, which I'm sure you have your reasons to believe they are, what evidence is there of Jimmy being involved? Or for that matter, why come to me about it at all?"

"Because I think you've been doing exactly the same sort of thing with your heart patients, Francesca. And your buddy, Jimmy here, has been helping you as well, along with Paul Edwards and Adele Blaine."

This time Norris actually felt the room spin.

"What!" she shrieked. "Why, I'll have you up before the ethics council, charged with uttering malicious slander—"

"Good, because that's exactly where you can explain all those unwarranted caths you performed on patients with no symptoms of increasing angina—"

"You question my competence, Richard, after working with me in ER all these years?" She didn't miss a beat. "Why, I've got the best record in the hospital with my MI patients, and you know it," she continued. "In the country even. And so what if a few extra angios are the price of that excellence. For your information, I received no fees—"

"Spare me, Francesca. I think the lot of you set this nut from the Legion of the Lord on Hamlin, Lockman, Dr. Sullivan, and myself to cover your tracks. So don't waste your time trying to bullshit me."

"No!" Norris heard himself say, the word sounding strangled and far off.

Downs seemed to stop breathing altogether. "Oh, my God, you're not serious?" A look of horror crossed her face. Her incredulity appeared so profound that Norris had no difficulty telling himself it had to be authentic. "Richard, please, you can't think that I'd have anything to do with killing anyone. I've spent my whole career saving lives. I could never be part of that, not for anything."

"Not for anything? Why not to save your career? Or to be among the first to tap the miracle of regenerative medicine? Whatever the reason, you and your buddies have brought a maniac down on me and my own, so you'll forgive me if I don't exactly sympathize."

She grabbed his hands. "Richard, you have to believe me. If I could do anything to stop that murderer, to keep you, Chet, and Dr. Sullivan from harm, I would."

"Then tell me who he is."

"I don't know."

"Damn it, Francesca, stop playing games! The only way you can help yourself out of the mess you're in is to tell me what you know about this killer."

She looked up at him, still clasping his hands, her eyes glistening on the verge of tears and her cheeks flushed. Then the expression on her face slowly vanished, replaced by a blank mask. "I've had enough," she said, "and insist you leave my office immediately."

Norris found the neutrality in her voice chilling.

Richard ignored her and turned on him again. "How about you, Jimmy? Feel like fessing up, now, while you've got the chance to help yourself?" He leaned in until there was less than six inches separating their noses. "After all, it doesn't look good for you. There's a record of your visiting all these patients of hers who, a few months later, seemed to outgrow their heart failure. A lot of nurses noted your comings and goings. Just dropping in for social chats, were you?"

"You'll be hearing from my lawyer," Norris said, trying to mimic the same show of outrage his lover had mustered. He knew as soon as the words were out of his mouth that he'd failed and only managed to make himself sound all the more scared.

"Oh, good, a court of law this time," Richard said. "Maybe we can talk about medical assault, negligent homicide, conspiracy. Let's see, how did it probably work? Edwards supplied the embryos. Jimmy, you harvested and grew the cells for Hamlin and your girlfriend here, then you lured Lockman into the game because you required an angiographer willing to go along with doing the infusions. And, of course, Adele Blaine provided the ideal setting with her institute for you to hustle your subjects away to. That got them far from prying eyes at NYCH. At her institute you could follow them in private and cover up any nasty surprises, no? Except Hamlin's DOAs started coming into ER. What were his reasons for doing Kathleen? Save her life, then out of gratitude I was supposed to go along with hiding his mistakes?"

"Richard, you're out of your mind," Downs said quietly, shaking her head in a perfect show of sadness and sympathy.

Richard studied her. "Oh, am I?" he said after a few seconds. Her sudden calm appeared to unsettle him.

"Yes, you are. And given all that's happened to your son and Dr. Sullivan, I suppose you can be forgiven. But it's affected your judgment and you've read this all wrong."

"Like hell I have!"

He's defensive, Norris thought. And all at once Francesca was smooth as silk again. Clearly she had found a way out.

"I have no idea what Hamlin and Lockman were up to," she continued, "but you were right about Jimmy and me doing stem cell research."

Norris felt his throat tighten again.

Richard went very still.

The cop shifted his weight off the cabinet and leaned forward, his eyes widening with interest.

"Except our work is with stromal cells." She paused, and seemed to savor the look of astonishment on Steele's face for a few seconds. "Last summer a Scandinavian team of scientists succeeded in isolating them from a subject's femoral marrow, and successfully implanted them back into that person's heart. They weren't treating anything, just doing a trial to prove the procedure could be done safely. Since that development, we've been harvesting them from the femurs of an adult mouse, successfully inserting them back into the scar tissue of myocardial infarcts experimentally induced on the same animal, and restoring much of the lost function. In fact, we've been so successful, we're now ready for human trials. All those visits of Jimmy to my patients? We were looking for a suitable candidate. And, recently, we've finally found one who's willing to proceed and try the technique. In fact we were just discussing holding a press conference to announce the news." Her voice held exactly the right blend of enthusiasm and pride.

It was Richard's turn to flush. "Your numbers already show fantastic results for two years, Francesca. And I'll bet if we questioned your patients from the last twelve months, we'd find they've all undergone samplings of their femoral marrows."

"Of course, some have. In addition to our work with mice, we had to be sure we could isolate and culture human stromal cells for when the time came for human trials. All these subjects signed releases showing informed consent, each one stating that he or she was fully aware we were extracting tissue for research purposes that might one day help people like themselves. They also signed a confidentiality agreement."

Richard opened his mouth, but McKnight interrupted.

"Could someone explain that in English?"

"I'm sure Richard can," she said sweetly, "but if you'll excuse me, I really must get to work. With a media event of this magnitude, there's a lot of phone calls to make."

She walked over to Richard and placed a hand on his shoulder.

He watched her fingers the way someone might look at a tarantula.

"Richard, Jimmy and I are as upset as you about this psychotic who's running around. One thing our work might accomplish is a way around such malicious assholes."

Richard glared at her hard enough to bore through diamond. "I'm not through with this, Francesca," he finally muttered, and left the room.

Norris watched him go, and felt himself exhale as if he'd been holding his breath the whole time.

McKnight, who'd gone back to leaning against the cabinet, pushed off it and said, "You should report this break-in to us." He gestured toward the twisted metal around the locks on the files. "We could check for prints, question your staff—"

"But I'm sure it's nothing to do with the murders," she said, offering the man her hand.

He took it, enveloping it in his huge ebony fist, and flashed her a startlingly disarming smile. "Well, now, how could you know that?"

"What happened back there?" McKnight demanded as they walked upstairs.

"She stood her ground. I couldn't touch her."

"What's all this stromal cell stuff."

"I'll tell you over coffee. No matter what she says, I know I'm right about them all being in cahoots with each other. But if she's using stromal cells, then she's bypassed the wrath of the antiabortionists."

"Is that what they call adult stem cells—what all the right-wing conservatives keep calling on scientists to use instead of embryonic tissue?"

"That's right."

"So she wouldn't be a target for the Legion of the Lord."

"If they've done their homework, they should be leaving her alone, but who knows with fanatics like that?"

"Was Hamlin using these adult stem cells as well?"

"I doubt it. His cases would be emergencies. There wouldn't be time to harvest and cultivate the necessary tissue from the patient's own marrow. Norris had to keep lines of embryonic cells at the ready. Otherwise why continue to involve Paul Edwards at all? In fact, even Downs was probably using them up until she learned what the Scandinavians were doing a year ago and switched. Pretty slick, overtly recruiting her patients to donate the marrow she and Norris needed for preparation of the infusions. It makes her story bulletproof."

McKnight whistled. "I see what you mean about our not being able to touch her. But if Francesca Downs is considered a good citizen by those Legion of the Lord creeps, wouldn't that make it easier for her to set them onto Hamlin and Lockman without endangering herself than for Norris, Edwards, or Blaine to do it?"

"I suppose so. What are you getting at?"

"She might even have manipulated the Legion of the Lord's fanaticism to her own ends, convincing them it was in their interest to remove you and Dr. Sullivan as well, so as to keep her secret safe. That way she'd remain free to champion the use of nonembryonic stem cells. The argument should have appealed to at least some of the 'soldiers.' "

"I guess. She also could have simply fed them a story making me part of the stem cell scheme, saying I agreed to cover up Hamlin's DOAs in ER in exchange for his treating Kathleen. But I still don't see your point."

"She's the only one of the bunch who could mobilize the LOTL and have a hope they wouldn't also kill her. Norris, Edwards, Blaine—their risk of becoming targets themselves is too great."

"So?"

"Downs could be acting alone in involving our killer, and she may be sending him after more people than you and Dr. Sullivan."

Richard slowed his pace. "Now that's an interesting way to look at it."

"Nothing special for a cop. Just a matter of trying to hook together opportunity and means as well as motive. I'd say the lady has a big edge over the others on those two counts."

"So what do we do?"

"Her former partners might be getting pretty nervous. What say we talk with them as well."

"You mean maybe they're scared enough to have a chat."

McKnight grinned. "It crossed my mind. You could meet with them in private and—"

"Come on!" Richard turned and started for the elevators.

"Hey, the coffee shop's this way."

"First I want to drop in on Edwards. See how he reacts to a surprise visit."

McKnight hurried to catch up with him. "Okay, but you can't come on the way you did back there with Downs and Norris. That almost verged on police harassment—"

"You didn't say anything."

"I was in the room. One of them could lodge a complaint."

"I'll swear you never said a word. Besides, with Edwards, I won't be leaning on him, just suggesting that not only has Downs unleashed a pack of mad dogs on his buddies, but he might be next. You can go on record again that you're only with me as my police protection."

"That's wafer thin and you know it. My being there scares the shit out of the person you're badgering. Hell, I thought that Norris guy was going to crap himself."

"So, he's got diarrhea, or a guilty conscience. How can any cop-complaints department fault you for that? Ah, here we are." He led the way up a side corridor.

"Speaking of Norris," continued McKnight. "He seems pretty weak. I'd like to question him alone."

"He may be scared, but I doubt he'd betray Downs, even to save his own hide. They've been lovers for over a year, and he's pretty besotted by her."

"You'd be surprised what the inside of a police station can do to love."

Richard smiled. "Maybe. But getting Edwards to rat on her, now that's a real possibility. He's much more addicted to his creature comforts. I bet he'll fold like a lawn chair if he thinks you'll go easier on him. If we can nail Downs with criminal charges based on his testimony, she might be less the Ice Queen we saw back there and more inclined to make a deal as well. Then maybe she'd give us the killer."

A chuckle rolled out from the depths of McKnight's massive barrel chest. "Doc, stick to medicine and let me handle him. You've seen too many gangster movies."

The passage led to where a severe looking woman dressed in a tangerine-colored jumpsuit commanded a desk blocking a set of mahogany doors as high as the ceiling.

"What lives in there?" McKnight whispered. "Godzilla?"

"Dr. Edwards isn't in yet," the woman informed them.

"When do you expect him?" Richard asked.

"I honestly don't know. He's never late, and," she added, a trace of anxiety in her words, "when I phoned his home, the housekeeper said he didn't come in last night."

Alarms went off in Richard, and, judging from the look on McKnight's face, he hadn't taken the secretary's information lightly either.

On their way back to the coffee shop, McKnight said, "By the way, what did you make of that alcohol smell? Is it normal for her office to reek of it like that?"

17

Gordon Ingram paced around his austere office. "Damn! I figured there was something screwy about Hamlin's statistics," he said. "I could shoot myself for not following up on them sooner."

"You knew?"

"Just the general morbidity-mortality numbers. His peculiar behavior around Dr. Sullivan got my antenna up. I wondered if he was over-medicating other cases as well, so I looked up his records. Then that bizarre argument between him and the others in the cafeteria that left him so ashen made me figure for sure there was some kind of trouble brewing, so I checked out all their stats."

You would, thought Richard, getting a sore neck following the man's progress back and forth. Yet it was precisely this suspicious nature and predatory determination that made him the one person in the hospital who might help.

"I was looking for bad news," he continued, "so supergood results were a pleasant surprise. But I still intended to check them out, especially the two recent DOAs under Hamlin's name. The diagnoses bothered me just as they did you. But the ethics caseload has gotten so heavy lately. Everyone's afraid to give an aspirin without a consult, and patient complaints are skyrocketing—well, I don't have to tell you the pattern. Poking through good news looking for problems was a luxury that had to wait."

"So what do we do now?" Richard asked, hoping his question would reign in Ingram's tendency to pontificate and get him focused on specifics.

Ingram flopped back into his chair, breathing heavily, and shoved his wire-rimmed glasses to the top of his head. Rubbing his eyes, he looked tired, more so than he ever had when he'd worked solely in ICU. Always a meticulous dresser, his dark jacket and charcoal shirt complemented his black eyes and hair in the best of style, but the outfit seemed to hang a little looser than usual on his slender frame, enough that Richard wondered if he'd lost weight.

"I suppose we can convene an emergency board meeting," Ingram said, "and demand they call in all Hamlin's patients who we think received stem cells. You say there's only eighteen?"

"Sixteen, not counting the two DOAs."

"It shouldn't be too hard to get MRIs on that many. And we can request exhumation orders and autopsies on the deceased. Finding out why they died will be the first priority."

"Do you think the hospital lawyers will let NYCH admit its liability just like that?"

"I'll argue that the real liability these days is sitting on a possible problem and not being forthright. Tell them we'll have our institutional ass in a sling if we don't warn everyone at risk immediately. Let's just pray we can offer something to prevent the sixteen from ending up like the first two."

Richard thought of Kathleen and winced.

"Sorry," Ingram said. "I didn't mean to be callous. You must be worried sick about Dr. Sullivan."

"What I'm worried about most right now is finding the killer before he gets another notion to attack her or tries again to get at me through our kids. For that I need Francesca Downs. I think she may have been using the son of a bitch to rid herself of potential witnesses."

Ingram flipped his glasses down onto his nose and looked at Richard as if he'd let out a bad smell. "You think what?"

"You heard me."

"Francesca in league with a killer? You're out of your mind."

"No I'm not. You saw her numbers. If you take a look at her individual charts, there's no other explanation but that she's been using stem cells for the last two years, probably stromal over the last twelve months."

Ingram pursed his lips and slipped his glasses back up on his forehead, then seemed to contemplate his bare desktop. After a few seconds he looked directly at Richard. "Suppose I bought the story of her using stem cells, which I'm not saying I will until I've looked at all her records myself. It's still a hell of a leap from there to her recruiting a homicidal zealot to get rid of people who might turn her in. Do you have proof of that?"

"No. Just that she's got motive, means, and opportunity."

"That's cop talk. Don't tell me *they* buy your theory."

"Not exactly."

"Not exactly? Are they doing anything about it? Bringing her in for questioning? Making her an official suspect as a conspirator in the killings?"

"No."

"So they haven't any proof either, but are thinking about it."

"You could say that."

He leaned back in his chair and exhaled his frustration. "Homicide detectives thinking the worst of her I can understand. It's their job. But you, Richard. Christ, you've worked with her. I don't condone her violating the usual protocols if she's done what you say with her patients, but she's a kid at heart and she's got stars in her eyes. Maybe she's capable of taking a big shortcut to grab the fame and glory. I mean, you can understand the lure, the potential of this stuff to give people their lives back is so magical, it's a wonder more doctors haven't jumped the gun. After all, just getting approval of phase-one clinical trials can take a year, and back when you say she started, the conservatives in government were threatening to ban stem cell research altogether. So yeah, I can see her rebelling against the rules. But commit murder to cover up for it? Never. She's been a celebrant of life in everything she's ever done, and you know it."

Richard said nothing. The man's words resonated deeply with what had always been his own instincts about the woman. But he had other instincts, too, ones forged in the crucible of ER where he couldn't allow himself to be swayed by feelings, where he had to be ruthlessly analytical and consider all diagnostic possibilities, however unpalatable they might be—or fatal mistakes would be the result. McKnight's assertion that Downs had motive, means, and opportunity couldn't be ignored, whatever Ingram said.

Except an inner voice cautioned that he wasn't in ER now. Maybe in this case relying solely on logic was misleading in itself. He smiled, remembering how Luana had always warned him against measuring life outside emergency with a clinical yardstick.

"As for Jimmy Norris," Ingram continued, "he's also a bit of a dreamer, an idealist. Even though everyone knows he's so bewitched by Francesca she can lead him around by the nose, he's hardly a killer either."

Richard's instincts also had no problem with that conclusion.

"Now Paul Edwards and Adele Blaine, those two would carve up their own mothers if it proved to be in their interests. I wouldn't put it past one or both of them to unleash some crazy assassin to save their own skins. Especially with the financial rewards they'd have at stake."

Richard had been so preoccupied with the who, what, and how of the case, he hadn't given much thought to the money details, other than thinking there must be a ton of it to be made off this stuff. If anybody could explain the skinny of it to him, he'd pick Ingram. Ethicists by the nature of their turf come face-to-face with every scam going. "Suppose you tell me your take on the economics of it all, Gordon. I'm afraid I don't have much imagination when it comes to getting tricky with the market aspects of the healing profession."

Ingram grinned as he usually did when offered an opportunity to show his erudition about anything. It was a lip-licking, savoring, *I'm going to enjoy this* kind of smile. "Trust me. The potential for profits from stem cell products is nothing short of staggering. I sit on committees reviewing the submissions for clinical trials, and these days biotech labs are crawling all over each other to be the first with commercial offerings of different cell lines. Everything from preparations to regenerate brains and nerves to infusions for restoring hearts, kidneys, bones, pancreases, and livers—well, you know the possibilities, we've been reading about them for years—they're rushing them all to market. And what a market."

Richard chuckled. "Baby boomers. All us baby boomers refusing to accept mortality are ready to pay anything so we won't grow old and die."

Ingram smiled. "Exactly. And as a result, private pharmaceutical companies are not only after guys like Norris who could harvest and successfully replicate cells, they need doctors like Francesca and Hamlin willing to refine techniques for their clinical use. So given that Paul Edwards and Adele Blaine have always been the kind of doctors who are preoccupied with the business side of medicine, I suspect the only reason they're involved in this at all is that they put together some sort of commercial package to take care of the entrepreneurial part of things—say, such as secretly selling the findings to one of these labs. And when Hamlin's shit hit the fan, maybe those two decided to eliminate witnesses to assure they'd remain out of jail and have a chance to enjoy the returns on whatever deal they cooked up."

Richard played with the idea that Downs and Norris acted frightened not from fear of getting caught, but of getting killed for what they knew, by Edwards and Blaine.

"Okay," Richard said finally. "Suppose it has gone down the way you say. Edwards may have disappeared, flown the coop. He hasn't come in, and his secretary says his housekeeper reported he wasn't home last night. For the moment, then, that leaves Adele Blaine. But she'll be disinclined to admit anything because there's nothing to connect her with the others apart from the patients going to her institute afterward. So I still need Downs, for what she knows. With her testimony against those two, maybe the police could at least pressure Blaine into telling us who this killer is in exchange for a lighter sentence."

"Sounds complicated."

"It is," said Richard, leaning forward in his chair and rubbing his face with his hands. "To make matters worse, I'll bet by now she and Norris are all lawyered up after our set-to this morning and won't talk to me or anyone about this business unless they're forced to. That's where you come in."

"Me?"

"Yeah. You could officially sweat her, put her on the hot seat for all those extra angiograms she did. Force her to answer questions. Maybe that would shake her up enough that she'd let something slip. You could even appeal to her celebration-of-life side, challenge her to fess up and help stop a killer."

"You know as well as I do that Francesca's got ice in her veins when it comes to a crisis. An ethics hearing isn't exactly going to set her trembling in her OR boots."

"I know, but it's all I've got right now. As I said, it's anybody's guess what this guy's going to do next if we don't grab him fast."

He nodded. "Of course. I'll do what I can."

Having succeeded in getting what he came for, Richard rose from his chair. "By the way, I owe you big-time for taking care of Kathleen's tracheotomy. So much has happened since you helped out that night, I never got back and thanked you properly."

Ingram gave a dismissive wave of his hand. "Glad to be of service. Dealing with airways and tissue is so refreshingly clear-cut compared to right and wrong, it's like a vacation for me."

Richard smiled at him. Sometimes the yearning in the man's eyes for his days of being a tireless lion with the physical stamina to take on all that ICU could throw at him was painful to look at.

"By the way," Ingram said, "did any of Hamlin's patients strike you as more appropriate to start with than others, in terms of giving us the best chance of finding out what he did to them?"

"Not really. But there's one case I was in on from the beginning. My having had hands-on involvement might give us an advantage in spotting something out of line."

"Sounds good. Remember the name?"

"Abraham Paxton."

"I'll let you know as soon as we get him in."

2:10 P.M.

Richard heard McKnight's rumbling voice when the doors to ICU slid open.

". . . but there's no need, now that we know what Hamlin was doing—"

"Do you know . . . who the killer is . . . where to find him?"

To his surprise he could also make out Kathleen's voice from the entrance, it was so much stronger.

"No, not yet. And that's a good reason to stay away," McKnight answered.

"Stay away from where?" asked Richard, parting the curtains and stepping into the cubicle. To his surprise he found Jo O'Brien was also there. She sat protectively by Kathleen's side on the bed, her glasses parked halfway down the bridge of her nose. Jo's stare over the top of the gold rims was as bristling as her short gray hair. Kathleen's gaze was just as pointed. Uh-oh, he thought, recognizing a common front when he saw one.

McKnight spun toward him, a look of relief passing over his dark face. "Dr. Sullivan's still insisting on going into Blaine's institute as a patient."

"What?"

"And I'm going with her," Jo said.

"Wait a minute—"

"It's all arranged . . . I've hired Jo . . . as a private nurse."

"But why?"

"Because I'm not . . . waiting for . . . another attempt . . . on the children . . . because this sick monster . . . can't get . . . at you or me. . . . I'll lure him . . . to a trap instead."

"But Chet and Lisa are under police protection."

"That doesn't . . . always work."

"It's a secure hotel. I left them there this morning. They're well guarded."

"This guy . . . seems to have a way . . . of getting past police."

McKnight's jaw clenched at that one, but he said nothing.

"So you'd use yourself as bait?" Richard continued, realizing he was on his own as far as carrying on the argument. "That's nuts."

"Think about it, Richard. . . . You told me yourself . . . Blaine's even less likely . . . to talk . . . than Downs or Norris. . . . So let's change tactics. . . . If she's behind the killer . . . let her try . . . to set him on me . . . at her institute. . . . If she does . . . Detective McKnight's people . . . can grab him."

"Ah-ha! You just said police protection might not work."

McKnight looked affronted, but he stayed stubbornly silent.

"Better it fail . . . with me . . . than Chet and Lisa."

Richard swung over to Jo. "Surely you're not going to go along with this?"

"I think Dr. Sullivan is going to go to Adele Blaine's whether we agree or not," the grandmotherly woman said in a voice that had the iron determination of a marine. "I'm just going to help her the best I can. A nurse can blend in and still be close enough to spot any funny stuff."

"But you being there will put Blaine on guard."

"She's already on her guard, wouldn't you say? Especially if Downs or Norris has already talked to her. From what I understand, with all due respect, you were about as subtle as a cruise missile with those two this morning."

"Oh, Jesus," said McKnight, his eyes rolling.

Clearly Kathleen had told Jo everything.

"It's one thing to be guilty of a plot to use stem cells on unsuspecting patients," Jo went on. "It's quite another to be manipulating a psychopath to commit murder. If she's only the former, her nervousness about having Kathleen, me, and the police around will be nothing compared to her fear she's become a target as well. We might even persuade her that it'll be safer if she comes clean and gets protection from him herself."

"And if it's . . . the latter . . . well . . . as I said . . . the police will be ready. . . . Either way . . . it's our best chance . . . to grab this guy."

Richard gaped at them both. He was outnumbered and out-argued. They'd rehearsed this, he thought, incredulous at Kathleen's determination to put herself in harm's way. But he had to admit he'd do exactly the same thing if he thought it would draw out this maniac and lead to his capture. "Look, Kathleen," he said, "I can see I'm not going to change your mind right now. Just give me a chance to come up with a better idea."

"You do . . . what you think best. . . . It changes nothing . . . as far as . . . my plans are concerned."

He found himself swallowing and casting about for a reply. She was distancing herself from him again, just like last night. It left a hollow burning in his chest, as if she were slowly withdrawing a knife.

"So, Detective, since I'm going to be around, shouldn't we liaise, or something?" said Jo, mercifully breaking the frosty silence that had settled into their tiny space. "Your people call my people, that kind of thing."

"Really Mrs. O'Brien—"

"It's Miss O'Brien."

"Ah, yes. As I started to say, Miss O'Brien, civilians have no place in a police operation—"

"Nonsense. You use informants all the time. Not that I'm a snitch, but the precedent for turning to the public for help is there. Now this is where you can reach me," she said, snapping a folded piece of paper out of her breast pocket and giving it to him, "my home number."

She wrote it out beforehand, Richard thought. Yet another detail in her and Kathleen's well-prepared plan.

McKnight seemed about to try and give it back, then shrugged, and slid it inside his jacket. "Good afternoon, ladies," he said with a nod of his head. "I've a three o'clock debriefing with my officers." His big frame left the curtains hanging open after he shoved his way through.

He was halfway to the exit when Jo leaned over to Richard and gave him a wink. "Tell me,"she said in a stage whisper that would have carried to the back row of the Lincoln Center opera house, "Is there a Mrs. McKnight?"

4:00 P.M.
NYCH Lecture Amphitheater

Though ostensibly for the media, the assembly had attracted every physician, resident, and intern in the hospital who didn't absolutely have to be somewhere else. Packing themselves into a high semicircle of steeply raked seats, they created a wall of white before Francesca Downs, who stood on the small stage at their feet. She also wore a lab coat, but unlike the creased, wrinkled garb that usually marked the end of a busy day on the wards, hers appeared crisply pressed, elegant almost, and a red business suit underneath set off her blond hair and brown eyes.

The cameras must love her, Richard thought as he looked down at the array of media surrounding the slender woman, her face flushed a radiant gold, her voice assuming the elegiac tones of someone summing up.

". . . and so, ladies and gentlemen of the press, as we cross this exciting threshold into a world of medicine where we can regenerate and restore ourselves, I invite you to imagine the possibilities. Victims of heart disease who can't walk across the room without getting short of breath might once more regain a youthful stride. A productive and healthy old age could become routine as researchers apply the applications of stem cell therapeutics to other fields . . ."

It was certainly exciting stuff, Richard granted. He thought of all the patients he'd seen who would otherwise end up battling to breathe, their lungs filling with fluid as they raced every few weeks to ER to save their very lives. He found himself seeking out Gordon Ingram in the audience, wondering what possibilities he must be imagining. But Ingram sat motionless, leaning forward, his chin propped on his hand, his thin face inscrutable. The guy had to be feeling excited, Richard thought. ICU provided a showcase of what stem cells could prevent, both for themselves and their patients. He let his own imagination roam over the possibilities. How many people might now be spared a relentless decline into end-stage heart, kidney, or liver disease, hopelessly clinging to life with a sodden body invaded and drained by machines, the only prospect death? Even Ingram's personal fate as set out in whatever scars were on his own myocardium could be rewritten.

". . . speedier and more complete recovery from devastating strokes of all kinds, whether they be hemorrhages, embolic, or atherosclerotic . . ."

Yanked back to the less than glowing prospects of Kathleen's future, Richard let his gaze drift down to where Jimmy Norris sat at an otherwise empty conference table behind Downs. The man repeatedly shifted in his chair and seemed self-conscious, his eyes continually searching the crowd in front of him. He looked as if he weren't entirely certain what some of them might do.

". . . regeneration of myelin around the nerves stripped bare by MS, restoration of bony surfaces ravaged by arthritis, and possible cures for diseases such as diabetes. Thank you very much."

Applause broke out, but not as enthusiastically as Richard would have predicted, given the momentous message everyone had just heard. Instead it quickly dissipated into a low discontented rumbling as the white-coat set headed for the exits.

"Bloody dog-and-pony show," someone muttered, shoving past him. "Didn't tell us any specifics. And precious little science . . ."

". . . fucking circus. They're a few in administration who ain't happy with her either. She apparently called the media on her own without going through channels . . ."

". . . I'm surprised at Downs, pulling a publicity stunt like this. She'll be on the talk shows next . . ."

But there was nothing muted about the dozens of people dressed in civilian clothes who converged on her with cameras flashing and fistfuls of microphones waving in her face. Their shouts filled the room.

"Will stromal cells deflect attacks from groups such as the Legion of the Lord?"

"Were Doctors Hamlin and Lockman working with you?"

"Were their murders or the bomb attack on Dr. Richard Steele's house related to stem cells in any way?"

Her face quickly lost its warm hue. "Those matters are better discussed with the police," she said. "I'm here to discuss science."

Their questions grew more strident.

"Why have you not identified the prospective patient?"

"Because he's very ill and has a right to privacy."

"Will stromal cells be as potent as those originating from embryos?"

"I can only say that in the case of restoring heart muscle they seem to work fine."

"Are you calling for a halt to the use of live embryos as a source for stem cells?"

"Of course not."

There wouldn't be much science discussed in this free-for-all, thought Richard, moving down the aisle against the current of all the doctors who were leaving. Making his way to where Downs continued to hold court with the reporters, he saw Norris's restless gaze lock onto his progress. For a second it looked as though Norris might move forward to head him off, but a stocky reporter with bushy black hair who'd been questioning him laid a restraining hand on his arm and kept his attention.

As soon as Downs spotted Richard she blanched, her eyes widening with alarm. She continued to engage the reporters, yet seemed more hesitant with her replies and kept sliding uneasy glances in his direction. Finally she said, "Excuse me, someone is signaling me that I've got a case in ER. Dr. Norris will have to answer the rest of your questions." Before anyone could protest, she broke free of them, took Richard by the elbow, and led him in the direction of the nearest exit. "For God's sake, Richard, not here!" she whispered as she hurried him along.

"Relax. I just came to say maybe I judged you too harshly yesterday. The Francesca I thought I knew wouldn't kill anyone."

She stopped in her tracks. "You're serious?"

He nodded.

Relief suffused her face. "Thank God, you finally believe me—"

"Oh, I still think the lot of you were using stem cells on unknowing patients. What's changed is that I'm willing to consider it's Blaine or Edwards who unleashed a madman to cover their tracks."

Her eyebrows snapped into another frown. "Really, Richard—"

"Hey, aren't you Dr. Steele?" interrupted a woman with a video camera standing outside the ring of reporters that had now besieged Norris.

"No, I'm the orderly," Richard answered, grabbing Downs by the arm and leading her the rest of the way to the door. "We need a cardiologist in CMU immediately."

Entering the corridor he pulled her to a recessed cubbyhole housing a coffee machine. "And the Francesca I knew wouldn't stand by and not do everything in her power to prevent this nut from killing again," he whispered, feeding the slots with enough quarters to buy them both cappuccinos. "So give the police what they need to press Blaine about who the killer is. Or Edwards for that matter, if we ever find him."

She glanced to the right and left as she sipped the coffee he'd just handed her. For the moment the passageway remained free of anyone within earshot. "Okay, Richard. Suppose you're right about Hamlin, Lockman, Edwards, and Blaine. I still can't help you."

"You can't stop a killer?"

"I won't put myself in jail for something I had nothing to do with."

"Cut the crap, Francesca. And it's not so much jail you have to worry about. It's this killer. Don't think your going public about stromal cells will protect you from becoming one of his targets if that's what this press conference is all about. You're in as much need of police protection as Kathleen and me. All Blaine or Edwards have to do is tell him you were once using embryonic tissue, and you'll be in his sights if you're not already."

"Trying to frighten me won't change my mind, Richard. If he kills me, so be it, as long as my work succeeds, intact and untainted."

"What?"

"You heard me."

"You'd rather die than admit what happened?"

She grimaced. "Of course I don't want to die." The lines around her eyes and mouth softened. "Richard, I'm going to try and make you understand, make you see why I couldn't ever do what you're asking."

"I'm listening."

She took another sip. "Suppose, just for argument's sake, I've done what you suspect. But unlike Hamlin, who was in too big a hurry and willing to cut corners he'd never have gotten away with in a properly monitored study, I did my trials on animals, refined a procedure that worked, and took all necessary steps to make sure I would, above all, 'do no harm.' "

"Except you left out informed consent."

She ignored the jibe. "If however, on the eve of delivering the benefits of this work to the world, I had to testify against what he did, there's no way I could keep my technique from getting lumped in with his, at least in the public's eye. His mess, by association, would cast a cloud of suspicion over my results, no matter how impeccable they were, and a miraculous treatment that could save millions of lives a year might be discarded along with his garbage, or seriously delayed at the very least. I couldn't risk that, even to save my own life."

"So you admit you've used stem cells on patients?"

"I admit nothing. I'm simply trying to persuade you to back off, trying to explain as nicely as I can how even if your fantastic story were true, I can't let myself get caught up in other people's mistakes."

"But this guy nearly killed my son."

"Then go after him. Make Blaine tell you who it is. Just don't jeopardize a breakthrough of this magnitude by bad-mouthing me."

"You heartless bitch!"

"Yes, I suppose I am, from your point of view," she said, her voice as cool as if she was discussing the weather.

She was nuts, he thought. A fucking martyr in waiting. A prima donna on a mission. He couldn't imagine a single other thing he could say that might change her mind. Against this kind of resistance, his idea of trying to shake her up by an ethics review board was a joke. "Then at least tell me this. Have you or Norris warned Blaine or Edwards that I'm onto them."

"Now why would I do a thing like that?"

"Francesca!"

"Of course not. At least I haven't. And I doubt Jimmy would either."

"Do you know where Edwards is?"

"No, Why would I—"

"Have you any idea why Hamlin's two patients died?"

"No. I doubt even Hamlin knew. If he did, he sure never told me." She gave a little smile that even the Mona Lisa would have envied. "But I'm the last person he'd confide his screwups to. He knew I wasn't a big fan."

"Dr. Downs," a woman coming out of the amphitheater called.

Richard recognized Edwards's secretary.

"They told me inside you'd come out this way," she said, stepping in front of Downs. "There's someone phoning long distance for you from Mexico City."

"For me? I don't understand."

"It's a Dr. Ramiros. He heard your press conference on CNN, and wants to talk with you."

"Why me?"

"He initially demanded to speak with Dr. Edwards, but when I explained we'd no idea where he was, the gentleman insisted he speak with you immediately. Says he's the CEO of an outfit called Fountainhead Pharmaceuticals."

"Oh, Francesca, there you are," called another woman, also exiting the amphitheater. Richard had seen her over the years in the clerical pool at the cardiology department. "I've just received a slew of messages for you and Dr. Norris. Every corporate drug company in the country seems to be after you."

Downs looked truly puzzled.

"Congratulations," Richard said. "Your little performance today has unleashed a bidding war."

"Oh, my God! That's not what I intended."

"Then you were naive." He spun on his heel, cheeks burning, and returned to the amphitheater, unsure now if even in her moments of apparent frankness she hadn't been conning him.

But what infuriated him the most was her cold self-assurance that he couldn't touch her—especially since she was right.

Back inside the large room he looked for Norris, hoping to provoke a confrontation with him that might prove more productive. Then Richard saw him disappearing through one of the far exits with the bushy-haired reporter he'd been talking to earlier.

Even researchers, he knew, tended to vacate their labs by five on a Friday evening. This said, he kept Norris talking for a half hour longer, just to be sure the place was deserted. The man seemed especially eager to show off his own works, probably from his feeling a little jealous of all the attention paid Francesca Downs. After a request to actually see stromal cells, in no time the scientist was hunched over the eyepiece of a microscope and projecting fuchsia-colored slides of pulsing cardiac tissue onto an overhead screen. "We don't let them reach this stage for the injection into the host's myocardium, of course," he explained. "But as long as the tracks of undifferentiated cells we lay down in the scar tissue also have contact with normal surrounding heart muscle, they'll receive their orders to form new cardiac cells, link up with each other, and start pumping, exactly like this . . ."

It would be a simple matter to step up from behind, yank his head back by the hair, and slit his windpipe with a scalpel.

Not enough to kill. Simply to render him silent, exactly as he had with Lockman. Because for Jimmy Norris, mass executioner of the Lord's seed, he had a special vengeance in mind, and hours to carry it out.

". . . in a matter of weeks we see the first signs of improvement, but full benefit, enough to make a clinical difference and increase the strength of a living heart, takes months."

He fingered the instrument's handle in his pants pocket, sliding the plastic sheath off the razor edge, and moved closer, eyeing the man's neck. The skin looked leathery, the sort toughened by sun and weather, and might prove hard to cut. He also noticed wiry gray bristles from the lower edge of the man's beard extending below his Adam's apple to where they would interfere with a sideways stroke.

"The patient who we'll be treating," Norris went on, "ought to feel a profound reversal of his heart failure after ninety days." Norris smiled proudly and looked up from the microscope at his guest. In turn the man approvingly beamed at the researcher and moved as if to give him a hug.

Norris never saw the scalpel.

His visitor had reached around and brought its tip to the hollow below his voice box from the other side of his head, grinning as he made the move.

The pain burned all the way down Norris's chest and up to his ears. He attempted to scream, but only a massive hissing noise exploded out the front of his throat. Instinctively his hands flew to the wound and clasped the lacerated opening, blood spilling down his shirt.

But surprisingly little, he reassured himself, frantically exploring the damage, his fingers awash in wet warmth. The major vessels had been completely spared, he realized. He needn't die from this. He looked into the wildly exuberant face of the man still grinning at him. Or was he simply sentenced to remain alive longer than Lockman?

Before he could start to struggle, a quick pull toppled him and his stool backwards, dashing his head against the linoleum floor. The blow set off a blazing light inside his brain, but didn't knock him completely unconscious. He could hear a ripping sound and feel his arms and legs being taped together.

"Now I can take my time with you," he heard his captor say from far too close, and he could sense a warmth against his cheeks that had a sour smell.

He snapped open his eyes; the man's face floated inches above his own. He tried to wrench himself free, straining and bucking against his ties. He again attempted to yell, producing only rasping noises out of his windpipe.

"Do you understand why you are to be punished, Dr. Norris?" the man demanded, continuing to hover over him.

Norris violently shook his head and managed to back up a few feet.

"Then I'll cite your crimes," his captor continued, scurrying forward, keeping them almost mouth to mouth. "You are guilty of destroying the Lord's seed, ripping out the cells that would form their hearts, their brains, their eyes, their very limbs . . ." He paused. "It's a long inventory of debts to pay."

Norris heard himself letting out loud chuffs of air and felt tears running down his cheeks. The fire in his throat spread to his face, and a coppery taste filled his mouth, making him choke. He started to shake his head. No! No! No!

"But the Lord is quite clear on the rendering of such accounts."

The blade flashed under the fluorescent lights.

"Do you recognize me, from when I used to work here?"

Norris gave another shake of his head.

He reached in his pocket and pulled out the worn photo.

"Recognize him?"

Norris seemed to study the picture. Eventually he shook his head.

"No? Well, it doesn't matter. He was a lot younger then, and the pictures in the paper when they killed him didn't do justice to the man. One hell of a soldier though. It was him who taught me how to shoot. I helped him pick off a half dozen abortionists before they cornered him. Happened outside of Rochester after our last job. He held off the troopers long enough for me to get away, then took his own life rather than be captured. But he'd be proud of my taking the fight to guys like you. 'The next war' he used to call it."

Norris was passing out again.

"Hey! Wake up. Tell me, have you had enough? Do you want to die now?"

His victim swallowed, sending rivulets of blood out the corners of his mouth. After a few seconds he nodded yes.

"Well, that's just too bad, because I won't be letting you off that easy. You get to be buried alive with your old pal Edwards. You and all your pieces. It'll be days before they find you, plenty of time for you to repent before finally meeting your maker. By then the others on my list will be dead. Maybe you'll linger long enough and be the last to go, and they'll all be waiting to greet you in hell."

Norris parted his lips and mouthed the same word over and over. It took a few minutes, but eventually the shape of what he was saying became clear.

Who?

"Who sent me? Besides God?"

He nodded.

"Don't worry, Jimmy. If I have my way, she'll die, too. That kind of woman doesn't obey. That kind of woman violates His natural order of things and the female's place in it. That kind of woman drove my father to his death and abandoned me. I'll take care that her sort pays any way I can."

The lips moved again.

Who?

"Francesca, of course. She used you Jimmy. And I'll bet she didn't always use stromal cells. Tell me the truth. Didn't Edwards and you supply her fetal tissue the way you did Hamlin?"

The man's tears came again.

"My, my, still protecting her, even after she's betrayed you?"

Norris doubled his efforts to move, writhing his way between two workbenches where he knew there was a phone. As he tried to raise himself up, his tormentor knocked him down again with a vicious kick to his shoulders.

As he lay on his back, thrashing his head, choking and gurgling on his own blood, his lids clenched shut against the imminent cut of the blade, he heard the snaps of a briefcase open, followed by the high-pitched whine of a bone saw.

It took him hours to clean up and dispose of Norris the way he'd planned. Then he wrapped up his bone saw with the white sheet before packing it in his briefcase, changed his clothing, and simply left the hospital through one of the maintenance doors.

Safely back in his new lair, he checked his e-mail. Well, well, he thought, recognizing from the logo of an East Village Internet café that his informant had seen fit to contact him again. He clicked on the accompanying paper clip insignia to open the attached document. It contained a portion of the hospital's admission and discharge records along with detailed instructions about what he was to do next. And there was a commendation to him for having dispatched Edwards.

Francesca Downs? he wondered, still not certain, despite what he'd told Norris solely in the hope it would drive the man mad as he died. Whoever it was, he wondered how she or he would like his latest work?

After rereading everything carefully, he lay down on his bed and thought well into the night about how best to proceed. Despite the fact he suspected this sender of still having a private agenda, it was a good plan, one that would take out the final three targets and wrap everything up in a most public, symmetrical way. At last His message will be unequivocally clear, he told himself, once I make sure the press gets it right. He reviewed his ideas for the communiqué he would issue, outlining the crimes of the executed and warning there would be more of the same for any doctor, patient, or institution that dared harm human embryos for any reason. And the plan involved his finally meeting the informant.

So much the better. If it was Francesca Downs, he'd execute her as well.

He set his alarm for six A.M., and fell into a deep, dreamless sleep.

18

"**D**r. Sullivan, the ambulance is here for your transfer to Dr. Blaine's institute."

Kathleen struggled to open her eyes. She'd been dozing off and on for an hour since they'd given breakfast, a bottle of beige sludge through a tube into her stomach. "Now? But I thought . . . Dr. Blaine meant later today . . . at least. . . . It's not a full . . . forty-eight hours—"

"Your numbers are good—the residents cleared them at rounds this morning with the staff doctors—and all the transfer orders are written. I'd think you'd be glad to be out of here."

"You've got . . . that part right . . . but—"

"Am I coming, too?" asked the policewoman who'd taken over the morning shift. She gave her red hair a shake. It hung like tiny flames over the collar of her dark blue uniform.

"I think so. . . . Detective McKnight . . . insisted . . . I would have protection . . . there as well."

"I'll have to check with him." She put on her hat, then walked over to the nursing station and picked up a phone.

"I'll notify Dr. Steele," said the nurse, busily bundling up the few toilet articles that Kathleen had been allowed to keep at the bedside.

"Yes . . . if you don't mind. . . . He'll want to know. . . . And could you tell Jo O'Brien as well? She'll be . . . in ER."

"What about the patient consent form? We've got strict orders from

279

him that we do nothing with you without his okay. Should I wait until he signs for you and approves the transfer?"

The question irritated her. "No . . . that won't be necessary. . . . I'm the patient . . . after all. . . . It's me who decides . . . these things now."

The nurse shrugged. "Suits me. If we lost this ambulance waiting for him, I don't know when we'd get another. Heading into a weekend, they get busy on the road with real emergencies." The nurse helped her with the signature. "What about these personal belongings? Do I ship them with you or pass them onto him?"

She somehow found this question annoying as well. "With me, please."

As they transferred her IV bottles, tubes, and monitors to the waiting stretcher, she wondered about her resentment at their wanting to refer everything to Richard. It shouldn't have bothered her—after all, she'd welcomed his vetting what they did with her in the beginning. But she didn't want that anymore, she thought, oddly troubled at how quickly her emotional reflexes had fallen in line with her decision to . . . to what really? Not break off, but rather distance herself so he'd be free to leave. Come on, Kathleen, she told herself. You have to be consistent. She'd always taken pride in making her head rule, so why should this be any different? Of course her feelings toward Richard would shut down as she pulled away. They had to.

She sighed. She supposed it was all part of the necessary process, even one that started in her head. Yet it saddened her. She'd so loved him and his caring.

The nurses clamped a set of oxygen tanks to the side frame just in case.

"All set?" the attendant asked.

"All set."

8:15 A.M.

Department of Radiology

"Hi, Doc," said the young man lying on the stretcher in an examining gown. He propped himself on his elbows and added, "Long time no see."

Richard couldn't reconcile the handsome smile with the distorted features and twisted gaze that had stared up at him during the "Hail Mary" intubation a little over a year ago. He could spot a few subtle asymmetries in the folds bracketing his former patient's mouth, but otherwise saw no major defects in the movement of his head or eyes. A pair of walking canes leaning against a nearby counter, however, testified to more significant permanent damage.

"Well look at you," Richard exclaimed. He stepped over and shook the man's hand. The returning grip had half the strength of normal. The patient's wristband read ABRAHAM PAXTON.

"Not bad, eh? And I'm still in therapy. My walking continues to improve, though not as quickly as at first."

Richard shook his head. "I'd say you've done one hell of a gutsy job getting yourself better. I'd no idea how great it was when we talked on the phone yesterday. And I want to thank you again for agreeing to come in."

"Hey, I never would have had a chance at all without what you did, and Dr. Hamlin of course. Jesus, I was shocked as hell to hear about his being murdered. And all that stuff in the papers, about the killer maybe being an antiabortion fanatic. Then this morning's news linking it all with stem cells—I mean, what the hell is going on?"

Richard sighed. They were alone in the anteroom to the MRI, or magnetic resonance imaging chamber, and while he intended to be candid with Paxton, he was determined not to fuel anymore rumors by letting the technicians who were preparing the machine in the next room overhear what he had to say. He lowered his voice. "I'm afraid no one is too sure, but Hamlin, along with some other doctors, may have prematurely been using stem cells on patients without their knowledge or consent."

"What?"

"The reason I suggested you submit to an exam is that it's possible you were one of his subjects."

Paxton looked as if he'd been kicked in the gut. "You've got to be kidding."

Richard said nothing, letting him digest the fact.

"What does it mean, if he has? Are there side effects?"

"We don't know. In fact, your incredible recovery may have been on account of what he did."

He flopped back and kept his eyes fixed on the ceiling, his pleasant expression of a few seconds ago replaced by a wooden stillness. "What about other patients he may have done this to? Did you find anything in them?"

"They're going to be called as well, through hospital channels. I took it on myself to suggest we start with you, since I was familiar with your case."

Paxton continued to look at the ceiling, seeming to withdraw into himself. "Then let's get started," he said about half a minute later.

She hadn't inhaled air free of hospital smells or felt the sun against her skin for over two weeks. Both felt like a bath in honey for the thirty seconds it took for the attendant to wheel her across the parking lot to where the ambulance waited.

"Glad to see the light of day?" the policewoman who walked beside her asked.

"You bet. . . . What's your name?"

"Carla Reid."

"Carla . . . I like your hair. . . . It catches the light . . . so beautifully."

"Why, thank you."

"It reminds me . . . of my daughter's."

They loaded her in the back, leaving the head of the stretcher upright, and through the small rear windows she could see the hospital recede in the distance as they drove north on First Avenue. She felt a spark of defiance at having survived the place, and relief to be out of there. Even the familiar sight of the line of flags snapping in the breeze along the curved facade of the United Nations gave her a marvelous sense of freedom.

At Seventy-second they cut a block east to York Avenue, then continued north, and she got to see the rows of shops and Irish pubs where Lisa had often insisted they go shopping together and have a beer afterward.

The memory made her smile, reconnecting her with what might be possible again. God, she missed those times.

Another right turn at Seventy-ninth, then north again, this time on East End Avenue, and soon they were racing under the trees hanging out over the street from Carl Shurz Park. She could see small children playing within its gates under the watchful eyes of women standing about in groups or sitting on benches chatting. She envied the shady serenity.

The vehicle slowed down and swung left. As it turned, she caught a glimpse of the East River, its gray surface gleaming slick as grease, yet sparkling at her from the other side of the park grounds. She even saw Gracie Mansion, the stately wooden house with peeling yellow paint where the mayor lived.

Then they pulled inside an ambulance entrance, the attendant recruited the help of an orderly lounging nearby to unload her stretcher, and Carla carried the small bag of belongings. As they wheeled her to the front door, she saw it was a modern building a half dozen stories high made of gleaming white stone, the brightness offset by layers of black smoked glass running the full length of each floor. Like a vanilla layer cake with chocolate filling, Kathleen thought. It also looked as if it had been dropped on the otherwise leafy neighborhood lined with red-brick homes resembling country cottages. It sure was a well protected area, she thought, looking at the contingent of dark blue uniformed police stationed at the mayor's gate across the road.

Inside the foyer what first greeted her was a delicious aroma of fresh coffee and cinnamon. It came from the direction of a sitting area where a dark green-and-white awning sheltered a few dozen small tables. Behind them stood a lunch counter lined with plates of bagels amongst rows of glass jars filled with brown beans and metal scoops. The place resembled a bistro more than a hospital cafeteria.

"A caffe latte," said a man with a walker to a woman whose uniform matched the canopy above her head. She punched the order into an espresso machine, and it responded with a guttural hiss. A host of other people, some in housecoats, most fully dressed, sat around talking, sipping from cups, or reading the morning papers. A nearby array of sofas and comfortable chairs filled the rest of the space, everything gently illuminated by recessed lighting. Vases full of fresh flowers and a few plants added color and life.

Kathleen's mouth watered, and for the first time since the stroke she felt hungry. She would down one of those coffees, the real way, through her mouth, within a week she determined.

The Admissions Department could have been a check-in desk for a luxury hotel, she thought. The room was wood paneled, and the staff was dressed in business suits with not a white coat in sight. But the tedious process of taking all her personal information, starting with her mother's maiden name, proved typical.

"I'll just leave her on my stretcher," she heard the driver whisper to Carla as the clerk started filling out her forms, "and go for one of those great javas they got out front."

"No problem," replied the policewoman. "Looks like this will take a while."

"And I'll need the patient's social security number, plus health care information," the woman who was checking Kathleen in continued.

Kathleen reamed off the numbers she now knew by heart after giving them so many times.

Richard peered up at the images on the viewing screen. Each no bigger than the size of a passport picture, they showed cross sections of Abe Paxton's brain as clearly as if they'd dissected it open and taken photos of it.

"That's where he had the previous bleed and Hamlin operated," said the radiologist, indicating an area under the swell of the frontal lobes. "But look here," he continued, pointing to a round dark spot much smaller than a pea. "If I didn't know Hamlin had removed the ruptured aneurysm, I'd swear this guy had another one."

"Could he have missed it the first time?"

"No." He shoved another sheet of images up on the screen alongside the first. "Here are the post-op films from last year. Everything's resected."

Richard had to agree. The area they were looking at was clear in the previous scans.

"It sounds crazy," said the man at his side. "but it's as if this guy Paxton has grown a second vascular anomaly. That's impossible. At least, I've never heard of such a thing. Whatever that is, it's still very small, but we'll do an angio to make sure we're looking at a lesion in a vessel—"

"Thanks," said Richard, breaking off and rushing out the door. "Call me as soon as it's done." He knew what had happened.

"Look, slow down. You're losing me," said Gordon Ingram.

"It's because the stem cells Hamlin used took their cues of what to become from the surrounding vascular anomalies as well as the neurons. They became arteries in addition to brain tissue, and must have copied the same structural abnormalities that had led to the vessels bursting in the first place."

"That's a hell of a supposition."

"Isn't one of the fears about stem cells that they could copy errors? Hell, does anybody know for sure how these things will work on humans in any given circumstances? That's what research is for."

"Okay, okay. One thing's for sure, it's got to be checked out. And what you found in Paxton will fast-track getting all Hamlin's other patients in here. Heaven knows what we're going to do with them if we do find recurrences—"

Richard's new cellular rang. He fumbled getting it open to turn it on, not used to the more recent model. "Hello?"

"Get down to the morgue, pronto," McKnight said into Richard's ear.

"Why?"

"Just do it, and fast. We found Edwards's body."

"Shit!"

"Hurry, and bring your ER team. We also got Norris. Our killer's cut him to pieces, but I think the poor son of a bitch may still be alive."

The temperature of the locker was set as low as a fridge, intended to preserve meat, not freeze it. Hypothermia had saved Norris.

At least what was left of him.

His ear, the remains of an eye, and his hand, all taken from the right side of his body, lay in a little pile by his head, along with a stack of twigs.

He had no palpable pulse, and his respirations were so shallow they were barely noticeable. His skin could be kneaded and drawn into tufts like cold Plasticine, and he responded neither to words or pain. To the uninitiated he'd have been pronounced dead.

But the observant McKnight had picked up the clues. Norris's remaining eye, though staring straight ahead, had a normal-sized pupil. His limbs, though stiff and difficult to bend, weren't rigid with rigor mortis. He was mottled blue, but his underside had none of the deep purple coloring called lividity, the pooling of venous blood in the lowest points of the body when a person is dead.

Richard bent over the man's chest and listened with a stethoscope while he was still on the sliding steel tray. About every three seconds he heard a faint heartbeat. "Let's go, people," he said. "This guy's not dead until he's warm and dead."

Within a minute the man had IVs in his arms and legs, heated saline infusions coursing through his veins, and a slew of monitors wired to his chest. Richard did the intubation himself, prying open the man's jaw with about the same force it might take to manipulate a frozen chicken leg. Using the illuminated blade of a laryngoscope he pushed aside Norris's tongue and visualized the V of his vocal cords. In went the tube as usual, except he had the added sight of seeing its tip pass by the hole in the front of his patient's trachea.

"He's eighteen degrees centigrade," shouted one of the nurses wielding a freshly used rectal thermometer calibrated for low temperatures.

The lowest on record who had ever survived was fifteen, according to the journals.

As they wheeled him out of the morgue and rushed to the elevator, they attracted more than a few comments and stares from the pathology staff. But Richard and his team were too busy ventilating the man and briefing the residents to pay any mind.

". . . heat the oxygen to about forty-five centigrade . . ."

". . . raise his temperature no faster than one-point-five degrees an hour. The key word here is slow, and it's only the core temperature we boost. No hot blankets once you get him upstairs. That'll dilate the peripheral circulation and put him in shock for sure . . ."

". . . no unnecessary manipulation of the heart, so don't go shoving in any central catheters. The slightest irritation at this temperature will set the myocardium fibrillating, and we'll be pumping this guy for hours . . ."

As the door of the elevator slid closed, Richard heard someone in the hallway quip, "Slabbed another live one, have you?"

"She's left already?"

"Yeah, the ambulance came early, Dr. Steele. I left a message for you in ER."

"But I was supposed to be notified personally."

"I'm afraid Dr. Sullivan overruled you. She insisted on signing her own consent form. You know that's to be expected. She's making progress and isn't willing to be dependent anymore."

He stiffened at the free insight.

"Hey, she's okay," interrupted McKnight, slamming down the phone. "My officer's with her right now. Rode in back at her side the whole way, and they're admitting her as we speak. I've ordered a few more squad cars of cops to scout out the place to see what security we'll need there, and until they get on the scene, some of the guys watching the mayor's place are going to wander over and man the front entrance. But it's this place we got to worry about the most. Imagine that son of a bitch operating right under our noses. How soon do you think Norris will be able to talk?" He jerked his thumb in the direction of the cubicle where the residents continued to work on him.

"I'm not even certain he's going to live. But it would take days before he'd be alert enough to tell us anything."

"Shit! How the hell could this happen? Two extra bodies in the morgue, one of them for more than an entire day and headless, yet nobody noticed?"

"In a word, cutbacks. They're so far behind on posts, you're lucky they didn't wait until next week to pull those particular slabs."

"Jesus, this place is screwier than the NYPD! Well, let me tell you, there's going to be so much security around here from now on not even a cockroach will get in or out. As of immediately, all the exits are manned, and I don't care how many people it takes. Plus we're searching the whole building again. Maybe with a bit of luck the creep will still be here."

"You really believe that?"

"No."

"What about Blaine or Downs?"

"My men have orders to pick up Downs and bring her here. We'll see how she reacts to seeing lover boy here, then I'll question her myself. With what's happened, the gloves are off—"

"And Blaine."

"You and I go see her once we're finished with Downs."

"I don't want Kathleen over there now—"

"Hey, wherever you decide she goes, we'll protect her."

If she'll listen, thought Richard, feeling no more sure about his influence over Kathleen than he did the detective's ability to keep her safe.

"One thing going for us as of this morning," McKnight continued, "we got lucky in pinning down the creep's identity. All those composite drawings finally got a hit. His former landlord recognized him. Called us to report the guy's been renting a room on Canal Street, but hasn't been seen there since Wednesday morning when neighbors noticed him loading his computer into a truck. We figure he took off between attacking you in the hospital and setting the bomb in your house."

"So he's gone."

"But we got prints. Complete ones, better than that partial we lifted because of the torn glove. And when we contacted the FBI, their files have a match."

Richard's hopes ticked up a notch. "Really?"

"Yeah. They're identical to a set they found in a hotel room at Rochester a few years ago where some hood held off the local police, then killed himself. It was around the time that a gynecologist there got shot, the one I told you whose murder we thought the Legion of the Lord had a hand in. Except they never established a clear link between this guy and that shooting. However, they did figure someone else was with him, because of the second set of prints, and they're real interested in talking to our boy."

"Do you have a name?"

"He called himself Rob Lowe to the landlord."

Richard snickered.

"This is the good part. The guy who offed himself in Rochester was a wife-beating scumbag named Bobby Nappin with a lifetime achievement award in domestic violence—his old lady went into hiding a decade ago. But he had a son whom the neighbors said he was raising to be a chip off the old block. The FBI wondered if the second man might have been him."

"Holy shit!"

"There's more. We ran the name Lowe through the personnel list here at the hospital and got nothing. But when we tried Nappin, we found a close match. According to hospital employment records, a Robert Nape used to work in pathology as an autopsy assistant, then a few years ago went on to do a stint as an orderly in the Department of Reproductive Medicine. He received an official reprimand after he started passing out Right to Life pamphlets and harassing patients about not destroying their unused embryos. One night a few weeks later he was found trying to get at the frozen specimens themselves and Edwards fired him outright. People around here remembered him, but recalled he had long hair and a beard. When our sketch artist added them to the composite Dr. Sullivan gave us, we had Robert Nape."

He walked to the vehicle, removed the ambulance attendant's jacket he'd stolen, retrieved the folded wheelchair that he'd secured against the wall behind the driver's seat, and pushed it back into the rehab center. If somebody had looked closely they'd have seen the pipes taped to the chrome frame on the underside, but he knew it was highly unlikely that anyone would give it a second glance, especially in a place like this.

Certainly none of the patients paid him the slightest attention as he passed through the sitting area. He avoided Admitting entirely by heading directly to where the signs read ADMINISTRATION.

"Can I help you, sir?" a secretary asked. Black curls piled up on her head and a glistening red mouth made him think of Cher.

"Is Dr. Blaine in her office?"

"Yes, but she's expecting a patient."

"Robert Nappin, the second?" He'd phoned for the appointment himself not more than an hour ago. A quick visit, he'd said, just to discuss a million-dollar endowment Mr. Nappin wished to bequeath to Dr. Blaine. But Mr. Nappin was in a rush, leaving for the Bahamas, and always did his charity on impulse.

Her pretty face reflected surprise. "Why, yes, but—"

"I'm his driver. Mr. Nappin's very proud, and wanted to come in under his own steam. His nurse is back there, escorting him, but he'll need his chair once he arrives, and sent me ahead with it. Can I place it in Dr. Blaine's office? He's fiercely eccentric about how he presents himself and insists on walking right up to greet her."

"Why, I guess it's okay. Just let me check with Dr. Blaine." She got up and, knocking first, poked her head inside her boss's office. "Mr. Nappin's driver is here, and would like to leave the man's wheelchair in your office. Mr. Nappin himself wants to meet you standing up."

He couldn't see Blaine, but heard her throaty chuckle. "Honey, for a million dollars, I don't care if he hops in on one leg."

He relinquished the chair to the young woman, and turned to leave. Over his shoulder he watched until she'd taken it through the door. He quickened his pace, reaching inside his pocket and fingering the remote. As soon as he was safely out in the hallway he pushed the button.

The blast made a giant wump, similar to the sound a kerosene-soaked rag makes when it ignites. The force of the explosion, even though he was buffered from it by two rooms, threw him to the floor amidst a shower of ceiling tiles and light fixtures. As he got to his knees, he reached up to brush debris from his head, careful not to disturb his wig. Then he saw that his palm was smeared with blood. Within seconds people were running by him toward where they'd heard the detonation. Someone stopped and tried to help him to his feet. She was saying things to him, but the concussion had sealed his ears, and her words sounded like distant shouts.

He signaled that he was okay, and stumbled in the direction of the admitting area. His deafness immediately started to clear, and behind him, despite ringing in his head, he heard screams. It must be the ones who found the bodies, he thought. The two women couldn't have survived.

Up ahead the policewoman stood between him and Sullivan's stretcher, back to her charge, hand on her gun, confusion on her face.

But there was nothing vague about Kathleen Sullivan's stare. Her green eyes were locked on him like a pair of cruise missiles, one hand starting to flap as she tried to get the officer's attention, the other leaping to her throat so she could speak.

She knows, he thought. "Quick, ma'am, they need a cop in there," he screamed at the officer.

"But I shouldn't leave Dr. Sullivan," she said, shouting above all the noise, oblivious to Sullivan's gesturing and attempts to make herself heard. "What's happened?"

"I think it's a gas explosion. Everyone's panicking. They need you to take charge." He took her by the elbow and urged her on her way. "And don't worry. I'll get Dr. Sullivan to safety."

She looked at his head. "You're bleeding."

"I'm fine. Just go."

She started to run back the way he'd come. "Then I'll meet you at the ambulance," she called over her shoulder, "as soon as help arrives. Make sure someone's called 911."

He turned to look at Sullivan. She started to rock and slap the side rails, continuing to try and call out, but her breathy voice hadn't a prayer of making itself heard over the commotion.

He stepped up to the head of the stretcher and quickly started pushing toward the exit. Her legs bent and lifted, her arms flailed at him, and he marveled at how much movement she'd regained in a matter of days. But her fingers brushed helplessly off him, weak as blades of grass.

None of the people heading out of the building alongside them, some on crutches, others in wheelchairs, paid her any mind. She couldn't even attract the attention of a half dozen uniformed policeman pushing their way in.

As soon as he had her in the back of the ambulance, he brought out the syringe he'd been carrying in his breast pocket, plunged it into the side portal of her IV, and slowly injected the contents until her eyes closed and her limbs fell listless at her sides. But this was midazolan, not potassium, and he stopped short of giving enough to kill her. He needed her alive for the grand finale, as bait to lure in Steele.

Switching on his siren with the flashers, he had no trouble threading through the swarm of white-and-blue NYPD cars amassing in front of the institute. On East End Avenue, he headed south, past a string of on-coming fire trucks, sirens screaming. Minutes later he pulled into a line of ambulances parked outside Mount Steven's Hospital near Seventy-seventh and Lexington. None of the other drivers leaning on their vehicles and drinking coffee as they waited for an assignment paid any attention to him when he got out and opened the rear of his vehicle.

"Boy, she's out of it," said one of the men who helped him unload, looking a little too carefully at Sullivan's motionless figure as they ex-tended the wheel carriage on the stretcher.

"A transfer from NYCH with one of them resistant pneumonias, so don't get so close."

"Jesus," he said, recoiling from her. "Why didn't you tell me?"

"You didn't ask," he called back, already pushing her in the front door.

He followed the ground-floor corridors through a series of zigs and zags that took him back out the Seventy-sixth Street entrance. He saw the truck that he'd been told to look for. As he approached, the driver got out.

It wasn't the person he expected. But it made sense. A whole lot of sense.

They loaded her into the back and drove off.

Sirens from all over the city seemed to be converging on the upper East Side.

Jo O'Brien barged into his office without knocking. "Richard, we just got an alert. They're sending a nail bomb victim from Adele Blaine's institute."

"What!" His heart jackknifed into his mouth.

"It's not Dr. Sullivan. But Blaine herself is dead, and we're getting her secretary. She apparently had a pulse and not much else when the medics got to her."

"Jesus Christ! What about Kathleen?" He leapt out of his chair and rushed for the door. "I've got to find her."

"No other casualties they told me," she said, laying a restraining hand on his shoulder as he pushed by her. "Besides, she's probably already on her way back. The institute's returning patients to their referring hospitals all over the city. Better you stay put, Chief, and help the woman who took the blast. The ambulance guys said they were bypassing closer hospitals to bring her here."

That meant they thought she was dead unless they got her to the best trauma team in the city.

But he had to know Kathleen was safe. "Call McKnight. Have him radio that policewoman who's with Kathleen and verify all's well." He turned toward the resus room, the strains of a siren wailing in the distance, forlorn as a moan bowed on a violin string.

Richard looked down at the shredded face impaled with nails and wondered what the young woman once looked like. From her forehead to her chest the spikes had torn her skin and left it in strips. But her cheeks and eyes had taken the brunt. He couldn't even say what color the irises had been. She must have been bending over to examine the bomb when it went off, not realizing what it was. Her lower body, while singed and bloodied, remained remarkably intact. Even her hair, luxuriously black and cascading onto the pillow appeared almost normal, until he touched it and felt it crumble to fine cinders between his gloved fingers. And nothing could mask the stench of burnt flesh that she gave off.

She'd had a pulse, just as Jo said, but it was still too late. Despite his team further skewering her with central lines, chest tubes, various catheters, and an airway, her heart beat its last the moment she arrived. Even that organ they violated trying to save her, a grinning gash curving below her left breast marking where he opened the ribs and tried to coax her back to life with his hand.

Now he was waiting for her parents.

Normally he'd spend these minutes cutting off the various tubes close to the skin, leaving them in place for the autopsy, yet removing enough of the projecting bits that a sheet could be laid over the body. "*To make it presentable for viewing,*" the textbooks said. What the hell was *presentable* about a dead loved one? he thought, so angry he was trembling. It's obscene. Vile. Putrid. Worse for being the deliberate work of a ghoul in the name of a cause.

"Dr. Steele, they're here," said Jo O'Brien, sticking her head into the resuscitation room.

He didn't move. "I can't do this another time, Jo. I can't."

"You must, and you will. I put them in your office."

"Did you reach McKnight?"

"Yes. He was already on the way to the institute. Assured me the officials there were saying only the two injured and all the patients were out, just like I said. But he'll make the call to his office."

After taking a final look at the body, Richard started down the hallway and began to prepare what he would say to the mother and father. He took a breath, and once more submerged his soul in ice, knowing one of these times he wouldn't get it back. Because he'd seen it happen. There was a limit to shedding all feeling the way a snake slips from its skin. Sooner or later some part of the person stops caring. Whether the change is called depression or burnout, no one's entirely ever the same afterward, even when they appear to recover. The aftermath is a thing spouses or lovers and children notice, an empty stare, a silence, a being pulled away from the sunlight into a darkness beneath the moment. When he'd gotten lost in it himself through grief, he ultimately broke free, his own lapses remaining relatively rare. But he doubted he'd be so lucky when he succumbed to the sum of all the horrors he'd seen in ER. Moments like this, he knew, brought that reckoning closer.

A half hour later he emerged from his office and relinquished the grieving couple to Jo's encompassing arms. He leaned against the door frame, watching them shuffle toward the exit, their lives irreparably broken, and once more felt grateful, God help him, that he'd never had to face that loss.

When he turned, he saw McKnight standing off to one side in the corridor, studying him. His heart sank at the dread in the detective's eyes, and nearly stopped altogether when he heard the man say, "I think you better sit down."

19

She awoke in stages.

All of them painful.

First the familiar cold ache from the tranquilizer filled her head.

Then she felt burning numbness in her limbs.

I've had another stroke. Oh, my God, I can't move.

She opened her eyes to complete darkness.

And felt a small sense of relief. She wasn't paralyzed. She was tied up, but not any longer in the ambulance. Yet she was still in a vehicle of some kind, lurching this way and that as they turned, slowed, and accelerated. Along with the sounds of traffic outside, she judged they were still in the city.

Behind her head she could hear two men talking, her hearing as hyper-acute as ever. She strained, but couldn't make out what they were saying. She could distinguish the higher pitch of her attacker's voice from a second voice that was lower and had a familiar halting quality to its rhythm. Whoever it was spoke in short segments, almost the way she did.

All at once they came to a stop. She felt a slight weight shift and heard the slam of the passenger side door. Someone had gotten out. Then the vehicle took off again.

Why didn't they just kill her outright?

God, not fun and games like with Lockman. Please not that. A clean shot, an injection—anything but cutting me to pieces.

If this guy was as big a control freak with women as his brothers in the Legion of the Lord, she knew her chances weren't good.

Or maybe she could use his hatred. Grovel, beg, plead that he kill her.

Convince him his ultimate power trip lay in taking her life while she was fully aware, not half out of her head with pain.

Some option.

The vehicle—a truck—slowed, then came to a stop.

He stayed in the cab.

Outside she could hear kids laughing, and conversations came and went as pedestrians strolled by not three feet from where she lay.

The only call she could make was her pathetic wheeze.

"You've killed her, you assholes! You fucking, incompetent assholes! You let that monster take her from under your noses, and that means you killed her."

"Richard, please," McKnight said, "this isn't helping—"

"Do you want to see what he's capable of? Come on. Let's go next door. I'll show you his latest work." Richard was reeling in circles, raging and careening off the walls of his office.

The detective simply stood in front of the door and remained silent.

Richard came to a stop directly in front of him. "Say something, damn you! Or is barring my way out of here all you're good for? What are you afraid of? That I might go running off looking for her myself? Well, get out of my way. I'll do a better job—"

"Her photo has been dispatched by computer to every patrol car in the city. The entire force has been put on an alert to try and spot her. TV and radio stations are issuing bulletins as we speak, listing the stolen ambulance's markings and plate numbers, instructing listeners to call 911 if they see anyone moving a woman matching Dr. Sullivan's description—"

"Have you picked up Downs?"

McKnight hesitated, and tried to swallow. It seemed to take a lot of effort, as if he had no spit. "Not exactly."

"Not exactly? But she's probably our only link to this guy."

"We can't find her. The super at her apartment building said he saw her leave early this morning with a suitcase."

Richard felt he was about to suffocate. "Let me by, you bastard," he said, lunging at the man, "I've got to get outside."

The detective's big hands encircled his upper arms and caught him in what felt like a vise. "Doc, you've got to stay put in case he calls."

"I've got my cellular."

"There's nothing else you can do."

"The hell there isn't."

"Like what?"

Get away from McKnight, was what he thought. So when the killer did call, Richard could go to him alone. Him in exchange for her. No cops around to screw it up. Instead he said, "I don't know what. It's just staying cooped up in here is driving me crazy. I've got to take a walk. Clear my head, alone. Now release me and step aside."

The big man looked at him apprehensively. "Don't try anything crazy on your own, Doc. I beg you. You're angry as hell at us now, and Lord knows you've got cause, but working with us is still your best chance of helping her."

Richard fought the urge to scream at him again. "Just give me time by myself, Detective."

He released Richard's arms, but didn't budge.

"Look, McKnight, you can't keep me here—"

A knock on the door interrupted him, and Gordon Ingram poked his head in, banging the door against the policeman's back. "Oh, sorry, Richard. I didn't mean to interrupt, but tell me what I'm hearing about Kathleen isn't true."

"Gordon, I need to walk, and would appreciate your company," he replied, not taking his eyes off McKnight.

The police officer shrugged, and stepped aside to let him pass. "You have my number."

Ingram looked quizzically at him, then at Richard, obviously sensing the tension between the two men. "I'm afraid I'm not much for hoofing it these days," he said, "but I'll buy you a coke, if that'll help."

"Let's go," said Richard.

Richard outlined his plan to try and substitute himself for Kathleen, if the killer made contact. Ingram listened patiently and offered little advice.

The call came before they'd finished off a second round of sodas.

"Steele?"

There was no mistaking the high, whiny voice.

"Listen, you fuck. Hurt her and I'll send you to hell, the slow way—"

"Get to a window at the front of the hospital, then call me back. You don't call me in thirty seconds, or I see any sign of cops, I push a button, understand?"

"But where?"

The connection went dead.

He looked at the call display. It showed his old cell number.

"Come on!" he yelled to Ingram, and ran from the cafeteria, heading to a stairwell and the nearest window overlooking Thirty-third. His fingers shaking, he dialed while scanning the street. Five floors below, in a line of parked cars on the other side of the street near Second Avenue, he saw a plain delivery truck with no windows or logos and a man at the rear fender bringing a phone to his ear. He had frizzy black hair and a mustache.

He was the reporter who went off with Norris at the press conference, Richard realized. He was astounded at how well the broad face from the composite drawing had been disguised.

"See me?" the voice asked.

"Yes."

"Then look at this." He threw open the back doors, and climbed inside. It took no more than a few seconds before he closed them again, but it was enough time for Richard to have seen the end of a stretcher. "Now here she is," said Kathleen's kidnapper.

He heard her breathing before she spoke. "Richard . . . don't listen to him. . . . Call the creep's bluff. . . . Love the children for me—"

"That's it, Steele. You've got forty-five seconds to get down here and climb in back with your lady. I'll be within a hundred feet and able to see. If you're a second late or pull any funny stuff, up she goes."

"No, wait—"

Again the connection broke off.

As he watched, the man with the frizzy black hair jumped from the back of the truck, closed it up again, and walked away.

Richard's head reeled. He hadn't time to tell McKnight or anyone else.

He started down the stairs, counting seconds in his head.

"Richard," Ingram called from where he'd just arrived at the entrance to the stairwell. "Where are you going?"

"To Kathleen," he called over his shoulder without slowing down. "I've got to get to her. She's in a truck out front wired to detonate. Tell McKnight what's happened. Maybe he can do something. But for God's sake make him and the cops keep out of sight. The guy's watching."

"What!"

"Do it." And he ran out onto the ground floor. He figured he had half a minute left.

He used up ten seconds to reach the front door. Darting outside and crossing Thirty-third cost him another three. Wherever the creep had retreated to, he couldn't spot him. Running full out with his white coat flapping behind him, he covered the half block to the truck in less than fifteen seconds. His throat burned the whole way, and drawing closer he grew certain the bomb would go off the instant he got there, that the killer had baited him.

He approached from the driver's side.

Nothing happened.

A woman with a stroller was walking away from him, toward First Avenue. There were no other pedestrians. But a steady stream of traffic flowed at his back. If he hesitated, the watcher would blow the bomb up, and the people driving cars and crossing the street were doomed anyway, he decided, practicing the cold logic of triage. Gingerly, he opened the rear door.

The first thing he saw were Kathleen's eyes glaring at him out of the darkness.

But no explosion.

He climbed in.

Still nothing.

Taped to the undercarriage of the stretcher he saw four gray pipes, each at least two inches wide and several feet in length. Quadruple what had detonated in his basement.

He thought of trying to grab her in his arms and run for their lives.

Stripped flesh beneath a halo of black hair flashed to mind.

He stayed put, closing the door as he'd been instructed, shutting himself and Kathleen in darkness.

"It's okay," he said. "Help's on the way."

A few seconds later a key turned in the lock, sealing them in.

Someone got in the cab, the motor roared to life, and they were off.

He felt his way over to the stretcher. "The police know we're here," he whispered, finding one of her arms and immediately undoing the tape that restrained it.

"You fool!" she wheezed at him the minute she could cover her larynx. "Now . . . we both die."

"No! Now we think of something."

"Think of what?"

He didn't have an answer. He'd been too big an asshole, raging at McKnight rather than working out some sort of contingency plan. Idiot! He took out his frustration on the tape. In an instant he freed her other arm and was working on her legs. The lurching of the truck to the left, then right every few minutes kept throwing him off balance. The driver must be zigzagging through one street after another, making sure they weren't followed. Hopefully McKnight had called in a helicopter.

He had her ankles unbound when the vehicle all at once slowed and came to a stop.

Then his phone rang.

As soon as he punched RECEIVE, the voice said, "You make any noise, I run fifty feet away, duck, and press, got that?"

"No, don't—"

"Same goes for any attempt to call up your cop friends. Keep our connection open, or else."

Wait a minute, Richard thought. Cell phones could be monitored. Surely McKnight had someone tuned in on them. "Where are we going?"

he demanded, hoping to get the killer to start talking. Maybe the cops could triangulate where they were, or this guy would give away their destination. "Obviously you intend to kill us anyway. It didn't bother you before where the bombs went off."

A wheedling laugh came over the phone. "You'll find out where soon enough. Let's just say it'll be so noisy that no passersby will hear you as I mete out the Lord's punishment."

Oh, Jesus, Richard thought. Maybe it would be better if he goaded the son of a bitch into blowing them up right now. It would be quick, and they could take him with them.

The voices of people walking by blended with the noises of passing traffic.

Him and a lot of bystanders.

No. Not more flesh for this monster. "You're a fine one to talk about killing," he said instead, figuring it best to just keep the conversation going. "How many innocents have you slaughtered?"

"Casualties of war."

"But why come after Kathleen and me? We didn't have anything to do with Hamlin and the others."

"Oh no?"

"That's right."

"Not according to my information."

"What information? From whom?"

"I know what you did, or would have done, all to save your geneticist friend there. How many embryos do you suppose died for her? Why should she or you deserve to live after agreeing to that?"

"Neither she nor I agreed to anything."

"Bullshit! You'd have gone on working with Hamlin and the rest of that bunch, covering up their mistakes, all the while giving them new cases, and the killings would have continued."

"Who told you this crap?"

More laughter came through the receiver, shrill enough to hurt his ear.

"You'll find that out soon enough."

"Is it Francesca Downs—"

The click of the passenger door opening interrupted him, and the sound of the connection changed, went flat, as if the man on the other end had covered the mouthpiece with his hand. Richard heard muffled voices from the cab, and the truck creaked as someone climbed in up front.

"That's the person I heard him talking with before," said Kathleen, in a single rushed breath. "Listen to how . . . he breaks up his speech . . . like me."

Before Richard could appreciate what she meant, the motor revved to life, and they were off again. Minutes later the truck lurched right, then came to another stop. The previous street sounds seemed to have disappeared, replaced by the racket of a jackhammer. A sudden metallic rattling followed, ending in a slam that echoed a few seconds, instantly muting the din from outside. The two front doors in the cab snapped opened almost simultaneously, but as far as Richard could tell, only the driver got out.

He had to find a weapon.

Untape the pipe bombs and clobber him with them when he comes in after them? There wasn't time.

He needed something quick.

"Excuse me, Kathleen," he whispered, slipping his arms under her and lifting her off the stretcher. The lightness of her body shocked him, despite knowing she'd lost so much weight.

"What are you doing?"

He laid her gently on the floor of the truck. "Getting a torpedo, " he told her, lifting her IV bags off their poles and nestling them in her arms. Next he snapped all the electrical leads off her, freeing her of the machines piled on top of the mattress. He put the catheter bags between her legs. Finally, he placed his cell phone in her hand. "As soon as the fun starts, dial 911."

"But I don't know where we are."

"McKnight's probably already outside. Just tell them, 'come in now!' "

A key sounded in the rear door lock, followed by a loud click.

"I love you, Kathleen," he said, grasping her head gently between his hands and giving her face a quick kiss. He sprung to his feet and released the foot brake on the gurney. Grabbing hold of it, he waited.

The rear doors started to open. "I've got a gun, so behave," said the whiny voice.

As soon as he caught a glimpse of the man's silhouette in the semi-darkness of wherever they were, Richard rammed the stretcher with its load of equipment at him. It slammed out the rear of the truck, arched through the air and hit the driver squarely in the chest.

"Shit!" he screamed, reeling backward under its weight, all the monitors crashing down on him as well. The gun went sailing out of his hand to the popping sounds of video screens shattering.

Richard leapt for it, paying no heed if the second person was out of the cab and coming at him from behind. All that mattered was to reach the gun first or he and Kathleen were dead anyway. He landed on concrete a few feet short, letting out a bellow of pain as he scrambled toward where it lay.

"Do I call you Nappin or Nape, or just Robbie the creep?" he yelled, willing to say anything that might fluster the figure struggling to disentangle himself from the tubular undercarriage and win a few seconds's advantage. In the thin light he saw glittering splinters embedded in that broad face he'd so come to hate and blood pouring from around the eyes. The glass from one of the monitors must have smashed on the guy's head. He felt his odds soar.

But the taunt was a mistake.

The man exploded into a frenzy of shrieks and screams, extricating his legs and throwing off the remains of the debris that had felled him. He made his own dive for the pistol.

Richard grabbed it first, but before he could point it, his opponent gripped the barrel and wrenched it from his grasp, rage giving him the strength of five men.

"Look what I've got," he said, his mouth breaking into a bloodied leer as he started bringing the muzzle right way around.

"No, don't," screamed Richard, sure that he was about to die and leave Kathleen at this madman's mercy. "The police are on their way. You can't escape unless you run now. Get out fast—"

A shot, then two more exploded almost by his ear.

The burly man in front of him arched his eyebrows, swayed a few seconds, and managed to twist his face into a pained look of surprise.

Richard stared at him in amazement, having so often seen that same expression in sudden death.

The wig turned crimson, then the familiar broad features disappeared under a fresh wash of red, and he pitched nose-first into a broken cardiac monitor.

Richard turned to see Ingram standing at the back of the truck, slowly lowering a gun.

20

Relief made him dizzy. "Gordon! How on earth did you get here? My God, you saved my life."

Ingram swayed and leaned against one of the open rear doors.

Even in the bad light, Richard could see he was breathing with great difficulty. "Jesus, are you all right?" He started toward him. "Did the guy shoot you?" The gunfire had been so loud inside what looked like a large garage entirely lined with concrete it had been impossible to say if it had all come from one direction.

Gordon shook his head.

"Richard . . . what's happened?" Kathleen called from the vehicle's dark interior behind Ingram. "I can't . . . get a . . . connection."

"I'm fine," he replied. "Dr. Ingram somehow arrived here in time and managed to save the day. . . ." He trailed off as he got closer and heard the man wheezing. With little illumination creeping through grimy windows in the large sliding door, Richard drew closer to see Ingram's face. It was gray and gleamed from a sheen of sweat. "Christ, Gordon, what is it? Not another heart attack?"

The man eyed him, his gun pointing in limbo between the ground and Richard's waist. "Guess I overdid it getting here," he said in a rush between breaths.

"Where's the second guy? Did you shoot him, too?" He started toward the cab to look.

"Dr. Ingram . . . the man who . . . fixed my throat?" Kathleen called.

"Yeah, the man who fixed your throat. . . ."

He stopped midstride, his voice trailing off once more on seeing the empty cab.

He slowly turned and faced Ingram again.

Ingram had sunk to his knees and taken a tube of nitroglycerine spray out of his pocket, liberally squirting it under his tongue. "Forget the other man, Richard. . . . He ran off . . . shot in the arm. . . . I'm going . . . into pulmonary edema. . . . Help me."

Richard saw the veins in Ingram's neck bulging above his collar. The man's lungs were filling with fluid, his myocardium having been taxed beyond what it could pump. Nitro, on the other hand, would dilate his arteries, reducing the resistance in the circulation and lessening the heart's workload. That might be enough to reverse the process. But oxygen to help him breath, diuresis with IV furosemide to make him pee out the excess water, and a shot of morphine to reduce the volume of blood flowing toward the heart would increase his chances a lot more. Which meant getting him to an ER.

Yet Richard just stood there, taking his first good look at the gun in Ingram's hand. It looked identical to the one he'd been fighting over. "Where'd you get the weapon, Gordon?"

The man, desperate for oxygen, had begun to mouth-breathe, exhibiting what doctors call "air hunger."

"What are you bothering . . . about that stuff for? . . . Get those tanks off the stretcher. . . . I carry . . . my own syringes." With his free hand he reached inside his breast pocket and took out what looked like a billfold. He laid it on the concrete, flipping it open.

Richard recognized the kind of case diabetics use, designed to carry four prefilled insulin needles.

Ingram gestured at the contents with an open palm. "Furosemide and morphine . . . two of each." He gave a little grin. "This occasionally happens . . . so I'm a man . . . who comes prepared." His gun remained vaguely pointed toward the ground between them. "Perk of being . . . my own doctor."

A man with heart failure, Richard thought.

A man who had access to all the records.

A man who might have gone through Hamlin and Downs's charts "looking for trouble" after all and would have figured out what was going on as readily as Richard had.

Oh, my God, Richard thought, recoiling from where his mind seemed to be shoving him. But it pushed harder, dredging up the events of the last two weeks, connecting and reconnecting them into patterns that made sense despite not wanting to see them. His ideas slid inexorably toward a possibility that made Ingram as hideous as rot. *No, don't go there. It can't be,* he tried to tell himself. But he said, "Give me the pistol, Gordon."

The grin faded, and the direction of the muzzle became more definite, rising to take a bead on Richard's chest.

The movement confirmed all that Richard had been thinking.

"I knew such a lame set of lies . . . wouldn't work. . . . My original plan . . . was to let psycho Bob there . . . kill you and Kathleen . . . then I'd kill him. . . . But I hadn't counted on . . . getting like this either . . . and all at once . . . needing your services. . . . Couldn't let him . . . do you in just yet." With his left hand he reached inside his jacket and pulled out a six-inch key chain attached to a small black box the size of a lighter. It had buttons on it.

Richard didn't need to be told what it did.

In a white-hot second his fury at Ingram swelled into rage. Despite the gun and detonator, every ounce of him quivered to leap at the man's throat, and only his determination to somehow save Kathleen's life stopped him. "I'm not doing squat to help you," he said instead.

"Suit yourself. Maybe I can inject the drugs, at least for now. But that might not be the case in a few minutes. What's up for grabs is how Kathleen dies." He gestured toward the truck with his gun. "Quick and easy, or slow and painfully." His thumb glided across the buttons on the detonator.

Richard again considered his chances of jumping him, but more coolly this time. Better keep him talking, he decided. "What you did, it makes me want to puke."

"What I did . . . was protect a doctor . . . who'd secretly crossed the line into regenerative medicine . . . who could restore damaged hearts . . .

and was years ahead of anyone on the planet . . . in making stem cells work."

"You used your position of trust to betray Kathleen and me. An innocent policeman and secretary died. Hamlin, Lockman, Edwards, Blain—dead. Maybe Norris, too. All to keep Downs out of jail so she could help you."

Ingram, his chest heaving more laboriously now, studied Richard from under half-closed lids, his eyes burning with contempt. "Sure I wanted to help myself. . . . Otherwise I'd be looking forward . . . to an ultimate heart transplant . . . a lifetime of antirejection drugs . . . and still . . . in all likelihood die young. . . . But I also kept a doctor free . . . who can help millions . . . and intend to keep her that way." As he talked, he laid the gun on the ground within easy reach while he continued to hold the detonator in his left hand, thumb at the ready. With his free hand he grabbed a rubber tourniquet from his kit. Not once did he take his eyes off Richard. Rolling up his sleeve he attempted a one-handed tie using his teeth, the way junkies do to make a vein in the arm bulge. But he repeatedly fumbled it, his holding the detonator at the same time making the task difficult. After several tries he threw the band down and picked up the gun again.

"You don't follow . . . my orders exactly, Richard . . . we all go boom . . . including Kathleen." He caressed the remote with his thumb as he retook his aim at Richard's chest. "Rest assured . . . at this range . . . the blast will be . . . mercifully lethal . . . for us. . . . But for Kathleen . . . through the open end of the truck . . . it could still rip her inside out . . . yet leave her alive. . . . With all the construction . . . noise in the street . . . no one may even hear . . . the explosion. . . . She could suffer for days . . . so no notions of sandbagging me . . . to save her . . . because I can press faster." Extending his gun arm, he presented his veins while still holding the weapon, but slid his left hand with the remote back away from Richard. "Now inject the first dose of furosemide . . . then the morphine. . . . And stay on my right side."

Richard hesitated.

"Think I'm kidding?" said Ingram, reading his face. "Hey . . . I've nothing to lose. . . . I feel myself going . . . I take you with me. . . . As for getting caught and ending my days in jail . . . I'd rather die. . . . Pull any stunt that brings in the police . . . same result. . . . Better get busy."

Play for time, Richard kept telling himself. Without another word, he picked up the abandoned tourniquet and kneeling beside Ingram's right arm, wrapped it around the biceps. Ingram jammed the barrel of the gun into his ribs and rummaged it around a bit, making it hurt. In return, Richard, selecting the first syringe of furosemide, plunged the point of the needle into the skin as roughly as he could and poked it about before gently sliding the tip into an engorged vein. When he pulled a slight return of blood into the cylinder, he drove down the plunger, giving him forty milligrams of the potent diuretic. Leaving the needle in place, he detached the empty syringe and replaced it with one full of morphine. Ten milligrams. Plunge it in, he'd probably execute the man, stopping his breathing altogether and putting him in shock. But a little at a time, it gave the heart less to pump, and a chance to recover.

"Tempted?" said Ingram, finding a new pair of ribs to irritate, all the while holding the small remote well out of Richard's reach.

Both men knew a bolus of morphine would still give him time to press the button.

Richard said nothing and slid in two and a half milligrams, an appropriate initial dose, though a bit on the light side.

"Hey, a little more," said Ingram.

"Then do it yourself," he said, leaving the entire syringe dangling in place and walking to the overturned stretcher where he detached the cylinder of oxygen. Club him with it? Wouldn't be fast enough to prevent a flick of the thumb.

Ingram eyed the syringe of morphine hanging out of his arm, but didn't relinquish either the gun or the controller in order to give himself an additional shot. His breathing seemed to be getting worse.

Play for time, Richard told himself once more, gritting his teeth and hooking Ingram up to the tank. Though how a few more minutes would do any good, he'd no idea. What about Kathleen? So far she'd said nothing. But she must have overheard them and caught on. Maybe she still could make the cellular work. Yet Ingram didn't seem too worried about that. Had he forgotten about the phone? Or did he know that with all the concrete and virtually no windows, it couldn't work? Even if it did, Kathleen had no more idea where they were than he did.

Ingram moaned. "Christ, Richard . . . I'm getting worse. . . . I swear I'll blow it."

Richard gave more morphine. And if he pulled Ingram through, soon as he felt better, he would kill them—but maybe if Ingram knew he had a chance to live, he wouldn't be so ready to blow himself up. That would at least take the bomb out of play. With just the gun to worry about, Richard calculated, he might be able to jump him.

He continued to race through the possibilities, assessing options, selecting or discarding what he could and couldn't do just as he did with life-and-death choices in ER, yet he knew anything he tried here would be a "Hail Mary," long on odds, short on success.

She heard them talking and caught sight of Richard whenever he stood up. But Ingram, lying somewhere near the end of the truck, remained below her line of sight.

Despite her daily resignation to a death by stroke these last sixteen days, she was not ready to just lie here and be skinned in a hail of nails. She'd be damned if she'd let him decide when to push that button, she thought, having abandoned trying to make the cell phone work.

Surely there was something she could do.

First she had to free herself of IVs and tubes. Though weak, she managed to rip off the tape securing them, then pull out the needles. Blood ran onto her skin from the puncture sites, but she paid it no mind.

Next she reached down and undid the plastic bladder she'd detested since her admission. More fluids ran free. She couldn't care less.

Unable to roll herself from her back to her side, she used her elbows and heels to heave her trunk an inch sideways. A few more tries, and she added a slight turn to the maneuver, slowly rotating the line of her body so that instead of being lengthways in the truck, she edged toward lying across its floor. Each movement was an effort, and she breathed heavily after less than a dozen attempts, but the continuous sound of the jackhammer outside masked her huffing and scraping. Once she turned completely sideways, she moved directly toward the open delivery doors, though only an inch at a time. Richard occasionally looked in her direction, at least where she had been, and gave a wan smile of encouragement.

He couldn't see her in the dark, she realized.

As she inched closer, the bottom of Ingrams's legs came into view, splayed out where he lay. Every few seconds she caught sight of his hand rising up in the air as he held it away from Richard. In it was the tiny detonator he'd threatened to push.

If she had her muscles back, she could grab it.

No way now.

Then she noticed the key chain dangling below it.

He finished adjusting the flow of O_2. Returning to the syringe, he gently pressed the plunger, slowly giving Ingram another dose of morphine. "Was Francesca in on your cover-up?" he asked, wanting to distract him so he wouldn't notice the amount was less than the first. He'd settled on drawing out the resuscitation, keeping him in limbo, neither letting him slip too far nor improve too quickly.

"Francesca? No way. . . . You know she's the original . . . Girl Scout."

"Then why did she tie in with Hamlin?"

"She tied in with Norris. . . . He's the one who included Hamlin."

"You figured all this out by looking at their records."

"And hacking into their research files. . . . People think their cute passwords and numbers . . . keep them secure. . . . Not from me."

"What made her idea work and not Hamlin's?"

"Because Hamlin's an idiot. . . . Where Francesca restricted herself . . . doing to humans . . . even in secret . . . only the technique she'd perfected with mice . . . Hamlin never accepted such restraints. . . . He'd rushed ahead . . . prematurely trying what he hadn't proved . . . using untested, improvised procedures. . . . And with his DOAs starting to arrive in ER . . . it was only a matter of time . . . before the whole scheme would be discovered. . . . To protect Francesca . . . especially after his bone-headed play of using Kathleen to try and recruit you . . . I turned to Robert here . . ."

He was speeding up his talking, trying to get more words in between ever shorter breaths, Richard thought. And he was straying off topic. Sure signs that Ingram was growing worse. Whenever he saw it, this compulsion to talk as death approached, the physician in him always had put it down to delirium from a lack of oxygen. But sometimes it seemed as if the dying had to get their story out.

"... As chief of ethics I had Nape ... or Nappin Junior if you like ... and his previous indiscretions ... when he was an orderly in the reproduction center ... on file. ... It's dead simple, if you know how ... to track down his type ... on the Internet these days. ... Even back then ... I'd found his links ... with the Legion of the Lord ... so I knew he was hard-core ... and where to find him now. ... Well, you know the rest. ... The first two kills went well. ... He insisted on leaving a 'message.' ... I suggested a pile of 'stems' because I figured ... it'll make sense to him ... but nobody else will get it. ... Everybody will just put it down to some psycho's twisted thinking ..."

Much shorter gasps now. Ever more pressured speech. And the wheezing was louder, accompanied by bubbly sounds deep in his chest. Definitely worse. Got to get him back before he felt he was hopeless.

"... but then he stopped following orders. ... Figured I had to get rid of the creep as well ... Agreed to meet him ... Promised I'd help him get Kathleen to himself. ... Figured to shoot him, then blow the bunch of you up. ... Let the police figure out a story from the body parts. ... Whatever they made of it ... no proof against Francesca ... I already got a consult on Norris's case ... will make sure he doesn't talk ..."

"What do you mean?"

"ICU asked me ... to help treat him ... should be easy ... making sure ... he doesn't survive."

"I better tourniquet your other limbs," said Richard, resorting to an old-fashion way to further reduce the return of blood to the heart. He grabbed the strip of rubber he'd used before, this time cinching it tight around the other arm. He then whipped off Ingram's shoes and requisitioned the man's socks to tie around his thighs.

"I'm going, Steele. ... Damn you." He raised the controller.

Richard tensed, ready to make a lunge at it, but knew he'd never have time. "No, you're not," he lied and injected as much morphine as he dared. In ER he'd have had a slew of instruments and readings to tell him the response, guiding him, helping him determine which drugs to give and how much. This was like trying to land a plane in fog without radar. He couldn't even get a blood pressure, except Ingram's weak and rapid pulse told him it was low.

"This feels bad," said his patient, the key chain making a tiny clinking noise as he changed his grip on the remote and grew more agitated from lack of air. His hand with the gun started to move restlessly around the front of his chest, his index finger still on the trigger, but his thumb plucking at the buttons on his monogrammed blue shirt as if he thought loosening them would let him breath better. Soon the hand clutching the black box got into the act.

Christ, he was going to blow them up by accident. "Any urge to pee, yet?" said Richard, making him focus on something so the hands might go still.

"Yeah." He kept fingering his shirt buttons and collar.

"Then go. Just let it flow," said Richard, watching that left thumb. It was still squarely on the LOCK button.

"No. Get me a pot."

"I don't have one."

"Oh, Jesus. I can't breathe." He started to whimper.

"Piss your pants, damn you. This isn't a fucking hospital."

Despite his dark pants, an even darker stain began to spread in the crotch, and the unmistakable odor of urine rose around them. "I'm going to die," he cried.

"Gordon, you're liable to press that button by accident. Then for sure I can't help you. Better give it here."

"No!" he screeched, trying to hide it behind his back.

Defiant again. But a lot more scared than minutes before. And possibly easier to frighten. "Then why the fuck should I help you? You're going to kill me and Kathleen anyway."

"No, I won't."

"Bullshit!"

"I swear."

His defiance vanished again. His eyes pulsed wide with terror, frantically darting right and left as if looking for a way out, the way patients always do when they can't breathe. With the darkness all around them, Ingram seemed to be watching for something in the shadows that nobody else could see. "Oh, God, save me," he cried.

"God save you? I don't think so. But I can."

"Please!"

Time for the "Hail Mary." Richard grabbed the remaining syringes and stepped away from him. As he did, he saw Kathleen slide sideways to the back of the truck and lay along the rear edge of its floor. She turned her head toward him, her eyes flashing, and nodded, her lips silently mouthing *I love you*. With two moves, she positioned herself directly above Ingram.

Not sure what she had in mind, Richard continued to play his hand. "Then give me the gun and the remote, or I bash these on the cement."

"No, please!"

"It's not so easy to say you're ready to die once death is on your doorstep, is it Gordon?"

"Stop!" He started to cough. Red-streaked sputum flecked with bubbles came out his mouth. His useless gasps couldn't move enough oxygen to keep a canary alive.

"You know what comes next, don't you Gordon? You've seen it often enough. Blood and foam coming out your nose and mouth, no air, yet conscious for the longest thirty, forty seconds at the end of life as your heart slows to zero before you finally and mercifully die."

"No! No! No . . . I'll blow the switch first."

"You need nerve to do that, Gordon. You haven't the guts. You're desperate to live. So give me the remote and the gun while there's still a chance to get an ambulance here."

His whole chest heaved, the way an animal's does when it's trying to throw up. Red bubbles ballooned out of his nostrils and mouth like crimson soapsuds. His face grew dark purple around eyes bulging out big as golf balls.

But straining backward, keeping the key chain up in the air and away from Richard, Ingram still kept his thumb on the button and the gun pointed straight ahead.

Kathleen swung at the loop of the chain with fingers curled.

She hooked it and the whole thing flew out of his hand.

He reflexively pointed the gun up and behind him, firing three shots, all above Kathleen's head.

Richard flung himself at Ingram, easily wrenching the weapon from his grip. The remote continued to arch its way across the room. He held his breath as it struck the concrete, only to slide harmlessly a few feet across the floor.

At Richard's feet, Ingram's face, mauve as an eggplant, seemed to twist in on itself while his body jackknifed forward into a seizure. The frantic jerking lasted for half a minute, more foam seeping out between his locked lips and flying into the air around his head. Then the movements tapered off, slowing and becoming less violent, ultimately diminishing into little more than an occasional twitch. Despite all the wet spittle remaining in his throat, he gave up a sound dry as bones rattling in a gourd, and the muscles around his eyes pulled up his brow into a look of surprise.

21

Three Weeks Later,
Friday Morning, July 20

Norris was still heavily bandaged over his ear, his throat, and the stump of his right forearm. A patch covered where his right eye had been. He also was unable to speak well. The scalpal thrust into his neck had severed some of the motor nerves to his soft palate and tongue. The speech pathologist had been trying to do some rudimentary therapy with him in order that he could compensate for the deficit, but it seemed unlikely he'd ever talk normally.

"So where did Downs go to?" McKnight demanded.

I've no idea, Norris scrawled with his left hand.

"And she's made no attempt to contact you?"

No.

"So what's your best guess where she is?"

Norris simply shrugged.

The grilling had been going on for half an hour. Norris wasn't admitting or confirming anything. "Jesus Christ," McKnight muttered, then flipped shut his notebook. "This is fuckin' useless."

Norris snorted.

As McKnight pivoted and walked out of the room, Norris gestured to Richard and began to scribble something furiously on his pad. He ripped off what he'd written and held it out. *Don't worry about Kathleen. I didn't let Hamlin give her the same immature cells he used on his other patients.*

"What?"

More scribbling. *He initially used very immature cell lines. That was the problem. They replicated everything, including the abnormal vasculature. With Dr. Sullivan, I used cells that were already well on their way to forming precursors for neural tissue.*

"What do you mean?"

Harvested them from the neuronal crest in embryos at the eight-week stage. Those cells can only form neurons. She shouldn't have any trouble.

Richard thought a few seconds. "So why didn't he use the more mature tissue in the first place?"

He didn't know, hadn't done the proper long-term trials, was in too big a rush. But the remaining patients can be helped.

"How?"

Remove any recurrent malformation before it bleeds, then reinfuse more stem cells, but of the neuronal type, to assure whatever benefit they might have on long-term recovery will continue. That's what he planned to offer Dr. Sullivan, as an incentive to make you cooperate.

"Son of a bitch!"

The neurosurgeons here will be able to do the procedure for the ones who will need it.

"How much time will he get?" Richard asked McKnight as he rejoined him in the hallway.

"Who knows? We're still counting up the charges we can bring against him. What with conspiracy to commit medical assault and his being an accomplice in two accidental homicides, I'd say ten years easy, if not twenty. And his refusal to help us locate Downs isn't helping his case any. What did he say to you at the end back there?"

"Nothing. Just that he was sorry."

"Amazing!" said Kathleen, seated by her bed. Though the tube was still in place, she no longer had to cover her tracheostomy site to speak. Since she'd been breathing entirely on her own for weeks and no longer had difficulty swallowing her saliva or fluids, a stopper plugged the opening. The entire apparatus would soon be unnecessary, once she mastered solid foods. "So he went along with Hamlin purely to save my life, not to try and ensnare you in a cover-up?"

Richard nodded. "That's right."

"What a remarkable man. And now he's going to take the blame for everyone else."

"It looks like it."

"But it's so unfair."

"I know."

"Can we help him?"

"I don't see how, but I'm sure going to try."

"Yes. Me, too. Whatever it takes. Money. Lawyers. Speaking out on his behalf. Oh, Richard, it would be wrong to put him away."

How like her, he thought, not able to walk yet, and she's already charging to the aid of what's probably a lost cause.

They were seated across from each other in floral-patterned sofa chairs he had arranged to have brought to her hospital room from her apartment. The air was filled with the aroma of cappuccino he'd made for her on a newly bought machine. Around her were the fresh flowers he'd brought in every day, nicely arranged in the crystal vases he'd retrieved from his own house. While nothing could disguise the coldness of institutional decor, he figured it was possible at least to take the edge off it for her.

Kathleen tentatively raised a cup mounded with white foam to her lips. Being able to take a drink by herself was one of her recent accomplishments.

"You better watch how much of that stuff you down," he told her. "It's high-octane caffeine."

She took a swallow, then grinned at him with a white mustache. "Fruits of victory. It goes especially well with all the reading I've got to do." She gestured with her cup at a coffee table between them that was strewn with newspapers, scientific journals, and files from her laboratory. But there was a tautness to her voice that belied the smile.

"Then I'll get you decaf," he said.

Her legs were still unable to support her, and the physiotherapists thought it would be another three to four weeks before she could go home and attend sessions as an outpatient. Whether she would ever walk again they couldn't yet say, and he was sure that the uncertainty weighed heavily on her. She'd met his attempts to talk about the future with such an icy silence he'd learned to let it be.

Until now.

"You know, you're doing exactly what I did."

"Pardon?"

"Running."

She stiffened. "Poor choice of words, buster."

"Not really. You don't need legs to desert." He tapped his head. "Not if you do it up here."

"Richard, stop—"

"No way! Nothing stopped you from giving me a piece of your mind—full blast—when I needed it. You deserve just as good from me. And if you don't like it, it's your own fault. I'm your worst nightmare, a reformed duck-out junkie you helped to restore who's head over heels in love with you. That means I stick around and nag you out of the hole you're trying to dig us into."

"Us?"

"Yeah. Us. You and me, not to mention Chet and Lisa."

"Now that's not fair. You leave the kids out of this."

"Not fair? The kids are already in 'this.' We figure it's you who's not being fair to any of us."

Her jaw dropped. "Richard! You didn't discuss us with them, did you?"

"Of course I did. Or rather they demanded to know what was up. We all think you're nuts. I'm just the one who gets first crack at you."

"Now wait a minute—"

"No, you wait a minute. Did you really think we would let you kiss us off, Kathleen?"

"I'm not kissing Lisa or Chet off! I'd never do that. I simply won't be a burden—"

"You've never been a burden to anyone in your life, and never will. It's just not in your nature. You're take-charge Kathleen Sullivan, and what your muscles will or won't do isn't going to change that. Hell, I for one won't even see your wheelchair, if you have one."

"That's easy to say. Living it is different—"

"Of course, we'll have to make adjustments wherever we move, but we can more than afford any help we'll need. Only difference would be that I'd get to pick you up and carry you lots. No letting some hired hunk have all the fun of putting his arms around you."

"Richard! And that's another thing. What if we can't . . . I mean . . . if I can't . . ."

"Make love?"

Her face flushed. "Yes."

He got up, walked over to the door, and locked it.

"Richard, what the hell are you doing?"

He came back to where she was sitting and took the cup from her hands. "I'm showing you what a doctor with a good imagination can do." He slipped his arms under her and lifted. She still felt so light it startled him.

"Richard, put me down."

He laid her gently on the bed. While she'd gotten much of her color back, her face remained as skeletal as the rest of her. He almost abandoned what he had in mind, she looked so frail, and if she continued to demand he stop, he of course would. But her pupils widened, telling him something else. He smiled at her, and lay down at her side, his lips brushing her temples.

"What if someone comes and finds they can't get in?" she asked, glancing nervously at the door.

He kissed her softly on her lips. "They won't dare."

"But isn't this against the rules?" she murmured, kissing him back.

He caressed the side of her neck, "I'm chief of emergency. That gives me privileges," he whispered in her ear.

"Even with me?"

"If you want."

She didn't reply at first.

"Kathleen?"

"It does feel nice."

He reached down and undid the tie on her robe, then slid his hands underneath her top, over her emaciated rib cage to her breasts. Gently he circled his fingertips around one of her nipples, and felt it become firm.

"Oh, my God." She sighed, her eyes glistened as she ever so slightly arched her back. "It's wonderful."

"You sound surprised."

"I was afraid I'd never feel sexy again."

"Shall I continue?"

"Oh, yes."

"Like that."

"Oh, Richard."

"More?"

"Yes. And don't stop."

He raised her nightgown, and let his lips do the touching.

Sunday, July 22

"Do you want me to go up with you, Chet?"

"No, Dad. It's better I speak with him alone. Every time the poor guy sees a father and son together, it must be extra hard on him."

Richard smiled, impressed. "You're right."

They stood in the cavernous gloom of Saint Patrick's Cathedral where a memorial service for Ted Mallory had just drawn to a close. The actual funeral had been held weeks earlier, a private affair for family members only. Ted Mallory Senior, his face pale, his eyes and cheeks sunken, stood in a reception line staring blankly ahead and shaking hands with an endless stream of uniformed officers. At his side was a slender, dark-haired woman who looked equally sucked inside out by grief.

The fianceé, Cathy? Richard would have a word with her later, in private. Heartrending as it would be for her, he knew she would want to hear about Ted's final moments. The bereaved always did. He usually dressed it up for them, distilling from their loved one's final agony a story of dignified courage and noble last words, but in this case it would be true.

He watched Chet make his way into the line. When the boy reached the old man, they exchanged a few phrases, and Mallory Senior's face broke out of its porcelain mask into a look of astonishment. He instantly clasped the teenager by the shoulders, gave him a tearful smile, then pulled him into a hug. The young woman's features, rigidly dry-eyed until now, seemed to crumple as she joined in the embrace.

Chet hesitantly put his arms around them, and the rest of the people in the church went silent. Only the sobs of the father and Cathy filled the echoing interior.

After a few seconds Richard heard the man's broken voice say, "God bless you for coming and giving us a chance to meet you. Your being alive is the only thing that makes sense out of what our Ted died for."

Monday, July 23, 10:35 P.M.

Jimmy Norris had no idea why they were taking him for an MRI at this time of night. When he'd scribbled a note demanding an explanation, all anybody told him was, "It's been ordered."

Not that he cared much what they did with him anymore. His life was finished. Having nothing but prison to look forward to, his survival on that slab in the morgue had become a cruel joke. His only comfort came in knowing they hadn't gotten Francesca. He had no idea where she'd fled. Yet he spent hours fantasizing her finding a safe refuge someplace and continuing their work, thereby keeping a part of him free. Then he'd think of all the hurdles she would have to overcome—financing, security, censure in the world scientific community—and would sink back into despair knowing all they'd done had been for naught.

An orderly loaded him into the waiting wheelchair and off they went toward radiology, the policeman assigned as his guard trotting along behind.

"You won't be able to go in with him," said the man doing the pushing. He was a slight wiry fellow who seemed to enjoy rushing everywhere at double speed. "The force of the magnet will rip out any metal you're carrying and pull it across the room like shrapnel—"

"I know the routine." The cop puffed, running behind a belly that certainly suggested he sat around watching incarcerated patients a lot. As soon as they arrived at the anteroom to the imaging suite the big man found a seat, pulled what looked like the *Times*' crossword out of his pocket, and started to pour over it with a pencil.

The orderly shrugged, and helped Norris to his feet. "Give this to the radiologist," he said, handing over the requisition for the procedure once they were inside the chamber itself, a bare medium-sized area containing a giant tube over eight feet long that was the magnetic resonance machine. Then he left, closing a massive door behind him that sealed itself with the buzz of an electronic lock.

Like a gas chamber, thought Norris, all at once feeling claustrophobic. The only window looked in on him from a small control booth where a man in OR greens was hunched over a panel of dials, his back turned. Probably a technician cuing up the necessary settings.

He walked over to the stretcher-sized tray that would feed him into the cylindrical opening where he'd be expected to lie perfectly still for about forty-five minutes. It was a pretty cramped space.

Who the hell had visited this on him anyway? He held the requisition up to the light to see the signature.

Rachael Jorgenson.

What the hell? That was Hamlin's former resident and squeeze. She had no business writing orders on him. It had to be a mistake.

A buzzing sounded behind him in the direction of the control booth, and he spun around to see a small door open. In stepped the man he'd noticed a few seconds before, except now he could see his face.

"Evening, Jimmy," said Richard Steele as casually as if they were meeting for a round of golf.

"Whaa!" said Norris, forgetting his garbled speech and self-imposed silence.

"Now listen carefully, Jimmy. We don't have much time," Richard said. "Through that booth is another door leading to the radiologist's lounge. There you'll find a set of civvies, and a stolen pass card that'll open all the doors you'll need to exit the rear of the hospital. A car is waiting out there, and in it is a woman named Bunny and her pilot boyfriend who you know. They are going to drive you to a private airport where they've arranged for someone to fly you to Francesca, but you've got to hoof it. I figure just under an hour is all we have before someone comes checking."

Norris felt his heart quicken. Was this a joke? Surely Steele was tormenting him, teasing him with the possibility of escape and seeing Francesca, only to slam the door shut in his face if he fell for it. "Goh te hil!" he managed to drawl.

"Damn it, Jimmy, trust me. It's your one chance. Take it."

Richard didn't sound like he was kidding. Maybe he was on the level. Why not play along? After all, he had nothing to lose. He started for the door to the booth, barely daring to hope. Passing on through and into the lounge he found trousers, socks, shoes, and a shirt laid out for him. "Wy rr yu halping me?" he asked, hurriedly pulling on the clothing, the job hampered by his having only one hand.

"Without you, Kathleen would be dead. A lot of other people, too, probably. The bottom line is, given what you can offer humankind, it makes no sense to throw you in jail. Now go."

Norris felt something release deep inside him. Richard was playing straight, at no small risk. "Won u git n tubble?"

"Hey, residents make errors all the time, including writing orders on the wrong patient. The police will just figure that once here, you took full advantage of the situation, stealing the clothes and whatever else you needed to skedaddle. I'll have nothing to do with it."

"Wha ef Jorgansin tals?"

"She can't say anything about our arrangement; she has no proof. Besides, she owes me big-time for not pursuing a huge screwup of hers. A potential career-ender."

Norris fished the promised pass card out of his newly donned pants. Realization hit like a blast of oxygen directly to the brain: He stood on the verge of freedom. His head swam and a swell of elation filled his chest. "Than yu," he said, his eye filling with tears as he grabbed Richard's hand. It was his first shake as a southpaw.

"Just go!"

Minutes later he was out a rear exit on Thirty-fourth Street. A breeze off the East River flowed over him, cool as a fresh spring shower, and overhead was a moonless starry sky. A good night to fly, he thought. Half a block away he saw the headlights of a car blink on and off. Running toward it, he started to laugh, yet he continued to cry. In seconds he was speeding away, safely in the custody of Bunny and Ralph Coady.

epilogue

The New York Herald, *Sunday, September 2*

A pair of doctors on Grand Cayman Island made medical history last week by implanting adult stem cells taken from a patient's own bone marrow into his heart. The subject, Ralph Coady of New York City, is a 45-year-old former airline pilot who suffered a major heart attack 10 weeks ago. The event left him with moderately severe heart failure, or weakening of the cardiac muscle. The new cells are expected to restore the injured areas of his myocardium, returning them to normal function within 6 to 12 weeks.

What makes the occurrence all the more remarkable is that the two people who carried out the procedure, Dr. Francesca Downs and Dr. James Norris, are wanted by U.S. authorities in connection with a recent scandal at New York City Hospital where they allegedly carried out unauthorized stem cell research on unsuspecting patients. Authorities in Grand Cayman, however, have refused to comply with all requests for their extradition of the pair to America. Instead local officials have authorized their participation in a stem cell research and treatment center established on the island in conjunction with Fountainhead Pharmaceuticals of Mexico. A spokesperson for the newly formed institute reported that they have also recruited leading specialists in all fields of regenerative medicine from virtually every corner of the planet, and patients are inundating the recently opened facility with requests for appointments.

Dr. Francesca Downs put it most succinctly: "Clearly the demand is there. Obviously we will be opening more such institutes in other countries where regulations favor scientific progress. In all, Dr. Norris and I are delighted our life-saving work is free to flourish."

Kathleen Sullivan lowered the newspaper and looked over at Richard. How she loved him. How grateful she was for his devotion and protection that had saved her life. But, oh, my God, what had she and he set in motion by freeing Norris?

acknowledgments

Many people shared their time, their insights, and their research into regenerative medicine with me as I was writing this book. Thanks to Dr. Thomas Chang, Dr. David Gearhart, Dr. Lorne Kastrukoff, and Dr. Janet Rossant. A special thanks goes to Dr. Ray Chiu, who kindly educated me about the history of stromal (or adult) stem cells, and took me on a tour of his laboratory, where he is currently investigating their use in restoring function to damaged myocardium.

Again, a heartfelt thanks goes to Dr. Brian Connolly and Dr. Jennifer Frank, my longtime friends and colleagues, for their "second opinion" on medical matters.

And an equally big thank you to Johanna, Betty, Connie, and Tamara for their editorial comments.

Thank you to my tireless agent, Denise Marcil, and her wonderful associates, Deryk and Maura, for their invaluable feedback on successive drafts.

Last, and definitely not least, thank you to my editor at Ballantine, Joe Blades, for his generosity and expertise.